SWIMMING WITH SHARKS

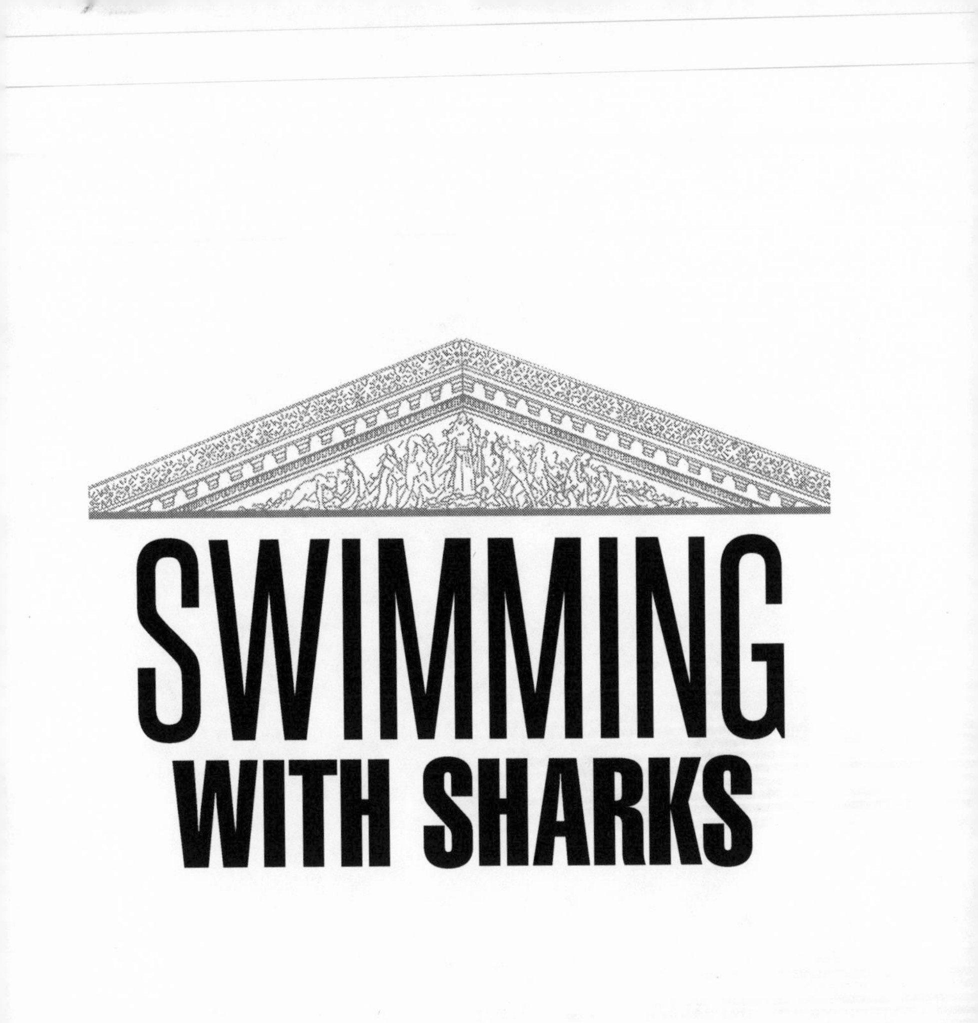

SWIMMING WITH SHARKS

NELE NEUHAUS

Translated by Christine M. Grimm

amazon crossing

The characters and events portrayed in this book are fictitious. Any similarity to real persons, living or dead, is coincidental and not intended by the author.

Printed in the United States of America.

Swimming with Sharks was first published in 2005 as *Unter Haien*. Translated from German by Christine M. Grimm. Published in English by AmazonCrossing in 2013.

Published by AmazonCrossing
PO Box 400818
Las Vegas, NV 89140

ISBN-13: 9781611099256
ISBN-10: 1611099250
Library of Congress Control Number: 2012920274

For Milla, my little sister and Matthias, my great love.

Letter to the Reader

A lot has happened since 2005 when this book was first published independently with a print run of five hundred copies. I've met many people who've accompanied and supported me along the way. I'd like to thank several of them here: First of all, my parents Dr. Bernward and Carola Löwenberg, my sisters Claudia Cohen and Camilla Altvater, and my brother-in-law Bruno Cohen, who translated this book into French—just for fun! Thanks also go to my agent, Andrea Wildgruber, and her colleagues from the Agence Hoffman literary agency in Munich. Special thanks to Susanne Hecker, who made particularly great contributions to this book. Susanne, you are simply wonderful! Thank you to Catherine Hackl for her work on reading the translated manuscript. And thank you to Gabriella Page-Fort, Declan Spring, and the entire team at AmazonCrossing—thanks to you all, my dream of bringing *Swimming with Sharks* to America has come true.

My biggest thanks go to my partner, Matthias Knöß. I'd only be half of what I am without you. I love you.

Nele Neuhaus

January 2013

PROLOGUE

February, 1998—New York City

Vincent Levy was lost in thought. He stared out the window of his office on the LMI Building's thirtieth floor. On this somber Friday afternoon, the Verrazano-Narrows Bridge was barely visible to the east. The Statue of Liberty raised her arm, and boats cruising New York Harbor drew white, foamy stripes in the churned-up black water. Snowflakes whirled through the air, and an icy east wind whistled around the glass facades of the skyscrapers. Vincent, in his early fifties, was already the fourth Levy in the firm. His great-great-uncle had founded the bank Levy & Villiers in 1902. Thanks to a prudent and conservative strategy, the firm had managed to safely navigate nearly a century's worth of storms and scandals in the financial world. But unlike his predecessors, Vincent Levy wasn't satisfied with simply leading a prestigious private bank. He started transforming the venerable private bank into a major investment bank during the mid-1980s, making the Levy & Villiers bank into the holding company of Levy Manhattan Investments. With a strong financial partner offering the possibility of becoming a global financial giant, Levy acquired competitors. He invested millions in computer technology and involved LMI in every important financial center of the world. Levy wasn't afraid of spectacular innovations. In fifteen years, Levy—with strategic skill, vision, and well-camouflaged ruthlessness—had successfully turned LMI into an investment bank with more than two thousand employees worldwide. Every department had a strong leader who knew how to get the best out of its employees, whether trading in foreign bonds, derivatives, securities, OTC, syndicated loans, index and risk arbitrage, futures, or private equity. LMI's reputation grew, with brokers on the NYSE trading floor and about two hundred traders on LMI's fourteenth floor generating enormous revenues and profits.

Although LMI was a major market player in many areas, Levy had failed to recruit a real rainmaker in the one that was dearest to his heart. Other players on Wall Street were pulling the strings in the field of mergers and acquisitions. Incredible amounts of money were flowing into people's pockets, sidestepping LMI in the current M&A boom—an almost unbearable situation! But this would soon change. The previous night he had heard that Alexandra Sontheim—the brightest star in Wall Street's M&A sky—had quit Morgan Stanley and was looking for a new job. Someone knocked on the door, and Levy's gaze turned from the harbor.

"Hello, St. John," he said to his visitor, and sat down behind his desk. "Have a seat."

"What's new, Vince?" Zachary St. John asked in the disrespectful way that always annoyed Levy. He glanced disapprovingly at his head of M&A, which, unfortunately, had no effect. St. John wasn't necessarily an ace when it came to his job, but he definitely knew everyone on Wall Street. Since joining LMI roughly nine years ago from Franklin Myers and Drexel Burnham Lambert, he had connected with almost every member of upper management at LMI. Levy didn't like St. John because he was a glib, money-hungry opportunist, but his contacts were extremely valuable.

"As you know," Levy began, "I have long wished for LMI to gain prominence in the area of M&A. Yesterday, I was told by well-informed sources that Alex Sontheim left Morgan Stanley after a disagreement."

He paused briefly to see St. John's reaction, but the latter appeared not to be impressed by his boss's sensational insider knowledge.

"I already knew that." St. John smiled smugly. "It was obvious she wouldn't stay at Morgan Stanley much longer, because she was tired of playing second fiddle to van Sand, that moron. And after he foiled her TexOil deal three days ago, she put the gun to Neil Sadler's head."

"Oh really?" Levy wasn't surprised that St. John was already familiar with some of the details.

"What else do you know about her?"

St. John leaned back and stretched his legs. He had just returned from a two-day business trip to the Bahamas. He had a deep tan. His short, reddish-blond hair was slicked back meticulously and had its usual perfect shine.

"Alex Sontheim," he said, "is from Germany. She is thirty-five and single, studied at the European Business School, and received a full scholarship to Stanford. She graduated at the top of her MBA class. She rose to the top in the Goldman Sachs associate program, and she could have easily stayed there. Any corporation would have loved to hire her, but she accepted the lowest-paying job at a brokerage called Global Equity Trust, working as a fund manager. After two years, she switched to Franklin Myers and did futures, derivatives, and a little M&A there. Then she went to Morgan Stanley, where she's been working exclusively in M&A for the past eight years. By now, everyone knows how good she is at her job."

Levy nodded with a thin smile. Alex Sontheim was *the* star in the field, and hardly any deal eluded her. Recruiting her to his firm would be a dream come true.

"She's ambitious and ruthless," St. John continued, "and that's why things came to a head between her and van Sand. Of course, everyone in the city knows that she makes the major deals, but Douglas is the big boss's son-in-law. She'll never get his job, and Alex isn't the type of woman who is content with second place."

Levy observed St. John with an expressionless face, but his brain was in high gear. He could already envision the headline of the *Wall Street Journal*: "Alex Sontheim Joins LMI…"

"Does she have any skeletons in her closet?" he asked.

"Not that I know of." St. John shook his head. "No alcohol-abusing ex-husband, no children out of wedlock, no previous convictions, no rumors. This woman lives for her work. She is clever and tough as nails."

"Why do you know so much about her, Zack?" Levy asked.

"Apart from the fact that I know a lot about most people in our industry," St. John said with a grin, his tone even more smug than before, "Alex and I were colleagues at Franklin Myers. I know her pretty well." He enjoyed playing Mr. Know-It-All. Levy squinted and observed him closely.

"Let's assume that we can convince her to join us," he said. "Then you would be out of a job, Zack."

"Well, I don't think so." St. John skimmed through his worn-out notebook with a languid smile before looking up. "I'm not a star like Alex Sontheim, but I would be the perfect managing director. What do you think, Vince?"

"Let's tackle this first," Levy responded coolly.

The position of managing director had been vacant at LMI since Gilbert Shanahan was literally crushed by a truck on his way to an SEC hearing—a year and a half ago. Poor Gilbert had been declared dead on the spot.

"I am *very* loyal." St. John leaned forward, and a brooding expression appeared in his eyes. "You know what I mean."

Levy's face was relaxed, but St. John's emphasis of the word *loyal* triggered an uneasy feeling in his stomach. St. John had never uttered a word about the details of this unpleasant matter with Shanahan; as a result, Levy had almost forgotten that this man knew almost everything about what had happened.

"We'll talk about that when the time is right," he said. He stood up to signal to St. John that the conversation was over. "I would like you to contact Alex Sontheim right away. Can you manage that?"

St. John raised his eyebrows mockingly and grinned.

"Are you joking, Vince?" He also stood up. "By right away, you mean today? Or is tomorrow early enough for you?"

Levy gave him a cold smile.

"Ideally, in an hour," he parried, and reached for the telephone receiver. St. John got the hint. He bowed slightly and left Levy's office. Levy waited until St. John closed the door behind him. Then he walked across his office to his fully equipped bar. He poured himself a scotch—straight, without ice—and stepped toward the window again. Recruiting Alex Sontheim was the perfect move. He would spare neither trouble nor expense to do so.

PART ONE

July 1998—New York City

Alex Sontheim didn't regret her move from Morgan Stanley to Levy Manhattan for one single moment, and she was sure Vincent Levy wasn't sorry he had won her over with his generous offer last February. With a fixed salary of two million dollars plus bonuses and commissions, Alex was among the best-paid investment bankers in the city, and she had already silenced any skeptics on LMI's board of directors with three spectacular deals.

Along with their revenues, LMI's reputation in the highly competitive M&A market went soaring. Levy was euphoric; it couldn't get better than this. General Engines and United Brake Systems were both blue-chip companies, and, through Alex, LMI successfully represented them. The *Wall Street Journal* called LMI a "serious competitor" to Merrill Lynch, Goldman Sachs, and Morgan Stanley in the field of M&A, and Alex was solely responsible for it. She had a keen sense for the markets, a sharp eye, ruthlessness, and experience—plus the necessary connections to remain at the top of the food chain in this business. From her office window on the fourteenth floor of the LMI Building, she had a fantastic view of the Verrazano-Narrows Bridge and the harbor. It was this breathtaking panorama that made her realize how incredibly far she had come in her career over the past years. She smiled in satisfaction. At the age of thirty-five, she felt well on her way to the top.

Now she was playing in the major leagues—and she had made it completely on her own. The telephone startled her out of her reverie. It was Zack, her former colleague at Franklin Myers and currently the managing director of LMI, to whom she more or less owed this job. He asked her to join a board meeting, scheduled at short notice on the thirtieth floor. Alex shut down her computer, grabbed her briefcase, and quickly rushed across the trading floor. It was already late on a Friday afternoon, and the normally hectic floor was deserted except for a cleaning crew. The traders had vanished into their weekends the moment trading closed on the NYSE. Alex swiped her badge through the reader next to the elevator door. Security at LMI was as tight as at the Pentagon; every swipe of the card was recorded by a central computer.

Alex assessed her appearance in the mirror, while the silent elevator transported her sixteen floors higher. It was far more difficult for a woman in her position to be accepted by colleagues and business partners than for a man. She had to be tough and unyielding, but without seeming masculine. She had perfectly mastered this balancing act after twelve years on Wall Street. She gave her mirror image a friendly smile. People in this city had long stopped making the mistake of underestimating her. Someone had once accused her of being cold and ruthless, but Alex saw this as a compliment—essential survival skills in this tough man's world.

The elevator stopped on the thirtieth floor with a subtle ring, and Alex took a deep breath. She walked along a mahogany-paneled hallway lined with exquisitely lit expressionist paintings—surely originals and worth a fortune. The thick Aubusson runner rugs over the reddish marble swallowed the sound of her steps. Every detail of the furnishings exuded solidity, power, and success. Anyone who sat on the thirtieth floor had made it. Alex smiled. One of these days, in the not too distant future, her name would also be on one of these doors.

She knocked on the door of the large conference room—it was as wide as the whole building—and entered. The windows stretched from the ceiling to the floor, and the view to the east across the river to Brooklyn was spectacular. Although she had been here a few times before, she was impressed anew by the vast space. The thought flashed through her mind that this room was designed not just to impress but to intimidate.

The entire board of directors sat around the giant, polished round table, which looked like it was carved from one piece—like the legendary Round Table of Camelot: CEO Vincent Levy, Vice President Isaac Rubinstein, CFO Michael Friedman, Head Analyst Hugh Weinberg, Legal Department Head Francis Dayton-Smith, Chairman of the Board Ron Schellenbaum, Director of Emerging Markets and International Business John Kwai, and Managing Director Zachary St. John.

"Hello," Alex said and smiled. "I hope I'm not late."

Vincent Levy jumped up and walked over to her with a smile. "Oh no, Alex," he said, extending his hand to her, "thank you for coming. I decided at the last minute to invite you to our meeting. After all, you made a major contribution to our recent successes."

Alex smiled as she look around at the group's benevolent but probing expressions. She couldn't figure out Levy. There was a core as hard as iron hiding behind his smooth demeanor. People didn't make it to the very top on Wall Street by being modest or friendly. She sat down between John Kwai and Zack. Her heart was beating in excitement when she realized that she was sitting as an equal among the most powerful men of the firm. Even though her job was exciting and satisfying, her next goal was to permanently establish herself in this circle. Levy spoke about the positive developments in M&A, but also about currency and equities trading and the underwriting of promising dot-com companies. Then Hugh Weinberg reported on his forecasts.

Levy had recruited Weinberg from Prudential Securities. Weinberg's opinion was highly respected and second to none on Wall Street—he was known and feared for his accurate analyses and proven forecasts. Alex was filled with pride that he had such high regard for her work. His market analysis was followed by Michael Friedman's dry report on the past quarter's revenues and profits. When at seven thirty Levy closed the meeting by thanking all of the attendees, Alex wondered why she had been invited in the first place. She was standing up, ready to leave, when Levy signaled for her to stay.

"We are very pleased with your work here, Alex," he began in a friendly tone once they were alone in the conference room. "Hugh is impressed by your profound market knowledge."

"Thank you." Alex smiled in acknowledgment. After all, they were paying her two million a year for that knowledge. But what did he really want?

"The efficiency and success of your work speaks for itself," Levy continued, "and as you know, we are willing to reward success."

His smile grew wider.

"We are considering a bonus of a hundred and fifty thousand dollars on top of your regular bonus payment."

Alex wondered if she'd heard him correctly.

"That's a significant amount of money." With some effort she concealed her surprise and maintained her composure.

"Yes, indeed." Levy smiled in a kind and paternal way. "But you work eighty hours a week and have delivered remarkable results in less than five months. Others need this much time just to get accustomed to a new company. Furthermore, LMI owes its excellent reputation in the area of M&A to you. Why shouldn't the firm reward you for that?"

"Well," Alex responded without batting an eye, "that's incredibly generous."

She had the feeling that she needed to be very careful. She had no idea where this intuition came from, but the feeling was there.

Finally Levy spoke. "I would like to make you an offer—here, between you and me. Nothing in writing. Let's call it a handshake agreement.

LMI could obviously give you the bonus in the customary form of stock options. But we could also transfer the money in cash, which means, well, tax free, to a foreign bank account."

He smiled innocently, as if he hadn't just suggested tax evasion to her.

"The decision is yours, Alex. Stock options are good. But considering your tax bracket, the advantage of a cash payment is obvious."

Alex wasn't quite sure whether she liked the proposal, but she slowly realized why Levy had invited her here today. He wanted to test her willingness to cross legal boundaries, to judge the extent of her moral scruples.

"Just slightly illegal, isn't it?" she said nonchalantly, and smiled.

"Illegal." Levy laughed quietly. "What an ugly word. By the way, I think that you already pay enough taxes, don't you?"

Alex nodded. Whenever a few investment bankers got together, they always talked about legal tricks and loopholes to avoid taxes. The cut taken in taxes from salaries this high was enormous. A bank account in the Bahamas, Cayman Islands, Switzerland, or elsewhere was the rule rather than the exception.

"Let St. John know once you make a decision," Levy said in a friendly tone. "But this is just one of two topics that I'd like to discuss with you. The other is the independence of your department."

"I thought that you expected personal initiative?" Alex was surprised.

"Oh yes, I do," Levy reassured her. "Please don't think of this as criticism! Discretion is vital in your job. And we are certainly more than happy. But in the future, perhaps you can manage to inform the board about planned deals before you enter into initial negotiations with a client."

He paused for a moment to let his words sink in.

"The board of directors," he continued, "would like to stay informed about the activities in every department of the firm. This is pure interest, not control. You make all of the decisions as before, after consulting the CFO and the legal department."

Alex looked at Levy for a moment and then nodded slowly. She was well aware of what one could do with information about imminent deals before other market participants could get in the game. There was a lot of money to be made by buying stocks of businesses prior to the public announcement of a takeover, which in turn would drive up the stock price. This was insider trading, and it was probably the most prohibited form of market manipulation. This is why investment banks were required to maintain "Chinese walls" serving as barriers between traders and investment bankers within a firm, so that undisclosed material information couldn't be abused prior to its public disclosure. Levy was more or less asking her to circumvent this Chinese wall. Alex noticed the LMI president was eagerly awaiting her response, and she decided to cooperate.

"That's no problem," she said after a brief hesitatation. "I'll keep you up to date."

The relief that rushed across Levy's face didn't escape her notice, though his friendly smile soon returned.

"Excellent," he said, satisfied. "I knew that we'd understand each other. You will report directly to Mr. St. John."

Zachary St. John wasn't particularly skilled in the banking business, but he very much understood the Wall Street power structure. He often threw parties at his penthouse apartment in Battery Park City, inviting only those he deemed important. Alex was invited for the first time this evening, and she was more than curious about who she would meet there. Invitations to Zack's legendary parties were highly coveted in the Wall Street community because people exchanged important news, made contacts, and arranged deals while enjoying the finest food and the most expensive French champagne.

Alex took a while to think about what she should wear. At first, she considered one of the business suits that she customarily wore in the office, but she finally decided on an outrageously expensive, tight red evening gown by Versace. Tonight, she intended to show everyone that she was a woman first and foremost—despite her cleverness and ruthlessness. She arrived at the penthouse at nine thirty. It never ceased to surprise her how extravagantly people lived in New York when they had the means. About two hundred guests were spread over five thousand square feet of luxury, sitting or standing in small groups, having a great time. Zack approached her with open arms, a broad grin, and a thick Cohiba cigar between his fingers. He welcomed her warmly, admiringly eyeing her dress and her lean, shapely legs. Then he showed her off to a few very important people.

The complete LMI board of directors was of course present, together with their wives, but also a diverse group of others: lawyers, brokers, analysts, and—of course—investment bankers from other firms. Alex's initial inhibition quickly disappeared after she realized how easily she was accepted into this illustrious circle. It felt like everyone was competing to speak with her. Zack reappeared at one point, just as she was absorbed in a discussion with Kwai and Weinberg.

"Sorry to interrupt," Zack said as he took Alex by the arm. "I'll bring her back in a minute."

"What's going on?" Alex asked in surprise.

"Come with me," Zack whispered with a mysterious grin on his face. "There's a very powerful man you should meet."

She was curious as she followed him through the maze of the penthouse and up to the sprawling rooftop terrace. A few men sat laughing together in comfortable rattan armchairs, drinking cognac, smoking the Cohibas that were offered in every room. Just as Alex stepped onto the terrace, one of the men turned around and their eyes met. The laugh on the dark-haired man's face faded. He placed his glass on the low table and stood up.

"Who's that?" Alex whispered into Zack's ear.

"Sergio Vitali. You've heard of him before, right?"

Of course she had. Everyone in New York City knew Sergio Vitali. His face was shown often enough on television and in the newspapers. He was one of the most powerful people in town—a billionaire real-estate tycoon, if the press was to be believed. He made regular headlines for his large donations to social institutions and presence at the glamorous benefits and banquets of New York's high society, where the most important deals were made. Sergio Vitali was a poster child for American business. According to *Forbes,* he was among the richest individuals in the United States. Half of Manhattan belonged to him. Vitali also owned hotel chains and casinos in Las Vegas, Reno, Atlantic City, and Miami. He ruled over a corporate conglomerate and traveled in his own private Learjets.

"Alex," Zack said, "may I introduce you to Mr. Sergio Vitali? Mr. Vitali, this is Alex Sontheim, head of the M&A department at LMI."

"I've already heard so much about you." Vitali's voice was pleasant, cultivated. "I'm delighted to finally meet you in person. Your excellent reputation precedes you, but no one warned me you were also an exceptionally beautiful woman."

Alex laughed in embarrassment and reached for his extended hand. His handshake was firm and warm. His touch ignited a fire in her that quickly spread throughout her entire body. She had never met a man with such strong sensuality. The attraction she felt confused her—it was irritating and deeply frightening. She preferred to have everything under control at all times.

"The pleasure is all mine," she responded, hiding her attraction behind a cool smile. No doubt, Sergio Vitali was the most attractive man she had ever met. His thick, black hair—graying at the temples—and the subtle wrinkles around his mouth and the corners of his eyes gave special character to his striking face. His profile was like a Roman statue. With this unforgettable face, he could have had a career in Hollywood. Yet, his steel-blue eyes were his most remarkable feature. Before they could exchange another word, Zack positioned himself in the widely opened terrace doors, clapped his hands, and asked his guests for a moment of attention. He gave a brief speech, but she didn't catch a single word of it. She noticed that Vitali's unsettling gaze rested on her, and she was torn between an instinctive aversion and a strange fascination. He unnerved her, and she wasn't sure whether she liked it. Nevertheless, he proved to be a very entertaining and attentive conversationalist.

Vitali introduced her to his friend and lawyer, Nelson van Mieren, who was the exact opposite of him: short, chubby, and bald, with a friendly smile on his bulging lips. His quick, small eyes, hovering above his plump cheeks, belied harmlessness. After midnight, van Mieren said good-bye. Suddenly Alex found herself completely alone with Vitali on the terrace. She had drunk much more champagne than usual, and her initial wariness quickly turned into a thrilling curiosity. It was two thirty when she realized that she had talked only to Sergio Vitali for the entire evening. She thanked Zack for the invitation and politely but firmly refused Vitali's offer to drive her home. Alex left the party with a tingly feeling, certain that she had left a lasting impression on one of the most influential men in the city.

On this Friday afternoon in September, Mark Ashton sat at his desk on the LMI Building's fourteenth floor. His boss sat behind office doors, while his desk was in a cubicle. But this didn't bother him. He enjoyed his work because it provided a welcome diversion from his private life, which was less than thrilling. About twelve years ago, the Harvard graduate and lawyer wound up on Wall Street. After six years at one of New York's law firms, he joined LMI. But he'd failed miserably on the trading floor because he wasn't cut out for the hustle and stress; he wasn't greedy and ruthless enough to be successful.

Human resources had moved him to a position in syndication at his own request, and he'd been quite happy there for three years. Detailed calculations, financial statements, and financial analyses were more to his liking. When the new head of M&A was searching for someone good at mundane number-crunching, Mark applied on a whim and got the job. He didn't regret it one bit. M&A was an exciting business.

Mark paused for a second, took off his glasses, and rubbed his eyes. Alex Sontheim was the smartest and most competent boss he'd ever had. She managed to motivate her team like no one else. She noticed every error and registered all weaknesses, but she never exposed anyone publicly. Ashton quickly realized that he shouldn't enter her office unprepared. Praise from Alex was a rare event, and the team she'd formed from this mixed group soon felt a sense of devotion that was unparalleled in the egocentric world of Wall Street. The entire department worked late into the night and on weekends without complaint. Closed deals were celebrated after work at the St. John's Inn, Luna Luna, or Reggie's at Hanover Square.

For the first time, Mark felt like an integral member of an efficient team, and he owed it all to Alex. If for no other reason than that, he decided to pledge loyalty to her. He especially wanted to find out whether she'd be interested in what he had uncovered about a potential client during his research. His findings seemed suspect, and Mark wasn't sure what to make of it.

The Wisconsin-based Hanson paper mill was one of the largest paper mills in the country, and they had shown interest in acquiring the prestigious, but almost bankrupt, American Road Map publishing company. Mark questioned the motivation behind this because he couldn't identify any good reason for it. In order to find out more about the company, he researched the Hanson paper mill and discovered to his surprise that it was owned by a holding company called SeViCo from Panama. SeViCo was owned in turn by a company called Sunset Properties, which had incorporated in the British Virgin Islands in 1985. No information was available whatsoever about Sunset Properties. None of this had mattered so far, but it was striking that American Road Map was already owned by Sunset Properties via a company called Sagimex S.A., of Monaco. Why should one company acquire another, both under the same owner? Mark chewed on his lower lip. Should he tell Alex what he had discovered about Hanson and American Road Map?

"No," he ultimately said out loud to himself, shaking his head. "It doesn't matter."

His job was to assemble the right numbers in order to prepare an attractive takeover offer. If the deal went through, the legal department would take care of everything else.

The day was pure hell. The market was inexplicably restless and had been for the past few weeks. The mad rush at the opening of the stock exchange was like the gates at the Super Bowl. Alex worked on the new deal under intense pressure, leading one telephone conference after another and poring over complicated financial reports. She scarfed down a sandwich for lunch, and if she wanted to avoid working throughout the entire weekend, dinner would have to wait. It was almost three thirty when her direct line rang.

"Yes?" she said and rubbed her burning eyes.

"Hello, Alex." The sonorous voice—so close and unexpected in her ear—automatically quickened her pulse. "It's me, Sergio."

"Hello, Sergio." Alex forced herself to sound relaxed. He had called her the day after Zack's party and invited her to lunch. His aura of power impressed Alex. She liked his attentiveness and was dazzled by the possibility of a closer relationship with him. This made her overlook the less-than-flattering rumors about the source of his incredible wealth—and the fact that he was married. During their increasingly frequent meetings, Alex noticed how fascinated he was by her and how he tried to impress her. She had acted cool and aloof until she was certain she had him hooked. Wielding power over a man like Sergio Vitali was more exciting than anything that she had previously experienced. Alex hadn't had time for a long-term relationship with a man. She spent an occasional noncommittal night with someone, only to disappear before dawn.

But Sergio Vitali was different from everyone else. He was definitely the Rolls-Royce of men, and he could be her ticket to New York's high society. When she'd arrived in New York at the age of twenty-three, her one and only goal had been to pursue her career. This dream had become reality some time ago. She was part of a multibillion-dollar game that was played every day behind magnificent facades. She was one of the major players of the financial world. She thought she would be satisfied once she was successful, but she quickly realized that it wasn't enough, and her ambition kept driving her. She wanted to be like the people who bought houses on Long Island, Westchester County, or Cape Cod; who were invited to the most important social events without a second thought.

Alex gave in to Sergio's persistent courtship after six weeks. It was easy for her to sleep with him. He was an exceptionally attractive man, and his breathtaking apartment on Park Avenue—once he finally brought her there—made him even more desirable in her eyes. Pure luxury spread over two floors with their reflecting thirteen-foot ceilings. The salons were furnished with the finest antiques, French crystal chandeliers, and thick carpets. Alex had heard of these stately apartments that only the super-rich could afford, larger than some country houses, but she'd never seen one from the inside.

The memories of her first night with Sergio sent pleasant shivers down her spine. To feel this well-composed man completely losing control of himself filled her with a thrilling sense of power. Sergio was crazy for her, and that in itself was flattering. But she'd left the next morning before he woke up so he wouldn't think he could claim his prize after just one—admittedly very exciting—night. Less than eight hours later he was standing at her apartment door to invite her to lunch at the Crow's Nest at the Water Club, which he had reserved entirely just for the two of them. "Impress me," Alex had challenged him on a date a few days ago, and Sergio had obliged.

"How are you, *cara*? How is work?"

"Suffocating." Alex signaled her secretary Marcia to put the files that she was carrying on her desk. "But I wouldn't have it any other way."

"I wanted to ask if you already have plans for tonight."

"Oh." Alex quickly scanned the mountain of files in front of her. "I still have a lot more work to do. It depends."

"It depends on what?"

"On what you are about to suggest." Alex smiled lightly. By now Sergio should understand that she wasn't the type to come running when he snaps his fingers.

"Hmm," he responded. "I don't know if you like things like this, and it's short notice, but I wanted to ask if you'd like to accompany me to the Stephen Freeman Foundation charity dinner at the Plaza tonight."

He said this in such a casual tone, as if he were inviting her ice skating. Alex straightened in her chair. She quickly forgot her work. She needed to reconsider her priorities, and the opportunity that Sergio offered her was clear. "But if you are too busy with work…" Sergio's voice sounded regretful, with a mocking undertone.

"My work isn't going anywhere," Alex replied.

"So you'll join me?" Sergio asked.

"Yes, I'd love to."

"Good," he responded. "I'll pick you up at eight o'clock."

Alex smiled in satisfaction as she hung up the phone. This would be another big step in the right direction: socializing with the city's most important people. Without a doubt, her first appearance on Sergio Vitali's arm would attract attention. Alex smiled triumphantly at her reflection in the window and then picked up the telephone. She had to look absolutely perfect. She had just four hours.

At dinner, Alex was seated between Sergio and Paul McIntyre, the commissioner of the New York City Department of Buildings. The other people at their table were Vincent Levy and his wife—who showed no surprise at seeing his head of M&A at Sergio Vitali's side—the famous real-estate speculator David Baines, Senator Fred Hoffman, and a few other important members of high society. After listening to Levy's and MacIntyre's wives discussing Cayman Islands vacations, and the building commissioner's wife raving about the wonderful luxury apartment that Vitali had generously placed at their disposal, she quickly wrote off the wives of these influential men as uninteresting. She had never cared for female companionship, and this type of women's talk seemed like the epitome of wasted time to her. Instead, she concentrated on the conversations among the men at the table as they discussed a construction project on Staten Island. As Alex's eyes wandered through the splendidly decorated ballroom, she noticed many celebrities. The realization that she was sitting among them filled her with an intoxicating sense of victory. But the other attendees were also eyeing her with curiosity, because it was scintillating for Sergio Vitali to appear in public with a woman who was both completely unknown and beautiful.

Alex enjoyed Sergio's undivided attention the entire evening. He made her laugh time and again with anecdotes about the people around them. The seven courses of the gala menu were exquisite, and the accompanying wines were wickedly good. After the official speeches were given, Sergio asked her to dance. Alex wasn't a particularly good dancer, so she was glad that they could hardly do more than turn on the overcrowded dance floor.

"Did you see Vince Levy's face when he saw us together?" Alex giggled. "What do you think he's thinking?"

"He probably thinks the same thing as everyone else here." Sergio smiled. His blue eyes examined her with an intensity that triggered a familiar sensation in her body. "Namely, that we're sleeping together."

Alex managed a relaxed smile.

"If I had known that you had such a bad reputation, I wouldn't have gotten involved with you," she said.

"Really?" Sergio raised his eyebrows. "I thought you didn't care about my reputation."

"Indeed, I don't," Alex said with a smile. "But I do care about *my* reputation."

"That's what I like about you, Alex," Sergio responded with amusement. "You remind me of myself. You'd do anything to reach your goal."

"Certainly not anything," Alex countered. "I might be ambitious, but there are definitely limits."

"And what are those?"

"Why don't you find out?" Alex stared deep into his blue eyes. Sergio returned her gaze. His hand slid from her waist to her bare back, and he pulled her closer to him. How had she managed to keep him at a distance for six weeks? She longed for him with every fiber of her being.

"You know I will," he murmured. His voice so close to her ear sent a shiver down her spine. "I want to find out everything about you."

They danced for a while without saying a word, until the music abruptly ended and the band took a short break. Sergio held Alex tightly in his arms, gazing at her while the other couples left the dance floor. They turned back to the table, her holding his arm. Time and again, Sergio—who apparently knew everyone there—stopped to introduce her to someone. Once they'd reached their table, Alex felt Sergio's body flinch at her side and stiffen for a split second. She followed his gaze. Paul McIntyre and Senator Hoffman, a white-haired giant, were talking to another man who looked vaguely familiar to Alex. The man stood up and put on a thin smile when he saw Sergio.

"Ah, good evening, Sergio."

"Good evening, Mayor Kostidis," Sergio responded smoothly.

Of course! That was Nicholas Kostidis, the mayor of New York City, who was incredibly popular but controversial. She had seen his distinctive face often enough on television and in the newspapers. Before he became mayor, he made a name for himself as a district attorney who prosecuted many investment bankers and who also earned a reputation for being America's most successful Mafia hunter. Alex studied him with curiosity. He was about the same age as Sergio, yet he wasn't as good-looking in a classic sense. He would have seemed almost insignificant at first sight—compared to the imposing appearance of Senator Hoffman, Paul McIntyre, and the handsome Sergio Vitali—if not for the forceful intensity of his fiery, almost-black eyes that impressed and unsettled Alex. Kostidis's posture exuded self-confidence and power. Sergio and the mayor sized each other up with cold looks. Alex could almost physically feel the tension between the two men, who were quite similar, despite their completely different appearances.

"Alex," Sergio finally said, "have you met our esteemed mayor, Nick Kostidis?"

Kostidis turned his gaze toward her. His eyes, both cool and burning, hypnotized her.

"No, I haven't." She returned his gaze with a smile. "My name is Alex Sontheim. It's a pleasure to meet you."

Sergio raised his eyebrows mockingly as she spoke. Kostidis's face showed skeptical interest as he extended his hand and held hers for a moment.

"The pleasure is all mine," he said politely, leaning closer to her. "It's always nice to see a new face among the all too familiar crowd."

Sergio interrupted before she could respond.

"I hear that you managed to bring the Zuckerman case up to the investigation committee," he said casually.

"Oh, yes!" Kostidis smiled, letting go of Alex's hand. "It took a lot of effort to convince them, but I think that it'll be worth it."

"I highly doubt it, but I wish you the best of luck," Sergio replied, also smiling. Alex looked back and forth between them in confusion. Pure hatred was boiling beneath their politeness.

The ferocity and fearlessness in Kostidis's eyes contradicted his friendly tone of voice.

"Thank you," he said, "but in my experience luck won't save you when you dive into a pool of sharks. In any case, I wish you a pleasant evening. Enjoy yourself. Miss Sontheim, it was a pleasure to make your acquaintance."

Alex simply nodded. Kostidis patted Paul McIntyre on his shoulder and moved on.

"Asshole," Sergio growled once the mayor was out of earshot. He pulled Alex's chair closer so she could sit down. She wasn't quite sure whether or not she liked Nick Kostidis, but he was an extraordinary man in any case. This is what she told Sergio after they sat down at the table again. Sergio looked at her with a mysterious expression in his eyes.

"Nicholas Kostidis is the plague," he said in a cold voice. Alex looked at him in astonishment. "He is a power-hungry, ruthless fanatic who is obsessed with the idea of turning this city into a children's playground."

"But safety and a lower crime rate are good things." Alex, who'd heard about the mayor's no-tolerance policy for combating crime, objected innocently. Sergio gave her a piercing look for a moment and then laughed.

"They certainly are."

"Kostidis is a demagogue and an agitator," Vincent Levy noted after ensuring that no one else was listening to him. "He's dangerous because he doesn't accept anything but his own truth. He is so popular with ordinary people because his truth is so simplistic."

He lowered his voice.

"He has turned this city into a police state and—"

"Kostidis can do whatever he wants," Sergio interrupted him, casually waving at a waiter, who immediately refilled their glasses. "Even with his tailored suit and silk tie he's nothing but a pathetic little Greek from Bed-Stuy, with a bark that's louder than his bite."

Both men laughed disdainfully.

"What investigation committee was he talking about?" Alex inquired.

"It's Kostidis's new obsession," Sergio said dismissively. "He's been after me for years. He keeps trying to intimidate my employees, hoping that someone will reveal a dark secret in my past and serve it to him on a silver platter. His hatred of anyone who has an Italian name is pathological. Maybe he was beaten up by an Italian bully as a child."

He laughed carelessly and raised his glass.

"Here's to our mayor and his incredible ambition, which will someday do him in."

Alex saw the cold sparkle in Sergio's eyes, but she preferred to keep silent. There was no reason for her to side with Kostidis.

A half hour later, she excused herself. She smiled as the motion of the crowd ushered her through to the foyer; she had almost forgotten about her encounter with the mayor. It was a great pleasure for her to belong among these privileged people who don't think twice about spending more money on a dinner than an average worker earned in half a year. She wandered around the long corridors of the Plaza for a while before she realized she was lost. She found herself in front of the entrance to the kitchen, turned around, and almost collided with two men who were moving quickly toward a door with a sign that read Personnel Only. To her surprise, Alex spotted Nick Kostidis. It seemed that the mayor was trying to leave the hotel through the back door.

"Oh!" Kostidis smiled once he recognized her. "Did you plan on inspecting the kitchen, Miss Sontheim?"

He remembered her name! The other man's cell phone started ringing, so he walked a little further away to take the call.

"No, I…I'm just a little lost," she replied. Kostidis was only slightly taller than Alex. She couldn't stop staring at his dark eyes. He had unusually long and thick eyelashes for a man.

"You're not from New York, right?" he asked.

"No, I'm from Germany. But I've lived here for twelve years."

"Germany!" Kostidis gave her a friendly smile. "The land of poets and thinkers! What brought you here of all places?"

"My career," Alex responded.

"Do you work here?" He raised his eyebrows.

"What did you think?" She gave him a mocking look. "I'm not a rich heiress. I was with Morgan Stanley for six years, and now I work at LMI."

"Aha. Banking. The big money." Kostidis laughed, but his eyes remained serious and inquiring.

"I like my job." Alex suddenly felt the need to justify herself. "I like this city, too. New York is so alive."

"Yes, indeed it is." Kostidis nodded. "My parents came from Greece, but I was born and raised here and never had the desire to live anywhere else. I spent some time in Washington DC for professional reasons, but I felt like I was in exile there. For me, there's just New York. I love this city despite all of its shortcomings. And I put all my energy into making New York a more beautiful and livable place."

Alex stared at Nick Kostidis. She was amazed at his sincere excitement and passion. He gestured with his hands when speaking, and his lively mannerisms captivated audiences. She remembered again that Levy had called him a demagogue and thought about Sergio's contemptuous words. Now that she had met Kostidis in person, she was no longer surprised at how he had won the mayoral elections with such an overwhelming majority. He had an almost magical magnetism and the rare talent of making a person feel like the most important human being in the world. The people of New York loved and worshipped him because his words were followed by actions. He had done more for public safety and improving the quality of life than his predecessors had accomplished in ten years.

"Nick?"

The young man with the thin blond hair and the smug look on his face had finished his phone call and was coming toward them. He eyed Alex with a mixture of curiosity and suspicion.

"Are you coming, Nick? We have to go."

"I'm coming," Kostidis said, without averting his penetrating stare from Alex. "I'll catch up with you, Ray."

"Okay." The man obeyed reluctantly.

"My babysitter." Kostidis smiled regretfully. "One appointment chases the next, and Mr. Howard makes sure that I show up everywhere on time and stay long enough. I don't envy him."

He extended his hand to Alex.

"It was a pleasure meeting you, Miss Sontheim."

"Yes, I…I think so too," she stuttered and sensed to her chagrin that her cheeks were turning red like a schoolgirl's.

"Allow me to give you some advice, even though we hardly know each other." Kostidis leaned forward slightly and lowered his voice. "Be careful with your choice of friends. Though it may be exciting, swimming with sharks is dangerous. Unless you are a shark yourself, which I don't believe."

He let go of her hand and smiled again.

"By the way, you'll find the restrooms by going downstairs from the foyer." He winked at her one more time before opening the door and disappearing. Alex was stunned. She dealt with important and influential people on a daily basis and had long stopped being easily impressed by them, but Nicholas Kostidis just managed to do exactly that.

Sergio Vitali entered the warehouse at the Brooklyn docks. The sign above the entrance door said Ficchiavelli & Sons—Italian Wine and Food Company. The last thing he wanted was another pointless discussion with his wayward youngest son, but Cesare had screwed up big time once again. Nelson had bailed Cesare out of jail that morning, and Sergio ordered him to bring the boy to Brooklyn. The offices, warehouses, cold-storage rooms, and loading ramps were deserted on this Saturday morning. There were three men waiting for Sergio in the front office. He greeted Silvio Bacchiocchi and Luca di Varese with a nod and scrutinized his youngest son, who looked back with a mixture of defiance and fear. He remained seated with crossed arms while Silvio and Luca stood up. Cesare was twenty-one, a handsome young man with the same blue eyes and sensual mouth as his father, but unfortunately, he didn't have the slightest inclination toward any kind of work. In contrast to his older brothers, Massimo and Domenico—who both graduated from high school and college with determination and now worked for their father's company—Cesare wasn't particularly bright. Besides that, he had an unpredictable temper that got him into trouble. Sergio was often forced to use his connections to help Cesare. Over the years, he'd donated large sums of money to seven different schools in hopes his son would at least manage a high-school diploma, but all his efforts were in vain.

"Hello, Cesare," Sergio said. He was not in the mood to deal with this spoiled brat.

"Hi, Papa," Cesare responded.

"Stand up when I talk to you."

Cesare raised his nose and remained seated. Sergio's expression turned as cold as ice. His cheek muscles tensed. Silvio Bacchiocchi was particularly familiar with this expression and he feared it. Silvio was in his late forties, blond and blue-eyed like so many of his Northern Italian ancestors, and had a tendency to gain weight. He had worked for Sergio for twenty-five years. Thanks to Sergio, he'd become a wealthy man, and he showed his gratitude with unconditional loyalty. No one who knew the friendly and constantly cheerful Silvio would have thought it possible that he managed his boss's business fearlessly and with a iron fist, stopping at nothing.

"Come on, stand up when your father talks to you," he said to Cesare, who obeyed reluctantly. Sergio looked at his son and noticed his runny nose and the thin layer of sweat on his forehead.

"You're using that goddamn stuff again, aren't you?" he asked. Cesare rubbed his hands nervously and wiped them on his jeans while evading his father's gaze.

"Answer me right now!"

"Sometimes. But not much."

That was a lie. Sergio had seen enough cokeheads in his life to recognize the tell-tale signs of abuse. He wasn't even surprised. Behind his loud mouth and his brutality, Cesare was a weak person.

"You got yourself arrested, you idiot! Why didn't you run away?" Sergio was enraged at his stupidity. "You actually still don't get it? Your last name is Vitali. You know what that means. Why didn't you throw the stuff away once the cops showed up? The press will jump on this, and once Kostidis gets wind of it, no one will be able to help you. You're such an idiot, Cesare!"

There was complete silence in the small office. Cesare's dumb, confused grin made Sergio even more furious. Kostidis had been after Sergio for years and was only waiting for a weakness, the slightest mistake, or a moment of foolishness—something like this—in order to strike.

Sergio knew all too well that Cesare's mindless behavior could shake his well-established power structure. When it came to assault, the cops sometimes turned a blind eye, but dealing drugs was a crime they addressed with full force. As a result of the fanatic mayor's tough policies, drug dealing was almost considered worse than murder, and even small-time crack dealers from the Bronx or East Harlem were severely punished.

"Silvio will get a lawyer for you," Sergio said to his son, "one who has no ties to us. Then we will see what he can do for you. If the cops dig in their heels, then unfortunately there's nothing that I can do."

"What does that mean?" Cesare's grin vanished.

"That you'll go to the slammer for a while." Sergio stood up. It was pointless to talk to the boy any longer. He turned away.

"Hey!" Cesare grabbed his father's shoulder. He quickly turned around as if electrified and pushed his son away. The disgust in Sergio's eyes made Cesare back off. He had never seen his father so furious.

"Papa," he began, "you can't let me—"

"I've given you every conceivable chance," Sergio said, trying hard to keep his composure. "I hoped that you'd grow up one day and understand what life is all about. But instead you get into fights like a child, snort cocaine. You drink your life away. You're getting dumber by the minute. I despise stupidity. It's the worst thing on earth."

Cesare's face turned red, and he clenched his fists. His father was the only person on this planet he feared. But he hated him to the same degree.

"Don't act like you're a saint!" Cesare yelled at him. "Do you think I don't know how much money you make with this stuff? You don't give a crap!"

"Correct," Sergio said, looking at him coldly, "but I've never used it myself, and I have definitely never let myself be caught with drugs by the police. That's the difference."

"What am I supposed to do now? I'm your son! You have to help me!" Sheer panic shone in Cesare's eyes. He'd been dead certain that his father only had to make some phone calls to straighten things out.

"I've come to the painful conclusion that all of my efforts to make a sensible human being out of you are a waste of time." Sergio's voice was gruff with contempt. "You don't even consider for a second that you have endangered all of us. I don't feel like rescuing you anymore. All that I have ever received from you in return was ingratitude. If you don't want to follow my rules, then don't expect me to help you."

The corner of Cesare's mouth twitched nervously. He was freezing and sweating at the same time.

"When they send me to prison," he said, giving his father an anxious glance, "and ask me about you, then I'll tell them everything I know."

Sergio's expression turned to ice. Silvio and Luca exchanged a troubled glance. That was the worst thing he could possibly have said. Cesare suddenly realized that he had made a huge mistake. His last remnant of confidence fell away, and tears sprang into his eyes.

"Papa!" he cried. "I didn't mean to say that."

"But you just did."

"I would never do anything to hurt you!"

"That's not possible." Sergio grimaced. He smiled contemptuously. "You have never cared for anything but women, drugs, and fistfights. Just keep on like that."

"Papa!" Cesare whined. He stretched out his hands. "I'll never take drugs again, I swear to you! Please, don't go! I'm your son!"

"Unfortunately, you are. But I have to leave. I have appointments." Sergio looked at his watch. "Luca, you come to the city with me. I still need to discuss something with you."

Sergio scowled at his son.

"You've failed to understand my most important rule, Cesare."

"Rule? What do you mean?" Cesare nervously looked back and forth between his father and the other two men, who were standing next to him with blank faces.

"Don't shit where you eat."

His father's uncharacteristic outburst of vulgarity made Cesare wince.

"Keep me posted, Silvio," Sergio said and left the room accompanied by Luca. Cesare sank down in his chair and began sobbing.

Luca di Varese sat down next to his boss in the back of the limousine. He sensed what Sergio wanted to talk to him about. Luca was a silent and slender man, thirty-eight years old. He came from the South Bronx and was orphaned at the age of four when his parents died in a building fire. His mother was the cousin of Sergio's wife Constanzia. Sergio had gotten to know the child and noticed his intelligence. He sent Luca to a good school, paid for his college degree in business administration, and made him the CEO of the Crown Regal Corporation at the tender age of twenty-six. This corporation managed all of the hotels and casinos that Sergio owned throughout the country, but the illegal part of his business was also embedded in it. Luca di Varese supervised illegal gambling, prostitution, and drug dealing for his boss, as well as laundering the funds that came from these lines of business.

"This boy is turning into a serious threat," Sergio said after a while, shaking his head pensively. "He can't stay in the city under any circumstances."

"You really won't help him?" Luca asked.

"Of course I will," Sergio sighed. "I hope that I can straighten out this matter by the end of today. As soon as the charges against him are dropped, he must get out of here for a while. I've thought about Europe."

"He could work for Barandetti in Napoli," Luca suggested, "not for us, of course, but in fish wholesale or his warehouse. Drive around a forklift. Things like that."

"Call Michele. If he doesn't have anything for him, try Stefano Piesini in Verona. It wouldn't hurt Cesare to spend a summer working in a vineyard."

Luca nodded. They sat silently in the back of the limousine.

"However, I doubt that he'll stay in Europe for the whole summer." Sergio's voice had a gloomy undertone. "His mother will take him in again. As usual."

He turned his head toward Luca and looked at him sternly.

"I will say this only once and only to you, Luca"—his voice was quiet—"but if the situation arises, I expect that you will not hesitate, not for one second."

Luca looked at his boss without flinching.

"I don't care whether he is my son or not. I will sacrifice him before he causes me serious trouble with his stupidity. Do you understand that?"

Luca nodded.

"Will you promise to take care of this personally?"

Luca di Varese's face didn't reveal what he thought about his boss's decision. He didn't ask any questions or try to put in a good word for Cesare. Luca's loyalty was unconditional, devoid of criticism.

"I promise, boss."

Alex was drenched through to the skin when she returned home with her groceries late that afternoon. She placed the four grocery bags on the kitchen table and transferred their contents to the fridge. It was totally empty, as usual. Sergio had actually planned to spend the day with her, but then another appointment had gotten in the way and he had someone drive her home at nine thirty. Whenever Alex came from his Park Avenue apartment to her place in Greenwich Village, she felt like Cinderella, and she was annoyed that she didn't have time to look for a nicer place. She lit a cigarette and thought about the past evening. She grinned as she remembered the many admiring and curious looks. People were curious because Sergio Vitali only had eyes for her the entire evening. Half of New York was surely speculating about who she was and what kind of relationship she had with Sergio. It was simply unbelievable how far she had made it! She felt like she was walking on air. The ringing of her cell phone startled her out of her thoughts.

"Good afternoon." It was Zack, and he sounded smug. "Did you enjoy your excursion into the world of the rich and beautiful?"

"What do you mean by that?" Alex played dumb. How could Zack know where she'd been last night?

"Vince told me that you were with Vitali at the Plaza. He was somewhat…surprised."

"I'm an adult. I can go out with whoever I want," Alex responded more coldly than she had intended.

"Of course." Zack laughed in a suggestive manner. "So do you fancy Vitali or just his connections?"

"That's none of your business, Zack," Alex snapped.

"It isn't," he admitted. "But now I understand why you keep brushing me off. Why would you waste your time with me if you've hit the jackpot?"

"Are you out of your mind?"

"Don't flatter yourself," Zack said in a spiteful tone. "Vitali fucks any woman he likes."

"Are you mad because you don't do it for me?"

"Nonsense," Zack said with a laugh. "You're not even my type."

Alex's laughter was forced. Zack *was* upset. Not because she consistently brushed off his overtures, but because she was in the process of passing him on her way up the social ladder. She'd spent the entire evening sitting at Vince Levy's table at the Plaza and he had not. Maybe he was jealous about her success and her favorable position with LMI's board. She realized she needed to deal with him very carefully in the future. He was an enigma, and it wasn't good to have him as an enemy.

"Listen," he said, "I actually wanted to talk to you about Micromax. I heard from a reliable source that they have serious management issues and that last quarter's numbers were dressed up considerably. There are a couple of major film companies that are more than eager to get their hands on Micromax. This could turn out to be a good deal."

Alex hesitated. Was Zack trying to meddle in her deals, or set out bait with this information?

"That sounds pretty interesting," she answered. "Let's talk about it on Monday. Okay?"

"Right." Zack's tone was no longer smug or upset. "And Alex, can I give you some advice?"

"What's that?" Something inside of her went on the defensive.

He hesitated for a moment.

"Stay away from Vitali."

Another warning! First Kostidis and now Zack. Why would he warn her about Sergio? Was he simply jealous, or was she doing him an injustice?

"Thanks, Zack," she said, "you don't have to worry about me. I know what I'm doing."

"I hope so. See you on Monday."

Nelson van Mieren sat sweating under an umbrella on one of the terraces at Sergio's luxurious villa on his private Cinnamon Island, part of the British Virgin Islands. He was disgruntled as he watched his boss and this Alex Sontheim walk up from the bay to the villa holding hands.

They'd been cruising in Sergio's snow-white, one-hundred-foot yacht *Stella Maris*—on which they'd come down here six days ago. Meanwhile, Nelson had been sitting around uselessly. Sergio had called him yesterday morning in New York and asked him to come here, although he very well knew that Nelson hated the climate and the entire island.

Nelson flew to Tortola and took a helicopter to the island, only to be the third wheel all night. With growing unease, he observed that Sergio had changed. Even a blind man could see how crazy he was about this blonde bitch. Nelson hoped that he could leave that same evening, but Sergio didn't appear to be in a rush to tell him why he wanted to speak with him so urgently. It was almost unbearable for Nelson to watch Sergio in action. When Sergio jumped into the pool with this broad after dinner, playing around and making out like a teenager, Nelson retreated.

Nelson had never seen Sergio behave so childishly in all the forty years they'd been friends, and he felt something almost like jealousy. The two met at an all-boys Catholic boarding school in Philadelphia, where they were sent at the age of six. Nelson van Mieren was much more than a simple lawyer. He was well versed in both commercial and criminal law, and he had been Sergio's right-hand man for almost thirty years. They had built an enormous empire together.

Nelson didn't like Alex Sontheim, and he was less and less pleased with how she had turned Sergio's head. There was no doubt that she was exceptionally beautiful and very intelligent, yet that was exactly what worried him. It would have been different if she were a dumb bimbo, but intelligent women were dangerous. While the two of them enjoyed their day together, Nelson came to the conclusion that he needed to put a stop to Alex's influence. He couldn't allow Sergio to listen to people other than him, especially not a woman.

Alex finally disappeared into the house. Sergio poured himself a whiskey and joined Nelson on the terrace. He wore a relaxed smile and looked years younger in shorts and a T-shirt. They talked for a while before Nelson cut to the chase and asked Sergio why he had called him here.

"I'd like to ask you for your opinion in a personal matter," Sergio responded. Nelson was in a state of red alert.

"I have never felt so content in my life." Sergio leaned back and stretched out his legs. "Since I met Alex, I feel like I'm thirty again. She's incredibly good for me."

"Well, well," Nelson replied.

Sergio kept smiling and swirled the ice cubes in his glass. "What do you think of her?"

The question sounded casual, but Nelson was instantly aware how critically important it was for him to give the correct answer. He wiped the sweat from his forehead with a handkerchief. The tropical temperatures put a strain on his circulation.

"I would appreciate hearing your honest opinion," Sergio said.

Nelson hesitated.

"She's an attractive woman," he answered elusively.

"Yes, indeed, she is"—Sergio nodded, somewhat impatiently—"but there are many other things that I love about her. I'm thinking about divorcing Constanzia."

"You can't be serious!" Nelson stared at his friend in disbelief. "You mean that you want to marry that girl?"

"I've never met a woman like her before." Sergio smiled dreamily. "She has her own will. She is successful. Just thinking about her makes my heart beat faster. This has never happened to me before. I'm fifty-six now, and I've realized that I don't want to continue my life as it was before. Everything is much more fun with Alex."

"Fun!" Nelson snorted derisively. Now he was seriously concerned. "You sound like an eighteen-year-old! I've never heard you talk like this. What has this woman done to you?"

He kept an eye on his friend. It wasn't enough to bad-mouth Alex. He needed to instill some doubts about her in Sergio's mind.

"What do you know about her, her origins, her motives? Does she like you, or is she only after your money, your power? What girl wouldn't be thrilled to cruise on a hundred-foot yacht to the private island of one of America's richest men?"

"Why do you say that?" Sergio straightened up and threw an indignant look at his lawyer. His smile had vanished, and a deep groove formed between his eyebrows.

Nelson answered carefully. "Because I want you to realize what you put on the line when you carelessly trust someone you hardly know."

"I've never been careless!" Sergio replied vehemently.

"That's why I'm even more surprised about what you just said." Nelson observed his friend attentively. Sergio was usually very good at hiding any type of emotion, but at this moment Nelson could read his friend's face like an open book. Sergio was dangerously serious about this woman.

After hesitating briefly, Sergio said, "Over the last few weeks I have given some thought to Alex assuming Shanahan's role. She does an excellent job at LMI, and she's clever and cold-blooded—"

"For God's sake, Sergio!" Nelson interrupted him. "Think about what you're saying!"

"What do you mean?"

"Sergio." Nelson leaned forward, and his voice was insistent. "You know how risky this is. Please, think about it! How well do you know Alex? How much can you trust her? What will you do when she suddenly has scruples? We can't afford another situation like we had with Shanahan."

Sergio was silent for a moment. He also knew that Levy's mistake with Shanahan had cost him a bundle and was not so easy to sweep under the rug.

"For as long as I've known you," Nelson said as he laid his hand on his friend's arm, "you have never let yourself be guided by personal emotions, and you've always done pretty well with that approach. Fine, you bang the girl, you like her. She's definitely beautiful and clever, but that's exactly what makes her dangerous. You have to watch out for clever women."

Sergio grimaced. This wasn't exactly what he wanted to hear.

"So you don't like Alex?" he asked.

"It doesn't matter whether I like her or not," Nelson countered. "Women have no place in our business. They are too unpredictable. And I think that Alex is especially unpredictable. Maybe it would make a difference if you weren't involved with her. To be honest, I think that this is far too risky for you and for all of us."

Sergio stared at his friend.

"You asked for my advice," Nelson said coolly, "and here it is: keep her away from your business. It's enough if she does her job well and Zack takes care of the rest."

Sergio was silent. Emotion and reason fought a violent battle behind his impassive face. He stared off without saying a word. The only sound to be heard was the chirping of cicadas in the hibiscus below the terrace. Nelson hardly dared to breathe. Finally, Sergio released a depressed sigh.

"You're probably right," he said reluctantly, and Nelson had the feeling that he had just barely avoided a catastrophe. His trip down here suddenly seemed worth the exertion.

"Come on, don't make such a face." He sneaked a glance at his watch, trying to decide if he could catch a flight back to Tortola before Alex reappeared with a phony smile to invite him to stay another night. "Enjoy her company for few more days. But don't let her wrap you around her finger. A little distance won't hurt."

Sergio nodded slowly.

"Thanks for your advice, Nelson," he said convincingly. "I'm probably just getting old and sentimental."

"Nonsense. Alex is a pretty girl. Keep her for the bedroom if you like." Nelson heaved his corpulent body out of the rattan chair. "I'll leave the two of you alone now. I have an appointment with Chester Milford to get to on Tortola about the terms for the new IBCs. I'll see you in the city in a couple days."

When Nelson left, Sergio poured himself a whiskey at the bar and gazed out over the emerald-green water. He had been hoping for a very different response from his friend. Maybe Nelson was right. But maybe not. Sergio had never asked for advice on his personal life before, but he also had never experienced such intense and confusing emotions.

Since their first meeting, Alex haunted his thoughts. For the first time, a woman had appeared in his dreams. Her initial standoffishness had driven him wild. Most women offered themselves as willing prey once they realized who he was, taking the thrill out of the chase. But Alex had kept him on tenterhooks for six long weeks. The combination of restraint and passion when their eyes met provided continuous fuel to the wildfire she set inside him. He courted her persistently, and their first night together proved that the wait was worthwhile. Sergio had been with many women, but his experience with Alex was beyond comparison. Their pent-up desire had discharged like thunder and lightning. They'd done things together that he—who was more old-fashioned—had never dreamed of and had even felt a prudish reluctance to try. They'd made passionate love through the night. They finally fell asleep, breathless and exhausted, as the sun was rising. Sergio knew he was in love. This made for an even harsher realization when he woke to discover she had simply left. She had done just as he always did—she'd slept with him and left, not asking if they would meet again. He was offended, but her resistance made him even crazier about her. For the first time in his life, Sergio couldn't understand what was going on inside of him, but he determined that morning that he would possess this woman at all costs. In the weeks that followed, he was happier than ever before in his life. The days on the *Stella Maris* and Cinnamon Island confirmed his suspicion that Alex was the love of his life.

He had expected Nelson to validate his actions, to give him some type of blessing. But Nelson's words had sobered him and instantly dissolved his euphoria. He suddenly felt like a sentimental fool who had been seduced by a woman. Angry, Sergio downed the whiskey in one gulp. Nelson was right. He needed to keep Alex at a distance.

May 1999

Alex and Mark sat on a bench enjoying a lunch of chicken sandwiches from Bandi's Deli. They were soaking in the warm sun at Battery Park, just like many other employees from the nearby financial district. Alex stretched out her legs, wiggled her toes in the comfortable sneakers that she had put on in place of elegant pumps, and watched a horde of tourists embark on one of the Circle Line ferries heading for to the Statue of Liberty.

"Mark, have you been to the Statue of Liberty?" she asked.

"Of course," he answered. "Three times."

"I've never been," Alex said. "What's it like?"

"Well," Mark said in between bites of his sandwich, "you have to wait in line forever because there's only one elevator that holds a maximum of two people. Or you can squeeze up the narrow stairwell with the crowd and have a fantastic view of the butt ahead of as you climb step by step for about an hour."

"My God," Alex said, dismissing the idea, "that's settled."

"My grandmother arrived in America on a ship from Europe in 1943. She's Jewish," Mark said. "When she first saw Lady Liberty, she realized that she had escaped the Nazis, the war, and the bombed-out cities, and that she was finally free. She told me and my brothers about it so many times that I had to see it for myself."

Alex swallowed the cynical remark at the tip of her tongue when she sensed Mark's honest emotion. And she had assumed he was an unemotional and somewhat boring person!

"The Statute of Liberty is a symbol of our democracy," he continued, "and whenever I see her, I feel a sense of humility and gratitude that I am able to live here and not in Africa or, say, Russia."

"You're a real philosopher," Alex replied, teasing him. He responded to her sarcasm with a skeptical look.

"Haven't you ever thanked God that you have so much good fortune in your life? That you are healthy, smart, good-looking, and managed to take advantage of your opportunities?"

Alex suddenly felt uncomfortable. She crumpled the sandwich wrapper and tossed it into a trash can next to the bench. What did God have to do with her success? She was the one who worked so hard and sacrificed so much!

She tried to lighten the tone of the conversation with a joke. "What, are you a Jehovah's Witness or something? A Scientologist?"

"No," Mark countered seriously, "I'm Jewish."

"That was supposed to be a joke." Alex grimaced.

"I don't joke around about God or faith."

She looked at him and shrugged, but his comment called to mind the values that her strict Catholic parents had instilled in her. She hadn't set foot in a church for years, though there were more than twenty-five hundred churches in New York. Suddenly she had a guilty conscience. She glanced at her watch, brushing off feelings of embarrassment.

"Lunch is over," she said. "Duty calls!"

"I hope I didn't upset you," Mark said as he straightened his tie. "I didn't mean to—"

"Forget it," she said. "Let's go."

They walked back through the park without exchanging a word. A man walking by stopped in his tracks.

"Mark? Is that you?"

They turned around. Alex had never seen this man before. He was in his midthirties, with tan skin; he was wearing mirrored sunglasses. With his jeans, Knicks T-shirt, light-brown Timberlands, and a backpack over his shoulder, he looked like a tourist.

"Oliver?" Mark asked in disbelief. When the man nodded, both of them laughed and hugged each other heartily.

"Alex," Mark said, "may I introduce an old friend of mine, Oliver Skerritt? We were law school roommates at Harvard. Ollie, this is my boss, Alex Sontheim."

"Hi, Alex." Oliver took off his sunglasses and reached out his hand with a smile. He had a nice face, with a thin goatee. He exuded a casual confidence.

Alex responded with a smile. She instinctively felt his gray eyes judging her and she wasn't sure she liked it.

"How long have you been back in the city?" Mark inquired.

"Three weeks," Oliver replied, grinning. "There's nothing worse than working where other people go for vacation."

"Where were you?" Alex inquired politely.

"The Caymans." Oliver grimaced. "On business, unfortunately. Luckily, I had the chance to do a bit of diving."

"Oliver works for the *Financial Times*," Mark explained.

"Really?" Alex was surprised. "So what were you doing in the Caribbean?"

"A piece about offshore companies," he said vaguely. "I'm somewhat familiar with the subject."

"That's a gross understatement," Mark interjected. "Oliver was with Simon, Weinstein & Cooper. He specialized in corporate law. After that, he was a fund manager at Trelawney & Hobbs and managed speculative and high-risk hedge funds."

Alex looked at the man with renewed interest.

"Why are you working for a newspaper now?" she asked. Oliver smiled, but his eyes remained serious.

"I was simply tired of my job," he replied. "You are drilled to be a ruthless and unscrupulous machine, and it's all about more money and financial success. I wanted to preserve a shred of humanity for myself. I like the whole business much better from the outside, and I finally don't have to keep my mouth shut."

"Did you get fired?" Alex asked directly.

A mocking look sudden flashed in his gray eyes.

"No." There was a hint of amusement on his face. "I simply quit, bought a house on Martha's Vineyard, a loft in the Village, and turned my hobby into my profession."

Alex couldn't understand how someone would trade a position at Trelawney & Hobbs—the world's largest investment company—for a job at a newspaper, and she suspected that he had been fired after all. "And what's your hobby?"

"Uncovering scandals," Oliver said with a smile, "and making them public."

Oliver and Alex sized each other up disdainfully.

"So you're a whistle-blower," she declared, and he became serious.

"If necessary, I also do that," he said, "and this is why I advised Mark to quit his job at LMI as soon as possible."

"Oliver," Mark started to say, "how could you say that in front of my boss—"

"It's okay, Mark." Alex stared firmly at Oliver. "Can you explain to me why?"

"I'd give you the same advice," he answered. "You still have a good, clean reputation in the industry, but that could change very soon if you keep working at that place. I've uncovered some pretty sensitive details that are directly tied to LMI. And this isn't about market manipulation or tax evasion, but substantial fraud and at least one life lost."

"Is that so?"

"Have you ever heard the name Gilbert Shanahan? No? Just ask Mark about him."

Mark's face looked like he would prefer the earth to open up and swallow him.

"Imagine," Alex said, growing impatient, "that I'm not interested one bit in this Gilbert. I have a well-paid, fascinating job, and I have worked very hard to get to where I am today."

Oliver gave her a penetrating look.

"A couple of years ago I had the same reaction," he said. "It hurts to admit that you are just a cog in the wheel of a giant criminal machine."

"Please listen closely, Mr. Skerritt," Alex interrupted Oliver harshly. "You could get into serious trouble if you keep making insinuations that you'll be hard pressed to prove."

"Shanahan was targeted by the SEC," Oliver replied, unmoved, "because he moved funds of unknown origin to various offshore tax havens. He was on his way to an SEC hearing when he was run over by a stolen truck with stolen license plates. The truck was found a few weeks later burned out in a parking lot in Vermont. Shanahan's widow claimed that her husband acted under orders of LMI's management, which they obviously vehemently deny. At the time, Levy assured the police that Shanahan was not acting in a professional capacity."

"Stop it!" Alex hissed. "I have no interest whatsoever in your absurd conspiracy theories. Let's go, Mark. Our lunch break is long over, and we have a lot of work waiting for us. Have a nice day, Mr. Skerritt."

She turned on her heel and marched off, not deigning to give Oliver Skerritt another look. Mark only caught up with her at the park's exit.

"Alex, I…I'm so sorry." He was out of breath. Alex stopped abruptly and looked at her employee.

"I don't want to hear another word about this," she said emphatically. "LMI is paying us both handsomely, so we owe them our loyalty. If you happen to disagree with me, I suggest that you take your friend's advice and hand in your notice. Have I made myself clear?"

"Yes." Mark nodded and lowered his head.

Alex started walking again. Why did Skerritt's words get to her? She should have just brushed them off with a smile and a shrug. But suddenly there was this tiny, nagging doubt planted deep inside her, a whispered warning that called to mind her private conversation with Levy. At the time, she'd accepted the bonus and decided to have it paid in stock options instead of cash. And she'd asked herself ever since how a serious investment bank could offer a hundred and fifty thousand dollars of unaccounted money. Why did Zack fly to the Bahamas, the Virgin Islands, or Grand Cayman every few weeks? Damn it! A chill overtook her, but then she chased off these gloomy thoughts. She didn't want to know anything about it. She wanted to do her job without being disturbed. Forget Oliver Skerritt!

It was difficult for Mark to focus on his work for the rest of the day. The encounter with Oliver at Battery Park was by no means a coincidence. He had carefully arranged it. Over the past weeks, his doubt had grown about the legality of the deals that he was working on. During his research for the current Micromax deal—which appeared to be unspectacular at first—Mark had discovered that Finley Desmond, the majority shareholder of the Los Angeles-based Ventura Film Corporation who wanted to acquire Micromax, already owned a large equity stake in Micromax by means of a dubious Canadian company. This Canadian company was in turn owned by a familiar player, namely SeViCo Holdings, which was owned by Sunset Properties. This was a rather strange coincidence; it almost looked like money laundering. Mark didn't like the thought of working for a company that was involved in shady business. It was becoming clear to him that something wasn't quite kosher at LMI.

When he told Oliver about his suspicions, Oliver shared many more details with him. He suspected that Alex knew about everything. Mark refused to believe him, but he was deeply disappointed that Alex wouldn't even listen to Oliver.

He vividly remembered how Gilbert Shanahan had changed in the weeks preceding his death. Before joining LMI, he was the top equities trader at Cantor and owned multiple Ferraris and a mansion on Long Island. Before he died, this pompous man had turned into a bundle of nerves, a shadow with bloodshot eyes who twitched every time the telephone rang. He couldn't handle the pressure that he was under anymore. Mark saw Shanahan every day and observed his growing panic, expecting him to have a breakdown. Was Shanahan really involved in illegal activities on his own account? Or should he believe Oliver's version—that Levy used Shanahan and ultimately sacrificed him when it seemed the shady wheeling and dealing might blow up?

Was Alex possibly involved in the same business as Shanahan? Mark stared at the wall. He admired his boss. It wasn't as easy as it had been ten years ago to find a well-paying job if you didn't specialize in a particular field. These two factors had prevented him from following his friend's advice. But what if Alex really did know about the dubious connections between her clients and—

The ringing of the telephone pulled him out of his thoughts. It was Alex. She was waiting for the LMI profit forecasts to finance the Micromax deal for Ventura. Mark grabbed his files and left for Alex's office. He would continue to observe everything. That was all that he could do.

May 17, 1999

Alex was dead tired as she rode the subway home. Earlier that day, she had finally closed a major deal she had been working on around the clock for the past week. Yet, she left the party with her team at Luna Luna after just one drink. She didn't feel like celebrating. She felt simultaneously burned-out and electrified. The stress didn't bother her, but the article in the *Post*'s gossip column someone had placed on her desk during lunch did. Alex boiled with rage after reading it. Sergio had attended a charity golf tournament last weekend on Long Island with supermodel Farideh Azzaeli on his arm for the third event in a row. Sergio had asked her to make time for him, which she did. She even turned down two other invitations so she could be with him. But he stood her up and she was left at home waiting for his call. Since their return from Cinnamon Island, Sergio had completely changed his behavior toward her. Before the trip, he had sometimes called her three times a day just to say hello, but since their return he called only once in a while to get together for sex. Alex couldn't understand what changed. She was hurt, and she was incredibly angry that she—who was so competent and powerful in her job—had lost control of the situation and let a man humiliate her like this.

Alex climbed the subway stairs at the corner of Broadway and Eighth Street and picked up some pasta from an Italian restaurant and a bottle of Brunello di Montalcino, stubbornly ignoring the repeated humming of her cell phone as she made her way home. When she finally checked, she saw that it was Sergio. She had no desire whatsoever to talk to him. She was well above playing second fiddle to a starved, cow-eyed model. She turned at the corner and saw the bicyclist too late. He tried to brake, but the front wheel and handlebars slammed into her hip and elbow. The bag with the pasta and the bottle of wine slid from her hands.

"Damn it!" she yelled at the bicyclist, who almost crashed. "Open your eyes!"

"You could watch where you're going, lady!"

This voice sounded familiar to Alex, and she took a closer look. After a few seconds, she recognized Oliver Skerritt.

"Oh, it's you," she said in a sarcastic tone. "Are you chasing after another conspiracy? Why are you in such a rush?"

Then he recognized her and grinned.

"What a coincidence," he said. "Honestly, I was just grabbing some food at Giovanni's. I'm sorry."

"You just ruined my dinner."

Alex bent down to pick up the broken glass.

"Wait, let me help you."

"No thanks, I've got it. Ouch!" Alex cursed as she cut her finger. Her emotions overcame her: she was mad at Sergio and feeling tired and hungry. Tears welled in her eyes.

"Here." Oliver handed her a clean tissue, which she wrapped around her bleeding finger as they both continued picking up the remnants of her dinner.

"What are you doing?" she asked.

"I can't stand to see girls cry." He looked up and smiled, his face level with hers. She realized that he had beautiful eyes. His hair was a little shorter than it was a few weeks ago, and looking closely, she found him quite attractive.

"I'm not crying anymore," she replied, "but now I have to find myself something to eat."

"How about a plate of *tagliatelle al salmone* over at Giovanni's?" Oliver straightened up. "As compensation for damages, so to speak."

Alex looked at him suspiciously for a moment and then shrugged her shoulders. She didn't feel like sitting in her apartment alone hoping Sergio might possibly appear at her door because she wouldn't answer the telephone.

"I'm really hungry," she said, "but I'm in no mood for an evening of abstruse conspiracy theories."

Oliver looked at her bemusedly and then adopted a solemn expression.

"I swear," he said, raising his hand as if making a pledge, "that I will not utter a single word about LMI or Gilbert Shanahan."

"Okay." Alex had to smile reluctantly. "It's a deal. But if you mention them even once, I'll get up and leave on the spot."

"I would never risk such a thing," Oliver responded and picked up his bike. "I'm a journalist in my heart and soul, but I'm not an idiot."

He really wasn't. He was downright entertaining and had a good sense of humor. Over big bowls of pasta and a bottle of Chianti, he told her about his childhood in Maine, where his father owned a few fish trawlers, and his student days at Harvard and in Europe. He had lived and worked in Paris, London, Frankfurt, and Rome over the course of his career. He and Alex got to talking about Frankfurt, ordered a second bottle of Chianti, and then a third. Alex's cell phone was turned off, and she was surprised how quickly the time passed. It was after midnight when they left the restaurant. Oliver had kept his promise and not said a word about LMI or Shanahan. Alex struggled to walk in a straight line and stumbled over the curb. Oliver let go of his bike just in time to grab hold of her.

"Oops," she mumbled. "I think I had a little too much to drink."

His embrace felt good. They stared into each other's eyes and before she knew what was happening, he leaned forward and kissed her. She could not contain the flash of lust that coursed through her body. She wrapped her arms around his neck and returned his kiss with passion. They broke apart and shared a moment of breathless eye contact. The second kiss was longer and more passionate than the first. She liked Oliver. Very much. Sergio had cheated on her and stood her up with some model. Ha! In less than a half hour since discovering his infidelity, she'd gotten back at him.

June 14, 1999

Sergio Vitali looked silently at the photos spread on his desk. He flipped through them slowly and was annoyed to notice his hands shaking.

"Who is this guy?" he asked, trying to control his voice.

"His name is Oliver Skerritt," Silvio Bacchiocchi responded. "He's a freelance journalist for the *Financial Times* and he lives on Barrow Street in the Village."

A wave of jealousy washed over Sergio. For days now, he had been trying to reach Alex to no avail. Her secretary kept making excuses, and his voice mails remained unanswered. So he had sent Silvio to follow her, and now he had to face the fact that she was running around hand in hand with another guy! He had done what Nelson suggested. With this nitwit Farideh Azzaeli, he had been trying prove to Alex that he didn't need her, even if it was terribly difficult for him to do so because his longing for Alex almost drove him crazy. Sergio was annoyed by his obsession; he couldn't bear the thought that she was seeing another man.

"How often does she see him?" he asked.

"Three times last week," Silvio said. "Tuesday, Thursday, and Friday. They spent the entire weekend together. They went to Central Park, a couple of bars, the Washington Square Arch, and went shopping."

"Did she also…stay overnight?"

"Er…yes."

Sergio swept the photos off his desk and stood up. With a stony expression, he stared down over the city from his office window on the top floor of the VITAL Building. The thought that she may have talked to this guy about him, maybe even laughed about him, was eating away at Sergio. This humiliation was a defeat that he could hardly bear. "What do you want me to do?"

Kill the bastard, Sergio thought, but then he relaxed.

"Nothing," he said without turning around. "Watch him and keep me posted."

Silvio picked up the photos and left the office. Sergio sat down at his desk and buried his face in his hands. Nelson was so right about her! He had almost trusted Alex! He really thought that he meant something to her! Now, she was more interested in a miserable newspaper hack who rollerbladed in the park! For the first time he could remember, his private life consumed him to such a degree that he neglected his business—which made him even angrier. Alex had developed into a dangerous obsession.

Alex couldn't get out of the annual charity event sponsored by LMI at the Metropolitan Museum of Art, though she considered every conceivable excuse. A personal invitation from Vincent Levy was an order. For a moment, she considered asking Oliver to join her so that he could get a closer look at these Wall Street sharks—whom he loved to observe and disparage—but then she decided against it. She really liked Oliver. He was funny, sensitive, and intelligent. She didn't feel an unpleasant pressure to play any role with him. The last weekend—the third they'd spent together—might not have been as spectacular as the ones with Sergio, but it was much more relaxed and entertaining. She and Oliver went rollerblading in Central Park, visited the Frick, shopped at Zabar's, and spent an entire afternoon people-watching in Washington Square Park. And the day built up into a great night together. There was no tense competition for dominance between them, no tactics, no acting as with Sergio. Sergio! He was the real reason Alex didn't want to attend this event, but she couldn't avoid him forever. For three weeks, she had consistently ignored his phone calls, voice mails, and the flowers that he sent to her office.

When she arrived at the Met, the tension was almost unbearable. Sergio was suddenly right in front of her. She had almost forgotten how it felt to be in his presence. He looked breathtakingly handsome. If she thought her time with Oliver would erase all her feelings for Sergio, then she was mistaken.

"Good evening, *cara*," he said. The sound of his dark voice made her shiver. "I was hoping I'd see you tonight."

"Hello, Sergio," Alex replied with a tentative smile. "I hoped so, too."

"You look stunning." Sergio didn't say a single word about how Alex had been obviously avoiding him. He pretended everything was just fine. They chatted for a while, just like distant acquaintances, until he finally posed the question that seemed to burn in his soul.

"Why do I get the feeling that you've been avoiding me the past few weeks?" He made it sound casual, taking two glasses of champagne from the passing waiter's tray and handing one to Alex. She noticed that Zack was roaming near them, curiously watching from the corner of his eye.

"Why should I avoid you?" she asked.

"I was wondering the same thing." He sipped his champagne and observed her closely.

"I'm very busy at work." Alex lowered her voice. She knew Zack's ears perked up. "And when I saw in the paper that you'd rather be accompanied by Farideh Azzaeli, I figured you were tired of me."

He smiled, but his eyes were penetrating.

"Are you jealous?" he inquired.

"No, I'm not. I certainly know other men besides you." She said this with a sense of malicious satisfaction as she watched the smile fade from his face. "I don't need to be stood up. There was a time when I thought that you cared about me, but you obviously don't. I don't feel like playing games."

Sergio raised his eyebrows.

"Games?"

"Exactly. What else would you call this? A relationship? First you call to tell me to keep my weekend open, and then I read in the newspaper that you're screwing this skinny bitch!"

He didn't like her vulgarity, but as usual, he hid every emotion behind his expressionless face.

"I didn't have sex with that woman," he said.

"Oh really?" Alex grimaced in disgust. "I don't believe that for a minute."

"But it's true. And after all, you stood me up first."

"I have a tough job," Alex said, without averting her gaze from his blue eyes. "I work eighty hours every week, and I can't always be available whenever you feel like it."

"What do you expect from me?" Sergio asked.

Yes, what did she expect? Did she expect anything at all from him anymore? Alex suddenly lost interest in this childish trial of strength. She didn't feel like arguing with him.

"I don't know," she said with a sigh. "Let's talk about it some other time. I had a long day."

Sergio took a long and close look at her, and then he nodded.

"I'll call you tomorrow," he said. "It would be nice of you to stop having someone else make excuses for you."

Alex suddenly thought of Oliver, and she felt even more miserable. She had not even talked to him about Sergio. To her own surprise, she wished she was courageous enough to tell Sergio to leave her alone. Before he could say anything else, she pushed through the crowd toward the coat check.

Alex stood on the steps of the Metropolitan Museum and took a deep breath. She longed for Oliver. Suddenly, she grabbed her cell phone and dialed his number. But she got his voice mail. Disappointed, she put her phone back in her purse. She sat down on the steps with a sigh and lit a cigarette. She didn't care if anyone saw her. After a while, she started to feel better. She flicked the cigarette butt and went looking for a taxi. She leaned on a telephone pole, taking in the mild night air, but no taxi passed.

She was just planning on returning to the museum to tell Sergio to forget about calling when a piercing scream startled Alex out of her thoughts. In the dim light of the streetlamp, she saw two men attacking a woman who had just left the museum. Without thinking, Alex jumped up, slipped her heels off her feet, and ran over to them. The woman was lying on the ground while one of the men pulled at her purse and the other—a scruffy white guy with rotten teeth—kicked her. Alex rammed her elbow with full force into the kicking man's back. He fell, hitting his head against a wall. His buddy let go of the purse in surprise. Alex had finally found an outlet for her pent-up frustration. She took a swing and slammed her purse into the other guy's face and then kicked him in the groin. This sent him to his knees with a gurgling groan. With sheer panic in her eyes, the woman crawled to the side.

"Are you okay?" Alex asked the woman.

The two men had run off.

"I...I think so," the woman whispered. Her skirt had slipped up, and her knee was bleeding. She was in a state of shock, her purse pressed to her chest. Tears ran down her face. She was probably in her early forties and appeared very refined. Some passersby had stopped on the other side of the street, and two men ran over to them.

"Could you please call the police?" Alex shouted, leaning over the woman, whose entire body was trembling.

"My necklace," the woman whispered and felt her neck. "They tore it off me."

"It can't be too far from here." Alex stroked the woman's arm to calm her. One of the passersby from the other side of the street found the necklace on the pavement. Seconds later, a police car came rushing up with the siren howling. Another appeared shortly thereafter. The police officers asked the woman how she was doing and what had happened.

"I was at a charity event in the Metropolitan Museum," the woman said quietly. "I thought I could walk home from here. It's only three blocks away."

The woman, who was still holding firmly onto Alex's hand, starting crying again.

"You're lucky this lady came to your rescue."

"I'm so grateful to you!" The woman wiped her tears, smudging her makeup with the back of her hand. "How can I possibly thank you?"

"Anyone would have done that," Alex replied. "It's okay."

"Unfortunately, that's anything but the norm," one of the police officers said. He seemed impressed. "Most people quickly move on when they see someone in trouble. Besides, those guys could have been armed."

"But they weren't." Alex looked at her watch. "Can you take this lady home? I have to pick up my shoes and go home."

"Please!" The woman grasped Alex's hand again. "Please come with me! I live on Park Avenue, not far from here. Our driver can take you home from there, so you don't need a taxi."

Alex hesitated. She didn't want to be celebrated as the Great Rescuer. After the police took more information, and sent a squad car to track down the muggers, Alex was surprised to discover that she had rushed to the aid of world-famous opera singer Madeleine Ross-Downey. She decided to get into the police car after all, which took them to 1016 Park Avenue. Alex knew the area because Sergio's apartment was in the building right next to the Downeys'. Park Avenue between Sixtieth and Eightieth Streets was the finest and most expensive area in the city. The rich and powerful lived in large, historic buildings that would better fit a gorgeous Paris boulevard. This elitist microcosm was shielded from the poverty and desperation of East Harlem, just a mile away. Security personnel and private bodyguards made sure that Park Avenue was just as secure as a small town. The doorman of 1016 was shocked when he saw the battered Mrs. Ross-Downey climb out of the police car. She was past the initial shock, and she assured the worried doorman that she was fine.

"Is it all right if I leave you here, Mrs. Ross-Downey?" Alex asked.

"Oh please, call me Madeleine." The opera singer gave her an unsure smile. "And please, come upstairs for a moment. My husband wouldn't forgive me if I failed to introduce him to the woman who rescued me."

Alex was curious about the apartment and Madeleine's husband, Trevor Downey. The papers called him "Manhattan's Department Store

King," the heir of the department-store chain with the same name. The two of them rode up in the marble-clad elevator to the third floor. The doorman had called upstairs, so Trevor was waiting in the open apartment door. He embraced his wife in both shock and relief, and she started to cry once again.

When Madeleine regained her composure, she introduced Alex to her husband. Trevor Downey was in his mid-forties, and he had thin sandy hair and friendly brown eyes. They went into one of the salons, which was dominated by a massive fireplace, and sat down on soft leather armchairs. Trevor poured a glass of cognac each for his wife and Alex, which they both gladly accepted. While Madeleine eloquently described the mugging and Alex's courageous actions, Alex looked around at the luxurious apartment. With its shiny wood floors, artfully illuminated paintings in splendid golden frames, and valuable antiques, it seemed friendlier than Sergio's cold marble palace in the adjacent building. Through the opened wing doors, she noticed a snow-white concert grand piano in the neighboring salon. Trevor wrapped a wool blanket around his poor wife's shoulders and stroked her cheek. It was obvious that the Downeys shared a deep love and respect for each other. Alex felt a sting inside that felt almost like jealousy. For the first time in her life, Alex sensed that money and success weren't everything.

"I can't believe that I could be so careless." Madeleine clutched her cognac glass with both hands. Her face was pale and tear stained, but she seemed to be fairly calm in her familiar environment. "Don and Liz, who went with me, wanted to take me home. But then I thought that a short walk wouldn't hurt. When you live in such a protected world, I guess you lose your perspective."

Trevor put his hand on her shoulder.

"The important thing is that nothing worse happened to you, thanks to your rescuer." He smiled at Alex.

"That was incredibly courageous of you, Alex!" Madeleine's eyes sparkled with admiration, and then she giggled quietly. "You really went after those two crooks! Weren't you scared at all?"

"Everything happened so fast that I didn't have any time to think about it," Alex admitted. She briefly thought about her raging anger at Sergio and her entire situation, which she'd unleashed against those two men. But she decided not to mention her dark thoughts to these cultivated people. It was better to let them think of her as the noble rescuer.

"My wife and I would like to thank you for your courageous and selfless intervention, in any case." Trevor sat down next to his wife, and they held hands.

"We'll tell Nick all about it," Madeleine said. "He'll be shocked because he works so hard for safety in this city. And then something like this happens, to me of all people!"

"Mayor Nick Kostidis and his wife Mary are close friends of ours," Trevor explained. "Pardon my rudeness, Alex, but in all this excitement I forgot your last name."

"Sontheim. Alex Sontheim."

"Ah." He leaned forward and looked at her with renewed interest. "Yes, of course! Alex Sontheim. This evening's event was organized by your employer, after all. I've heard a great deal about you. You have a remarkable reputation on Wall Street."

"Thank you very much." Alex smiled humbly. She enjoyed that even Manhattan's Department Store King knew her name. If he was a friend of the mayor, she realized that he couldn't possibly be a friend of Sergio.

"Wall Street?" Madeleine asked in astonishment. "Do you work at the stock exchange?"

"No, an investment bank," Alex responded. "I'm the head of the mergers and acquisitions department at LMI."

"How fascinating!" Madeleine exclaimed.

"It's nothing to write home about." Alex shrugged her shoulders.

"It certainly is." Madeleine looked at her with curious eyes. "I always thought that just men were involved in that business. Somehow I had a completely different image of investment bankers."

"And I thought that all opera singers look like Montserrat Caballé," Alex countered with a smile, which finally broke the ice. They liked each other straightaway. All three of them laughed, and Trevor poured another round of cognac.

It was two thirty in the morning. Alex glanced at her watch and was amazed to realize how late it was. Trevor insisted on having his chauffeur drive Alex home. She gratefully accepted this offer after the Downeys made her promise to get together again. Alex sat in the back of the limousine and stared out the window in contemplation. The past three hours that she had spent with the Downeys showed her with great clarity what was missing in her life. She had never before wasted a single thought on marriage and friendship because her career was always more important, but she had felt lonely many times during the past few months. She had no real friends in her life. She no longer had any idea at all what she really wanted, which was a strange and oppressive feeling. On an impulse, Alex asked the chauffeur to drive her to Barrow Street. She hoped that Oliver was at home and wouldn't be angry with her for showing up at his place in the middle of the night. It took a while before he came to the intercom half asleep.

"It's me, Alex," she said. "Sorry that I'm waking you this late, but can you let me in?"

If he was surprised, he didn't show it. He answered the door in his boxer shorts and smiled with sleepy eyes. Without saying a word, she wrapped her arms around his neck and kissed him. His skin was warm and smelled slightly like sweat. Suddenly she was overcome with the desire for him on the spot, to be as intimate as Madeleine and Trevor. They fumbled their way to his bed and made love tenderly.

"And now you can tell me everything," Oliver said as they rested side by side, holding each other tightly, pleasantly exhausted. Alex barely mentioned the event at the museum, but she described in detail how she'd virtually knocked out the two men, how the police showed up, and her surprise when she discovered the identity of the woman she had rushed to help. She told him about the Downeys and their apartment, while Oliver listened with an impressed look on his face. Alex felt very close to him and decided to reveal a little more about herself.

"I was embarrassed at how often she thanked me and how they treated me like a noble and selfless rescuer," she said.

"But that's what you were," Oliver objected. "I wouldn't have dared to attack two guys. Honestly. That's courage."

"No." Alex turned to the side so that she could see him better in the half dark of the night. "It was more an impulsive reaction. I was so incredibly mad that it was simply an outlet for my anger. If I'd had a baseball bat instead of my purse, I would have beaten those guys to a pulp."

Oliver looked at her with sleepy eyes and stroked her arm.

"It makes you furious watching helplessly while someone gets mugged," he said. He didn't understand.

"It had nothing to do with the mugging," Alex said as she shook her head. "I ran into the man I'd been…er…seeing for the past few months at the event."

"I thought that was me." Oliver smiled.

"I haven't talked about him because I didn't know exactly what to say," Alex said. "It's a strange thing with him, nothing serious. He's married."

"Not good."

"I never planned on having a serious relationship with him," Alex explained. "When I met him, I told myself that it would be fine to go out every once in a while and have some fun. Besides that, he knows many important people, and I thought that I could benefit in some way."

Oliver was no longer sleepy. He looked at her with his full attention.

"I admit that I was flattered by his interest in me," Alex continued. "He once reserved an entire restaurant for us. We flew in his private jet to see a boxing match in Las Vegas and to the Academy Awards. It was totally crazy and exciting."

"He wanted to impress you." Oliver put on his glasses.

"Yes, I'm pretty sure that's what he wanted to do."

"And why were you so mad at him tonight?"

"Because he stood me up three weekends in a row while I sat at home waiting for his phone calls."

"Aha. And when you were really mad and hurt, I came along."

"You ran me over with your bicycle," Alex reminded him and smiled. "But that night it became clear to me that I didn't feel anything for him. It was simply exciting to be with him. An excursion into high society."

"Great." Oliver acted unimpressed and sat up in bed. "But how could this man—for whom you supposedly have no feelings—make you so angry that you went after two men just to let off some steam? Wouldn't you have to feel something for him to get so angry?"

Alex looked at him in bewilderment. Was he mad at her now?

"Would it have been better not to say anything?"

"You show up here at two thirty in the morning, have sex with me, and then you tell me about another guy," replied Oliver. "What should I make of that?"

"Okay, then I won't say another word."

She smiled and stretched out her hand toward him.

"Does this Park Avenue guy also have a name?"

"Yes. I'm pretty sure that you've heard it before. His name is Sergio Vitali."

"Holy shit!" Oliver suddenly threw back the blanket with a jerk. He fished for his boxers and jumped up. He turned on the light switch and left the bedroom. Confused, Alex squinted into the bright light. She got up and followed him into the kitchen.

"What's wrong with you?" she asked. Oliver turned around quickly. There was no trace of a smile on his face, and his gray eyes were ice cold.

"It would be better if you got dressed now and left," he said, opening the refrigerator door. Alex instantly regretted her honesty, because she felt true affection for Oliver. She didn't understand what had made him so angry.

"Leave!" he repeated, not looking at her. "I'm better off if I forget you as quickly as possible."

His voice sounded bitter.

"You can't just throw me out like this," Alex began timidly. "Just because I—"

It was very important for her to stay in his good graces. She didn't want to leave now with such hard feelings between them. Oliver slammed the refrigerator door and turned around. Alex was frightened when she saw the angry glint in his eyes. What had set him off?

"You've breached my trust," he snarled.

Alex stared at him without understanding.

"I promised not to mention any of those monstrosities at LMI that I uncovered over the past months and years. I accepted the fact that you didn't want to know anything detrimental about your employer, hoping that you'd recognize it yourself one day, and preferably before it's too late. I really started to like you. Not in a million years would I have thought that you could be involved with *Vitali*!"

Alex was taken aback and swallowed hard.

"I've formed a pretty comprehensive opinion about this guy over the past few years because I kept stumbling across his name over and over again during my research. This man has his fingers in almost every criminal business in this city. Among other things, he's a shareholder of LMI. His entire empire is built upon blood and crime. He's an unscrupulous and brutal gangster. I just can't associate with people like that. It's a cruel twist of fate that I would end up in bed with a woman who lets *him* fuck her!"

His brutal frankness hit Alex like a slap in the face.

"What a shame, Alex, it's really a shame." Oliver let himself sink onto the kitchen chair. He looked at her with a mixture of pity and disgust. "I really thought that you were different. But you're apparently just another one of those women who close their eyes and ears to reality, driven by pathological ambition."

She was shocked by the coldness of his words.

"None of this is true," she responded. "Sergio has nothing to do with LMI."

"Are you kidding me, or are you really that naive?" Oliver shook his head and burst out laughing, but it wasn't a happy laugh. "He sits on the board of directors!"

"Yes, I know, but he sits on a dozen boards. I would know if he had something to do with LMI's business," Alex whispered, perplexed. "He would have told me!"

"Unbelievable," said Oliver, more to himself than to Alex. "I've banged a gangster's whore!"

This left Alex speechless for a moment. *Gangster's whore!* How outrageous! Hot anger rose within her.

"How dare you!" she screamed, and tears sprang into her eyes. "Who do you think you are to judge other people so harshly?"

"Incidentally, this is a free country, and I can judge whomever I please." He stood up and pushed past her.

"I wish you the best of luck," he said and opened the front door. "Go to your Mafia lover! If you keep on like this, you'll be on LMI's board in no time. I hope that it's worth your investment. Good-bye."

"Can I get dressed first?"

Oliver didn't respond. He seemed to have lost all interest in her. Alex's blood hissed in her ears. She let her tears run freely only after she had closed the apartment door behind her. Oliver's cold contempt and hurtful words stung like salt in a wound. The sky reddened to the east as she stumbled along the street, blinded by tears and bewilderment. *A gangster's whore!* The insult echoed in her ears, and she cried angry tears of desperation and humiliation. Why did she always end up with the wrong men? First Sergio, who stood her up, and now this! The tears stopped, and a paralyzing chill took hold of her. The clicking of her high heels on the pavement echoed in the empty streets, and she felt more miserable with every step. Oliver's reaction had struck a sore point she preferred not to think about. She had managed to mentally block any speculations about Sergio's connections to the underworld she saw in the press. She had refused to listen to Oliver's accusations against LMI. But Alex suddenly realized that she couldn't ignore these signals any longer. She realized how lonely she was. She had no one to talk to, no one to trust. Her whole world started to crumble before her eyes. Her certainty that what she was doing was right had just vanished.

Three hours later, Alex was at her desk with swollen eyes and a pitch-black cup of coffee. The week ahead promised to be very exciting. A hostile takeover battle involving merger negotiations between the country's two leading waste management companies was coming to a head. For weeks, United Waste Disposal had been defending itself to the best of its ability against Waste Management's advances. Alex observed this attentively and called Fred W. Watkins, CEO of A&R Resources, to suggest he step in as a white knight. Watkins, who'd met Alex a couple of months ago through Sergio, was more than excited by this proposal. A&R Resources was a highly specialized company that primarily handled military waste disposal, but Alex found out Watkins was looking to diversify his business in order to expand. Without hesitation, Watkins hired Alex and LMI to work on the acquisition of United Waste Disposal; as a result, she was now involved in this hard-fought takeover battle.

The atmosphere on Wall Street was tense as bankers anticipated a Federal Reserve interest rate hike. Alan Greenspan had hinted at an increase to combat inflation. Investor nerves were on edge waiting to see whether such an interest rate hike would lead to consolidation or plummet to a crash. The noise on the trading floor was deafening as traders tried to placate their clients. The NASDAQ started sliding in the first few minutes after the opening bell. Alex hadn't even turned on her Mac yet when Marcia entered with a pile of notes.

"The appointment with the A&R lawyers is confirmed for noon," she announced. "Mr. Watkins and Mr. Levy will be there, Steve Cavanaugh from Schuyler & Partner asked for a call-back, as well as Franklin Mills and Mr. Weinberg. And Mr. Vitali called. I told him that you're still in a meeting. Was that right?"

Yes. No. Alex rubbed the bridge of her nose with her index finger and thumb. Marcia had been on strict orders to put Sergio off by all possible means for the past three weeks.

"He said that he'll call again."

"You can put him through then." Alex typed in the password on her keyboard and was happy that Marcia hadn't mentioned her disastrous appearance this morning. By now, last night seemed like a crazy nightmare or a bad movie that she had watched half asleep and could only recall in fragments. She obviously should have talked to Oliver about Sergio a long time ago, but she still felt incredibly humiliated and hurt by his reaction. Alex really liked Oliver, but that made her even angrier. How could he insult her this way without giving her a chance to justify herself?

Just as she was checking her e-mails, Marcia transferred a phone call to her. It was Sergio. Her heart fluttered.

"I spent the whole night thinking about what you said," he began, not even bothering to greet her, "and you're right. What would you say if we scratch everything that happened so far and make a fresh start?"

"Do you think that's a good idea?"

"Join me for dinner tonight, *cara*. Let's talk about everything in peace and quiet. Please."

A light was flashing on Alex's telephone.

"I have one appointment after the other today," she replied with hesitation. "The board of a new client from Texas is in town."

Sergio couldn't let her get away with such a lame excuse. Despite all of the doubts that Oliver had sown in Alex's heart, Sergio was still the most important person in her life.

"I need to see you, *cara*," he said in a pleading tone that Alex had never heard before, "and I have a surprise for you."

Alex hesitated. Sergio's surprise could turn out to be a trip to Las Vegas or dinner in Miami.

"Okay," she said halfheartedly.

"Wonderful. I'll come over to your place at eight. *Ciao, cara*."

The spacious penthouse apartment with a terrace and winter garden was located directly on Central Park West at Sixty-Sixth Street and offered a magnificent park view. Eight tastefully furnished salons on two levels were distributed over more than three thousand square feet. They were pure luxury, the dream of millions of New Yorkers. A single elevator led from the parking garage directly to the penthouse, and the all-around rooftop terrace was accessible from every room. A starry night sky arched across the city, and the air was mild and soft. The luxuriantly blossoming roses twining around a pergola exuded a bewitching fragrance.

Sergio observed Alex as she walked through the rooms in amazement and finally stepped out onto the terrace. He could tell she had spent the night with that guy again. Silvio had seen her arrive in a limousine at two thirty in the morning and walk into the building on Barrow Street. The hidden cameras that Silvio's men had installed throughout the apartment recorded her doing it with this guy. Sergio watched the tape thirty times, listening in cold anger to what she'd said to him. *"On that night it became clear to me that I didn't feel anything for him. It was simply exciting to be with him. An excursion into high society."*

Sergio also heard what the guy had said, and the sheer desire to kill him had risen up inside of him. After much drama, Alex had left the house shortly after five and walked home.

While he and Alex had a sophisticated dinner at Le Cirque, Oliver Skerritt had a painful encounter with three of Silvio's men. If someone had already found him, he was certainly in the hospital by now. With a feeling of spiteful satisfaction, Sergio thought about the images of Skerritt's disfigured face Silvio had sent to his cell phone about an hour ago. The bastard would stay away from Alex in the future. He was pretty sure about that.

"Do you like the apartment?" He leaned against the open terrace door and looked at her.

"Are you kidding?" Alex turned toward him. "Who wouldn't like such an apartment? Who lives here?"

Until three days ago, some other tenants lived here. But Sergio had them thrown out without notice so he could show Alex an apartment that she would definitely like.

"You mentioned once that you would like an apartment with a view of the park," he said casually. He grabbed a bottle of champagne from an ice cooler. "And when I heard that this apartment was vacant, I thought of you. You can have it."

Alex leaned on the railing and smiled. Her smile attracted Sergio like a compass needle is drawn to the North Pole.

"I can't afford an apartment like this."

"You don't even know what it costs yet." Sergio poured champagne into two glasses and held one of them toward her.

"Are you serious?" She tilted her head in disbelief.

"It's a coincidence that the entire building belongs to me," Sergio responded. "I would rent it to you for twenty-five hundred a month."

"That sounds like a bad deal for you."

"I never make bad deals." He was standing very close to her. "So?"

She gave him a look that was hard to decipher. Her thick, glossy hair fell over her shoulders. She was so beautiful and desirable that he could hardly bear not to touch her. Strangely enough, he didn't even care that she had slept with someone else not even twenty-four hours ago.

"When can I move in?"

This made Sergio smile. She had swallowed the hook.

"Today, if you like." He took the glass from her hand. Before she could say a word, he lifted her up and carried her into the bedroom.

Long past midnight, as they were lying on the bed exhausted and breathing heavily, their sweaty bodies wrapped around each other, Alex remembered the things that Oliver had said about Sergio. She decided to take advantage of this moment of intimacy.

"Sergio?" She kissed his naked shoulder.

"Hmm..." He was lying on his back and smiling sleepily.

"I'd like to ask you something, but please only answer if you're telling the truth."

Sergio's eyes opened wide.

"Okay."

"They keep writing in the newspapers that your father was a Mafioso."

"Yes, he probably was." He turned his head so that she could see him better. "His bad reputation still haunts me today, as you've noticed. Unfortunately, people automatically think that you're with the Mafia if you have an Italian name and are successful."

"They claim that your father killed many people."

Sergio looked at Alex pensively.

"I was nineteen when my father was shot," he said slowly. "I think that he deserved it because he killed a lot of people."

Alex shivered. "That sounds intense."

"Intense?" Sergio grimaced. "My father was a hit man. He came to America from Sicily as a young man knowing nothing but tending sheep and handling weapons. He did that in order to survive, because legal jobs were hard to come by back then. Life in the 1930s was very difficult. Honest work was hard to come by and poorly paid."

"Did you like your father?"

Sergio contemplated for a moment before he replied.

"To be honest, I don't remember. I hardly knew him. He sent me off to boarding school when I was six. My brother had been killed, and he didn't want me to get into any kind of trouble. For ten years, I just came home for Christmas. I didn't move back to New York until after my father was dead."

They lay next to each other in silence. Far below them, the city that never sleeps was bustling, and they could hear the muted sounds of street traffic.

"Have you killed anyone?" Alex asked quietly. Sergio looked at her with a spark in his eyes.

"Why do you want to know that, *cara*?"

"There are so many stories in the newspapers," she replied, "all these things about the Mafia and crime syndicates. I want to know if any of it is true."

Sergio kissed her, gently disentangling himself from her, and got up. Somehow his naked body didn't make him seem defenseless or ridiculous. He held himself with the nonchalant self-confidence of a classical statue.

"Is it important to you?" he asked.

"Yes," she said as she calmly returned his look, "it's important to me."

"Would it make a difference to you if you found out that I am all the things that the press claims? Would the past matter so much that you wouldn't want to see me anymore?"

"No." Alex shook her head. "It has nothing to do with that."

She knew he had secrets, and it didn't bother her. But since Oliver said those harsh words last night, she felt the need to know some general truths.

"What is it then?" Sergio asked, and Alex straightened up. She thought about the Downeys and the trusting affection between them.

"I want to hear from you if what the newspapers write is true. If it's the truth and you tell me, then I can live with it. I simply want to be able to trust you."

Sergio sat down at the edge of the bed and looked at her. For a split second he felt tempted to tell Alex what she wanted to hear, but then he remembered Nelson's warning and the guy with whom she had cheated on him. Reason regained the upper hand. He was still as unable to read Alex's face as on their first meeting. He knew he desired her like no woman before. He wanted to own and dominate her, but that was exactly what she didn't allow him to do. No, he must not show any signs of weakness. He could not possibly tell her the truth because he had learned never to trust anyone very early in his life. Generosity and openness were weaknesses that could be deadly. Since the potential for false friends was high, Sergio preferred not to have any friends at all. He had reliable business partners with whom he had no emotional ties. But people who knew too much about him could possibly hurt, weaken, or even destroy him. He couldn't really trust anyone, even within the ranks of his own family, and Cesare's ridiculous threat was proof of that. The tough struggle for survival growing up on the streets of Little Italy and the Lower East Side and the brutal murders of his brother and father had changed him forever. This made it impossible for Sergio to be completely open with anyone.

He knew that he wouldn't hesitate to leave Alex if the circumstances required it. But he hoped that this would never be the case. All this went through his head while Alex stared at him, waiting for a response. For a brief moment, Sergio felt ashamed as he prepared to lie to her.

"Listen, *cara*," he said and looked at her openly, "I had to fight very hard all my life to get to where I am right now. I lead a major corporation and am responsible for thousands of people. When I was young, I made a questionable deal or two. But what person who made it to the top hasn't done such things?"

Alex nodded.

"When the newspapers write disparaging things about me, it's just because of envy and frustration. Try as they might, they can't dig up any dirt on me. That's why they keep bringing up these old stories about my father. Entire books have been written about Ignazio Vitali, like *Murder Inc.*, and it's no secret that he and his colleagues killed dozens of people during Prohibition. But that is not my legacy. I conduct my business in the manner of other legitimate businessmen around the world. Maybe I'm more cunning or more ruthless, but I pay my taxes and present my financial statements to whoever cares to read them. I have never been convicted, and I'm no criminal. All this tabloid talk about the Mafia and the underworld will sell newspapers, but it doesn't correspond with reality."

Sergio looked calmly at Alex, and everything he said sounded plausible in her ears.

"Are you happy now, *cara*?"

She nodded.

"You do your job and I do mine," Sergio continued. "We are both successful. When I see you, *cara*, I'd rather not think about business, but about you. This is not about concealing anything from you."

"Hmm," Alex said as she wrapped her arms around his waist, "so what's your involvement with LMI?"

Sergio was prepared for this question because he knew that Oliver had told her about it.

"I'm on the board of directors," he said as he pulled her close and kissed her, "just like I sit on twenty-four other boards. My companies also do business with LMI every now and then. That's all."

Alex sighed. To hell with Oliver and his conspiracy theories! If Sergio had denied any business involvement with LMI, then she wouldn't have believed anything else either, but now she felt sure Sergio was being honest. And that was enough for her.

Alex woke up the next morning and needed a few seconds to realize where she was. Her eyes fell on Sergio, who was still in a state of deep sleep. She'd made a decision during the night. Her brief affair with Oliver was over. It hurt too much when he threw her out of his apartment without giving her a chance to explain herself. Sergio had much more to offer. A penthouse overlooking Central Park, a private underground garage for her Porsche, and a table at Le Cirque without a reservation! Sergio Vitali made everything possible, and there was no point in pretending that she didn't care about him. The intimacy of their night together made her feel like this could be the loving relationship she longed for. Sergio opened his eyes and squinted into the bright sunlight. He reached for her and Alex snuggled into his arms.

"What are you thinking about, *cara*?" he whispered.

"All kinds of things." She stroked his tousled hair and was tempted for a split second to tell him the whole truth about her feelings. But then she thought about Oliver and what her honesty led to with him. No, she couldn't tell him—it didn't matter how close she felt to him.

"Does it have anything to do with me?"

"No," she lied. "I'm thinking about how I could raise thirty-two million dollars for A&R. Maybe I could—"

Sergio bolted into an upright position.

"You are really unbelievable," he said. "You lie in bed with me and all you can think about is business!"

He shot her such a hurt look that she paused in fright. Sergio untangled himself from her, jumped up, and walked across the room. Alex bit her lip as he disappeared into the bathroom. She really wanted to run after him and tell him the truth—that she had been hurt by his behavior and had cheated on him with another man only because she'd hoped that would banish him from her mind! Impossible. No, she had to keep pretending that he was just an acquaintance with whom she enjoyed spending a few hours now and then.

Somewhere in her clothes, which she had carelessly tossed on the floor, her cell phone started ringing. She jumped up, rummaged through her clothing, and found it in her coat pocket, under the armchair. To her surprise, it was Madeleine Ross-Downey. Alex walked out on the terrace. Madeleine apologized for calling so early, but she had to travel to the West Coast for three days and wanted to say hello before she forgot. She thanked Alex again for her courageous intervention and invited her to dinner at their home that Friday evening. Some other friends were also coming, and it would be a casual evening, but she and Trevor would be delighted if she could join them.

Alex's first impulse was to excuse herself, since she almost always turned down invitations, but she had instantly liked Madeleine and her husband. Furthermore, the thought of getting to know some friends of Sergio's enemy Kostidis intrigued her. When she turned around, she saw Sergio standing in the open terrace door.

"It was Madeleine Ross-Downey," Alex said. "She invited me to come to her apartment on Friday evening."

"Really?" Sergio raised his eyebrows. "How did you achieve this honor?"

Alex told him about the incident at the museum two days before.

"Unbelievable." Sergio looked at her with a mixture of amazement and amusement. "You charged two street thugs with your bare hands? I should hire you as my bodyguard." He grinned.

"Don't mock me," Alex said, annoyed. "I could hardly pretend I didn't see anything."

"I'm not mocking you," Sergio answered. "I really mean it! There aren't many people who would do the same. I'm sure Trevor was happy nothing happened to his Maddy."

"Yes, he certainly was. I also visited their home that night. Do you know the Downeys?"

"Of course. I know everyone in the city."

Anyone else would have sounded arrogant making this kind of statement, but Sergio was simply stating a fact.

"Do you like them?"

"Madeleine is really a magnificent singer—I admire her art very much," he replied, but then his voice filled with contempt. "On the other hand, Trevor Downey is weak and spoiled. He lucked into a department-store chain because his older brother who inherited the business was a hemophiliac and passed away at twenty. Moreover, he is a close friend of our highly esteemed Mayor Kostidis."

"I hate it when you're so sarcastic." Alex noted the mocking glint in his eyes.

"And I hate it when you think about business while you lie in bed with me," Sergio responded.

"To tell the truth, I wasn't thinking about business," she said quietly.

"Then why did you say that?"

"Because…" She fought with herself for a moment and avoided looking at him. "Because I didn't want to admit that I was thinking last night was one of the most beautiful nights of my life."

Sergio didn't respond. He walked back to the bedroom to get dressed. She followed him, annoyed by his silence.

"Do you want to know why I didn't tell you the truth?" she asked, trying to restrain the angry tremble in her voice.

"Yes." He sat on the edge of the bed while tying his shoelaces.

"Because I was afraid that you would react exactly like this. With no reaction at all. You expect honesty from me and don't say a single word yourself."

A shadow drifted across Sergio's face, and when he looked up again he had dropped his mask. He was attentive and tense, and he looked surprisingly vulnerable. He grabbed her wrists.

"Alex," he said softly, "are you really being honest with me?"

She hesitated. She had an opening to confess that she'd had an affair with Oliver because she was jealous and angry. She could choose this moment to tell him the details about Oliver's accusations that had caused her doubts. And she could admit how much she longed for his love and his trust. But she was afraid to let her guard down, and so she let this opportunity pass by.

"I think," she answered instead, "that I'm as honest with you as you are with me."

Sergio sighed. He let go of her wrists and stood up. "Well then, let's leave it at that," he said. "But I *can* tell you one thing in all honesty: it was a wonderful night. I enjoyed it very much."

August 15, 1999

Sergio Vitali entered his office at the VITAL Building. His oldest son Massimo and his lawyer Nelson van Mieren were already waiting for him. He smiled briefly when they wished him a happy birthday, and then he sat down behind his desk.

"So?" he asked, looking at his son. Massimo was courageous and intelligent, but his uncontrollable violent temper led him to make mistakes time and again. Fortunately, his screwups had not yet triggered any major consequences. "We have a problem at the port," Massimo said without introduction. "Johnnie Craven—president of the dockworkers' union—isn't keeping his end of the bargain."

"What did he do?"

"A shipment from Germany arrived yesterday—Russian Kalashnikovs and control mechanisms for ICBMs. They were declared as 'cooling units' as usual. Craven normally makes sure that the stuff clears customs, but yesterday he didn't."

"Did you talk to him?"

"Yes." Massimo leaned forward. "He claims that his people somehow forgot to keep the customs officers from boarding. But he lied to me. It's no one's fault but his. That's what we pay him for, and not too shabbily at that!"

"Go on…"

"Ficchiavelli was listed as the delivery address. The cops searched all the warehouses. We were lucky that the last shipment was already out for delivery, so they didn't find anything. I claimed that they must have mixed up the cargo in Germany."

"Nelson?" Sergio looked at his lawyer.

"They can't prove that the weapons were meant for us. The shipping documents for the cooling units were okay. But we do have a problem in that the Port Authority Police has involved the FBI and confiscated the entire shipment."

"Where was the delivery headed?"

"Houston." Massimo clenched his fist. "Tommasino was mad as hell when I told him that we can't deliver for at least three more weeks. Not only has a two-and-a-half-million-dollar deal gone down the drain, it looks as if we might also get into trouble with the dockworkers' union."

"Can we reason with Craven?"

"No. He said that he wouldn't let himself be bossed around by fucking wops."

"Is that so?" Sergio raised his eyebrows. "Then let's not waste our time with him. Who is second in command after Craven?"

"His name is Michael Burns. He's the up-and-coming man. The dockworkers have a lot of respect for him. And it also appears that we owe this disturbance to him."

"Can this man be persuaded?"

Massimo understood what his father meant and shook his head.

"He's Irish, Papa."

"Hmm." Sergio thought for a moment. The port was strategically important, and they couldn't face the risk of losing more valuable shipments. Above all, they needed the port for drug imports from Colombia and the Far East. They could hardly afford any trouble.

"Do we have a reliable man on the docks?"

"Yes." Massimo nodded. "Angelo Lanza, Giuseppe Lanza's nephew. He's a good man."

"Good. Burns must disappear, and it should happen today. I don't want any trouble at the port," Sergio said. "Nelson, Luca should have Manzo handle this."

Nelson van Mieren nodded.

"But we have one more problem, Sergio," the lawyer said, clearing his throat, "and it's pretty serious."

"What is it?"

"David Zuckerman."

"I thought that was taken care of a long time ago." Sergio threw an indignant look at Nelson.

"I thought so too," van Mieren said, raising his shoulders. "They must have grilled him pretty bad, because last night he agreed to testify in front of the investigation committee. They offered him immunity in return. Our contact at city hall just called me thirty minutes ago."

Sergio jumped up. His face reddened in murderous rage.

"Damn it! We have Kostidis to thank for this," he exclaimed angrily. "That rotten bastard doesn't know when to quit! The state attorney wanted to close the case a long time ago, but Kostidis insisted on digging deeper. I could kill him myself!"

"They must have pressed him really hard." Massimo made himself heard. "David would never talk."

Sergio pretended not to hear this comment. He had a completely different opinion about Zuckerman than Massimo. The boy still had a lot to learn about human nature.

"How dangerous is Zuckerman, Nelson?" he asked.

"Extremely dangerous," the lawyer responded. "He was there when we bribed some of the media. He knows that McIntyre is our man. He knows about all the arrangements and the amounts of money that we paid. He's known it for years. He could blow everything up."

"Can we get to him?"

"He's in a hotel in Midtown." Van Mieren shook his head. "He has more protection from the FBI than Fort Knox. It's near impossible."

"There's no such thing as impossible," Sergio said harshly. "When is the next committee meeting?"

"Next Monday. Kostidis did everything in his power to bring the members back from their vacations early."

"I want him to disappear today. Nelson, give the contract to the Neapolitan. I don't care how he does it. I want his report by tonight."

"But Papa," Massimo objected, "David is—"

"He's become a major threat to us," Sergio interrupted, giving him a cold stare. "He'll talk. We can't afford any leniency. You know that as well as I do."

Massimo sighed and nodded. He knew that any decision his father made was irrevocable. With a tinge of genuine regret, Massimo thought about David Zuckerman, whom he liked very much. David's wife and his own wife were good friends, and their children often played together. This would not be easy for him. But the die was cast.

"I'll see you later tonight at your party," Nelson wheezed as he got up.

Sergio waited for the two men to leave his office, and then he turned and gazed out the window. The foundation of his power was a fine network of connections, but thin as a spiderweb. To build and maintain it had cost him many years and much money. Very few men knew enough about him to pose a threat. And most of these men would rather go to prison than open their mouths. Nevertheless, there was a weak link every now and then, and Zuckerman had become one. It was a shame, because he was a good man, an ace when it came to generating business in the construction industry. Sergio owed many lucrative contracts to him. But Zuckerman had recently caught the attention of the authorities, which made his services useless. Sergio knew that this man was a coward who paid too much attention to his social standing. Zuckerman would rather betray Vitali than go to prison for a year or two. He had apparently forgotten to whom he owed his mansion on Long Island, his weekend house on Cape Cod, and his life of luxury. But it was too late now to remind him. He was a liability.

Alex steered her black Porsche convertible on to the Henry Hudson Parkway, which later turned into the Saw Mill River Parkway. She drove through placid, wooded hill country and passed the exclusive suburbs of Bedford Hills and Mount Kisco. She had been thinking for days about whether she should actually accept the invitation to Sergio's birthday party at his house in Westchester County. She didn't quite feel comfortable facing the wife of the man with whom she was having an affair, but her curiosity about Sergio's house and his family was ultimately stronger than her fear. Sergio told her that there would be many interesting guests, and that it wouldn't hurt her to meet some new contacts.

She turned onto a narrow asphalt road near the Mount Kisco exit. Properties here in Westchester County were so large that you couldn't see the houses from the road. After Alex had been driving for some time along a ten-foot-high yew hedge, she figured that she'd taken a wrong turn somewhere. But then a big gate appeared with several men in dark suits with walkie-talkies. She stepped on the brakes, rolled down her window, and showed her invitation to the security guard. With her heart pounding, she drove through the wide-open cast-iron gate. The estate was enormous. The gravel driveway wound through a meticulously designed landscape—the artfully trimmed bushes and lush green lawns reminded her of a golf course, interspersed with patches of trees.

Alex was amazed when she turned the corner and saw the brightly lit house on the hill. In the twilight, it looked like a French castle. Cars were parked in the large space in front of the mansion, and a man wearing sunglasses assigned her a parking spot. Alex had suspected that the cream of the crop of New York's society would be gathered at this little garden party. Just at that moment, a bright red Ferrari Maranello pulled in next to her, and Alex recognized Zack. She was actually relieved to see him here.

"Hello, Zack," she said, looking him up and down. With his deep tan, he looked more like a playboy than an investment banker in his light linen suit. "How was your vacation in the Caymans?"

"Vacation," he said as he kissed her on both cheeks and laughed, amused, "you're too funny! It's hard work profitably reinvesting all the money that you industrious bankers bring in!"

"You look like you've been working very hard," Alex noted sarcastically. They walked toward a broad flight of stairs with two stone lions enthroned at its base.

"I admit," Zack laughed happily, offering her his arm, "that I enjoyed some time on the beach in between. What do you think about this shack? It's even better inside!"

"It's unbelievable that some people live like this," Alex replied.

"Well," Zack said, pursing his lips and throwing her a quick side glance, "Vitali isn't a normal person."

"What do you mean by that?"

"My God, Alex, you know him better than I do," Zack said. "You can't possibly measure him against normal standards."

A butler opened the thirteen-foot-high white wing doors. They entered the spacious, black-and-white tiled entrance hall. Muted music could be heard in the distance. Alex saw Sergio surrounded by a group of people. She was impressed to recognize Robert Landford Rhodes, governor of the State of New York, who resided in Albany, and Clarence Whitewater, the chief judge. Charlie Rosenbaum, one of the city's biggest real estate speculators, stood next to him, as well as Carey Newberg, the publisher of *Time*. When she entered with Zack, Sergio excused himself and approached her, smiling. Alex had butterflies in her stomach.

"Alex! Zack! I'm glad you could make it!"

He extended his hand to Alex first, then to Zack. The sight of his steel-blue eyes made her shiver. They congratulated him on his birthday and chatted a little. Zack wandered off.

"I'm very happy to see you here," Sergio murmured to Alex.

"Nice little party," she said with a grin. "Is there anyone who isn't here?"

"Very few," he responded with amusement. "I'll see you outside in a minute."

He squeezed her hand one more time before turning to greet the newly arrived guests. Alex looked around curiously. The tasteful yet impersonal furnishings of the house might have been a masterpiece of interior design, but the entire place somehow reminded her of a mausoleum.

"It's incredible, don't you think?" Zack grinned. "I want a house like this someday."

"I'll say," Alex said, raising her eyebrows. "This is no house, it's a temple!"

"Well, it's impressive. If you live like this, you've really made it."

He was right about that. They walked down a few steps to the large terrace. It offered a breathtaking view across a parklike garden, decorated with antique white statues, a large white marble swimming pool, and a pool house. People were crowded around tables and benches on the grass between the terrace balustrade and the pool. A band played Italian folk music on stage risers, and an opulent buffet was served under big white pagoda tents. Everything was beautifully decorated with colorful paper lanterns, burning torches, and splendid flower arrangements. A bar surrounded by cocktail tables was right next to the pool. It was the perfect setting for a high-society summer party.

They met almost the entire board of LMI on the terrace. Vincent Levy, Isaac Rubinstein, and Hugh Weinberg were here with their wives. A bit later, Michael Friedman and Max Rudensky—owners of a famous brokerage and arbitrage firm—also arrived. The mood was relaxed, and when Levy suggested that they take a look at the buffet, everyone but Alex turned toward the steps. From the corner of her eye, she saw that Sergio had stepped out of the house and stopped at the terrace's balustrade. The warm air smelled like lavender, and swallows shot through the gorgeous misty twilight.

"How do you like my house, *cara*?" Sergio asked as he stood behind her.

"It's imposing." She turned, and a mocking smile flitted across her face. "It seems to me that you've built a mausoleum for yourself during your lifetime. Like the pharaohs in ancient Egypt."

"That's what I appreciate about you." Sergio said, smiling at her. "Anyone else would have said how fabulous it is."

"We're probably beyond the stage of courteous phrases."

"Yes, we probably are." Sergio leaned next to her on the balustrade. Alex gave him a probing look. He seemed relaxed and in a good mood, but she saw an attentive tension in his eyes. She suddenly remembered what Oliver had said to her that night: *Are you kidding me, or are you really that naive?* She was just about to pepper Sergio with some hard questions when she sensed him noticing someone approaching behind her.

"Ah, here's my wife," he said. Alex froze for a second, and then she forced a friendly smile. Constanzia Vitali was a cultivated woman, and her elegant dress concealed her round shape perfectly. She might have been very pretty once, but her beauty had long since faded. At fifty-five, Sergio was so incredibly attractive and full of energy that his wife looked like a withered rose next to him. He casually pushed himself away from the wall.

"Constanzia," he said as he put his arm around his wife's shoulders, "may I introduce Alex Sontheim? She is one of Vince Levy's best employees. Alex, this is my wife, Constanzia."

The two women shook hands. Alex felt a twinge of guilt at Constanzia's inquiring look.

"You work at an investment bank?" Constanzia Vitali's face was friendly and without any expression. "That must be quite exciting."

"Yes, it certainly is."

Constanzia Vitali turned toward her husband and said something in Italian. Alex, who spoke Italian quite well, understood that Constanzia was asking her husband to give his speech. Sergio answered her in a low voice, whereupon Constanzia turned around without neglecting to throw another probing look at Alex.

"Unfortunately, I have to look after my other guests now." Sergio placed his hand briefly on Alex's arm. "Can you take me to the city with you later?"

"Maybe. I don' know whether I'll stay that long."

"It would make me so happy."

For the rest of the evening, Alex only saw Sergio from a distance. He was in a splendid mood, joking with his business partners' wives and his friends, dancing with his wife. He was the perfect host. Even without him on her arm, Alex enjoyed the evening to the fullest. Just a week ago, she had moved into the penthouse on the Upper West Side. Now she was a guest at a private party of one of the country's richest men, and she was treated as someone who quite naturally belonged in this crowd. She felt flattered that so many of the people at the party knew her name.

While the wives listened in boredom, Alex conversed with their husbands about the expected rate hike by the Fed, the higher leverage in option trading versus stocks, the rapidly rising prices of technology stocks and the resulting opportunities for the market, and the consequences of political decisions on the stock market. She was sitting at a table with Zack, Levy, Weinberg, Friedman, David Norman, a board member of the NYSE, and a young man named Jack Lang from a brokerage firm called Manhattan Portfolio Management. The food was provided by New York's best catering company, and the heavy French red wine was pure poetry; the cocktails, perfectly mixed, contributed to Alex's failure to notice how quickly time passed.

It was already dark when she looked around for Sergio. He was nowhere to be seen. With one ear she overheard Zack, Rudensky, and Jack Lang whispering about the sensational profit margins possible when investing in venture capital companies. They talked about international business companies, or IBCs, that were incorporated in offshore financial centers such as the Cayman Islands, Samoa, Labuan, or other exotic locations. Alex didn't jump into the conversation because she was more interested to know where

Sergio was. His wife sat a few tables away and was engaged in a conversation with an older gray-haired woman.

Alex eventually excused herself and walked toward the house to find the restroom. As she walked through the vast salons and long hallways, she realized that she'd had too much to drink. She winced as she noticed a man standing across from her. He was smaller than she was; he was skinny, and his ferret-like face was disfigured by acne scars. An ice-cold shiver ran down Alex's spine. It wasn't his ugliness, but his strangely lifeless eyes that instilled fear in her.

"*Buona sera*," he said with a coarse voice, walking past her. Alex stared after him. What kind of horrible person was this? Suddenly sober, she had the feeling that she needed to get back to the other guests as quickly as possible.

Cesare Vitali was in a bad mood. The laughing hordes annoyed him just as much as the schmaltzy Italian music, but he was especially mad at Silvio, Luca, and his brother Massimo. They treated him like a child. They had walked past him on their way into the house about a half hour ago. When he asked where they were going, Massimo replied that they had something to talk about. The men simply left him behind and disappeared into the house, where his father was likely expecting them like a king waiting for his subjects—confident, fearless, and powerful. Cesare wanted to earn his father's attention and respect, but he somehow always screwed up. His buddies respected him, and the prostitutes on the Lower East Side feared him—which felt good—but in his father's eyes, he was a failure who had to be kept away from the family business.

Despite the warm temperature outside, Cesare was suddenly freezing. He needed a line of coke desperately. The white powder could make his bad mood disappear instantly and turn him into the big man he wanted to be. He dumped his whiskey over the terrace railing in disgust and stood up. He had a burning interest in what they were talking about in there. Nelson was there too. Something big was brewing. In a surge of anger, he briefly considered just barging into the library. Wasn't he, just like Massimo, also one of Sergio's sons? Didn't he also have the right to be part of those meetings? But he wasn't invited. He wouldn't put it past his father to kick him out in front of his brother and the others.

In the guest bathroom, Cesare quickly fished out a tinfoil packet of white powder, tapped some onto a small pocket mirror that he always carried with him for that purpose, and formed two lines with a golden razor blade that hung in a case around his neck. Then he skillfully rolled up a dollar bill and snorted the powder forcefully. It burned in his nose and brought tears to his eyes. Cesare relished the bitter flavor of the cocaine at the back of his throat and took in a deep breath. The chill disappeared from his body, replaced by an intoxicating heat. A wonderful feeling of security enveloped his body. He smiled at his reflection in the mirror and opened the door.

Alex wandered through all the colossal salons until she realized that she was at the far end of the house and nowhere close to the terrace. She was just about to turn around and retrace her steps when she heard muted voices from an adjacent room. She didn't usually eavesdrop at doors, but this repulsive man with his yellow predator eyes had sparked her curiosity. She held her breath and stopped in front of the room's double doors. Through the narrow crack between them, she could see a library. Sergio was standing behind a massive desk made of marble and glass with floor-to-ceiling bookshelves behind him. Alex recognized three of the men.

One of them was Nelson van Mieren, Sergio's lawyer, the other Massimo, Sergio's oldest son, and the third was Luca di Varese, one of Sergio's confidants. The skinny man with the acne scars and yellow eyes was standing in front of the desk.

"Do you have any news for me, Natale?" Sergio asked in Italian.

"It is done," the man responded in a coarse voice. "Zuckerman won't utter another word."

Alex caught her breath. At first she thought she'd misheard him.

"Bene," Sergio triumphantly. "What about the Irishman at the docks, Luca?"

"As they say in the movies, he's sleeping with the fishes," Luca replied, "and no one will find him."

"Good work." Sergio nodded and sat down at his desk. Alex felt a wave of horror pulsing through her. Her heart was beating so loudly that everyone must have heard it. Confused thought fragments whirled around her head. The men in this room were talking about people who had been murdered! Today, on this beautiful August day, two men had died. Someone had given an order to kill them. Alex closed her eyes. This someone was no other than Sergio Vitali. He had assured her that he had nothing to do with these rumors circulating about him in the press. She had believed him because he was so convincing. She had *wanted* to believe him. Now she realized that he had shamelessly betrayed her trust. She remembered Oliver's words again: *His entire empire is built upon blood and crime. He is an unscrupulous and brutal gangster.*

Alex's mouth was dry from fear. She was miserable, but she couldn't run away. Some part of her pleaded to learn the opposite of what she'd just heard was true. She didn't want to think badly of Sergio. Maybe she'd simply misunderstood his words…

"I'm very satisfied, Natale," Sergio said. Alex could see his face through the crack in the door. She couldn't understand the ugly man's response, but she certainly understood his salutation.

"I wish you a happy birthday and a joyful evening, Don Sergio."

Don Sergio. Sergio acknowledged this man's reverence with a casual nod. Alex felt the ground shaking beneath her, and it seemed like an ice-cold hand had grabbed her heart. None of the stories in the papers were invented. They seemed to be grossly understated. *Gangster's whore,* she thought. Oliver was completely right, but she'd refused to believe him! She, Alex Sontheim, was the mistress of a Mafia boss, a man who hired killers to solve his problems. She turned around to flee from this house, but then she froze in shock. A man stood in front of her and gazed at her with frightening blue eyes.

"Are you lost?" He looked her up and down in an obscene way.

"I…err…I'm looking for the restroom," Alex stuttered. The voices of the men in the library could be heard through the doors. She snapped out of it and tried to sneak past the man, but he grabbed her by the wrist.

"Not so fast," he said suspiciously. "What were you doing in front of this door?"

"I told you that I was looking for the restroom." Alex thought she might pass out any moment. "Would you please let go of me now?" she asked, with all of the assertiveness she could muster.

"Oh no, I won't. Because I don't believe that you got lost. And I don't think that my father will be amused when he finds out that you're eavesdropping at the door."

My father…

Alex stared at the young man, and she recognized the astonishing resemblance. This is exactly how Sergio must have looked at twenty-five. The young man was Sergio's son. She felt sick with fear. She had overheard the men in the adjacent room talking about two murders. She thought about the Mafia movies that she had seen in which accidental witnesses were thrown into the East River with a concrete block strapped to their feet. *Sleeping with the fishes.* And Sergio, the man she thought she knew, was Don Sergio—the godfather of New York. It would be very easy for him to make her disappear.

"Listen," she whispered, "this is nothing but a misunderstanding."

"We'll see about that in a minute." Without knocking, the young man pushed the door open and dragged Alex with him. Sergio stopped midsentence and stared at his youngest son and Alex in surprise.

"Cesare, what is this?" Sergio snarled at his son.

"Papa!" Cesare exclaimed in triumph and tightened his grip on Alex's wrist. "This woman was standing outside the door eavesdropping!"

Sergio looked at Alex in astonishment.

"Let her go!" he ordered. Cesare obeyed reluctantly and gave her another push that almost made her lose her balance.

"I wasn't eavesdropping at all," Alex sputtered. "I was looking for the restroom and got lost, and suddenly this guy grabs me and drags me in here."

"Cesare, you are a goddamn miserable idiot!" Sergio said in Italian, trying hard to contain his anger. "Why do you bother my guests? Were you snorting cocaine again?"

"She was standing outside the door, Papa!" The young man suddenly seemed insecure. "You should thank me for—"

"Thank you?" Sergio hollered so unexpectedly that Alex winced. Never before had she seen him this angry. He was truly terrifying in his rage. He spoke Italian so fast and used so many colloquialisms, she could barely understand him.

"You brought her here, you stupid, brainless idiot! She doesn't understand a single word anyway, but what will she think now? Why the hell can't you use your head for once? I honestly believe that you've boozed your brain away!"

Cesare looked hurt. He said nothing. No one in the room moved. Alex was not a fearful person, but at this moment she was overcome by a terrifying dread. Sergio was a stranger; these men were strangers. Cesare laughed hoarsely. His glassy eyes sparkled with hatred.

"You're telling *me* that!" he said to his father in Italian. "You're the one who screws this whore and then invites her into Mama's house."

His face was twisted in anger and disappointment.

"Shut up!" Sergio shouted.

"Why should I shut up?" Cesare asked with a nasty laugh. "You think that I don't know what you're talking about? You think that I'm a little boy, but—"

Sergio raised his hand and slapped Cesare's face, which sent him reeling.

"Get out of my sight, Cesare," Sergio said, his voice muted to an angry whisper, "before I lose it and do something that I'll regret. Get out of my house!"

Cesare held his cheek and stepped back. His eyes darted around furiously.

"You'll regret this! All of you will regret this! Fuck you all!" he screamed.

Luca and Silvio jumped up, looking at their boss.

"Let him go," Sergio said in Italian. "He doesn't know anything. He's nothing but a coked-up idiot."

He walked over to Alex and put his arm around her shoulders.

"I'm sorry he scared you," he said, and then he turned toward the men and sent them out. He let go of her and walked over to the small bar in of one of the bookshelves.

"Would you like something to drink?"

"Yes, please." Alex tried to get her panic under control and stop her trembling. She had to get out of this house right away! She wished she could fly home to her parents in Germany this very second. What the hell had she gotten herself into? Sergio handed her a glass of whiskey and observed her with a penetrating look. He seemed to be wondering if she'd really eavesdropped at the door.

"Did you understand anything I just said to Cesare?" he asked her in Italian. Alex's brain was still functioning and instinctively reacted the right way.

"I don't understand what you're saying," she said with a slight smile. "Maybe you could speak English with me."

"No, it's all right." Sergio smiled and took the empty glass from her hand. Then he put his arms around her and kissed her cheek. She almost pushed him away, but managed to control the impulse.

"Cesare is somewhat overzealous at times," Sergio said softly. "He scared you."

"He tried." Alex managed to smile. "But people don't scare me that easily."

After everything she had learned about Sergio, nothing in the world could frighten her anymore. Senators, bank executives, the governor of the State of New York, judges, and lawyers were sitting out there. There was no way that they knew the whole truth about Sergio Vitali! Don Sergio, indeed, commanded an army of killers, paving his own path with money and murder.

"Come, *cara*," Sergio said, "let's go outside to my guests. We'll drink another glass of champagne and enjoy ourselves."

"Yes," Alex mumbled, a little dazed. "Yes, that sounds good."

A dark shadow had fallen over her entire life that evening. In desperation and dread, she asked herself what she should do.

Frank Cohen yawned and rubbed his eyes. His watch read quarter past ten. Besides him, only security guards and cleaning crews were still at city hall. There was such a flurry of activity at the mayor's office during the day that Frank saved matters requiring more concentration for the evening. The last two evenings, he had been researching Donald Coleman—an African American preacher from Harlem who was stabbed outside his church by unknown assailants fifteen years ago. His death had nearly triggered a riot at the time and made a martyr out of Coleman. Tomorrow

Mayor Kostidis would inaugurate a youth center named after Donald Coleman. The East Harlem center would employ social workers to look after street kids in one of the city's poorest neighborhoods. The building had a library, a computer lab, and a counseling center for teenagers who were down on their luck or addicted to drugs. The printer spewed out four pages containing all the information about Donald Coleman that Frank was able to gather. The mayor would skim through them for two minutes tomorrow—two minutes attention for at least eight hours of work—and then give a brilliant, affectionate speech about Coleman for the opening ceremony's guests, as if they'd been close friends for many years.

Gathering his papers and turning off the computer, Frank smiled to himself. Without a doubt, Nicholas Kostidis was the most impressive person he'd ever met. He'd gotten to know him about twelve years ago, when Kostidis was an assistant US attorney at the Department of Justice in Washington DC. Frank had just graduated with honors from law school and had managed to snag one of few highly coveted internships at the Department of Justice. Frank was assigned to work on Kostidis's staff, and he was immediately fascinated by his boss. He had inexhaustible energy, cunning intelligence, and inspiring charisma. Nick Kostidis was straightforward and incorruptible, ambitious without seeming arrogant. Fighting crime was dear to his heart—in contrast to many other people who had only their political careers in mind. It was typical for him to work sixteen-hour days, and he demanded complete loyalty and hard work from all of his staff members. In return, he was an unconventional and generous boss. He hated pedantry and bureaucracy almost as much as organized crime and drug trafficking, which he had combated directly as the US Attorney for the Southern District of New York. Nick Kostidis's enthusiasm was often called fanaticism by his adversaries, and Frank had to admit that it sometimes really seemed that way.

Frank vividly remembered the winter of 1984. After months of intense preparation for the RICO indictment against the city's leading

Mafia bosses, Kostidis had been just a shadow of himself—pale with dark lines under his eyes, driven only by his almost inhuman energy. He lived for his work. Sometimes it was downright frightening to see him in his office ready to accomplish his mission after five hours of sleep, setting a pace that even much younger staff members couldn't sustain. Nick Kostidis set very high standards, yet he was tough and courageous, and willing to give it all he had. Moreover, he had an infallible instinct for dealing with the media. He was never afraid to state his opinion bluntly in front of running cameras. The majority of New York City's population loved him for it, but there were also many people who hated him because he posed a threat to their lucrative—and in most cases illegal—businesses. Over the years, Frank had come to the conclusion that you either had to love or hate Nick Kostidis. At the very least, you couldn't be indifferent to him.

Frank never regretted that he hadn't become a lawyer like his father or his brothers. Fate had introduced him to Nick Kostidis, and Frank was grateful for that. Although his job was stressful and didn't pay particularly well, the position as the closest assistant to the mayor of New York City held new challenges and assignments every day. Frank was confronted in his work with a sense of life's incredible highs and lows that could only exist in a metropolis like New York. Wealth and misery, crime and charity bloomed and faded rapidly like colors in a kaleidoscope. The biggest bright spot was Nick Kostidis, this incredible man who never neglected humanity because of politics. Frank would never let Nick down in his tireless effort to fight for improving people's lives in New York.

The telephone rang.

"Good evening," he answered.

"You're still there," said an unpleasantly droning voice.

"Hello, Mr. McDeere." Frank closed his tired eyes. "What can I do for you at this late hour?"

Truman McDeere was the FBI agent who'd been assigned to guard key witness David Zuckerman. Frank didn't like this bald man with his grim expression and jaundiced face. He'd met him during the indictment of the city's Mafia bosses and was happy when their collaboration ended.

"Where can I reach the mayor?"

"He's out on private business tonight. Would you like to leave him a message?"

"I have to speak to him urgently. Something happened that he should know about."

It was very unusual for the otherwise arrogant McDeere to stammer so sheepishly.

"Did something happen to Zuckerman?" he asked and opened his eyes.

"Yes, God damn it! He's dead. We had fifteen men in the freaking hotel!"

"My God!" Frank jumped up so violently that he hit his knee on the desk drawer. "You're kidding, right? Was it suicide?"

"No," McDeere said meekly. "He was shot—with a suppressed forty-five."

"Shit." Frank sank down on his chair and rubbed his hurt knee. His thoughts raced. Nick had put all his hopes on Zuckerman's testimony. He was sure that he could finally get Sergio Vitali with the help of this man. Zuckerman's initial arrogance wore down during his months in jail. He'd virtually fallen apart over the past weeks. Last night, he had made the surprising decision to testify in front of a grand jury. He announced that he would reveal everything about the corruption scandal case surrounding the construction of the World Financial Center, which had fizzled out due to a lack of evidence. Zuckerman had rambled about bribery and extortion, falsified building applications and plans, excessive cost calculations, and price fixing. His testimony would have been more than unpleasant for Sergio Vitali. At the first grand jury hearing in November of last year,

Zuckerman had taken his lawyer's advice and pleaded the Fifth Amendment. Although this was considered a clear admission of guilt, the US Attorney's Office closed the investigation. Kostidis's anger went through the roof. He did everything he could to keep Zuckerman locked up and to reopen the case. He'd succeeded in appointing a new investigation committee to make absolutely certain that Vitali wouldn't be able to get away this time. There was no doubt that Nick would be devastated to hear of Zuckerman's death.

Just two days before, Zuckerman had been transferred from the Metropolitan Correction Center to a hotel in a cloak-and-dagger operation while guarded by fifteen FBI agents. Their job was to keep him completely shielded before his testimony. And now he was dead. Shot dead. It was quite clear that Vitali had found out about Zuckerman's decision to cooperate with the authorities, contracted an assassin, and duped the FBI. Frank sighed. He would have liked for his boss to spend a quiet evening with his wife, but he had to deliver the bad news right away before the mayor read about it in the morning newspapers.

"I'll inform him right away," Frank said to the FBI officer. "Thanks for calling, Truman." He hung up and rushed out of his office.

"Fucking bullshit," he muttered on his way out the door.

A half hour later Frank was standing with his boss. He had been expecting a fit of rage over the FBI's stupidity, but instead Nick Kostidis merely acknowledged the news with a resigned nod of his head. He let himself sink onto one of the benches outside Central Park's Delacorte Theater and rubbed his eyes wearily.

"Vitali is behind this, there's no doubt," he said in a somber tone.

Muted voices and applause could be heard from the theater's fully occupied semicircular pavilion.

"I'm really sorry," Frank said quietly. In the bright light of the park lanterns, he noticed the wrinkles and dark shadows on Kostidis's face, and saw that the fire in his eyes had gone out. Kostidis looked as if he had aged years in the past few minutes. His energy and enthusiasm had vanished. Kostidis stared at his closest staff member for a moment and then sighed.

"Sometimes I wonder whether I'm doing the right thing or making big mistakes because I'm too zealous."

"Mistakes?" Frank was taken aback. He didn't think of his boss as someone who doubted himself.

"Yes." Kostidis leaned back and closed his eyes. "Zuckerman would still be alive if I hadn't insisted on keeping him locked up for so long until he came clean. Now his wife is a widow and his children are fatherless. He's dead, and we still haven't made any progress."

Frank was shocked.

"Vitali is stronger than me," Nick Kostidis continued. "He's stronger because he's ruthless. Because he has no conscience and doesn't give a damn about human lives. What have I done?"

"But Nick," Frank objected, "we did the right thing. How could we possibly know that Zuckerman would be murdered? With his testimony, we could have killed *ten* birds with one stone."

"Do we really have the right to risk someone's life in the name of justice?" Kostidis opened his eyes. "I'm not so sure about that anymore. I used to think that I was doing the right thing."

His boss's doubts and dejection affected Frank more than any fit of rage could have, but he couldn't think of what to say to console him.

"Go home, Frank." Kostidis placed his hand on the younger man's shoulder. "You've more than earned your time off after work."

Frank nodded. "I didn't mean to spoil your evening, but I thought that it would be better for you to hear the bad news from me than the radio."

"Yes, you're right. Thank you." Nick Kostidis sat up straight, now that the first spectators poured out of the open-air theater. "Call Jerome Harding and Michael Page. I'd like to meet them tomorrow morning at ten o'clock in my office."

"On it," Frank nodded. He said goodnight to his boss and headed home with much on his mind.

Mary Kostidis slowly flowed with the crowd and searched for her husband. Once again, something so important had happened that it couldn't wait until morning. She hadn't been able to follow the rest of the theater performance because she wondered what was going on. When she finally caught sight of him, his facial expression said everything.

Mary had known her husband for thirty-two years. She had always supported him and admired his dedication, but she observed with concern how hard he fought. The wrinkles in his face had grown deeper, and the first gray strands had begun to appear in his thick dark hair. As the mayor, he was more vulnerable than ever before. He was always in the public eye, and any small mistake he made was greedily seized upon and mercilessly exploited by his enemies. He had been so tense the past few weeks that he didn't often really listen to her. Something occupied his mind, but she knew that pushing him for information was pointless. He would tell her if he deemed it necessary. On the outside, Nick appeared as strong and fearless as ever. His circumstances and the grueling years of fighting had made him hard as granite, but on the inside, he remained a sensitive and compassionate human being who suffered when his efforts failed.

Mary was often worried about her husband because he antagonized many powerful men. He had never been afraid. She still loved him as much as when they first met in the reading room of the New York Public

Library. Mary admired his ambition and straightforwardness and loved his ability to admit defeat gracefully. Time and again, he foiled other people's business with his plans. He had been at the receiving end of many death threats, hostile newspaper articles, and anonymous phone calls. But none of this ever deterred Nick from doing what he thought was right. Mary was worried, but she never bothered him with her concerns. If there was anyone who knew what he was doing, it was Nick. She'd support any actions he took to fulfill his lifetime dream of improving the quality of life for the residents of New York.

"What happened?" she asked when she reached her husband.

"David Zuckerman, the man who agreed to testify in front of the investigation committee, was shot," Nick said after they had been walking for a while. "Frank was here and told me."

"My God!" Mary knew how much it meant to her husband to find a witness to provide testimony against Sergio Vitali and to nail his powerful enemy—who had triumphed over him time and again. "That's terrible."

"No," Nick said, walking with his head down. "It's sickening."

They left the park through the Metropolitan Museum exit. Passersby greeted Nick, but he didn't respond. Nick was normally in his element in public, known for having an open ear for anyone, but tonight he looked exhausted. They crossed the street, and Nick signaled the passing taxis.

"I wonder whether Frank has a private life at all," he said pensively.

Mary smiled and shrugged her shoulders.

The third taxi stopped.

"Christopher is coming home this weekend," Mary said as the yellow taxi turned from Fifth Avenue onto Eighty-Sixth Street toward Carl Schurz Park, the location of Gracie Mansion.

"Oh," Nick mumbled, lost in his thoughts, "how nice."

"He's bringing his girlfriend." Mary noticed that her husband wasn't really listening. "He wants to introduce her to you. You can spend some time with them on the weekend, right?"

"Pardon me?" Nick gave his wife an apologetic look. "I was just thinking about something."

Mary sighed and patiently repeated what she'd said.

"Chris has a girlfriend?" Nick asked in surprise. "This is the first time I've heard about it!"

"That's why he's coming to the city," Mary replied. "Her name is Britney Edwards, and she's studying art history and philosophy at Harvard. Her family lives somewhere in the Hudson Valley, and her father is a high-ranking officer at West Point."

"Aha. And how serious is Chris about her?"

"I think he's very serious. He told me he wants to marry her."

"Get married?" Nick stared at his wife in irritation.

"Why not?" She laughed. "After all, he's already twenty-nine. We were already married and had a child at that age."

"Yes, sure, but..." Nick shook his head. Unbelievable that their boy was already twenty-nine. It felt like his first day of school was just yesterday. How quickly time flies! Christopher was a good kid who had never caused him any trouble. High school, Air Force, and medical school. Now he had a good job at Washington Memorial Hospital—his résumé was exemplary. And he had never reproached Nick for spending so little time with him. He'd never blamed his father for rarely going to the ballpark or the movies like his friends' fathers did.

"You realize how old you are when you look at your kids," Nick said and wiped his hand across his face. "I have so many plans for the future, but more and more, I feel that time is running out."

"You're not old, my love," Mary said, grabbing his hand. "You're a man in his best years."

"That's tactful." Nick's smile was bitter. "I feel ancient. Everything's getting harder. I used to be so enthusiastic, so sure that I would be successful. And now..."

He fell silent.

"Don't take Zuckerman's death personally."

"I don't. It's just the situation. I've failed. It's not like in the movies where the good guys always win."

"Are you sure that Vitali is behind this assassination?"

"Yes, I'm pretty sure." Nick sighed. "Somehow he found out that Zuckerman agreed to testify. And he acted immediately. I blame myself that I pressured this man into cooperating with us. I'm responsible for his death."

"No, you're not. He was the one who got involved with criminals."

"That doesn't change the fact that he'd still be alive if I hadn't pushed him to testify."

The grim expression on her husband's face made Mary feel queasy. She anticipated that there was more than this man's death behind his dejection.

"But it was the US Attorney's Office that decided to keep him in custody," she said carefully. At least he was talking to her instead of falling into his gloomy silence of recent weeks.

"De Lancie wanted to let him go six months ago." Nick made a dismissive gesture. "He had no interest in pursuing this. In fact, he seemed uneasy about upholding the charges against Zuckerman."

"Uneasy? He could have revealed a bribery scandal!"

"That's exactly what bothers me." Nick shrugged his shoulders and stared out the window. "It almost seems that this is exactly what de Lancie wanted to prevent."

Mary cringed.

"Do you think that de Lancie…"

"Yes. I have the suspicion that he's on Vitali's payroll."

"My God, the US attorney?"

"You can buy anyone with enough money."

"Not you." Mary touched Nick's hand, but he didn't react to her affection. He didn't feel like being comforted, so she pulled her hand back again.

"Yeah"—Nick laughed unhappily—"Not me. I'm the idiot tilting at windmills. Not only do I have all of the powerful people in the city against me, but worse—I also have a traitor among my ranks."

"What makes you think that?"

"Vitali found out about Zuckerman's change of heart within twelve hours. Only the FBI and my people—no one else—knew about it."

"And de Lancie?"

"I suspected him at first, but he was in Europe and wouldn't have been informed."

Mary was taken aback. She remained silent. A traitor among his own ranks—a mole! Now she understood why her husband was so discouraged. He was capable of fighting the enemies he knew without fear, but it was a terrible realization that someone on his staff—a confidant—had been secretly informing the enemy.

"I won't win this," Nick said quietly. Mary saw the gloomy expression in his eyes illuminated by the headlights of oncoming traffic. "I've won so many times when it seemed impossible, had so many unexpected victories. But this time I'm going to lose. I know it."

"That's not true," she whispered.

"Yes, it is." He shook his head without looking at her. "They're stronger. They'll do everything to destroy me because I'm in their way. I can't defend myself if they corrupt my closest staff members."

He sighed wearily. Sometimes he had the feeling that he was bailing water from a sinking ship with a teaspoon. The second he filled a hole, a bigger one opened up somewhere else. He couldn't have imagined that trying to keep his campaign promises could be so frustrating and hopeless. He certainly could have done the same thing as so many of his predecessors. He could have made deals with people like Vitali, instead of fighting them and wearing himself out in the process. But Nick knew that he wouldn't be able to look at himself in the mirror if he did that. Many of New York's prominent individuals from business, finance, or politics had approached him more or less openly, but he categorically rejected anything that could have been misconstrued as a payoff.

Just two weeks ago, he'd had a dispute with Charlie Rosenbaum—one of the city's biggest real-estate tycoons—at one of those pompous receptions. The party was nothing but a business development meeting disguised as a charity event. Rosenbaum had promised to build a kindergarten in Harlem. When Nick asked him the price of such generosity, Rosenbaum answered that it would be nice if the Department of Buildings could retroactively issue a permit for six additional stories that had been built on top of his new downtown skyscraper "by accident." This was how things worked in New York, but that's exactly what had always bothered Nick. The rich got away with everything; laws and prohibitions didn't apply to them. They put money on the table, and then they could do whatever they pleased. They drove drunk, ignored building codes, cheated, lied, stole, and even killed people.

"I promised my constituents I'd make New York a more honest place," he had replied to Rosenbaum. "I intend to keep this promise."

"What's dishonest about the deal that I'm proposing?" Rosenbaum's eyes were wide in fake surprise. "I treat the city to a beautiful new kindergarten that's modern, bright, and equipped with all the bells and whistles. This is great publicity for both you and me. In return, I get a retroactive permit. Tax-paying businesses will move into those six stories. There are only benefits for the city. Who really cares whether a skyscraper has a hundred and sixteen or a hundred and twenty-two stories?"

"It's the principle."

"The principle! Nick! The city needs private investors because it's broke. I invest, but I expect consideration in return. That's how business works. No one can live on charity alone."

"That's bribery."

Rosenbaum's face took on a sinister expression.

"An evil word for such a good deed. It would provide a safe place for many children who'd just be hanging out in the street and smoking crack in a few years, and then becoming criminals."

It was all too tempting! The city's coffers were indeed chronically empty, and a new kindergarten in the South Bronx or Harlem was simply not feasible due to a lack of municipal funds.

"Charlie," Nick said, "how can I get you this permit without my constituents accusing me of being an opportunist? Of course, I would love to have a new and beautiful kindergarten that doesn't cost the city anything, but I can't just walk into the Department of Buildings and say, *Hey, Mr. Rosenbaum has built six more stories than originally planned on his building. He's very sorry, but now he needs a permit even if you rejected it during the planning stage.*"

"You're the mayor, Nick. You can do this."

"I can't do it without losing face in the process. I'm sorry."

"I'll get the permit. It's only a question of time, and it will cost me a lot of money. Money that I'd rather spend on a kindergarten than on lawyers and appraisers."

"I can't do it."

Rosenbaum shrugged his shoulders with a thin smile on his face.

"I've always taken you for an intelligent man. But apparently I was mistaken. You're harming this city with your stubbornness and unwillingness to compromise. The financiers and investors will go somewhere else. To a place where they are welcomed with open arms and a good deed isn't considered bribery."

Rosenbaum had expressed his opinion more clearly than anyone before him, and Nick painfully realized for the first time that because of his strict morality, perhaps he wasn't the right person for this job. For the benefit of the city and its citizens, he would have been forced to agree with him and forget his black-and-white thinking. Hundreds of children would benefit from this new kindergarten, and it probably wouldn't bother anyone that a new skyscraper turned out to be a bit taller than initially planned and permitted. Nevertheless, if he accepted this bargain just once, then he wouldn't be able to say no the next time. He'd once called his predecessors "the establishment's corrupt puppets." The people of New York had voted for him because he promised to be different.

"It's a shame," Rosenbaum said. "I thought that you'd been around long enough to understand that you won't get anywhere with these small-minded policies. You'll go down in history as the mayor who ruined this city with his exaggerated moral standards."

Nick had mulled over Rosenbaum's words ever since. Serious doubts about his approach had tormented him. He lay awake at nights thinking, but Nick ultimately decided that he couldn't compromise if he wanted to stay true to himself.

The taxi stopped at Gracie Mansion, and Nick paid the driver. The security guards saluted the mayor and his wife politely. They were used to seeing Nick taking taxis or the subway, rather than traveling by private car. Mary and Nick silently strolled toward the house, which looked like a Southern mansion, with its surrounding veranda and white railings. The fragrance of lilac mixed in the air with that of the roses. The foliage was so thick and dark that the driveway seemed narrow. It was a beautiful night.

But Mary's search for comfort in the beauty of the garden was in vain. Her husband walked next to her like he was a stranger, with his hands buried deep in his pockets and his eyes downcast. She was desperately searching for the right words to liberate him from this mood that she knew all too well. Recently, he suffered from these bouts of melancholy more often. He closed himself off, and he got this empty, bitter look on his face, which hurt Mary very much.

"Nick," she said. She couldn't take his silence anymore. Moths were flitting around the streetlight, and the unceasing sounds of the city could be heard as a muted mumbling from the distance.

"Yes?" He avoided looking into her eyes.

"It hurts me to see you so desperate and discouraged. You've always kept fighting no matter how hopeless the situation seemed. You can't give up now!"

Nick didn't answer.

"I love you," Mary said softly. "I don't give a damn what other people say."

Nick was silent and shook his head.

"I have to accept that I'm not the right man for this job."

"But that's nonsense! You're the best mayor this city ever had!"

Nick's gaze, helpless and scornful at the same time, hit Mary like a slap in the face. He laughed mockingly. "Well, at least one person thinks so."

Then he turned and quickly walked to the house. Mary followed him slowly. He had never rebuffed her this harshly before. Tears burned in her eyes, and a lump rose in her throat. He was distancing himself from her, and she couldn't understand why.

The next morning, Nick Kostidis passed the gate and assured the two security guards—as he had done so many times before—that he was quite capable of getting downtown himself. He walked along Eighty-Sixth Street to the subway station at the corner of Lexington Avenue. He rushed down the stairs with quick steps, just barely catching the downtown express train, and sat down on an empty seat in the very last car. At this early hour on a Sunday morning, the subway was deserted save for a few early-rising tourists. The train rattled and raced through the dark tunnels, flying past the brightly lit local stations.

Nick leaned back and closed his eyes. He'd hardly slept last night. He woke up drenched in sweat from a nightmare at four in the morning. He couldn't remember the details, but he could still feel the dream's sensation of powerlessness. Until the crack of dawn, he'd lain awake in his bed wondering which one of his employees was double-crossing him. Who knew that Zuckerman was brought to that hotel and that he had agreed to testify against Vitali?

The train came to a screeching halt and the doors opened, just to close again seconds later with a pneumatic sigh. Coming out under the blue sky at City Hall Park, he squinted into the bright August sun. He stopped for a short moment and looked at his office building with a mixture of pride and resignation.

Thinking about how many mayors before him had tried to govern this incomparable city more or less successfully since 1821 filled him with awe and respect, as it always did. At the same time, he felt that the arrogant proximity of the modern glass-and-steel skyscrapers towering so mightily above city hall was symbolic. The people sitting in these skyscrapers—the banks and corporations with ruthless men at their helms—held the true power over this city.

Nick Kostidis sighed and walked up the steps to city hall. A horde of press people lurked in the entrance hall, immediately storming toward him when they saw him coming. They had somehow heard he would be there.

"Mayor Kostidis!" an eager young woman yelled. "What do you have to say about the accusations that you had something to do with David Zuckerman's death?"

Within seconds, he found himself trapped by reporters, photographers, and camera crews pushing their microphones into his face. How the hell did the press already know about Zuckerman?

"Nick!" It was John Steele from Network America. "There are rumors that Zuckerman was killed by the Mafia. What do you think?"

Nick raised his hands and waited for the yelling to subside.

"First of all, good morning." He tried to put on a friendly face. "I can't comment at this point in time because all I know right now is that Mr.

Zuckerman was shot dead last night. I'm on my way to have a meeting with the police commissioner right now. We will release a statement later today."

"Mr. Kostidis," the eager woman persisted, "there's a rumor that you were involved in Zuckerman's death. Is there any truth to these allegations?"

Nick saw an unprofessional lust for sensationalism in her eyes.

"These allegations are nothing but hot air," he responded. "Zuckerman was charged with aiding and abetting fraud and bribery. This matter is solely the concern of the US Attorney's Office. I'm the mayor of New York. This case doesn't fall under my jurisdiction."

"But," the eager woman persisted, "according to some people, Zuckerman worked for Sergio Vitali. It's well known that you and Mr. Vitali—"

"Listen," Nick interrupted her impatiently, "you apparently know more than I do. Why don't you wait until I find out what this is all about? Okay?"

With these words, he pushed himself through the crowd of journalists. He swiftly disappeared into the hallway leading to his ground-floor office. Frank approached him at the door.

"How did the press find out about this?" Nick yelled at his assistant in a rage. "What the fuck is going on?"

"The press?" Frank gave him an astonished look.

"Yes, damn it." Nick quickly paced along the hallway. "They ambushed me in the entrance hall, bombarding me with questions. I wasn't prepared. They asked me whether I was involved in Zuckerman's death!"

"You?" Frank asked, surprised. "Who gave them that idea? How did the press find this out anyway?"

Nick stopped so abruptly that the young man almost ran into him.

"That's exactly what I'd like to know. It looks like no secret whatsoever is safe here! Not even ten hours have passed, and everyone in the city appears to be better informed than I am!"

His eyes flashed angrily, but he wasn't really mad. He had a sense of futility, as if someone had taken the helm out of his hands.

"By the way, Truman McDeere has been waiting in your office," Frank said, "for the past half hour."

They reached the west wing of city hall. The hustle and bustle usually reigning here was absent on the weekend. The offices were empty. Only Nick's secretary, Allie Mitchell, sat at her desk, as well as Raymond Howard.

"The press is bombarding us with phone calls," Allie said to Nick. "And Mr. de Lancie called, and Governor Rhodes wants you to call him back."

"Great." Nick frowned. "They'll have to wait. I first want to hear what McDeere has to say."

He disappeared into his office, while Frank, Ray, and Allie exchanged telling looks.

Truman McDeere rose from the chair he was sitting in when Nick Kostidis entered his office. He looked even more pinched than usual.

"How could this happen, McDeere?" Nick snapped at the FBI officer.

"I'm not accountable to you, Mayor Kostidis," the bald federal agent responded sharply. "We're not guilty of anything."

"Except that a man who was supposed to be protected by fifteen FBI agents was shot to death."

McDeere's expression turned even grimmer.

"The men weren't informed properly about this operation. They were just briefed about the identity of this man on-site," he snapped. "They didn't know each other. Just your people and I knew about this."

"What interest would any of us have in seeing Zuckerman killed?"

McDeere shrugged his shoulders and lit a cigarillo. Nick watched him closely. He had known Truman McDeere for some time and he suspected that there was more to this story than the FBI agent was willing to admit.

"So, Truman," he said in a conciliatory tone, "what really happened?"

After a brief internal debate, McDeere took a deep breath and started to speak in a quiet voice.

"Our people were positioned throughout the entire hotel. At all of the back entrances, the kitchen, the underground garage, and the elevators. One man stayed in the room with Zuckerman the whole time. It was about eight thirty when someone knocked at the door of the room. That person knew the agreed-upon knocking signals, and he also reached the sixth floor unchallenged. So the officer opened up. The agent thought he recognized the man from the meeting the night before and assumed that he was part of the squad. When the agent was told that he should go to the lobby to report the changing of the guard, he left the room."

Nick closed his eyes. An old, brazen Mafia trick, and the Feds fell for it! McDeere apparently had trouble admitting the mistake.

"When the agent got downstairs to see the others, it was immediately clear that something was fishy. They rushed back upstairs, but it was already too late by then. Zuckerman was dead as a doornail. Two shots at close range to the heart and one to the head. The murder weapon was a .45-caliber Smith & Wesson with a silencer. We found it."

"Oh?" Nick opened his eyes again.

"It was in a cart with dirty laundry."

"Did you trace it?"

"We couldn't. It has no serial number, no fingerprints, nothing. Ballistics are examining the gun, but there's no way to trace anything by way of the weapon. This guy was a pro."

"Looks like Mafia."

"Definitely." McDeere nodded, his face sullen. "We made a mistake precisely because we wanted to be absolutely sure that nothing went wrong. This is why we only used officers who didn't know each other. And that was exactly the opportunity for the killer to do his thing."

"He must have known all the details," Nick said. His darkest fears seemed to prove true. Only Vitali could be behind this cold-blooded execution.

"Yes," McDeere replied, "Zuckerman's killer was well informed. Nothing can bring this man back to life, but I want to know who provided the killer with this information. There were very few people who knew the exact details, which narrows the circle of possible suspects considerably."

"Lloyd Connors from the US Attorney's Office knew about it, the police commissioner, and your people."

"And you."

"No." Nick shook his head. "I knew which hotel Zuckerman was brought to, but I wasn't informed about the operation's details."

McDeere extinguished his cigarillo in the ashtray.

"I admit," he said, "that we won't be getting any accolades for how we handled this, but I firmly reject the suspicion that any of my men divulged any information."

Both men looked at each other in silence.

"The mole," McDeere said, "is at the US Attorney's Office, the police, or here in city hall."

Nick wiped his hand across his face. He wished that he could reject the accusation of having a traitor within his own ranks as resolutely as McDeere did. But he couldn't. About fifteen of his closest staff knew about this matter—fifteen people whom he could no longer trust.

"Nick, unfortunately, there has always been corruption in the city administration," McDeere said. "If you want, we can check your people."

"No, no," Nick quickly silenced him. "I have to find out another way. Maybe it's someone from the US Attorney's Office."

He thought about his staff members, all of whom he had known now for many years. In the future, he'd have to suspect that anyone he spoke to could be an informer for one of his enemies. This was a terrible thought, and Nick wished that he had more influence on his people's paychecks. Given their immense workload, their salaries were downright laughable. No wonder one of them might be open to receiving additional sources of income.

McDeere said good-bye a few minutes later. Nick sat there in a very pensive mood. In the 1960s, John Lindsay—the mayor at the time—had called New York City ungovernable. Corruption, a disastrous infrastructure, the extreme contrast between rich and poor, high unemployment in the poverty-stricken districts, and a chronic shortfall in the city's budget all made reasonable government policies virtually impossible. Nick had never let himself be discouraged by this up to now. With much enthusiasm and a healthy dose of optimism, he vigorously tackled the problems that his predecessors had failed to resolve. He had already accomplished so much. Continued support from the majority of his constituents confirmed his actions.

Nevertheless, there were plenty of people who were displeased by his fight against crime and his strengthening of the police force. The police's tough stance was publicly criticized time and again, and only the obvious accomplishments of his no-tolerance policy could take the wind out of his enemies' sails. In just one and a half years, he'd managed to drastically lower the crime rate in the city, and the Mafia bogeyman had faded away thanks to his persistent crackdowns. But now three damned shots threatened the success of his work! Nick had a feeling that Zuckerman's murder would trigger active lively debate about safety in the city. He could already see the sensational headlines: "Mafia Murder in Manhattan," "How Safe Is the City?" People would question the effectiveness of his security policy, and all the positive things that Nick had achieved with regard to quality of life and infrastructure improvements would be forgotten. He buried his face in his hands. He was a fighter. For his entire life he'd had to fight, but he didn't mind it. Now, the terrible suspicion of having a traitor in his own ranks deeply discouraged him.

"Mr. Harding is here, sir," Allie announced over the speakerphone.

"Send him in," Nick replied, "and bring us some coffee, please."

He stood up and walked toward the police commissioner. Jerome Harding, the head of the New York Police Department, was in his late fifties. He began his career as a patrol officer in the Bronx and built himself a reputation as a tough cop. His powerful stature and striking face with a protruding chin gave him an aggressive appearance. With his tailored suit and expensive silk tie, Harding looked civilized, but underneath this facade he was still a brutal bruiser from the Bronx who didn't forgive or forget. At the age of twenty-five, he'd joined the police academy. After that, he worked his way up to become a chief homicide detective. Ambitious as he was, he studied law by taking evening classes and applied to the US Attorney's Office for the Southern District of New York, where he quickly rose through the ranks to become the head of the securities fraud department. Nick met him there and soon came to appreciate his effective work, although he didn't particularly like him as a person. The feeling was mutual, but both men were professional enough to put their career goals above their personal aversion. Harding was known for his hot temper, but also for his perseverance. He was an energetic and merciless investigator who was never overcome by remorse. He was behind the successful criminal prosecution of an insider-trading scandal on Wall Street in the 1980s, And as the police commissioner, he'd become one of Nick's most important partners in the fight against crime.

"Jerome," Nick said as he extended his hand toward the red-faced man with a smile. "I'm sorry you had to come here on a Sunday morning. Thanks."

"No problem." Harding laughed and winked at him. "As you know, the police never sleep."

The two men sat down at the large conference table while Allie served coffee.

"So, what's the matter? How can I help you, Nick?"

Nick interlaced his fingers. He caught himself questioning the degree of Harding's loyalty, but he immediately brushed his doubts aside. The man sitting in front of him was known for his uncompromising disdain for all criminals. Harding might have a few unpleasant attributes, but he wasn't corrupt!

"I'm sure you've heard about the FBI's blunder in the Zuckerman matter."

"Yes, indeed"—Harding waved his hand in contempt—"The Feds screwed up. But you insisted that the FBI should handle Zuckerman's protection."

Nick ignored this pointed remark.

"How is it possible that a killer can get this close to a man being guarded by fifteen agents?"

"These idiots fell right into a classic Mafia trap!" Harding laughed maniacally. "The killer was probably among them from the very beginning, and they didn't notice!"

"That's exactly what gives me a headache! We've been in this business long enough to know that something like this should never happen!"

Harding darted a piercing glance at Nick. "What are you trying to get at?"

"The killer's contractor knew about Zuckerman's imminent testimony, the secret location, and the details of the entire operation. Let me make myself clear, Jerome. I'm not so much interested in catching this killer, which we probably won't manage to do anyway. I want to know how it was possible for confidential information to be leaked so quickly, and I want to know who leaked it!"

Harding seemed to hesitate for a split second before offering his unexpected response.

"You're taking this thing way too personally." He took a sip of his coffee and leaned back. "The FBI has disgraced itself, but you and I have nothing to do with it."

Nick was silent. Was Harding right? Did he take all of this too personally because Vitali had once again managed to slip through his net?

"No," he replied, "that's not true. This episode will bring us a lot of negative publicity. My main promise to my constituents was that I would make this city a safer place. We've already achieved quite a bit, but my political adversaries will use this to tear us to pieces. You know yourself that many people disapprove of the police's hard line, and now they'll reignite public discussion about the purpose of certain police operations."

The smirk vanished from Harding's face.

"You're being too dramatic. We succeeded in convincingly shutting up those damn liberal sissies, and we'll continue to do so."

"So you think we shouldn't do anything?"

Harding nodded. "Correct. Give the press some meaningless report, and point out the responsibility of the FBI and the US Attorney's Office. Let's wait and see. Just don't make any statements that could heat up this whole story in the public's eye."

Nick looked doubtfully at the police commissioner. Harding seemed unusually reserved. His recommendation to keep calm was completely out of character.

"I'd really like to know who provided the killer with the details," Nick insisted.

"Jesus, Nick"—Harding impatiently clicked his tongue—"Do you really want to set off an avalanche and provoke a public discussion about corruption? That would harm you a lot more. Let the Zuckerman matter rest."

Nick was anything but happy with the result of his meeting, and his phone calls with US Attorney John de Lancie and Governor Rhodes didn't lift his spirits any. It seemed he was the only one bothered by the death of this key witness. Zuckerman's testimony would have certainly stirred things up.

There was a knock at the door, and Michael Page—Nick's chief of staff—entered.

"I've prepared a statement for the press," he said, handing three pages to the mayor. "We won't leave any room for speculation."

"Hmm." Nick looked at the pages pensively. "Harding, de Lancie, and Governor Rhodes think that we should let this matter rest."

"Really?" Page was surprised. "And what do you think?"

"I don't know. I *do* know that there is more to this than meets the eye."

"I can change the press release."

"No, wait. Let me read it first." Nick delved into the text. Soon a smile spread across his face.

"It's brilliant, Michael," he said after he finished. "I stand against everyone else with this statement. We have only lost a battle instead of the entire war."

"Exactly." His chief of staff nodded, satisfied. "Public outrage will be shifted toward the likes of Vitali and Rosenbaum. We won't let them point the finger at us."

Sergio Vitali sat at his desk on the eighty-sixth floor of the VITAL Building and read the paper. The cover story headline read, "Mafia Murder in Manhattan?"

> *Late last night, well-known real-estate speculator David Zuckerman of New York City was shot dead by an unknown perpetrator at a hotel in Midtown Manhattan. Zuckerman, 42, was charged for his involvement in questionable business deals in the mid-1980s, especially during the contract award process for the construction of the World Financial Center. He was scheduled for questioning at a hearing before the US attorney's office investigation committee in*

Manhattan on Monday. In October of last year, Zuckerman was charged with at least four counts of bribery, illegal price fixing, and fraud. After Zuckerman—who owns a mansion on Long Island and a luxurious weekend house on Cape Cod—pleaded his right not to incriminate himself under the Fifth Amendment, the US attorney's office wanted to release him due to a lack of evidence. Mayor Kostidis, who himself served as the US Attorney for the Southern District of New York for many years, ordered the reopening of procedures due to a reasonable doubt of the defendant's innocence. The suspicions were substantiated on all counts by new evidence.

Many of the city's construction companies are involved in this corruption scandal, first and foremost VITAL Building Corp., which was awarded the contract for the construction of both World Financial Center subsections. Its owner, Sergio Vitali, has previously been accused of bribery and illegal price fixing in connection with several construction contract awards. However, the affair involving the construction of the World Financial Center is the largest and most comprehensive case in which many well-known companies and banks have been cited for their involvement. With the help of Zuckerman's testimony, the US attorney's office hoped to shed light on this case and finally bring Vitali to court for "his dubious and criminal business dealings."

"*Merda*," Sergio growled, then finished the article.

The FBI still has no leads in their search for the perpetrators. At yesterday's press conference, Truman McDeere, the head of the task force, said, "This was a cold-blooded, brutal murder that carries the Mafia's signature. Someone quite obviously feared that Zuckerman's testimony in front of the investigation committee could bring some inconvenient truths to light."

"I didn't think that the Feds would make so much noise about this," Nelson van Mieren said, concerned. "Their failure was rather embarrassing."

"This is not the FBI." Sergio slapped the newspaper with a flat hand. "This article is Kostidis's creation."

He let out a sinister laugh.

"He thought he finally had me, and now he sees that I slipped through his fingers once again."

"I don't like this at all, Sergio," the lawyer objected. "This talk about the Mafia and corruption damages your reputation. This is a godsend for the media."

"So what? I don't give a damn." Sergio stood up and crumpled the newspaper. "No one will remember this in a couple of weeks. Kostidis can suspect as much as he wants, but he can't prove anything. And he very well knows it."

"I don't think they will let it rest so easily this time," Nelson replied, "because it's an opportunity to discredit you publicly. You know yourself how sensitive this topic still is. It'll become difficult to maintain the support of our friends if the press picks up on this. Politicians hate negative publicity."

"But they love my money." Sergio laughed. "I don't give a damn whether or not they like me. I own them. I know way too much about them and their secret tax-free earnings for them to stab me in the back."

Nelson van Mieren let out a sigh. It had taken him years of hard work to build a legal and serious facade for Sergio's empire. Just a few negative words in the headlines and television coverage could cause a great deal of damage. And these headlines were sure to come, because the press was virtually starving for sensational stories in the summer.

"The building commissioner just called," Nelson said.

"He's starting to freak out," Sergio said, sitting in his armchair again and leaning back with a sinister smile. "We gave him twenty-five thousand dollars last month! What's he going to do? He won't bite the hand that feeds him."

He turned his chair to the side to behold the Empire State Building and the skyline of Midtown Manhattan.

"Look at this, Nelson," he said, "my city at our feet! I'm the king of Manhattan. Anyone who wants to do business here must get past me first!"

He laughed, but there was an icy glint in his eyes.

"Nelson, I'm not a megalomaniac, you know that. I've made it here from the streets of Little Italy, and nobody helped me. I'm used to a headwind, and I'm not scared of it. Quite the contrary—I like to fight! And I like to win. I'll win this time."

"Kostidis will try to crucify you."

"He's been trying for years." Sergio waved his hand, dismissing him. "I don't care. I'll stay backstage pulling the strings just like I've always done. Do you know what would really be bad, Nelson?"

"No, I don't."

"If I were in a position where I needed to hand this all over—that would be bad. But I don't." Sergio smiled, musing. "I could have retired a long time ago. I've seriously considered the idea, but..."

"But?" Nelson looked at him attentively.

"Massimo isn't ready to lead all of this yet." Sergio made a sweeping gesture. "And besides that, I still enjoy this game way too much."

Nelson looked at his friend with an uneasy feeling. He had witnessed Sergio's unstoppable rise and knew how ruthless he could be. But Sergio was wrong about one thing: he could not afford to ignore his reputation, because many of his business partners wouldn't allow themselves to be linked with a man who was called a Mafioso in the press. Sergio's empire—based on brutality and bloodshed—had become so mighty and powerful because he understood how to convince influential men to side with him. Assuming that nothing could shake it was a mistake. He'd made many enemies on his way to the top, and Nelson was convinced that many of these bought friends were just waiting for the moment when Sergio's empire started to rock to quickly jump ship. There were no bigger opportunists in the world than politicians.

"What's the matter, Nelson?" Sergio asked. "Don't tell me this newspaper scribbling scares you."

"I think you're taking this much too lightly," his lawyer replied. "We can't afford to make any mistakes that could threaten our key connections."

"What are you trying to say?" Sergio's ice-blue eyes seemed to pierce van Mieren. Nelson shuddered. It was inconceivable to imagine what would happen if someone who really knew something decided to get out. Vincent Levy, for example. Would he risk the reputation of his bank by publicly supporting Sergio? Never! Levy was a businessman, and he wasn't Italian. He was a Jew. If push came to shove, he would switch sides to ensure his own survival. But it was pointless to argue with Sergio because he refused to accept any reality but his own. Nelson realized that Sergio had stopped heeding his advice a long time ago.

"Nothing," he said, "you're right. Chances are that no one will still be talking about this in a few days."

Sergio smiled.

"Nelson, my old friend, you're not going to lose your nerve on me, are you? Speculation over whether I have something to do with the Mafia is less damaging than the testimony of a man who knows facts and figures. The dust around Zuckerman will settle, and then the bootlickers from politics, justice, and the administration will return. Ancient human greed has always bound them to me."

He stood up and stared out the window. Even if they avoided him for a while, they would never revoke their loyalty. One person who had planned on doing so was now lying stiff and cold in the morgue at the Department of Forensic Medicine. Sergio Vitali was no one to mess with.

"What about the woman?"

Sergio looked at Nelson in surprise.

"Alex?"

"Yes."

"Nothing. What about her?"

"Is she on your side?"

"I don't know." Sergio shrugged his shoulders. "She does her job, and she does it well. I don't talk about my business with her."

Nelson breathed a sigh of relief. He had secretly feared that Sergio had given in to weakness and let her in on his secret business deals.

"Are you worried that I would risk everything because of a woman?" Sergio laughed out loud.

"Well," Nelson replied, "after all, you toyed with the idea of confiding in her."

"But I decided against it. It was a sentimental moment. It passed."

He sat down at his desk again, but the smile had vanished from his face and made way for a grim expression.

"Get me McIntyre on the phone," he said to Nelson. "I'd better talk to him before he flips out."

"Sergio!" Paul McIntyre exclaimed in a low voice that had the sound of sheer panic. "Have you read the paper?"

He didn't hear the typical arrogance in McIntyre's voice.

"Yes," Sergio replied, "I have. Is there something in it that should interest me?"

"Jesus." McIntyre lowered his voice to a nervous whisper. "Zuckerman is dead! No more investigation committee! Kostidis is mad as hell, and now they'll certainly come after me."

"Nonsense. Who would come after you?"

"The US attorney, Kostidis—who knows!"

"Nobody will come, Paul, I can promise you that. Now calm down. I'd like to discuss something with you."

“Calm down!” McIntyre laughed desperately. “The entire city is standing on its head, and you tell me to calm down!”

“How was your vacation?” Sergio leaned back into a comfortable position in his chair; he put his feet up on the reflective top of his mahogany desk. “Was everything arranged to your liking?”

McIntyre instantly got the hint. He hesitated for a moment; then his voice sounded calmer.

“Of course. It was perfect, as usual. My wife even went diving.”

“I’m glad. I hope that she spent a lot of money.”

“Hmm…yes…”

“I heard that another little tidy sum has been transferred to your account in Georgetown.”

“Great.” McIntyre was still tense, but he had himself under control again.

“Paul,” Sergio said, “I need a favor. A friend of mine has a small problem.”

The buildings commissioner was silent. These words coming from Vitali were familiar and were meant as anything but a request. However, Vitali rewarded those who did him favors royally. McIntyre was aware of that. He’d complied for the first time with one of Vitali’s requests about fifteen years ago, when he was a clerk at the Department of Buildings, and he had never regretted it. He was able to send his kids to private schools instead of the run-down public schools, and his family vacationed at hotels Vitali owned throughout the world. In addition, they were always treated as if they were Vitali’s close relatives. McIntyre had by now added a respectable chunk to his retirement savings. Although he still needed to be careful not to live beyond his means, he would retire in luxury.

“So what can I do for you?”

“Charlie Rosenbaum is having problems with his new skyscraper on Fifty-Second Street,” Sergio began.

"For heaven's sake! God knows that I can't do anything about that! The mayor himself just asked last week whether Rosenbaum had applied for a retroactive permit."

Sergio felt the hot anger rise up in him whenever he heard of this man. Kostidis! Didn't he have enough work on his hands without assuming the jobs of the attorney general and the buildings commissioner?

"And?" He forced himself to remain calm. "Did he?"

"No."

"See? Go ahead and issue a permit for him now. Kostidis has other things on his mind at the moment and won't ask again for a while."

"Impossible!"

"I'm not familiar with that word, Paul."

"This could cost me my job."

"I've promised my friend I'd put a good word in for him."

Rosenbaum had offered Sergio two magnificently run-down apartment buildings in Morrisania and Hunts Point at a truly special price in return for his help as an intermediary with the Department of Buildings. Of course, Rosenbaum couldn't possibly know that these areas of the South Bronx were earmarked as priority redevelopment projects in city hall. In a few years, perhaps even sooner, these properties would be worth hundreds or even thousands of times more after the decrepit apartment buildings were demolished. Sergio owed this information to his absolute favorite informer sitting right in Kostidis's office. This informer made up for all the trouble Sergio had with the mayor. A strange twist of fate had made Zachary St. John's old college friend a member of Nick Kostidis's inner circle. It was easy enough for Sergio to recruit the unhappy man with St. John's help. In addition to regular payments, Sergio promised he would support his ambitious political aspirations. Thinking about this made Sergio smile in satisfaction. He had an eye and an ear directly in the mayor's office. He'd never before had a mole that far up the ladder in city hall. Whatever Kostidis did, Sergio was immediately informed about everything and able to take countermeasures, if necessary. Without a doubt, the 107th mayor of New York City would go down in history as the least successful of them all.

"So, Paul, how about it?" Sergio asked. McIntyre sighed, and Sergio knew that he had won. The buildings commissioner argued a little for appearance's sake.

"By the way," Sergio said, playing his trump card, "I found that house your wife has been dreaming about for years. Right on the coast of Long Beach with an ocean view. It's a real beauty, with its own dock and private beach."

This eliminated any remaining doubts.

"Okay," Paul McIntyre said, giving up his resistance, "tell Rosenbaum to call me."

"You're my friend, Paul." Sergio tapped the miniature bronze Statue of Liberty on his desk with the toe of his shoe. "And you know that I never forget my friends."

Alex also read the article in the paper. The hint at a connection between Sergio and the Mafia was anything but speculation; it was the absolute truth. The ugly man whom she'd encountered at Sergio's house was David Zuckerman's killer. Sergio had no doubt lied to her. She had believed his reassurances because she had *wanted* to believe him.

On Saturday night, she had managed to escape from his house unnoticed. Driving back to the city, she briefly contemplated calling Oliver, but she didn't. The memory of his contempt was still too vivid, and she wouldn't have been able to bear it if he slammed the door in her face. She had been wide awake all night as she sat in her dark apartment, trembling with fear and trying to gather her thoughts. Sergio didn't suspect that she'd found out the truth about him, and he must never find out. Once again, the fear crept up inside of her. Were all the guests at Sergio's party really as clueless as she assumed? Or was she the only one in the dark? It seemed impossible to her that the governor, the publisher of *Time* magazine, even LMI's board members, could turn a blind eye.

Alex got to the office early the next morning. She was biting her lower lip, contemplating how she could cool off her relationship with Sergio without raising suspicion, when she heard a knock on her glass office door. Her nerves were so tense, she jumped up as if someone had just shot her.

"Hi, Alex." It was Mark. He was surprised by her frightened expression. "Here are the documents about Xiao-Ling Industries and Midway Porter."

"Okay, thanks." Alex nodded absentmindedly. Fortunately, she was going to be able to get away from Sergio for eight days. She had to take a business trip to Asia and Europe with John Kwai, and this would give her time to develop a strategy.

"How are you?" Mark asked in a concerned voice. "You look sick."

"I'm feeling great," she replied and forced a smile. It occurred to her that Mark was friends with Oliver. Had Oliver told him about the embarrassing episode in his apartment?

"Is there anything else?" she asked Mark, who was still holding the files in his hands and looked like he had something else on his mind.

"There's something that I'd like to talk to you about," he said.

"Is it urgent? I have another meeting, then I need to leave for the airport."

"Maybe it's important," Mark answered in a serious tone. "I've compiled some information that you should read. There are inconsistencies that I stumbled upon during the last few weeks. I know that you don't want to hear about it, but I'm sure that this will interest you."

He placed a large envelope on her desk.

"What kind of information is this?" Alex eyed her employee suspiciously. She saw Zack strolling around the trading floor. Mark also spotted him. It was still relatively quiet because the stock exchange had not yet opened, and Zack was talking with some of the traders.

"It would be better if St. John doesn't get a hold of this envelope," Mark said. An uneasy feeling suddenly overcame her.

"Why are you giving me this now, of all times?" she asked. Mark threw a quick glance at the trading floor.

"I want you to know that you can trust me," he said, lowering his voice, "but probably not many others in here. Please, Alex, take a look, but don't speak about it to anyone."

At that moment, Zack stepped into Alex's office, whereupon Mark excused himself and left. Alex put the envelope into her briefcase together with other documents she needed for the trip.

"You left so quickly Saturday." Zack sat down on one of the visitor's chairs unasked, and his eyes curiously glanced over her desk. "You missed the fireworks. It was phenomenal."

"I'm sure," Alex said, trying to act relaxed, "but I was dead tired all of a sudden. And I need to fly to Hong Kong today."

While Zack made small talk about the fireworks and the party, Alex had the feeling that there was a ticking bomb in her briefcase, and Zack's warning suddenly entered her mind: *Be careful with Vitali.* She wished she could ask him what he'd meant by that. Did he know about Sergio? She didn't know what to believe anymore.

Alex had no idea how she would act toward Sergio when she returned to New York. As expected, the press jumped on the scandal that the Zuckerman murder ignited during the summer slump. Regardless of the respectability of the newspaper or television station, the topic of the Mafia in New York was gleefully exploited. Alex bought every American newspaper she could get her hands on and vigilantly followed the reports while she was abroad. Sergio was publicly accused of involvement in the murder at the Milford Plaza, and his father's criminal past was once again covered extensively. Although every accusation raised against Sergio was dug up out of the archives, none of the journalists dared to call him a gangster. But the intense speculation was enough to portray him in an unfavorable light.

Alex had opened the envelope the moment she reached her Hong Kong hotel room. It contained a neatly bound stack of copied newspaper clippings about Gilbert Shanahan. Alex broke out in goose bumps as she read them. She also found a list of all the deals she had completed in recent months: Camexco, Hanson, American Road Map, National Concrete, Sherman Industries, Seattle Pacific Woods, Inc., Diamond Crown, Redwood Lumber, Storer, Hale-Newport, A&R, and Micromax. Mark had researched meticulously and discovered that either the Panamanian holding company of SeViCo or a company called Sunset Properties was behind every client. Sunset Properties had been incorporated in the British Virgin Islands since 1985. He had created a diagram of arrows that all converged into one point.

Alex was perplexed and shook her head. What was this supposed to mean? Additionally, there was a list of investment funds launched by LMI in recent months. Many of these funds were issued as a way to finance their deals. One of the funds—Private Equity Technology Partners—was highlighted in yellow marker; with five hundred million dollars in capital, it was larger than the average fund. It was highly speculative and invested in new technology-oriented start-ups. This included another fund called Venture Capital SeaStarFriends Limited Partnership.

Alex lit a cigarette and stared at the area highlighted in yellow. She didn't understand the connections and turned the page. Then she suddenly froze. *Are you kidding me, or are you really that naive?* SeViCo. Sergio Vitali Corporation. The hand holding her cigarette started to tremble. *Some of my companies also do business with LMI...* This is what Sergio told her when she asked him whether he was involved with LMI. Here it was in black-and-white. SeViCo was behind every single deal that she'd worked on and closed over the last few months. Alex flipped back a few pages. Venture Capital SeaStarFriends Limited Partnership. Sea Star—*Stella Maris.* Was all of this a coincidence? She turned to the last page of Mark's summary, holding her breath. On the top of the page it said in handwriting:

> *NBC Broadcast Satellite Corp. acquired 100 percent of the shares of the Tallahassee News Group in April 1997. The buyer in this deal was represented by LMI. TNG's stock price rose to an all-time high of $23\frac{5}{16}$ in March 1997 and subsequently fell to $7\frac{15}{16}$. Simultaneously, an IBC called Magnolia Limited Partnership was incorporated in the British Virgin Islands with $320,000 in capital. These strong price fluctuations in TNG's stock were then investigated by the SEC. Gilbert Shanahan was summoned and run over by a truck the day of the hearing. As it turned out, the legal department at LMI had prepared the articles of incorporation for Magnolia, whose sole shareholder was Gilbert Shanahan. LMI claimed in front of the SEC that they knew nothing about it, and by doing so passed the buck to Shanahan, who was—quite conveniently—already dead at that point in time.*

Alex skimmed over the next page. Mark had listed the stock prices and the corresponding dates of her deals. She felt a chill come over her. The stock prices rose slightly every single time before the acquisition or merger was made public. At the bottom, Mark had written: *Who knew about these deals before their announcement?* Alex broke out into a cold sweat. She knew who it was, and this someone knew it solely and exclusively from her. It was Zack, and it looked like he was taking advantage of this knowledge. There was only one question left unanswered: For whom was he doing these insider trades—for himself, or Vincent Levy?

She stared at the wall of her hotel room, and slowly the confusion in her mind cleared. The pieces of the puzzle started coming together, and she suddenly saw things clearly. Sergio had been at Zack's party. That's where she'd met him. She'd never asked herself what he was doing there. Besides, he had also invited Zack to his birthday party. Why? Because they were close business partners? Did Zack also supply Sergio with information, which she gave him on Levy's order? If Sergio, through SeViCo, was behind these deals, then he already profited handsomely through Zack—and illegally and tax-free at that! This was incredible! Her bewilderment turned into rage as she realized how naive and blind she had been. Was Sergio even responsible for her being hired at LMI? Possibly. Levy had tested to what degree she would be willing to participate in these dirty business deals, and she had let herself be bribed with his dubious bonus. If Mark was right and she had interpreted the findings of his research correctly, then she was nothing but a willing puppet. This was fraud of epic proportions. Alex sat motionless on her hotel bed for a long time. It would be quite simple to find out. She would set a trap for Zack. If he fell into it, then she'd know.

Alex threw her keys on the table, slipped her sandals from her feet, and took off her blazer. Without turning on the light, she walked straight to the kitchen and opened the refrigerator door. She took out a bottle of milk and allowed herself a big gulp. The evening with Madeleine and Trevor had been very entertaining, but she had downed more red wine than she could handle. The Downeys had invited her to their house on Long Island for the weekend, and Alex had been happy to escape the humid city. She had a great time in Amagansett, horseback riding on the beach with Madeleine and sharing meals with her and Trevor.

Alex walked barefoot into the living room and pressed the light switch as she passed it. She froze and nearly dropped the bottle of milk in shock. Sergio was sitting on the couch.

"Jesus!" she exclaimed. "Why did you scare me like that? Why are you sitting here in the dark?"

"Hello, *cara*." He smiled, his white teeth flashing in his dark face. "I've been waiting for you for three hours. Your cell phone was turned off."

"Did we have a date?" Alex put the milk bottle on the floor and noticed that she was trembling. This was the first time she had seen him since that terrible evening at his house. Although she was horrified by him now that she knew the truth, she had to keep her composure.

"You haven't called me since you got back from Asia, and I was simply longing for you. How are you?"

"Good." She remained standing next to the light switch, watching him. "And how are you?"

"Excellent."

"It's unbelievable what they write in the newspapers," she said coolly.

"Newspaper scribbling," Sergio said and laughed. "I've never cared about that."

"They say that you're somehow connected with the murder of this real-estate guy." Alex was trembling inside. She could hardly resist the urge to throw everything she had found out about him into his face.

"I'm sure that they'd love to put the blame on me."

Sergio crossed his legs and grinned. Although he'd never admit it, this vicious press campaign was really getting to him. Being defenseless made him angry. And on top of that, he could hardly endure how self-righteous Mayor Kostidis appeared on television. On Monday, the IRS criminal tax investigation unit showed up once again at Ficchiavelli and turned the entire place upside down. Massimo had attacked one of the agents in one of his temper tantrums. That had cost Sergio endless phone calls with all kinds of influential people on his bribery payroll to keep this situation from leaking to the press. He also realized that some of his "friends" were avoiding him, which was a clear indication that Kostidis's smear campaign was having an impact. There were problems in every direction, and he also couldn't reach Alex. Sergio was tense beyond all measure and irritated. He wanted to have sex with Alex and release the pressure.

"This bastard Kostidis has been leading a personal crusade against me for the past fifteen years," he continued. "He's obsessed with the idea of locking me up behind bars. During his time as the US attorney, he tried everything in his power to denounce me. It wasn't enough for him to drag New York's entire underworld and half of Wall Street into court—he wants me too."

He stood up without taking his eyes off of Alex. At first glance, he seemed as confident and relaxed as usual, but his eyebrows were tensely furrowed.

"He's tried everything already: He accused me of all kinds of Mafia activities, bribery, extortion. He tried to frame me with fraud and union manipulation. All to no avail. I don't know how many years the US Attorney's Office spent fabricating accusations. It was all in vain."

His expression became sinister.

"I pay my taxes, provide work for thousands of people, and carry a great deal of responsibility," he said, his tone angry, "and then this miserable Greek idiot brings his righteous anger upon anyone with an Italian name, calling me a gangster and Mafioso. He's already caused me enormous damage with his slander, but I don't get upset about him anymore. Let him make a fool of himself with his missionary zeal."

Sergio laughed grimly.

Alex knew that this was anything but ridiculous, yet she secretly admired Sergio's performance. He withstood her stare without blinking an eye, and if she hadn't known better, she would have believed him. *Don Sergio,* she thought, and a shiver ran down her spine.

She had to play along with his game. “Why don’t you defend yourself against these accusations? Why do you let them drag your name through the mud?”

“I don’t need to justify myself over things that I’m not involved with.” He smiled, but his blue eyes were flinty.

“But a tarnished reputation hurts business.”

“That’s nonsense,” Sergio said contemptuously, shaking his head. “The people I do business with aren’t small-minded philistines easily intimidated by sensationalist newspaper articles.”

Alex didn’t say a word.

“What is it, *cara*?” He put his hands on her shoulders and gazed intensely into her eyes. “Do you actually believe what they say about me?”

“I wish I could say no,” Alex replied.

He grabbed her wrists.

“Does it really matter to you what’s written in the newspapers?”

“No,” she said, shaking her head. “I’m as unconcerned with that as you are. I wouldn’t care if you would just be honest with me. But I have a feeling that you’re not.”

Sergio let go of her.

“Why do you want to know things that are none of your business?”

He put his hands in his pockets, and his smile had vanished.

“Do you think that I’m accountable to you just because I have sex with you every once in a while?”

Alex stared at him in disbelief.

“I’ve never asked you to explain anything about yourself to me. But you ask me to believe you. The press has been writing and reporting otherwise about you for weeks. Why should I believe you when you don’t trust me?”

“It’s exactly like I’m telling you.”

“Just like in the Bible, right?” Alex laughed and suddenly felt a chill. “True to the words, ‘Blessed are those who haven’t seen and yet have come to believe’!”

Sergio gave her a serious look. His handsomely sculpted face looked like it was chiseled from stone.

"I love you," he said unexpectedly.

"No, you don't." Alex shook her head. "Maybe you desire me, but that's all."

She thought about the natural and loving comfort with which Trevor and Madeleine treated each other. Sergio was completely incapable of such affection. She suddenly didn't want to see him anymore. She was tired and wanted to sleep.

"The past few days have been rough," she said and turned away. "I'm tired. You should leave now."

Sergio's anger, which he had struggled to hold back, flared up. He approached her with three large steps and grabbed her arm harshly.

"Let me go," Alex said. "I want to go to bed."

"I do too." Sergio pulled her toward him and pressed his lower body against hers. "With you."

"But I don't want to do this with you." She pushed her arms against his chest, but he wouldn't let go of her. He raged with lust. She kicked and punched him in a fit of panic, but any pain that she caused intensified his wild desire. It was a crazy, angry, downright fierce fight, and Alex lost. She endured his brutal passion, her faced turned away. As he climaxed with a muffled panting, she knew that she hated him. Furious, she watched him get up, calmly zip his pants and then straighten up his tie.

"You asshole," she whispered. "You just raped me!"

Sergio leaned over her and turned her face so that she was forced to look up at him.

"You should remember one thing very precisely, *cara mia*." He smiled, but the chill in his eyes was arctic. "I always get what I want."

Then he walked to the door and disappeared. Alex began to sob. Why hadn't she listened to all of the warnings, even when she'd sensed deep inside that the terrible rumors were true? She was no longer in control of the situation, and realized she actually never had been. She learned the hard way: Sergio Vitali was not a person to be gotten rid of that easily.

December 21, 1999

Shortly before Christmas, Alex closed one of the most spectacular deals of the year. Maxxam was a blue-chip company with a good international reputation, a conglomerate that was massively expanding in the computer technology sector. Alex had learned that Maxxam was interested in IT-Systems, a hardware giant from Texas, and she had managed to outdo all the competition with her clever and skillful negotiations.

The fact that she hadn't mentioned a single word to Zack filled her with a special sense of satisfaction. She was more than curious how he would react to her announcement at the next board meeting—the main topic of which was the presentation of the company's financial results at its annual press conference in January. LMI would represent Maxxam in this deal. Although it hadn't been possible for Mark and her to find out how the complex constructs of offshore companies were related to LMI, they were both firmly convinced that Zack brazenly abused the information that Alex passed on to him. This is why they had prepared and worked on the Maxxam deal in secret. By the time Zack heard about it today, it would be too late to build a position in Maxxam or IT-Systems shares. Alex had carefully prepared for this presentation. Even though she was on the brink of collapse after the intensity of a 120-hour week, she looked forward to the triumph that was certainly awaiting her. Before Vincent Levy officially opened the meeting, she rose from her seat between John Kwai (the director of emerging markets and international business) and Ron Schellenbaum (the chairman of the board) and asked for everyone's attention.

"Gentlemen," she said, after the chatter died down, "I would like to make an announcement that should delight all of you. It's an early Christmas present, so to speak."

Everyone looked at her expectantly.

"I'm happy to announce that Maxxam Enterprises has given us the mandate to arrange a leveraged buyout for its acquisition of IT-Systems."

The large conference room was as silent as a tomb. Everyone was stunned as they stared at Alex. They had all heard about Maxxam's interest in IT-Systems, but only through rumors up to now. Suddenly, everyone started talking at once, and Alex barely managed to hold back a satisfied smile.

"I worked out an LBO price of forty dollars per share," she continued and immediately regained the undivided attention of everyone in the room. "We'll issue high-yield bonds to raise five hundred million dollars. LMI serves as the underwriter for this debt."

Levy asked CFO Michael Friedman if LMI was actually capable of financing such a gigantic deal. Alex thought that this question was hypocritical considering that the Private Equity Technology Partners trust alone managed assets worth five hundred million dollars.

"How is this supposed to work?" Zack asked, visibly irritated. "How could you work on such a deal without informing anyone about it in advance?"

"This is my job," she said, "and the Chinese wall prohibits me from sharing information about such an LBO in-house. Maxxam's management is enthusiastic, and I built a detailed financial plan with our colleagues from the corporate finance department."

Zack fell silent, but anger flashed in his eyes.

"Maxxam doesn't have sufficient funds of its own at the moment to acquire IT-Systems, which is why they need to finance the deal," Alex said in a loud voice. "IT-Systems is an excellent and profitable company and the market leader in the area of computer hardware. Unfortunately, it has been run into the ground by poor management. However, in addition to Maxxam, other industry giants such as HP and Microsoft were also interested in IT-Systems. I had no choice but to go with the higher-risk option. The interest rate that I demanded was one percentage point below that of the competition, which ultimately tipped the scales at Maxxam in our favor and resulted in the LBO winning the mandate. Gentlemen, the total volume of this deal is 1.2 billion dollars. In addition to the fees for our advisory work, we will generate about one hundred million dollars in financing fees from the bonds that we issue."

"Are you saying that we could earn as much money with this deal as with all of last year's deals combined?" Friedman's jaw dropped.

"That's correct." Alex smiled triumphantly. "If I have understood Mr. Levy correctly, he wants LMI to be a major player in M&A. With this deal, that will definitely be the case."

She opened her briefcase and pulled out a stack of photocopies, which she then distributed to everyone.

"This is irresponsible!" Zack jumped up. His cheeks flushed in anger.

"I think it's brilliant," Levy said, looking up from his document, "simply magnificent. How far along are the negotiations at this point, Alex?"

"The IT-Systems board of directors will meet tomorrow and approve the proposed LBO, in all likelihood. I just spoke at length with Bernie Ritt, the president of IT-Systems. Maxxam agreed on very favorable terms for the IT-Systems shareholders. They'll exchange the shares at a ratio of one to one and pay out a bonus stock dividend of one share per ten shares. All employees will be taken over, except for the management, who will receive generous severance packages. If everything goes well, then we should have the okay before Christmas. It's the biggest deal in years. LMI has the fish on the hook."

"And what if the management of IT-Systems doesn't approve?" Zack asked anxiously.

"In that case," Alex replied in a relaxed tone, "Maxxam's board has left no doubt that it will pursue a much less lucrative hostile takeover. Ultimately, the shareholders determine the future, but they won't get a better offer than this one from Maxxam. All of the other potential buyers would break up IT-Systems."

"Stop it, Zack," Levy said to his managing director. "Alex has done excellent work here, and we should acknowledge that, even if it comes as a surprise to all of us. I'm absolutely sure this is the largest deal that LMI has ever financed."

For the remainder of the meeting, the Maxxam deal was the main topic of discussion and pushed the annual report press conference into the background. Alex had done her job. Now it was up to corporate finance and the securities and fixed-income departments to put the leveraged buyout into practice and issue the bonds to their clients. After the meeting was over, Alex rushed to get out of the conference room. Her entire team was already waiting at Luna Luna to celebrate the completion of this gigantic deal. She said good-bye with a smile on her face, and everyone congratulated her—except for Zack. She wasn't surprised about that; this confirmed her grave suspicions.

"Alex!"

She stopped as she heard Zack's voice behind her.

"Come to my office!" he ordered. She obeyed, shrugging her shoulders. He sat down behind his desk, but didn't ask her to sit. He managed to disguise his anger behind a phony smile.

"Why am I hearing about such a deal this way?" he asked. "Didn't we agree that you'd inform me in advance?"

"It was incredibly hectic," Alex answered with a smile that was just as fake. "And you weren't in the city. I simply forgot to tell you."

"Forgot?" Zack opened his eyes wide in pretend astonishment. "I think you're overestimating your authority a little bit here, sweetie."

Alex stopped smiling. She put her briefcase down and leaned over with her hands on the desk. Zack crossed his hands behind his head with a slight grin.

"I suspect that you've misunderstood the meaning of a Chinese wall in the past," she said quietly, "because a birdie chirped in my ear that every single one of my deals was preceded by peculiar price fluctuations. This is a surefire sign of illegal insider trading."

Zack was an accomplished actor, but leagues below Sergio. Alex noticed a slight flicker of fright in his eyes, and the corners of his mouth twitched in brief panic.

"You take yourself very seriously," he said.

"No, I take my responsibility seriously." She straightened up again. "Because I have a responsibility to the financial markets. And your reaction confirmed my suspicion."

"You're an arrogant bitch!" Zack suddenly resorting to unprofessional insults made Alex grin.

"And you're a sore loser," she countered, grabbing her briefcase. "I'm going to celebrate with my team a little bit. They deserve it. Have a nice evening, Mr. St. John!"

Her entire department was already at Luna Luna, a cozy bar on Broad Street mostly frequented by brokers and bankers. They greeted Alex with applause and enthusiastic whistling when she entered. She asked for everyone's attention and then reported about the events at the meeting and the board's reactions.

"All right, people." Alex raised her hand, and it became quiet again. "Enough of this, let's move on to the fun part of the evening. You've all done a great job, and I'm incredibly proud of you. As a token of appreciation for all the nights and weekends that you worked around the clock, all drinks on me tonight! Celebrate your achievement! You earned it!"

After another surge of applause, the first round arrived. The mood was cheerful and boisterous, the alcohol flowed freely, and the inhuman hundred-hour work weeks were behind them. Christmas and New Year's were just around the corner, which meant even the financial district would be quieter for a few weeks. After a few drinks, Alex found a moment to speak with Mark.

"How did it go?" Mark inquired.

"Zack went berserk. He could hardly control himself."

"Bingo." Mark nodded seriously. "So you were right."

"Well," Alex said and let out a sigh, "but I still don't know how far up his little side dealings go. Does Levy know of them?"

"He knew about Shanahan," said Mark quietly, "and I'm sure that he knows about this."

Alex frowned. She was in this thing up to her ears. No one would believe that she was stupid enough not to know what Zack did with her information. If the regulating authorities caught wind of this, she would face a harsh fine in addition to possibly losing her work permit.

"Damn it," she said, her good mood swept away. "I was a pretentious idiot. I had it coming."

"Why is that?" Mark looked at her, surprised.

"Oliver tried to tell me about it months ago." Alex shrugged her shoulders. "But I refused to listen to him. He was right about everything."

"I didn't believe him either at first," Mark replied.

"Do you still see Oliver every now and then?" Alex asked. The alcohol had lowered her inhibitions, and she suddenly wanted to know whether Mark was aware of what had happened between her and Oliver, and what he thought about it.

"Not for a while." Mark threw a brief glance at her. "He left the city in May for a few months because..."

He stopped.

"Because of—what? Keep going, Mark!"

"I don't know. It…it's none of my business."

"What did he tell you?"

Mark struggled with himself for a moment, and then he looked at Alex. "He was attacked in May and beaten pretty badly. His apartment was ransacked while he was in the hospital."

"What?" Alex's blood froze in her veins. "When was this exactly?"

"I don't know if I should talk about it," Mark replied evasively, biting his lip. "It's really none of—"

"Mark!" Alex insisted. "Tell me what happened! Please!"

"Oliver told me that you showed up at his apartment one night and revealed to him that you'd had an affair with Sergio Vitali," he said, visibly embarrassed, "and that the two of you had a disagreement. The next evening, three masked men were waiting for him in the hallway and roughed him up pretty badly. One of the men told him to stop sticking his nose into matters that are none of his business and to keep his hands off of you."

"My God," Alex whispered in deep horror. Sergio knew about Oliver and her, but he had never spoken a word about it! The thought that Sergio had her monitored was so outrageous and frightening that she didn't dare to believe it. She tried to remember the day after the fight with Oliver. Yes! Sergio had taken her out for dinner at Le Cirque and showed her the penthouse apartment afterward. While she dined and laughed with him, Oliver had been brutally beaten. Her shock mixed with a feeling of cold fear. She knew all too well what Sergio was capable of. Did he still have someone trailing her? Was he tracking her every move? Involuntarily, she glanced around the packed pub, looking for a stranger among the happy faces of her team members.

"How…how's Oliver doing now?" she whispered.

"I think he's okay again," Mark answered, "but he was in the hospital for almost three weeks."

Alex's entire body shook. Her triumph over the sealed deal was forgotten. On top of her fear, she had deep feelings of guilt toward Oliver.

"Here," Mark said as he pushed another drink toward her, "drink something."

She raised her head and looked at Mark desperately.

"I'll never be able to make up for this," she said quietly. "I had no idea! Oliver will hate me for it because he thinks that—"

"No, he doesn't hate you," Mark said to her quickly. "Quite the contrary. But he's very worried about you."

Alex didn't believe that. She had put Oliver in jeopardy! Probably every man she spoke to was in danger if Sergio thought he was a threat to him. It was simply terrible, and she couldn't do anything about it. Right at that moment, Zack entered the pub with another man. He looked around and grinned when he caught sight of Alex. Then he pushed his way through the crowd in her direction.

"He's the last thing that I need right now," she muttered. "Don't even think about leaving me alone, Mark."

"I'll stay right at your side."

"Hello, gorgeous." Zack squeezed himself next to Alex at the bar. She could smell that he'd already had plenty to drink. His usual pristine appearance was disturbed, his tie hung lopsided, and the top buttons of his shirt were open.

"Zack, what are you doing here?" Alex pretended to be surprised.

"Ray," Zack said, turning to his companion, "what are we drinking? Vodka on the rocks?"

The man with the thin blond hair grinned and nodded. His face seemed vaguely familiar, but Alex couldn't place him.

"Bartender," Zack said, snapping his fingers, "two double vodkas on the rocks, not too much ice!"

Alex's only wish at that moment was to hole up somewhere. Zack observed her with a blurred gaze through bloodshot eyes. He took his glass and raised it in the air.

"Here's to our great, brilliant M&A chief," Zack said, his pronunciation garbled but loud enough for people to hear every single word, "who descended from a bed on Park Avenue to party with the common people. Very generous of her!"

"Are you crazy, Zack? What is this?"

"I admire you, Alex Sontheim, I admire you!" Zack put his arm around her shoulders as if he had permission to do so and whispered, "So, where's your rich lover now, hmm? Or do you have permission to be out alone tonight?"

"You're drunk." She tried to break free from him, but Zack had a firm grip on her.

"That was pretty clever of you, Alex; I give you that," he continued. "You got in bed with the right guy, hats off! Did you also make a play for Vince? He's eating from the palm of your hand, the bastard. Just like the entire rest of this stupid outfit, they'd all love to f—"

"That's enough!" Alex interrupted him brusquely. He laughed maniacally and downed his vodka in one gulp.

"Another!" he yelled over to the bartender.

"What's your problem?"

"I don't have a problem." He grinned, but his eyes shone with pure hatred. His lips touched her cheek, and he hissed, "I love to stand in your shadow. I love to be the idiot who does all of your dirty work. It turns me on when all I hear is *Alex, Alex, Alex!*"

She wiped his spit from her cheek in disgust. The grin had vanished from his face—Alex was shocked to realize the extent of his envy. He was jealous of her success and her standing with the board, and he was angry because he didn't have a chance with her. His friendliness had been a facade all along. Zack wasn't her friend. Quite the contrary. She slid off her bar stool.

"I'm leaving now," she said coolly. "You're completely drunk."

"Yes, I'm drunk." He was standing so close to her that she could see every pore in his face. "But don't think that I'm as stupid as all those other idiots. You conned me, you little bitch. I won't let you get away with it a second time!"

Mark stepped in. He pushed Zack aside, which nearly triggered a brawl. But all of the men from Alex's department kept Zack in check, allowing her to leave the bar unscathed. She stood on the street in the sleet.

"Is everything all right?" Mark looked at her with so much concern and empathy that she almost lost the last bit of her self-control. The events of recent days had simply been overwhelming. Discovering that Sergio knew about her and Oliver was the last straw, and Zack's mean vulgarities nearly sent her over the edge.

"Yes, everything's okay," she said, her voice trembling.

"I'll take you home," Mark offered. Alex thought about Oliver again. Maybe Sergio's spies were lurking around every corner. In any event, she wanted to prevent something happening to Mark.

"No, it's all right. I'll take a cab. Go back inside and celebrate a little more."

"I can't possibly leave you alone." Mark remained firm, waving at a passing taxi that looked empty.

"Yes, you can. It's all right." Alex managed to smile. "I'm okay."

"Can I at least call you later?" Mark was sincerely concerned. Alex nodded. Then she hugged him spontaneously.

"Thank you for everything, Mark. Thank you for letting me trust you."

Mark swallowed and nodded. Alex quickly climbed into the waiting taxi and waved good-bye.

It was early morning, and a pale-blue horizon arched across the sea. The December sun tried to provide a little warmth as Alex and Madeleine rode through the dunes down to the beach. Alex was happy that she had accepted Trevor and Madeleine's invitation to Lands End House on Long Island. During her visit in July, she'd fallen in love with the massive red-brick mansion—which wasn't pretentious despite its imposing size. Trevor's great-great-grandfather had built it in 1845 at the northern end of Long Island, between the towns of Montauk and Amagansett, and it had been owned by the family ever since.

Trevor and Madeleine had become good friends, and Alex felt protected and secure at their house. She enjoyed the cheerful family atmosphere in the house, with its magnificent Christmas decorations, the long conversations at the fireplace, and the unconditional sympathy that the Downeys were showing her, which Alex returned from her heart. Once, she had talked to them about Sergio because she thought that her friends had the right to know. She had anxiously waited for their reaction and prepared herself for outright rejection; instead, the Downeys accepted the situation without judgment.

"I'm terribly nervous," Madeleine said to Alex as they reached the beach. "I've been organizing this Christmas party for eighteen years now, but every time I'm worried that something will go wrong."

"Come on, Maddy," Alex said with a grin, "what could possibly go wrong? You're part of an experienced team, plus I'm here to assist you."

"I'm very grateful to you for that." Madeleine sighed, but then she laughed. "You're so pragmatic and always keep a clear head. I panic immediately."

"It's my job to stay calm even if things go haywire."

"Imagine, Cliff Gordon and his wife are coming over from Martha's Vineyard by helicopter."

Alex knew that Trevor was a college friend of Robert Gordon, the president's younger brother, and that the two aristocratic families had been friends for generations.

"You're so incredibly genteel."

"Ah, stop mocking me!" Madeleine grinned. "You know just as many important people as I do."

"Let's trot for a bit." Alex preferred not to speak about the important people she knew. The stiff breeze stirred up the gray sea and caused large waves to roll onto the beach. The surf's salty spray blew into both women's faces. Alex took a deep breath and smiled. Sitting in the saddle with the cold wind in her face and the endless sea before her eyes, she forgot about her problems for a while and once again felt just as free, as carefree, as when she was a child. The seagulls were struggling against the wind with their melancholy cries. The beach extended for miles all the way out to Montauk. A magnificent mansion appeared up on the dunes every now and then, but their inhabitants were still asleep at this time of the day. Alex's horse started bucking boisterously. It wanted to gallop.

"Just let him run," Madeleine said. "I'll catch up with you."

The two riders had reached the wide inlet of Stony Bay.

"Okay!" Alex winked at her friend. "Let's go!"

The chestnut gelding suddenly rose up, which would have thrown an inexperienced rider out of the saddle. But Alex leaned forward and held on with her knees and thighs. The horse thundered along the beach with long, galloping strides and pricked ears, racing against the stormy wind and the seagulls. Faster, faster! She laughed happily. The wind drove tears into her eyes as she ducked behind the horse's neck and enjoyed its magnificent, graceful strength.

Strolling on the dunes with a golden retriever, two early walkers watched her with faces aghast as she raced past them like an incarnate Valkyrie. She let the horse circle the entire width of Stony Bay before slowly reducing her speed and looking around. The two walkers had reached the beach, and Alex saw that Madeleine had stopped to talk to them. She let her horse gallop once again. Her ponytail had come loose during the wild gallop and her blonde hair was flowing in the icy December wind, just like the horse's flaxen tail.

Madeleine waved at Alex. She slowed down the gelding a few yards ahead of them, and both of the walkers stepped back out of respect. Breathless, with reddened cheeks, she stopped her horse.

"Isn't she an excellent rider?" Madeleine said to the couple. All three of them watched Alex with undisguised admiration as she calmed down the nervous horse.

"Yes, indeed," the man said, "quite impressive."

"Alex!" Madeleine called out. "Do you know Nick and Mary Kostidis?"

Alex turned her head, surprised. Sure enough, the man standing next to Madeleine's horse was the mayor of New York. He looked completely different in his blue down jacket and jeans, but she immediately recognized those dark, burning eyes.

"Hello," she said, smiling. "Yes, we've met once before."

"Alex Sontheim," Kostidis nodded, inspecting her closely, "at the Plaza. I remember."

Alex remembered how disdainfully Sergio had spoken about this man and how much he hated him. He called him a fanatic, an idiot, the plague. While Madeleine and Mary Kostidis talked about the horses, she wondered what the mayor was doing at seven thirty on Christmas morning on a deserted beach at the tip of Long Island.

"Is Christopher with you at your sister's place?" Madeleine asked the mayor's wife.

"No," she said and laughed. "He's spending Christmas with his future in-laws in the Hudson Valley."

Alex noticed that Kostidis watched her with steadfast eyes the entire time. She wasn't sure why, but his searching, serious gaze disturbed and irritated her. If he knew who she was, then he would also know about her relationship with Sergio Vitali. Did she detect contempt in his stare? She tried to appear relaxed and indifferent. Madeleine and Mary were chatting, but Alex didn't catch a single word of their conversation. Her eyes met those of Nick Kostidis. Their gazes interlocked for a few seconds. She felt a hot blush rising to her cheeks and turned away.

"We need to keep going, Maddy," she said. "The horses are sweating. They'll catch a cold."

"Of course!" Madeleine made a guilty face. "I really lack horse sense sometimes!"

"Enjoy your ride!" Nick Kostidis called to them. "See you later!"

Madeleine smiled and waved. Alex cantered next to her without saying a word. Why did Kostidis look at her in such a strange way? The expression in his eyes was hard to read. He was probably saying to his wife at this second, "Did you see her? She's Vitali's lover. *A gangster's whore!*" She hated to feel so insecure, and the prospect of Kostidis attending the Downeys' party ruined her excitement. She felt like packing her suitcase and disappearing to avoid running into him again.

Alex was still sitting in her room when the first guests arrived at Lands End House, and she contemplated whether she should go downstairs at all. She wasn't in the mood for small talk. The horseback ride had shaken off her tense mood for a moment, but the unexpected encounter with Nick Kostidis abruptly destroyed her feeling of happiness. Alex didn't feel comfortable in Kostidis's presence, but then she also had the urge to see him. She couldn't explain these conflicting emotions—this mixture of attraction and aversion. There was something in his eyes, an expression that she couldn't interpret. Was it ridicule or contempt? Or was she just imagining all of this?

She heard Christmas music and laughter from downstairs. She knew that Trevor and Madeleine would be disappointed if she didn't join the party, so she finally slipped into her Ferragamo cocktail dress, checked herself out in the mirror, and with a sigh opened the door to go downstairs.

The party was already in full swing. The Christmas gathering was as "small" as Sergio's birthday party had been. Everyone who was anyone on the East Coast was invited. But in contrast to Sergio's party, old money mingled here—the real upper class, America's aristocrats. Northern Long Island was once called the "Gold Coast." This name did not refer to the color of its sandy beaches, but to the wealth of its inhabitants. But it had been some time since bold-faced names or conspicuous wealth impressed Alex. She'd had to deal with gigantic amounts of money, and she knew the richest people in America. Somewhere in this crowd, she found Madeleine, who looked enchanting and girlish in her burgundy dress, her cheeks red with excitement.

"How do you like it?" she called out with glowing eyes. "Isn't it magnificent? I'm always nervous before, but once everyone is here, then it's simply wonderful! The president and the first lady just arrived."

Madeleine hugged her and rushed on. Alex took a glass of champagne and strolled through the large house filled with unfamiliar people. In the blue salon she caught sight of the president talking to Trevor, Senator Hoffman, Governor Rhodes, Congressman James Vaillant III, and Nick Kostidis—who had changed from his jeans into a dark-gray suit and a red tie. She was just about to leave the room when Trevor saw her and waved her toward him. He pulled her into his circle with a smile.

"Cliff," he said to the president, "may I introduce Alex Sontheim? She's a good friend of Maddy's and mine."

Cliff Gordon offered her a friendly smile and reached out his hand.

"I'm delighted to meet you, Ms. Sontheim."

"The pleasure is mine, Mr. President." Alex's heart was racing in excitement. Trevor also introduced her to the other gentlemen, and it occurred to Alex that she had seen the senator and Governor Rhodes at Sergio's birthday party. She was curious what they would say if she mentioned that now. Trevor was describing the unusual circumstances in which Madeleine and Alex met about six months ago to the president, and he was impressed. The president asked about her work and—to her amazement—gave Alex his undivided attention.

"You have an exceptional reputation on Wall Street," he said. "Our country needs more people like you, Ms. Sontheim. Intelligent young people with civic courage."

She smiled in embarrassment. Cliff Gordon invited her to the White House, and she trembled with excitement and pride. But then she met eyes with Nick Kostidis, and she thought that she sensed a hint of mockery. The pride that she'd felt a second ago vanished instantly. She was relieved that others crowded around the president, and she excused herself. She escaped the crowd and went into an adjacent room and sat down in an armchair at the window.

She could just kill Kostidis! He'd not only ruined her encounter with Cliff Gordon, but also her entire day! Alex Sontheim—the star of Wall Street, the selfless rescuer of the opera singer Madeleine Ross-Downey—was actually nothing but a girl from Germany who had gotten involved with a dubious social climber, Sergio Vitali, the godfather of New York City! What would President Gordon say if he found out she was the lover of a man who ordered murders?

With tears welling up she searched for a cigarette in her purse. Someone cleared his throat behind her and she turned quickly around. She could hardly believe her eyes when Nick Kostidis of all people, whom she'd just escaped from, appeared in the doorway.

"Hello," she said in a discouraging tone, "if you're looking for the restrooms, they're two doors further down."

Kostidis smiled.

"Thanks, I know," he said and entered the room. "But I was actually looking for you."

"Really?" Alex took a drag from her cigarette. "Why?"

She was mad about her teary eyes.

"May I sit down with you for a moment?"

She was about to tell him to go to hell, but she managed to keep her composure.

He sat down in the armchair across from her. There was a tense moment of silence between them.

"What can I do for you, Mayor Kostidis?"

"Call me Nick," he responded. "'Mayor' sounds so formal."

"Okay," Alex said with a shrug. "Nick. So, what can I do for you?"

"I'm not sure whether you can help me." Nick crossed his legs and gave her another piercing look. She longed to get up and run away.

"I hardly know you," Kostidis continued. "Well, as a matter of fact, I don't know you at all. But I've been following your professional career with great interest for quite some time now. And my friends Trevor and Madeleine speak very highly of you."

"Aha." Alex was at the edge of her seat.

"You're a successful woman. Intelligent, ambitious, and courageous."

"And now you ask yourself why I'm involved with Vitali," she interrupted him coolly. "That's what you're trying to get at, isn't it?"

If he was surprised, Kostidis didn't let it show, but then he nodded slowly.

"I know what you think of him," Alex said, "and probably you think the same of me."

She jumped up and stepped toward the window.

"No!" Kostidis shook his head. "That's not true. Like I said, I don't know you, Alex. I only know what the newspapers write about you and what my friends, the Downeys, say about you, and that's why..."

Alex turned around again and looked at the man who both impressed and intimidated her.

"Yes?" She tried to regain her usual self-confidence, but to her chagrin, her voice sounded thin.

"Alex," Kostidis said, leaning forward, "it's not my intention to interfere with your private life."

"It's none of your business anyway," she countered brusquely. Kostidis stopped smiling.

"Sergio Vitali," he said with a calm voice, "is a very dangerous man. Many people think that I'm obsessed because I've been trying for years to bring him to justice for his criminal dealings. I know a great deal about him and his business, but unfortunately, I've never been able to prove anything against him. Vitali doesn't hesitate to defend his position of power by using violence. We've had evidence against him many times, but key witnesses suddenly lost their memory overnight or simply disappeared. Some of them were found again as corpses."

Alex felt weak in the knees. *It is done. Zuckerman won't utter another word...* She felt the horror and nausea all over again. She knew all too well that Kostidis was aware of the truth.

"Why are you telling me all of this?"

"I want you to understand my situation," he replied in a quiet voice. "It's not a personal thing between me and Vitali, like the media keeps insisting. The stakes are much higher. One of my predecessors called New York 'ungovernable.' I work very hard to get a grip on the public debt, the poor infrastructure, and the disastrous social disparities. But the worst of all evils is the corruption. The reason that Vitali is so untouchable is because he bribes many influential politicians and judges. I can live with corruption to a certain extent, but now I'm afraid that Vitali has an informer within my inner circle."

He paused for a moment and rubbed his chin. He looked tired.

"A man was shot dead on August fifteenth," Nick Kostidis said. "He was still young; he had a wife who is now a widow, and two little children lost their father because of this killer."

Alex swallowed. She knew who Zuckerman's killer was. Strictly speaking, she was obligated to tell the police what she knew, but she was frightened Sergio would find out, and then she would lose everything. Even if she wanted to, she couldn't help Kostidis.

"This man," the mayor continued, "could have hurt Vitali significantly by testifying in front of the investigation committee. We were aware of that, so we brought him to a hotel under utmost secrecy to keep him completely protected until he gave his testimony. Very few people were informed about this. And still someone found out and silenced the man."

His words triggered a black, empty feeling inside of Alex, and she simultaneously felt a raging, helpless anger. What did Kostidis expect from her? He didn't care one bit about what would happen to her. He wanted to get to Sergio by any means, and he had taken a clever approach by appealing to her conscience. Her nausea intensified.

"I don't know anything about Vitali's business," she said. Did Kostidis know that she was lying?

"I want to be very frank," Nick Kostidis said, locking his eyes on her. "Based on Madeleine's and Trevor's descriptions of you, I had the impression that you would have the courage to do the right thing."

Alex stared at him in silence. Courage! What did this man know about how cruel Sergio could be? Everything had been so easy for her in the past—people were clearly good or bad—but now her entire world was in turmoil. Nothing was clear anymore. Her future, her career, even her life was at stake! David Zuckerman was dead, and even if she told the mayor who the killer was, it wouldn't bring this man back to life.

"This has nothing to do with courage." She had the feeling that Kostidis was able to read her mind.

"Then what?"

Alex couldn't bear Kostidis's gaze any longer. He'd succeeded in rattling her. She felt like pouncing on him, yelling at him to leave her alone. What in the world had she done to get into this situation?

"Listen, Nick"—Alex hoped she appeared relaxed and composed—"I'm not indifferent to your worries by any means, and if I could, I would certainly help you. But I can't. Do you understand that?"

Nick Kostidis nodded slowly and sighed.

"Of course," he said and smiled again, but there was an alert expression in his eyes. "I understand you very well. Forget what I just said."

Their eyes locked.

"You know where to reach me."

"Thanks, but that won't be necessary," she replied coolly. Kostidis threw her one last inquiring glance.

"But maybe it will," he said with a mysterious smile; then he turned around and left the room.

PART TWO

June 6, 2000—LMI

The glass door to Alex's office flew open, and Mark stormed in. He had a concerned look on his face.

"Hello, Mark." Alex looked up from her documents. "What's up?"

He closed the door behind him.

"Did you take a look at the price of PBA Steel today?"

"Yes, this morning." She looked at her usually calm employee in surprise. "It was at seventeen and a half."

"Two minutes ago it was twenty-six and three-quarters."

"Pardon me?" She turned toward her monitors and pulled up the ticker. In disbelief, she stared at the quote for PBA Steel—which had already risen by another dollar.

"That's impossible!"

She quickly ran this information through her mind. Her client Blue Steel, the largest independent steel company on the East Coast, had just offered last week to take over the ailing but long-established Pittsburgh steel mill for 21.8336 dollars per share on her advice. And all of this was still unknown by the public. PBA Steel's management was hesitant and wanted to ask its shareholders whether they would agree to the takeover by Blue Steel. Even for market professionals, nothing indicated that such a takeover offer was imminent because PBA was far from bankrupt and still valued as a solid and stable company.

On the other hand, Blue Steel was sitting on above-average profits generated by its new management and looking for investment opportunities to avoid taxes from eating into those earnings. For this reason, Alex had scoured the market and come across PBA Steel. All in all, it was intended to be an unspectacular and rather average deal. The telephone rang, and she picked it up with an uneasy feeling. It was Marty Freeman, the president of Blue Steel.

"Alex, have you looked at PBA lately?" he yelled into the telephone. "Was what you suggested to us some kind of joke? We offer twenty-one dollars per share, and now it's racing toward thirty! How can it be that a stock priced below twenty dollars for years suddenly takes off like this?"

"I don't know either, Marty," Alex said, trying to calm him. "I've been following PBA for weeks, and I looked back over the years. There were minimal price fluctuations of a few cents here and there. My calculations were perfectly in order."

"Let me tell you something," Freeman said, lowering his voice a few decibels, "someone got wind of this deal! We're not interested in a takeover if we have to pay fifty dollars per share. You know as well as I do that this scrap heap isn't worth that much!"

Their conversation went back and forth like this for a while as the stock price kept rising. It was already clear that PBA Steel was overvalued, and the SEC would invariably initiate an investigation—at the very latest after Blue Steel's public announcement of its takeover bid.

"That son of a bitch!" Alex cursed after Freeman hung up. "Now he's going too far!"

"Do you think that Zack is behind this?" Mark raised his eyebrows, and Alex nodded grimly. After keeping the Maxxam deal secret from Zack and demonstrating to him that she was in the know about him, she had continued to cooperate on trivial things. Neither of them had uttered a word about the incident at Luna Luna, but their relationship had been cool and purely professional since then.

"Mark," Alex said, thinking rapidly, "if it was Zack, we need to find out right now. I don't care how you do it, but I want to know. Preferably before the close of the market."

"And what if it really is him? Then what?" Mark asked.

"Then I'll teach him a lesson that he won't soon forget," Alex answered. Mark left, and she followed him across the trading floor. At this time of the day, the traders had their hands full. Phones were ringing; there were hollers, wild gestures, and waves. Some traders had a phone to each ear and another in hand. Alex threw a glance at the LED ticker at the front of the large trading floor, constantly updating the quoted values of NYSE-listed stocks. Marty Freeman must have taken her for a fool! Her thoughts were racing. On her way out the sliding glass door, which led from the trading floor to the hallway, she nearly collided with Zack.

"Oh, hello, Alex," he said, grinning in an overly friendly way. "How's business?"

"Excellent." She forced an equally phony smile. She knew he hated her since her magnificent success with Maxxam. But was he really so dumb as to use confidential information in such a blatantly obvious way? Or was he trying to trip her up? Insider trading was a serious violation. She swore to herself she'd only give him information one last time. But this one would be unforgettable.

"Can I buy you lunch?" Zack asked.

"Sorry, I'm busy. Maybe some other time."

"Well"—he casually threw his Armani jacket over his shoulder and turned away to leave—"good luck."

She watched him disappear in to the elevator. It was about time for her to stop this cat-and-mouse game. Levy *had* to notice that she had become suspicious. Depending on his reaction, she could determine whether he was a part of this, or if Zack was working for himself.

Alex went back to her office. After a moment, she dialed Max Rudensky's number and waited impatiently for him to pick up. Max had been a broker for many years in London and New York. After exchanging the usual courtesies, she cut straight to the point. She asked if he had heard anything about PBA Steel in the market. It wasn't unusual for her to ask him for advice, and in the past he had pointed out one or another good deal to her. But since seeing him at Sergio's party, she had realized that the deals he recommended were exclusively with companies in which the dubious SeViCo held shares. If she was really right about this, then Max would inform Zack about her call in no time. Or maybe even Sergio. This thought was far scarier. Up to now, she had still hoped that Sergio wasn't involved in any of this.

Just as Alex expected, Rudensky pretended to be clueless, but she didn't much care anyway. She was only interested in whether he would call Zack. While she waited for Mark to come back, she stared at her desk in a morbid mood. The PBA Steel deal had gone down the drain. An hour later, Mark returned and let himself sink into a chair, out of breath.

"Most of the stock purchases were made by a firm called Manhattan Portfolio Management," he reported. "Rudensky has been buying like crazy. None of our traders knows where the other purchases are coming from."

Alex nodded. She had expected Rudensky's involvement in this buying spree, but who was Manhattan Portfolio Management? She had heard this name before, but where?

"What are we going to do now?" Mark wanted to know. At that moment, Alex remembered. Manhattan Portfolio Management. Jack Lang. Sergio's birthday party! Zack had talked about offshore companies with him!

"We need to find out who's behind this MPM," she said with determination. "Zack knows this firm pretty well. I'm sure of it. But how can we find out?"

"We could try the commercial register," Mark suggested.

"That's a good idea." Alex sat upright and smiled grimly. "I'll let you take care of it, Mark. In the meantime I'll prepare a nice little trap."

She had a great idea to teach Zack a painful lesson.

When the market closed, PBA Steel had reached an all-time high at thirty-two dollars per share. Whoever had tried to push up the price acted exceptionally imprudently because PBA Steel was obviously the topic of the day. Alex dialed Zack's extension, and he answered immediately.

"Did you see PBA?" she asked innocently. "Unbelievable what happened there, right?"

"Yes, indeed," he answered, as slippery as an eel, "and all of this on the day after you told me that something could be in it for us with PBA."

"I have to admit I suspected that you were behind this rise in the stock price," Alex said and laughed. Zack joined in her laughter after a few seconds, but it sounded forced.

"In that case, we suspected each other."

"Nonsense," she countered, "what interest should we have in the stock price skyrocketing like this? The deal is dead, and the people at Blue Steel are pretty pissed off."

She waited for Zack's reaction.

"Vince won't be pleased if this deal falls through."

"Well, tough luck," Alex replied. "My calculations were based on twenty-one dollars per share. But it's not all that bad. Because I have something else in the works."

"Really? What is it?" Zack couldn't hide his curiosity.

"Hey, not so fast! I'm still working on it. It could be as big as the Maxxam deal, if not bigger."

"Are you going to tell me what this is about?"

"I'll tell you about it soon enough. I'm still in the initial talks. But this could turn out to be a sensation."

"Come on, don't torture me like that!"

Alex grinned. She could vividly imagine Zack sliding back and forth in his chair with dollar signs in his eyes.

"Okay," she said, "my prospective client is looking for opportunities to increase their share capital. They've made many large investments recently and are strained for cash as a result, but they still want to acquire a well-known company. I had the idea of creating a limited partnership and launching a fund that invests in promising start-ups. It's risky, but the returns could be gigantic. I also thought about high-yield bonds. Oh, I'm already revealing way too much."

"Sounds very interesting. You're a smart girl. How about having dinner with me tonight?"

Bastard, Alex thought. Everything that she'd just told Zack was a product of her imagination. There was no new client. She had laid the bait, and now she just had to wait for Zack to take it. Alex sensed a tingling excitement rising in her. She was a skillful strategist, with a hunter's instinct. Certainly she wouldn't let anyone force her into the role of the hunted. It was five thirty when Mark returned in an excited mood.

"Did you find anything?" Alex asked.

"Of course." He grinned mysteriously. "I have a friend who works in public administration. She looked up everything that I needed to know."

He rummaged in his briefcase and pulled out a copy of the articles of incorporation. Alex didn't want to know how he'd managed to get it, but the fact that he did proved how capable he was.

"The managing director of Manhattan Portfolio Management is a certain Jackson Patrick Lang, residing on Leroy Street in the West Village," he said. "And now hold on to your seat, Alex."

She looked at Mark expectantly.

"Manhattan Portfolio Management—abbreviated MPM—belongs to Venture Capital SeaStarFriends Limited Partnership."

"That's impossible," Alex said, shaking her head. "Some US citizen must be registered."

"No, not according to applicable law. I talked to a lawyer who specializes in corporate law, and he confirmed it." Mark excitedly leaned forward and lowered his voice. "Do you understand what this means? We found a connection to LMI! Funds launched in-house were invested in an offshore company incorporated in the British Virgin Islands called SeaStarFriends! Do you remember?"

Alex stared at him, speechless.

"Of course I do," she whispered. "I can't believe it."

"Now we only have to find out who's behind SeaStarFriends," Mark said, "and then we know whether Zack acts on his own account or on the orders of Vince Levy."

He turned around as if expecting Zack to appear behind him.

"It's quite obvious already," he whispered. "LMI wouldn't launch a fund with capital of five hundred million dollars to invest in a third-party venture-capital company. They want the money to stay in-house, after all."

"Of course."

Thousands of questions flooded Alex's brain. It was impossible to find detailed information about a company incorporated in an offshore location because there were no mandatory disclosures or accounting rules so long as the company only did business with other companies outside that location.

"Well, there's someone who's a real expert when it comes to offshore companies," Mark said, hesitating. Alex sighed.

"I know him too," she answered, "but I doubt that he'll help you once he finds out that I'm involved."

"Oliver is my friend," Mark said. "He can only say no."

She didn't feel comfortable asking Oliver Skerritt for a favor, but in the end her curiosity prevailed. She wanted to know who was making illegal money through her deals. The telephone rang.

"Answer it, Mark," she said quickly. "If it's Zack, tell him I just left."

It was Zack. Alex smiled bitterly. The fish was still carefully but greedily circling the bait. She scribbled some notes on a piece of paper that Zack wouldn't be able to miss when snooping around her office. Without a doubt, he had called just to see whether she was still there. He would wait a little longer and then come over to search her desk.

Have fun, Mr. St. John, Alex thought, stepping into the elevator with Mark. *I hope you burn your fingers on this one!*

Alex spent the next day in Baltimore trying to appease the management of Blue Steel. The PBA stock price had leveled off again at around eighteen and a half. This was probably due to her phone call to Rudensky, who had told his clients that she had pricked up her ears. So as not to ruin the deal completely, they had let go of their positions and the market calmed down.

Alex was completely exhausted when she arrived at her apartment that evening. She opened a bottle of Coors and walked out on the terrace. She called Mark on her cell phone in case Sergio had the land line tapped.

Time had passed since that incident with Sergio, and things had cooled off between them. She'd been extremely busy with work, and so had he.

Mark picked up after the second ring. Zack hadn't been seen in his department or on the trading floor that day. Furthermore, Mark hadn't been able to reach Oliver—who was still in Europe and wouldn't be back in the city until the beginning of July.

Alex sincerely hoped that Zack was behind this all by himself. He surely had the means to pull off such an operation. He had many friends and informers in the world of big finance. On top of that, she knew that there were no limits to Zack's greed for cash and his craving for recognition. But would he really risk betraying Levy, as well as Sergio?

The ringing of the telephone interrupted into her thoughts. The clock showed a few minutes after eleven. Just before the answering machine clicked on, Alex answered.

"Hello, *cara*." It was Sergio, as if he knew that she was thinking about him. "How are you?"

"Not so good," she replied. "I had a terrible day. I've probably lost a deal that I thought was wrapped up."

"What kind of deal?" he asked. Was he pretending, or did he really not know about it? Alex realized that she didn't trust him at all anymore.

"Blue Steel and PBA Steel," she said. "Everything was all worked out, and I even told Levy about it. But yesterday, the price of PBA more than doubled in no time. I was in Baltimore all day, but I didn't know what else to tell these Blue Steel people. And on top of it, I'm afraid that the SEC will get involved. It looks like we tried to drive up the price in order to earn higher fees!"

"Don't worry about the SEC."

Alex straightened up in her chair.

"What do you mean? The SEC has initiated investigations on much less before."

"I mean it just like I said. Forget the SEC."

Forget the SEC! She would have loved to ask him directly about SeaStarFriends, but his involvement in MPM was just speculation at this point. Sergio wasn't a banker, but he knew enough about business to fear the Securities and Exchange Commission, which monitored the trading of all securities. Especially if he knew that MPM and LMI were trading on insider information. Was his carelessness an indication of his naiveté or the exact opposite? Since her conversation with Nick Kostidis on Christmas at the Downeys' house, she'd thought about him many times. To her annoyance, she realized that she was listening for revealing undertones in every one of Sergio's words. She hadn't seen Kostidis since then, but she still owed her nagging guilty conscience to him—which she could have done without. She was relieved that Sergio was still in Chicago. When he said good-bye after fifteen minutes and said he'd get in touch when he was back in the city, it sounded almost like a threat.

Sergio had been in Las Vegas for the past three days and was extremely satisfied with the deal he had finally closed after long and tenacious negotiations. In addition to the Gold Nugget, the Pyramid, and the Southern Cross, he now also owned the fourth-largest luxury hotel on the Las Vegas Strip: the Venice. The negotiations had been tough, but Angelo Canaletti—the last offspring of the once important Canaletti family from New York, which had relocated to the West in the 1960s—lacked any sense for business. He had gotten too comfortable with his excessive lifestyle. He'd run the gold mine of the Meridian, with its six hundred beds and enormous casino, completely into the ground with his disastrous management. He was in deep because he owed millions of dollars to the IRS. This purchase was a bargain for Sergio; it just required some patience. After finishing the contract, he finally cemented his position of dominance in Las Vegas. Profits from the casinos were sizable and crisis-proof sources of income.

However, his meeting in Vegas with Jorge Alvarez Ortega had been much more important. Ortega had become the undisputed number one of the powerful Colombian drug cartel in Medellín after the violent death of Emilio Arqueros a few months prior. The negotiations with Ortega concerned the import of cocaine to the US. Due to Sergio's newly consolidated influence at the Brooklyn port, he was the only person who could guarantee Ortega a risk-free import of drugs from Colombia. The old routes via Florida or Mexico were too risky, and many couriers had been busted. But Sergio's people knew how to smuggle illegal drugs directly into New York in front of the customs agents and the police without any problems.

Sergio demanded thirty percent of the revenues for his services; Ortega only offered him fifteen. The negotiations with the Colombian dragged on through the entire night and seriously put Sergio's patience to the test. They wined and dined like kings, and Franco Cavalese—Sergio's man in Vegas—brought in the prettiest girls in town. With a mixture of contempt and amusement, Sergio watched the eyes of this South American peasant Ortega pop when he saw them. At three in the morning, the man disappeared into his suite with three very young blondes.

He and Sergio hadn't come an inch closer in their negotiations. Sergio left the hotel at three thirty in the morning and had a limousine take him to the airport. He didn't need to wait for this peasant! If Ortega wanted something from him, he would have to come to New York. To show that Sergio was serious about his thirty percent share, he would blow cover on the next delivery from Colombia.

When he arrived in Chicago, Sergio had received a message from Levy that St. John's reckless behavior threatened to trigger an investigation by the SEC against LMI and MPM. It was a bad situation, but Sergio had managed to control the damage with a few phone calls.

The fact that Alex now seemed suspicious was far more serious to him. Zack had Jack Lang from MPM and Rudensky go overboard buying the stock of a company that LMI intended to represent in a takeover. Zack usually acted on his knowledge more prudently, but this time he had made a mistake. Sergio urgently needed to speak to Alex and check whether she had noticed anything. After their conversation, he was overcome with a wild longing for her. She had never mentioned another word about his uncontrolled violation of last October and behaved normally toward him. Sergio was sure that she had forgiven him for his faux pas.

Despite Nelson's warning on Cinnamon Island, Sergio kept thinking about getting divorced from Constanzia. His biggest wish was to have Alex at his side day and night. His surveillance and monitoring of her telephone calls and e-mails turned up nothing. Alex went to work, came home, and met him occasionally. If Alex went out, then it was to after-work parties with her colleagues or a visit to the Downeys—with whom she'd spent a weekend on Long Island. There was no other man in her life besides him. Sergio poured himself a whiskey and contemplated whether he should skip his appointment in the morning. He longed for Alex with every fiber of his being, and at the same time he was mad at himself for being so obsessed with her. His anger at Ortega and St. John had caused him unbearable tension, and he desperately needed to let off some steam. After a third whiskey, he ordered a call girl to his room. The girl was young, blonde, and gorgeous, but Sergio suddenly thought about Alex. And although the little whore gave it her best effort, Sergio was horrified to realize that he couldn't get it up. Feeling terribly humiliated, he angrily sent the girl away. At that moment, he hated Alex with all his heart. She was to blame for his failure. She had jinxed him.

On Tuesday, June 14, 2000, US Customs caught a very big fish at the Brooklyn port. The customs agents had received an anonymous tip early in the morning to take a closer look at the Panamanian freighter *Cabo de la Nao,* which was coming from Costa Rica with a cargo of coffee beans. Sure enough, they found more than two hundred kilos of pure cocaine with a street value of several million dollars. The drugs, originating from Colombia, were sealed in plastic bags hidden in the coffee. The captain and the crew of the *Cabo de la Nao* were arrested on the spot and taken away for questioning; the entire shipment was seized. Time and again, customs and drug enforcement agents seized narcotics at the city's port or airports, but usually they only found a few grams or kilos. This discovery was surely one of the biggest in United States history.

Naturally, every news channel focused on coverage of the cocaine bust in Brooklyn. Mayor Kostidis proudly announced this significant blow to organized crime in New York. Sergio laughed disdainfully and turned away from the television.

"Excellent," he said to Massimo, Nelson, Luca, and Silvio, who were all watching the news with him at his apartment on Park Avenue, "this will force Ortega to give in."

"Or there will be war," Nelson said.

"Ortega can't afford that. He needs our connections at the port in order to bring such large shipments into the country. And he's certainly dependent on the North American market." Sergio shook his head and once again watched the mayor's grim face on the screen. "This idiot really believes that his cops pulled this off all by themselves."

"Maybe you should talk to Ortega again," Nelson said. "Now he'll—"

"Nelson!" Sergio looked at his friend in astonishment. "What's going on with you? You don't sound like the Nelson I know!"

"The idea of you starting a war with the Colombians makes me a little uneasy. They're dangerous."

"It sounds like you're getting scared in your old age." Sergio grinned.

"Call it what you want," Nelson responded, "but I'm not interested in an armed conflict with these people."

"It'll be all right." Sergio turned the television off impatiently and stood up. "Ortega will contact us. And then we'll negotiate."

"I hope you're right."

"Ortega is a businessman, Nelson," Sergio replied. "Going after us would claim too many victims and cost too much money."

Thursday, June 16, 2000

At eight thirty, Alex turned the computer off and straightened up her desk. She was the last one in the building besides the guards on duty. She and Mark still hadn't uncovered any more information about the mysterious partnership called SeaStarFriends. The price of PBA had stabilized after the SEC got involved. But it was strange that the investigation had been called off after just two days. All of the events surrounding PBA were more than mysterious, but the deal with Blue Steel would go through in the coming weeks. Alex was just about to leave her office when the external line rang. She hesitated briefly, but then she picked up the phone.

"Alex Sontheim," she answered.

"Hello, Alex, I was still hoping to reach you at the office." The voice was unmistakable.

"Hello, Nick." She sat down again. "You're lucky. I was just about to leave. How are you?"

"I'm fine, thank you," the mayor replied. "How's business?"

"I can't complain."

Why was he calling her? How did he get her extension?

"I just heard that you declined your invitation to the awards ceremony for the outstanding citizens of our city," Kostidis said. "I wanted to find out why."

Alex had received a letter from the mayor's office a few weeks ago, informing her that the City of New York wanted to honor her for her courageous rescue of Madeleine last year. Together with other extraordinary citizens, she was to be honored during a ceremony at city hall. Alex couldn't attend, so she had her secretary call to send her regrets.

"Don't tell me that you personally call everyone who cancels," she answered quizzically.

"No," he said with a laugh. "Definitely not. But then again, very few people ever cancel."

"I believe that." Her voice sounded sarcastic. "Most people love to see their name in the newspaper."

"Maybe," the mayor countered, "but they deserve it. All of the people who will be honored have accomplished something outstanding."

"Listen, Nick." Alex realized that this was turning into an unpleasant conversation. "I'd love to come, but I need to fly to Houston that day. I'm sorry."

"Then there's nothing that we can do about it," Kostidis replied. "What a shame. But the reason that I was actually calling..."

Alex felt herself getting defensive.

"I'd like to invite you to a dinner at Gracie Mansion on July fifteenth," he said to her surprise. "You'll obviously also receive a written invitation. My wife and I would be delighted if you could come."

"Thanks, but what have I done to deserve this honor?"

Kostidis didn't let Alex lead him astray with her sarcasm.

"It's a reception for the Canadian ambassador," he said calmly. "We always like to invite interesting people to such occasions. The Downeys will also be there, and my wife suggested that I invite you. Mary is very impressed with you."

Alex almost thought she could hear him smiling. Was he making fun of her? He had entirely different motives for inviting her, and it seemed just a flimsy excuse that this was his wife's idea.

"I assume that this invitation is just for me."

"Of course you can bring a guest," Kostidis replied smoothly. Alex couldn't help it, but this man simply provoked her to react in a sarcastic way.

"I'll check my schedule to see if I'm free that day," she answered coolly.

"Great. By the way, have you thought about our conversation?"

Aha. He'd finally gotten to the topic he wanted to talk about from the very start. This was certainly also the reason for his call.

"No," she said, "I haven't had time the past few months."

This was a lie. She'd been thinking about it incessantly.

"Too bad."

"Nick"—Alex lowered her voice even though she really wanted to scream—"I don't like to think that someone is trying to use me. I'm truly sorry, but if you've got problems, please contact the FBI or the CIA. I can't help you."

"I'm sorry if you think I'm trying to use you. That wasn't my intention." He paused briefly. "Have you heard about the narcotics bust at the Brooklyn port?"

"Yes." Alex was surprised about the sudden shift of the topic. "That's all people are talking about right now. What does it have to do with me?"

"FBI experts believe," Kostidis said, "that there will be an armed conflict between the Colombian drug cartel and the New York crime syndicates very soon."

"Why are you telling me this?"

He was silent for a moment.

"Because I'm afraid that Mr. Vitali is involved."

Alex shivered.

"I want to prevent anything bad from happening to you, Alex."

"You're really trying by all means possible," Alex replied in a frosty tone. "I appreciate your concern, but as I've assured you before, I'm in no way involved with Mr. Vitali's business."

Nick sighed. "All right then. Will you accept our invitation?"

"I'll let you know."

Alex's heart felt like it was about to burst when she hung up the phone. Why couldn't Kostidis just leave her alone!

Saturday, June 18, 2000

The doorbell rang. Soon afterward, the key turned in the lock and Sergio entered the apartment.

"Alex?" he called. "I'm here!"

"I'll be right there!" she yelled from the bathroom. She stared at herself in the mirror. Her long, dark-blonde hair was bleached and cut to chin-length. She hoped that Sergio would dislike it as much as the skin-tight, silver Missoni dress that was far too flashy for his old-fashioned tastes. Alex couldn't stand him anymore. The constant effort to disguise her feelings was nerve-racking, She had been postponing an important decision that she made weeks ago. Today she would end this relationship that had turned into true torture for her. She took a deep breath before she left the bathroom.

"Hello," she said.

"Hi," he replied, and his gaze slid from her hair down to the silver strap sandals and back up. He raised his eyebrows. He didn't smile, but kissed her cheek.

"What have you done to your hair?"

"I was at the hairstylist." Alex no longer felt that familiar pounding of her heart at the sight of him. "Can we go now?"

They rode the elevator down without saying a word. Luca was waiting in the lobby, and Alex nodded at him briefly.

"Since when do you need bodyguards when you go out with me?" she asked. Sergio's face turned grim for a moment.

"So no one can steal you, *cara*," he replied airily.

His limousine was waiting in front of the building with its engine running. Then Alex remembered Kostidis's words about the narcotics bust at the port. *I'm afraid that Mr. Vitali is involved in this...*No, that couldn't be. Sergio seemed as relaxed as ever, not exactly like someone who was expecting an armed conflict with South American drug dealers. Fifteen minutes later, the limousine stopped in front of Le Bernardin on Fifty-First Street. The owner of the posh French restaurant—whom Sergio called Jean—greeted them effusively. He escorted them to a table in a corner of the restaurant. Admiring looks followed Alex throughout the entire restaurant, and she registered that Sergio also noticed.

"Maybe your dress is a little too revealing for dinner," he said quietly. "Don't you think?"

"The other guests seem to like it. Don't you?"

"It fills me with jealousy when other men stare at you like that."

"Really?" She smiled disdainfully. "I thought you were above all that."

Sergio was absolved from answering her by the appearance of the head chef. Throughout the dinner, Sergio tried hard to be as entertaining as ever. Alex realized that his charm was bouncing off her, and she had to force herself not to look at the clock. She wanted to tell him what she had to say and get out of there as quickly as possible.

"What's wrong with you, *cara*?" Sergio asked after dessert was served. "Why are you being so standoffish? You could be a little friendlier after such an exquisite meal."

She looked at him pensively.

"I wanted to wait until we finished dinner," she said, "to tell you that I've made a decision."

"Aha." He smiled, unruffled, but an attentive expression appeared in his eyes. "What decision is that?"

"Since the incident last year," Alex said, "I have come to realize that our relationship is lacking something very important. You don't love me. You think of me as your property that you can use as you please. You don't respect me."

Sergio said nothing but just observed her carefully with his incredibly blue eyes.

"That evening," she continued, "when you raped me, I realized what kind of a person you really are."

"And what kind of person is that?" He managed to smile.

"You're an egoist. The only person who matters to you is Sergio Vitali, and no one else."

"I'm sorry."

"I don't believe you."

"*Cara*," he said as he leaned toward her and put his hand on hers, "in all my life I have never desired a woman as much as I desire you."

"And?"

"And?" He looked at her with an irritated expression. "What do you mean?"

"You desire my body," she answered, "but I expect more from a relationship than just sex. I'm almost thirty-seven years old, and I don't want to be just the sex kitten of a man who doesn't give a damn about my feelings."

"What do you expect from me?" The look in his eyes was hard to read. Was it insecurity? Or was it simply anger that he couldn't escape this conversation?

"Nothing," Alex said, shrugging her shoulders. "I don't expect anything from you. There will never be anything more than sex between us. You'll never accept me as an equal partner or a person you can trust. For a while I assumed it was because of me, but that's not the case. You simply don't want more from a woman than what you're getting from me. That's not enough for me in the long term."

Sergio was silent for a moment. His face was expressionless.

"I won't allow you to leave me," he said and then let go of her hand.

"What are you going to do? Force me to sleep with you with a gun to my head?"

He didn't react to this remark.

"Tell me what I can do to change your mind."

"Nothing. It's too late."

"I can't accept this."

"You shouldn't have lied to me," Alex said. "You keep lying to me. Why aren't we going out alone tonight? Why the limousine and the bodyguards eyeing anyone who walks into the restaurant?"

She exhaled with a deep sigh and shook her head.

"I was ready to love you, Sergio. If you'd been honest with me, I would have accepted the truth, no matter how bad it might be."

She realized from the expression in his eyes that she'd hit a sore spot.

"My wife has never asked me to tell her about my business in all our thirty years together," he said stiffly. "Why can't we just leave it as it is?"

"I told you why." She finished her drink. "I want to go home now."

Sergio swallowed. Under no circumstances did he want to lose Alex. She meant more to him than any other woman had in the past. Maybe he should cast Nelson's warnings aside and tell her the truth about himself. He would be invincible with her by his side, because Alex had all the traits that his son Massimo lacked. She was an excellent and cold-blooded tactician, and she was prudent despite her willingness to take risks. But how would she react to the truth? What if she suddenly had scruples? Then she would be a risk, and he would have no choice but to eliminate her. Women were difficult to gauge, especially Alex. Sergio needed time to think. The soundest approach seemed to be putting their relationship on hold, but the moment that he thought this, he felt an unbearably painful longing. Just the thought of another man touching her drove him crazy.

"Let's talk about this another time," he finally said, using all of his strength to force himself to smile. "I need to think about all this."

"Agreed."

It was a quarter past midnight when they left Le Bernardin. Luca and another man had been waiting in the lobby all night and moved outside as they saw Alex approaching. Sergio fell back for a quick conversation with the restaurant's owner. The weather was cool for June, and it was drizzling lightly. Sergio turned up his trench coat collar as he stepped outside.

"Where's the limousine?" he snarled indignantly at Luca.

"He had to drive around the block first," he replied. Alex felt chilly as she stood next to Sergio, and she raised her head when she heard screeching tires. An old brown Ford switched lanes at high speed and raced directly toward them. She noticed that the windows were down despite the rain. She remembered Kostidis's warning words, and instantly her brain starting churning through fragments of information. She instinctively felt danger emanating from that brown car.

"Sergio!" she screamed. "Watch out."

Warned by her scream, Sergio quickly turned around. Flashes from a submachine gun came from the car's interior. Alex heard the dry barking of the gunfire and felt a hard blow to her back as Luca pushed her to the ground. She heard the bullets pierce the car's sheet metal, and the restaurant's glass door burst into thousands of glass splinters; ricocheting bullets ripped through the air. This scene only lasted for a few seconds, but as it unfolded in front of her eyes, it seemed as if in slow motion. Then the nightmare was over. After a rev of the engine, the car raced away toward Rockefeller Center. The passersby who were still out on the streets at this late hour were screaming in panic. Cars stopped and honked their horns. Alex freed herself from Luca's grip and jumped up. Sergio and the other man were crouched behind a parked car that was now riddled with bullet holes.

"*Cara*," he said, extending his arm toward her, "did anything happen to you?"

"N…n…no." She was in shock and could hardly speak. "You?"

"I'm okay," he assured her. As he lifted himself up his face looked pale, but he remained as calm and composed as ever. A curious crowd gathered but kept a respectful distance. The restaurant's owner came out—white as a sheet from the shock—with some of the guests who had also heard the shots.

"Mr. Vitali!" the owner of the restaurant yelled. "Should I call the police? Or an ambulance?"

"No, no, never mind, Jean." Sergio patted the dirt off his coat with his right hand. "Everything's all right."

"Someone was shooting at you!" Alex's voice trembled hysterically. Only now did she feel the panic rising inside of her. The car had long since vanished in Midtown Manhattan's busy nighttime traffic.

"Everything's all right," Sergio repeated. He walked over to the limousine that had stopped at the roadside. Alex slowly realized how close she had come to death. This wasn't a movie, but real life! The owners of the damaged vehicles argued angrily, and someone called the police.

"You've got to call the police, Sergio!" Alex's voice sounded shrill. She was trembling in fear. "Someone tried to kill you!"

"No, I don't," Sergio replied without looking at her. "Like I said, nothing happened. Come on, get in."

Alex opened her mouth to object, but Luca—who had just saved her life—pushed her into the limousine. The door was hardly closed when the driver hit the pedal. Alex felt her heartbeat racing. She felt by turns hot and cold. She still couldn't completely grasp what had just happened. In the dim light inside the limousine, she stared numbly at her hand. She touched Sergio's shoulder. It was covered in blood. Sergio took off his coat and jacket with his face contorted in pain. Alex was horrified when she saw the rapidly expanding red patch of blood on his shirt.

"My God, you're injured!" she whispered. "You've been hit!"

"Armando, make her a drink," Sergio ordered and unbuttoned his shirt. "How about you guys? Are you okay?"

"Yep," Luca and Armando answered. Wide-eyed and silent with fear and horror, Alex stared at the men until her gaze stopped at Sergio. He had a bulletproof vest underneath his shirt.

"Why are you wearing that thing?" she whispered, but slowly her mind started to make sense of it. Everything Kostidis had told her on the telephone was true.

"Sergio!" she said again, but he didn't react at all.

"Have a drink, *cara*," he replied. Armando pressed a glass filled with whiskey into her hand. "That'll make you feel better."

Alex obediently downed the whiskey, and her trembling subsided.

Armando pulled out dressing materials from a first-aid kit, and Luca set about bandaging Sergio's intensely bleeding shoulder. They spoke quietly in Italian, and then Luca opened the glass partition and ordered the driver to head to a certain address in Brooklyn. Alex was in a state of shock. She hadn't noticed that the limousine was rolling over the brightly lit Brooklyn Bridge.

Luca made two quick calls on his cell phone. Sergio's eyes were closed, and he pressed his hand on the bandage, which was turning red beneath his fingers. The sight of blood usually didn't bother her, but this was something entirely different.

"Sergio." Alex leaned forward, trying to subdue the trembling in her voice. "Who were they? Who was shooting at you?"

"Don't worry about it." He opened his eyes and gave her a flat smile. "This is just a little scratch."

"You could be dead now!"

"Yes. But you warned me in time."

Alex said nothing. The car turned onto a deserted street. Alex could see elongated warehouses and the light of Manhattan on the other side of the river.

"Where are we?" she asked.

"Someone will take you home now." Sergio avoided answering her directly as usual and grabbed her hand. "You saved my life, *cara*. Thank you."

The car stopped.

"What are you doing here? Why don't you go to a hospital?" Alex was too confused to grasp what was happening. Armando opened the door, and Sergio clumsily got out. Although it was raining harder now and the air was cool, he had beads of sweat on his forehead.

Some cars approached through the rain with their headlights turned off; a few men got out. The rain moved sideways through the light of the lamp above the entrance. No one paid any attention to Alex, and so she followed them into the warehouse. Pressing herself to the wall of the small office, she recognized Sergio's son Massimo and Nelson van Mieren.

More cars arrived outside. Alex heard the sound of car doors slamming. Serious-looking men with determined, grim faces entered the warehouse and talked quietly amongst themselves in Italian. She could feel their tentative looks and saw that all the men were armed to the teeth. Up to now, the Mafia was no more than an abstract term with a negative connotation for Alex—and now she was right in the middle of it. She winced when Massimo suddenly addressed her.

"Dario will take you to the city now," he said.

"Can I see him for a moment?"

Massimo gave her a searching stare, and then he nodded. She followed him through a room in which files were stacked up to the ceiling on shaky shelves. Why did they bring Sergio here and not to his apartment or a hospital? Massimo knocked on the door. When it opened, he whispered something in Italian to Nelson van Mieren. Nelson shot Alex a repulsed look.

Sergio lay on a narrow bed. His upper body was exposed, and an older man was examining his shoulder.

"The bullet is still inside," he said, wiping his bloody fingers on a towel. "I'm afraid that an artery has been ruptured."

"We're taking you to Dr. Sutton, Sergio," Nelson said. "I've already called him. You're safe at his clinic."

Safe? From what? From another attempt on his life? Alex's knees started trembling. Kostidis had warned her. Now there could be no excuses, no sugarcoating, no doubts about Sergio's involvement with the criminal underworld. Just a half hour ago, she'd witnessed an assassination attempt that only barely failed. Nearly fifty heavily armed men were standing outside. The thought that she was at the Mafia's New York headquarters seemed almost grotesque.

"Okay," Sergio said, his face contorted in pain, "where's Natale? He should—"

Van Mieren made a gesture with his hand, and Sergio fell silent.

His eyes landed on Alex, who stood at the wall next to a filing shelf as if paralyzed, looking at him fearfully.

"*Cara*." Sergio extended his right hand, smiling with difficulty. "Come over here."

She walked toward him hesitantly and took his hand, which was unusually cold. His eyes had a feverish gleam. He was sweating even though it wasn't particularly warm. He was obviously weak, but he still had full control of the situation.

"I'm very sorry that you had to witness this," he said with a grimace, "but you wanted to know why I had bodyguards escorting us tonight."

Alex was speechless for a moment, and then her fear turned into furious anger. She pulled her hand away.

"You were expecting something like this to happen," she whispered, "but you didn't consider it necessary to tell me. I'm so unimportant to you that you carelessly put my life at risk!"

"I'm sorry."

Alex clenched her hands into a fist. She felt like punching his expressionless face.

"Go to hell, Sergio," she hissed.

She turned away before he could respond. The faster she could leave this dark warehouse, these sinister characters, this entire nightmare behind, the better.

Marvin Finnegan was playing cards with a few colleagues when an emergency call came in to the Forty-First Precinct in Morrisania in the South Bronx. It was around one in the morning, a relatively quiet night, and the officers who weren't on patrol killed time by playing cards. The area around the Forty-First Precinct was one of New York's most run-down neighborhoods, far removed from Manhattan's sparkling skyscrapers, the luxury boutiques on Fifth Avenue, and the Upper East Side's posh apartment buildings. The city's administrators rarely ventured to the South Bronx. Too few disillusioned and corrupt police officers barely maintained order here. Drugs were nothing unusual in the South Bronx. People living in the projects were embittered or had given up a long time ago. Most families had at least someone who was hooked on the needle. Many men boozed away the few dollars that they received from welfare. Violent family disputes were common in these tiny apartments, which sometimes housed more than ten people. The misery and neglect were depressing. The hideous apartment buildings were decaying because no one cared about maintaining them. Sometimes they burned down. Mountains of rubble were everywhere, and so were the prostitutes and hustlers at Hunts Point, the drug dealers, and the juvenile delinquents.

Most of the police officers were just as frustrated as the neighborhood's inhabitants. If they couldn't get out on sick leave or transfer to another precinct, then they took bribes from drug dealers and squeezed store owners for protection money.

Marvin Finnegan had been a police officer in one of New York's most miserable neighborhoods for sixteen years. He was born and raised here, and had only left the South Bronx to serve in the army and later attend the police academy. He was a tough but fair cop, and his name had long ago become a legend because he was incorruptible, determined to protect honest people from criminals.

"Hey, Marvin!" Patrick Peters, the lieutenant on duty, stuck his head inside the recreation room. "A woman from an apartment at the corner of Flatbush and Sound View Avenue just called. That gang showed up again. I sent over Hank and Freddie."

Finnegan put down his hand with a hint of regret. He had a full house, but that was tough luck.

Tom Ganelli, who had been Finnegan's partner for three years, grinned in excitement.

"Pat," Finnegan said, slipping into his jacket, "try to reach Valentine and Burns. I want them to come, but without the siren. We'll end the game these bastards are playing."

The patrol car stopped on a side street close to the apartment building just ten minutes later. The building was on one of those half-empty, dilapidated blocks, where working-class families lived alongside junkie squatters. Finnegan and Ganelli could hear screams and the sound of shattering glass from a distance as they approached. They scurried to the rear of the building in the shadow of the crumbling walls, while taking care not to stumble over rubble and garbage. They passed a burned-out car. Finnegan pulled out his gun. The past few weeks had seen an unusual accumulation of these nightly raids on dilapidated apartment buildings. Two buildings had been set on fire and burned to the ground because the fire hydrants in the vicinity had been intentionally blocked.

It was quite obvious to the men of the Forty-First Precinct that there was a coordinated effort underway to empty these buildings. After the tenants gave up and moved out due to the constant terror and fear, heavy machinery with wrecking balls moved in and razed the building to the ground. Property was scarce in New York City. New developments with expensive condos or offices would be built here eventually. This neighborhood would be cleaned up someday, and unscrupulous real-estate speculators, who bought these properties cheap, would make a killing. The poor people would be pushed to more run-down areas. The police officers coordinated their actions by radio and surrounded the building in a circle.

"How many, and where are they?" Finnegan wanted to know.

"They're inside the building," his colleague replied from the other side. "I think five or six."

They slowly approached the building.

"It smells like gasoline here," Ganelli said quietly. "They want to burn this shack down."

The glow of a fire lit up the night just at that moment. Windows were flung open, and people screamed in desperation.

"Call the fire department," Finnegan said, turning his radio on. "Everybody else move!"

Just as they approached the building, the arsonists tried to escape through the busted front door.

"Police!" Finnegan roared, charging ahead with his weapon pulled. "Freeze!"

Ganelli flared up a bright spotlight and aimed it at the men. The thugs were blinded for a second and stopped; then one of them pulled a gun.

"Get down!" Finnegan screamed, ducking. Not a second too late, because someone started firing in all directions. Finnegan aimed his .357 Magnum and pulled the trigger. A moment's remorse or the slightest hesitation could be deadly in this situation. He heard a stifled cry behind him, and then the spotlight went out. The other officers charged the five thugs, who now stood there like well-behaved choir boys.

"Tommy?" Finnegan leaned over his partner in concern. "Hey, Tommy!"

"I think I got hit," the young man whispered and moaned.

"Shit!" Finnegan raised himself up. "We need an ambulance! Tommy's been hit!"

Two police officers rushed over. In the light of Mendoza's flashlight, Finnegan saw that Ganelli had caught a bullet in his stomach. He'd forgotten to put on his bulletproof vest in the rush to the scene.

"God damn it," he cursed, patting his partner's face in desperation. "Hang in there, Tommy! You better hang in there! We're taking you to the hospital, kid. Everything's going to be all right."

Ganelli smiled slightly. The sirens of the fire trucks were already approaching in the distance. Curious bystanders appeared. Biting smoke came through the broken windows of the building's basement. The officers forced the five men against a building covered with graffiti, their legs spread. They searched them for weapons before handcuffing them. Jimmy Soames leaned over the man who Finnegan had shot.

"This one doesn't need an ambulance anymore," he remarked, putting his weapon back into his holster. "He's stone dead."

Finnegan squatted on the ground next to his injured partner in the drizzling rain that soaked his uniform. Blood was tricking out of the corner of Ganelli's mouth, and his eyes became increasingly glassy. He suspected that the twenty-eight-year-old man would die.

When they returned to the precinct, the news that a policeman had been shot was already making the rounds. There was an unusual frenzy of activity in the police station for this time of night. Hordes of reporters flocked like moths to light when they heard some guys were arrested in the South Bronx during an operation to forcibly evict tenants. An officer, Lieutenant O'Malley, stepped into Finnegan's path.

"You won't believe it," he said, "but one of those thugs is the son of Vitali, that real-estate tycoon from Manhattan."

"Oh really?" Finnegan grinned coldly. "That's the icing on the cake."

He pushed impatiently through the waiting press crowd without addressing any of their questions. In the basement near the holding cells, he ran into Patrick Peters.

"What happened to Tommy is terrible," he said to Finnegan compassionately. "They took him to Fordham."

"At least one of those bastards bit the dust."

"Yes," Peters nodded, "I heard. Shot to the head."

"But it was too late. He'd already shot Tommy."

Peters gave Finnegan a sympathetic look and then patted him on the shoulder.

"I think it would be better if you call it a day now, Marv."

"No, I'm not leaving until I see what happens with Tommy," Finnegan objected. "I'm all right, Pat."

Peters nodded. "It seems that you caught a big fish. We might actually be able to get to one of the guys pulling the strings."

"I already heard. Vitali's son," Finnegan replied.

"You should inform the mayor. That'll interest him."

"I believe that's Captain Tremell's decision," Peters said. "He's on his way here."

Finnegan put his jacket on the coat rack and walked over to the holding cells where the five arrested men were locked up. Lieutenant Peters walked upstairs to the police station to report the details to Captain Tremell, the commanding officer of the Forty-First Precinct.

"Where's Vitali Junior?" Finnegan asked the officer on duty. The latter briefly looked at his colleague's determined face and nodded toward the door directly across from his desk. "I'm getting myself a cup of coffee," he said.

Cesare Vitali looked at the three officers across the interrogation room with a taunting sneer, intending to appear self-confident. But Finnegan saw the fear in his dark eyes. Just one look was enough to tell him that this guy was high. He obviously didn't smoke crack or shoot heroin like the poor kids; he snorted coke. Mendoza and Soames positioned themselves in front of the door.

"I want to make a phone call!" the young man demanded.

"Not now," Finnegan countered calmly.

"I have the right to make a phone call."

"You have bullshit."

Finnegan hated these greasy wops, these spoiled rich kids with their expensive leather jackets, shiny gel in their hair, and flashy cars, who came to this part of town to cause trouble.

"Hey, cop. I want to call my lawyer," Cesare Vitali said and leaned back casually.

Finnegan also hated being called *cop*.

"Get up when I'm speaking to you, you stupid spaghetti jerk-off." Cesare looked over to the other two officers, and then he grinned.

"Kiss my ass, cop."

This was exactly what Finnegan was waiting for. With one quick step, he stood in front of the kid and grabbed him by his jacket. The fact that this little arrogant bastard had shot Tommy enraged him. Finnegan slapped him so hard that he fell to the ground.

"What did you just say?" he asked in a friendly voice. He calmly pulled out his baton and smacked it into his palm.

"When my father finds out how you're treating me in here, your days as a cop are over," Cesare said with naked fear his eyes.

"I'm shaking now," he said loudly, his eyes widening as he pretended to be afraid. "I want to know what you were doing in my neighborhood, you little wop rat!"

"I won't say a word without my lawyer." Cesare crossed his arms with a defiant expression on his face. With a quick swing of his arm, Finnegan bashed the baton on the boy's shoulder. Cesare cried out, writhing in pain. Finnegan kept hitting him until he whimpered and begged for mercy.

"Rat," he said calmly, "you better spit it out now. Otherwise, it'll be unpleasant for you."

Tears ran down Cesare's face. His self-confidence seemed swept away.

"Look who's crying now!" Finnegan taunted him. "Are you a girl or something?"

Fury flared in Cesare's eyes for a moment, but his fear was building.

"I'm not saying a word. You're in big trouble now."

"What for, if I may ask?" Finnegan's voice was smooth as silk.

"You hit me!"

"What?" Finnegan turned to his colleagues and they just grinned. "He claims that I've hit him! Jimmy, Freddie—what do you say about that?"

"Do you know what the dudes Marv has beaten look like?" Mendoza grinned. Cesare looked at him stunned, but then he understood. These cops weren't witnesses on his side. His cocaine high had gone away in one swoop. No one would believe him that a police officer had abused him. In front of a jury, he wouldn't have much credibility as a criminal who was caught in the act. Threatening him with his father was also completely pointless. Cesare knew that his father would explode with anger when he found out he'd been arrested. He had screwed it all up once again. He'd let himself get caught, but this time he was really in deep shit. He'd end up in jail, and his father would show no interest in helping him.

"You goddamn wops shot my partner," Finnegan said in a cold voice. "We don't like people who shoot at us."

He rolled up his sleeves, and Cesare looked around in panic. There was no way out. The other two cops at the door turned their backs on him.

"Are you going to open your fucking mouth now," Finnegan hissed, "or are you one of those Mafia scumbags who choose to die instead of saying anything?"

His baton bashed down, and Cesare felt his nose breaking and lips busting. He was in the worst nightmare of his life; he was in such a panic that he pissed his pants.

"I don't know!" he whined. "Please! I really don't know anything!"

"Funny, I still have a feeling that you're lying to me. I hate it when people lie to me."

The blows rained down on him again. They hit him everywhere, and Cesare could taste blood. He could hardly speak anymore, and he spit out a tooth. Finnegan raised his baton again.

"No! Please, no more! I'll tell you everything I know!" Cesare hid his face under his arms.

"There you go," Finnegan said with a grin. "You could've had it much easier. So, go ahead and tell me."

Dr. Martin Sutton's private clinic was located a few miles outside Southampton on Long Island; its expansive grounds were surrounded by head-high hedgerows. Dr. Sutton had been a world-renowned surgeon when he worked at the famous Mount Sinai Hospital on the Upper East Side. A scandal resulting from a patient's death during a high-risk abortion had ended his career. Only his good political connections prevented him from being barred from the National Medical Association and losing his medical license. He bought a mansion on Long Island and converted it into a private clinic where he made a name for himself as a cosmetic surgeon. The world's most beautiful women were among his patients. They appreciated the clinic's first-class reputation and its discretion.

Dr. Sutton had helped his old friend Sergio Vitali a few times before, stitching up wounded men shot in gunfights with the police or other gangs. Sutton never forgot what Vitali had done for him during the terrible abortion scandal. At a time when everyone had turned their backs on the once-celebrated star surgeon, Vitali stood by his side and pulled strings for him. Dr. Sutton owed it solely to this man that he could still practice medicine.

When Nelson van Mieren jolted the doctor out of his sleep at one in the morning, he immediately headed over to the clinic, not asking what had happened. If Vitali wanted to tell him, fine; if he didn't, then Martin Sutton wouldn't ask. He told the doctor on duty to prepare the operating room. According to van Mieren's account, Vitali appeared to be badly wounded. It was two thirty when he arrived, and he had already lost a lot of blood. Sergio Vitali was as tough as coffin nails; not a single moan came out as Dr. Sutton examined the gunshot wound. The nurse prepared a blood transfusion while Sutton took an X-ray of Sergio's shoulder.

"I need to operate immediately," he decided.

"I have a very important meeting tomorrow morning," Sergio said. His lips were dry as paper. He felt drowsy, powerless. At first, he didn't think that the injury was that bad, but the wound wouldn't stop bleeding. The freezing chill that had spread through his body was the worst thing.

"You've lost a lot of blood." Sutton shook his head. "The bullet has ruptured an artery. It'll be a few days before you're back on your feet again."

"Blood pressure one twenty over sixty-five," the nurse said.

"We start operating when the diastolic reaches eighty," Sutton said, changing a bag of blood plasma. "Call Dr. Johnson. Tell him to prepare anesthesia for surgery."

The nurse nodded and left the room. Dr. Sutton was concerned that the blood was seeping out through the shoulder wound almost as quickly as fresh blood was being infused. He couldn't wait much longer. Vitali would bleed to death if he did. The anesthesiologist entered the room, and the two doctors worked together to prepare Sergio for the operation.

Nelson van Mieren called Massimo at the warehouse office in Brooklyn.

"You should let your mother know, Massimo," the lawyer said, trying to disguise his concern. "It doesn't look good."

"Things were bad here, too," Massimo countered. "Cesare was arrested in the Bronx after setting fire to a building with some of Silvio's people."

Van Mieren felt an chill come over him. What a disastrous day this was! He'd had a bad premonition after the incident at the port, but Sergio only mocked him when he voiced his fears. This time, his boss was wrong. Ortega had lashed out with a determined act of vengeance. It was clear to Nelson that the Colombian was behind this attempt on Sergio's life. And to make matters worse, Cesare had been arrested! That was the last thing that they needed now. Nelson could already see the headlines.

Maybe Sergio is right and I'm really getting old, the lawyer thought wearily. *I don't have the nerve I had twenty years ago.*

He longed for his house in the country, his wife, his children, and his grandchildren. What was he still doing here? After all, Sergio didn't even listen to him anymore.

"I won't call Mama just yet," Massimo decided, "but you should go to the Bronx to get Cesare out before he risks his neck with careless talk."

"They'll set a very high bail," Nelson reminded him.

"It doesn't matter. Get moving right now, Nelson," Massimo said. "I'll send Silvio with enough money. Cesare needs to disappear before he does something even more foolish."

"All right. I'll leave Luca here."

"How's my father doing?"

"They're operating right now. The bullet ruptured an artery. He's lost a lot of blood."

"He'll make it. Papa is tough."

Nelson noticed that Massimo's voice was similar to his father's in these situations. He appeared to have everything under control. Still, as long as Sergio was out of action, nothing else should happen.

Nick Kostidis groped for the receiver, half asleep, when the phone rang at three in the morning. Very few people knew his private phone number, so he wasn't really surprised to hear Frank's voice on the other end of the line.

"Frank," he said quietly, throwing a quick glance at a sleeping Mary, "you don't rest, do you?"

"I do sometimes," Frank Cohen replied. "But I've been working on the program for Moscow's mayor."

"What's up?" Nick yawned and rubbed his eyes.

"Who is it?" Mary asked in a drowsy voice.

"Captain Tremell from the Forty-First Precinct called me," Frank reported. "It looks like they've arrested Vitali's son during an illegal operation to evict tenants in the Bronx. One police officer was seriously injured."

Nick was instantly wide awake.

"I thought this might interest you."

Could this be the long-awaited opportunity to finally get to Vitali?

"When did this happen?" Nick asked, turning on the light.

"It seems as if the guys from the Forty-First wanted to make an example of him and his accomplices. This gang terrorizes people in the neighborhood and burns down buildings, and they've been after them for months."

"I'm driving over there right away," Nick said.

"Oh, Nick, one more thing," Frank said. "All of the buildings that this gang targeted were in Morrisania and Hunts Point between Westchester Avenue and Boston Road. Does that ring a bell?"

"No, not at the moment."

"Last year, this area was declared as a priority redevelopment project."

"What are you trying to say?"

"If Vitali is behind the raids, then he was likely in the know about the redevelopment plans."

Nick felt a sudden chill. The mole was at work again.

"What happened?" Mary squinted sleepily into the bright light. "Do you really need to go?"

"They've arrested Vitali's son. This may be my chance to finally nail that guy." Nick's eyes were shining. Vitali was Nick's obsession.

Mary had hoped that this would stop when her husband quit his job as a US attorney, but no. It was Vitali over and over again. An indescribable feeling told her that a tragedy would occur one day because of this man.

"Don't go!" she urged. "It's not your job anymore!"

"Mary," he said as he sat down on the edge of the bed, "I've been after this guy for almost twenty years, and every time when I almost had him, he walked away with a smirk. Tonight, maybe it doesn't have to be that way!"

"I'm scared," she said quietly.

"Honey," he said as he stood up, "you don't need to worry. I'll be back in two hours."

The prospect of getting to Vitali through his son electrified Nick. He remembered all the times he had slipped through his fingers: the wasted hours, days, and weeks that he and his people had spent building a criminal case against him for his dirty deeds, only to be thwarted. Strangely enough, he also thought about Alex Sontheim—the beautiful and hard-to-read woman who had been stuck in his mind since their first meeting at the Plaza. Nick got dressed quickly. Instead of a suit and tie, he slipped into a white T-shirt and pulled a leather jacket out of the closet. Feeling sad and worried, Mary watched as he sprinted down the stairs. Her heart tensed with fear. She wished, for probably the thousandth time that her husband was a simpler man, in a simpler job, working far away from this brutal and violent city. The moment the door closed behind him, she began to cry.

It was four a.m. when the car stopped at the fortress-like building of the Forty-First Precinct on Simpson Street. Reporters crowded in front of the building's steps, holding umbrellas to ward off a steady drizzle. They immediately recognized the mayor despite his leather jacket and jeans. Flashbulbs flared and two camera flashes lit up the darkness of the night. The reporters charged Nick.

"Is it true that Sergio Vitali's son has been arrested?"

"Do you know whether the injured officer is still alive?"

"What do you have to say about last night's shooting of Vitali?"

"Do you think that this assassination attempt has anything to do with the drug bust at the port?"

Nick pushed himself through the crowd without saying a word. He took a deep breath when he entered the police station.

"What assassination attempt?" he hissed at Frank once they were safely behind closed doors.

"I don't know either." Frank shrugged his shoulders.

Captain Tremell, commanding officer of the Forty-First Precinct, approached them with a concerned expression. He was followed by Lucas Morgan, the deputy commissioner of the NYPD. Nick was astonished to see Morgan because he rarely ever left his office. In contrast to Jerome Harding, Morgan wasn't a man of the streets. A true bureaucrat, who had risen in a persistent, unspectacular way, Morgan was waiting patiently to assume Harding's job. Nick greeted both men.

"The press people are saying that Vitali was gunned down tonight," he said. "Is that true?"

"There was a shootout on Fifty-First Street just after midnight," Morgan confirmed, while the men walked into the captain's office. "Local residents told us that nobody was injured. But CSI found bullets in the wall, and the entrance of a restaurant was destroyed. Eyewitnesses reported that submachine gun shots were fired from a moving vehicle targeting three men and a woman coming out of Le Bernardin."

Three men and a woman! Alex! Nick was sure that Vitali had something to do with the drug bust in Brooklyn.

"And?" he asked.

"The men and the woman disappeared in a limousine. No one fitting their description was admitted with a gunshot wound to any of the city's hospitals." Morgan raised his shoulders. "We don't know if it was actually Vitali. The owner of Le Bernardin wouldn't confirm that Vitali was there for dinner."

"Let me know if you find out anything new," Nick said. He was relieved that Alex wasn't injured, if it actually was her.

"Mr. de Lancie?"

Manhattan's US attorney pressed the phone receiver between his shoulder and ear. He searched for his glasses and the light switch since he was still half asleep.

"Y...yes," he cleared his throat. "Who's calling?"

"This is Massimo Vitali."

John de Lancie's drowsiness vanished in an instant, and his heart started pounding.

"Listen, de Lancie," Massimo Vitali said in a harsh voice, "my brother was arrested last night in the Bronx. I'd like to ask you to make sure that he's released immediately."

"I...um...why are you calling me?" John de Lancie didn't appreciate Massimo's tone. Furthermore, he was startled that someone besides Sergio Vitali knew about their secret agreement. Vitali was anything but his friend—especially after the Zuckerman affair last year. And de Lancie had only dealt with Sergio himself so far, which is why he preferred to play dumb. This call could actually be a trap.

"My father was shot an hour ago," Massimo continued. "So I can hardly bother him with this. We need your help. My brother must not go to jail, do you understand?"

"What am I supposed to do? I'm sure you have a lawyer who—"

"I know that you owe my father a favor," Massimo interrupted him rudely. Apparently, he had no time to be polite. The wheels started turning in de Lancie's brain. How could he possibly show up at the precinct in the middle of the night and release a man who had been arrested for perpetrating a crime? After all, his job was to do the opposite.

"I'll see what I can do," he replied and hung up. Less than thirty seconds later, the telephone rang again. It was one of the junior attorneys from de Lancie's office confirming what Massimo just said. An apartment building had been raided. One police officer was wounded, and one of the gangsters was dead. Vitali's son was among those arrested, and the Forty-First Precinct had requested someone from the US Attorney's Office. John de Lancie found himself between a rock and a hard place. He was obliged to Vitali, but it would be extremely difficult for him to help in this situation without exposing himself. He'd promised Vitali his assistance, but he'd always pulled strings in the background. On the other hand, nothing much could happen to him. Most likely no one would notice yet another unsolved shooting in the South Bronx—such incidents were the order of the day. There was hardly a reporter who'd get up on a rainy night to wait for an arrest in the infamous Forty-First Precinct.

"I'll go there myself," he said to his staffer—who seemed astonished. "It's better if I take care of this personally. The press is sensitive at the moment when it comes to Vitali, and we can't afford any mistakes."

Lieutenant Patrick Peters broke out in a cold sweat.

"I can't do this," he said quietly. "It's impossible."

"You'll find a way." Luca di Varese didn't smile. "Here's three grand. There'll be more when it's done."

The police officer swallowed. Luca didn't like this, but his boss's order during their ride back from Brooklyn that day some weeks ago had been crystal clear. Vitali suspected Cesare would sing like a nightingale in jail out of fear and cowardice. The boss was willing to sacrifice his son to protect his business. This scenario had now come to pass. Sergio Vitali was too incapacitated to make a decision, so it fell to Luca to execute his order. Massimo, Silvio, and van Mieren mustn't know about this. After a moment's hesitation, Lieutenant Peters accepted the bundle of bills.

"You want him...dead, if I understood you correctly?" he whispered.

"That's right." Luca nodded, his face a mask. He turned around, left the parking lot of the Forty-First Precinct without anyone seeing him, and headed back to Long Island.

Captain Tremell reported on the previous night's incidents.

"Vitali Junior spilled the beans," he said in a low voice.

Nick couldn't believe it.

"It seems that he was part of all this by coincidence," Tremell continued. "These thugs raided and set fire to the building by the order of someone named Silvio Bacchiocchi. This guy Bacchiocchi is Vitali's strongman; we've known this for a while. He's got a few prior convictions, but small stuff; that's why we've got him in our computer system."

"Which means that there's a connection to Vitali," Nick stated. He had a hard time remaining calm.

"Well," Lucas Morgan said, nodding slowly, "we already have a warrant for Bacchiocchi, and we're going to ask him some questions. Vitali Junior gave us some information that Bacchiocchi needs to rebut, for starters."

"And this kid revealed all of this just like that?" Nick asked in disbelief.

"No, not just like that." Tremell coughed slightly in embarrassment. "My men are very upset. One of their colleagues was gunned down during the bust. They grilled Vitali pretty hard, and then he… hmm…came clean."

"A forced confession," Morgan cut in, "is useless in court."

"That doesn't matter," Nick responded vehemently. "Most important, we have a connection to Vitali."

There was a knock at the door.

"Captain," the lieutenant on duty said. "Vitali's lawyer is here demanding the kid be released on bail."

"No bail's been set yet," Tremell replied. "He won't be arraigned until tomorrow morning."

"This guy is enraged, sir." The lieutenant frowned. "He's screaming that this is unlawful detention and coercion."

"Tell him that we're allowed to keep Vitali in custody for twenty-four hours. There's reasonable suspicion of trespassing, arson, battery, armed resistance, and who the hell knows what else. He's going to remain in his holding cell until he appears before the judge in the morning."

"Okay, sir." The lieutenant disappeared again.

"How the hell does the lawyer already know that we've arrested the kid?" Tremell was pissed off. "We've ordered a complete news blackout!"

"If the reporters already know about it…" Morgan said.

"Vitali's reach extends even into the Forty-First Precinct," Nick said and sighed. Someone had informed Cesare's father—either one of the officers or even one of the police commissioners. The payees on Vitali's list of friends were everywhere. Not only in the police department, but also at city hall.

Captain Tremell, Lucas Morgan, Nick, and Frank walked toward the booking room. They could hear excited voices from a distance. It was Vitali's lawyer arguing with some officers, but the sergeant on duty wasn't having it. Three officers stood at the door blocking the reporters from storming the building.

"I demand," Vitali's lawyer screamed, "to see my client *immediately*! He has the right to legal representation!"

Nick stopped.

"Hi, Nelson," he said calmly. "Why are you so agitated?"

Van Mieren turned around quickly, staring at Nick in astonishment. But he quickly regained his composure.

"Ah, Mayor Kostidis!" he exclaimed. He had the sonorous voice of a defense lawyer projecting to the farthest corners of even the largest courtrooms. "I should have expected I'd find you here!"

Nick and van Mieren had faced off in the courtroom a few times before, and Nick had always gotten the short end of the stick. But tonight he felt strangely confident because van Mieren seemed unusually shaken. There was a look of panic in his eyes, and he seemed to have aged by many years since their last meeting. He had lost weight in his face, but not around the belly; he looked sick, and his suit hung loose around him.

"You're here too, Nelson," Nick replied, "despite the fact that a complete news blackout was ordered. I guess the bush drums are in good working order."

"I demand to see my client," van Mieren insisted, ignoring Nick's remark.

There was renewed commotion at the door of the police station, and then a man appeared. Nick was surprised to recognize John de Lancie—the US Attorney for the Southern District of New York.

When he arrived in front of the police station, de Lancie instantly realized that he'd made a big mistake. A swarm of reporters huddled in front of the massive granite facade on Simpson Street. A flurry of flashbulbs went off as he pushed his way through the intrusive crowd, silent and grim. De Lancie's anger mixed with cold fear when he saw the mayor—of all people—in the waiting room. He was still measured against the success of his predecessor, and he felt in this moment that he was a pale comparison. It was too late to sweep this incident under the rug, and he could hardly leave now. He had to somehow make the best out of this without raising the suspicions of that clever fox Kostidis. Never before had he felt such an impotent anger; never before had he broken out into such a fearful sweat. De Lancie didn't care about Cesare Vitali at all, but he needed to focus in order to avoid a tactical mistake; the consequences could prove fatal. "What's actually going on here?" he asked, irritated.

Nelson van Mieren repeated his complaint.

"You're going to see your client soon enough," de Lancie said, but he stared at Nick. There was anger in his eyes; Nick thought that he also detected a hint of insecurity.

"What are *you* doing here?" de Lancie asked in a harsh tone. "You want your old job back, or you're just coincidentally in this neighborhood at this time of night?"

His voice was oozing animosity.

"Call it curiosity, or even personal interest."

Nick wondered why the US attorney was so irritated by his presence.

"I don't understand why the mayor, the deputy police commissioner, and the US attorney are called over here because a few hooligans tried to burn down a tenement in the South Bronx," de Lancie sputtered. "What's the big deal?"

"One police officer was seriously wounded, one person is dead, and there was significant property damage," Tremell interjected. "Furthermore, I requested someone from the US Attorney's Office, but not you specifically, sir."

John de Lancie turned to face him. He opened his mouth for a sharp rebuttal, but when faced with Nick's inquiring gaze, he chose to remain silent.

"Well," he continued in a more subdued tone, "as far as I can tell we're here because the son of someone who has much power and influence in this city has been arrested. I'm less concerned about the incident than damage control in the public eye."

"Pardon me?" Nick thought that he misheard. "A police officer is fighting for his life in the hospital! What kind of damage are you trying to control?"

"My God, Nick." Drops of sweat appeared on de Lancie's forehead. "It's not even clear yet whether this young man shot the officer. Just because his father is your enemy, we shouldn't allow ourselves to be accused of overreacting!"

Captain Tremell's and Lucas Morgan's jaws dropped in surprise. The nightly raids on apartment buildings where people's lives were threatened could hardly be considered a trifle!

"Vitali's not just my enemy," Nick responded. "He's an unscrupulous criminal. And I haven't changed my opinion. I still believe that we need to put a stop to him if we want to establish a minimum level of safety and order in this city."

Nick noticed de Lancie's nervousness, saw the sweat on his forehead, and remembered his suspicion that Vitali had bought de Lancie. It was hard to believe, but seemed to be true. Vitali had sent the US attorney to make this issue disappear as fast as possible, and it probably would have worked if Kostidis hadn't come running. De Lancie was grinding his teeth, and his face had an unhealthy ruddiness.

"I'd like to talk to the kid," Nick said to Captain Tremell.

"No, you won't." De Lancie was vehement.

"And why not?"

"This is outside your jurisdiction!" De Lancie was sweating even more. The collar of his shirt was completely soaked through.

"I'm the mayor of this city," Nick said, unmoved, giving his successor a piercing look. "I'm responsible for the security of my citizens. I want to ask this kid a few questions."

The US attorney stared at Nick. His mind was spinning feverishly. He had to prevent the mayor from speaking to Cesare Vitali under all circumstances. De Lancie knew Kostidis all too well. He'd admired him in earlier days as a US attorney because hardly anyone else was as successful in the courtroom. He could slip into the role of thundering prosecutor or understanding friend, and his summations were famous and brilliant. He played every role that promised to lead him to success. He knew how to influence the jury and manipulate witnesses into making statements they never intended to make. The secrets behind his legendary success as an attorney were his knowledge of human nature, his ability to empathize with his counterparts, his perseverance, and his computer-like memory. De Lancie knew that Cesare Vitali would be completely defenseless against this man. He responded to Kostidis's gaze with powerless anger, clenched his hands into fists, and opened them again.

"No one will talk to Mr. Vitali until he's been presented before the judge." Captain Tremell closed the discussion. "Not even the emperor of China!"

"I'm the chief federal law-enforcement officer for the Southern District of New York," de Lancie insisted. "We've taken over the investigation in this case, and I demand to see this man right now!"

Captain Tremell exchanged looks with Lucas Morgan and then shrugged his shoulders. He led the men to the interrogation rooms.

"*You* will get out of here!" De Lancie pointed with his index finger at Kostidis. The latter looked at the US attorney for a moment, and then he shrugged his shoulders.

"Get me Mr. Vitali's lawyer!" de Lancie snarled at the police officer standing at the door. "This man has a right to legal representation!"

Lucas Morgan wondered why de Lancie was acting so strangely. Furthermore, he seemed to be afraid of Kostidis—but why?

"Why is this taking so long?" De Lancie looked nervously at his watch, pacing the room with long strides.

"I need to wrap this up, too," Nick said. "Fortunately, the kid already confessed to everything. It looks as though we have nearly enough evidence to take on Vitali."

De Lancie turned around quickly. His Adam's apple jumped up and down nervously, and rivers of sweat ran down his forehead. "You should be happy, John," Nick said with feigned innocence. "I've been after Vitali for twenty years and never had such good evidence against him as you have today."

"This isn't your job anymore, Kostidis!" de Lancie hissed. "The work of the US Attorney's Office is no longer any of your business!"

Nick turned around in the door frame.

"Sometimes I wonder," he said slowly, without letting de Lancie out of his sight, "which side you're on."

The US attorney was speechless as he stared at Nick. His nerves were about to explode. Nick walked over to Frank, who was waiting for him at the sergeant's desk.

"Let's go," Nick said to him. "Vitali has already confessed anyway. He did so under pressure, but we know that these guys worked under the orders of Vitali's henchman. So the connection is there."

Frank stared at his boss.

"De Lancie is Vitali's man," Nick said in a low voice. "I had a hunch. He knows that I suspect him too. I stepped on his toes pretty badly. I'm afraid that now he won't leave a stone unturned to discredit me in public."

"Hmm." Frank had a concerned expression on his face. At that moment, commotion broke out near the holding cells. Captain Tremell and two officers came running from the cell block with faces as white as sheets.

"Goddamn, shit!" The otherwise calm commanding officer of the Forty-First Precinct was beside himself. "Vitali hung himself in his cell!"

"What?" Nick and Frank asked as if speaking with one voice.

"Yes, goddamn it! They forgot to take away his belt! He hung himself from the heating pipe!"

De Lancie lunged out of the interrogation room, his bloodshot eyes bulging out of his face.

"What is this bullshit!" he roared. "Am I surrounded by idiots?"

The police doctor who just happened to be there at that time of night ran past them, followed by van Mieren and the other officers. De Lancie's gaze fell on Nick.

"This suits your plans exactly!" he said spitefully.

"No, not at all," Nick replied. "He would've been far more useful to us alive. Good night, John."

"Go to hell!" de Lancie growled after the mayor. Despite his fear, he was secretly relieved that Cesare Vitali was dead. Now he only had to deal with a corpse instead of keeping a guilty criminal from going to the slammer.

"This stinks to high heaven," Nick said as they walked up the stairs.

"De Lancie will try to cover up this whole thing," Frank said. "If your suspicion that he's Vitali's man is correct, then he won't let the truth come out under any circumstances."

"Shit." Nick stopped, contemplating this. "And we have no way of preventing it."

"Yes, we do," Frank replied. "They can't cover it up if Cesare Vitali's arrest and confession is covered in tomorrow's newspaper."

"Tomorrow's newspapers are already printed."

"Crews from NBC and NY-1 are waiting outside."

Nick thought for a moment, and then he grinned.

"Okay. That's how we do it. Come on, Frank."

John de Lancie didn't get a wink of sleep that night. When he entered the US Attorney's Office building on St. Andrews Plaza behind the federal court on Foley Square at nine on Sunday morning, he felt absolutely exhausted. Shortly after the medical examiner determined Cesare Vitali's death and issued the death certificate, de Lancie left the police station through the back exit. He had no desire to face the vultures from the press and was glad that he didn't run into Kostidis again. It wasn't Cesare Vitali who gave de Lancie stomach pains, but the fear that the mayor saw right through him. An agitated crowd bombarding him with questions was waiting outside his office, but he forced his way through indignantly.

"What's going on here?" he asked his assistant irritably. "Why are all these people here?"

"But you were there last night," the woman replied in surprise. "Didn't you watch television this morning? Yesterday's incident in the Bronx is the lead story on every channel!"

An uneasy feeling overcame de Lancie. He opened the door to his expansive, mahogany-paneled office. Autographed head shots of Ronald Reagan, George Bush, and J. Edgar Hoover hung on its walls. De Lancie stared at the television screen, which stood on his bookshelf alongside his legal books. Almost instantly, Nick Kostidis appeared on the screen, standing on the steps of the Forty-First Precinct police station. That same second, de Lancie realized that he had made a grave mistake leaving the building through the back exit. He had ceded the stage to Kostidis without a fight, and the media-obsessed mayor naturally took advantage of it.

"As the mayor of this city, I'm responsible for the safety of its citizens," Kostidis was saying. De Lancie felt a murderous rage, but it quickly gave

way to a feeling of helplessness. *"I cannot and will not allow ruthless criminals to terrorize law-abiding citizens in this way. This group of six young men attempted to set an apartment building on fire—a building in which many families live. One of them was shot by the police after he critically wounded an officer in the line of duty. The other five perpetrators were arrested."*

"Is it true that Sergio Vitali's son is among them?" a young female reporter asked.

"Yes, that's correct," Kostidis replied. Standing there in the drizzling rain, unshaven in his leather jacket, he fit the image of a man who sacrificed himself for his constituents. De Lancie reluctantly acknowledged that Kostidis was anything but a bland politician. Time and again, Kostidis managed to turn even the most trivial incidents into media events. In contrast to his predecessors, the many other politicians who seemed artificial in front of a camera or microphone, Kostidis seemed completely authentic. His enemies cynically called him a gifted actor who was a better fit for Hollywood than New York. But they also had to admit that he was the most popular mayor since Fiorello LaGuardia.

"Is that why you're here now, Mayor Kostidis?" one of the reporters asked. As usual, Kostidis didn't shy away from telling the truth.

Or what he believes to be the truth, de Lancie thought bitterly.

"Yes, this is one of the reasons. We've had reason to believe that Mr. Vitali was involved in numerous recent raids on apartment buildings in the Bronx, and the participation by his son Cesare in last night's events offers conclusive evidence. Cesare confessed that he and his accomplices acted under someone's orders. Real-estate speculators keep trying to oust tenants from their homes in order to raze those buildings and repurpose the properties. This is pure terror, which I won't tolerate in my city!"

Kostidis's eyes sparked angrily.

"It is a well-known fact," one of the reporters began, *"that you and Mr. Vitali aren't close friends—"*

"This is nothing personal!" the mayor interrupted the journalist. *"I fought vehemently against* any *type of crime during my tenure as US attorney, and the fight continues to this day. As mayor, I am responsible for the safety of the citizens of our city. It makes no difference if the son of Mr. Vitali or anyone else is involved."*

"US Attorney de Lancie is also here tonight. It seems as if this case is a political issue."

"Without a doubt, this arrest has a heightened political profile due to the involvement of the son of such a well-known figure as Sergio Vitali," Kostidis said plainly. *"At the very least this could prove Vitali's connection to illegal business, even if he continues to deny it publicly and invest large sums of money in protecting his image."*

He spoke with confidence and eloquence. His lively facial expressions and gestures said more than he expressed in words. He was careful not to communicate his suspicions directly, but the way he spoke allowed viewers to connect the dots.

"Besides, I believe that Mr. de Lancie shares my opinion that this case should not be handled any differently than that of any other perpetrator. A prominent name doesn't protect a criminal from the full force of the law."

De Lancie felt by turns hot and cold. That goddamned son of a bitch! If only lightning would strike him down. He couldn't have possibly handled this in a more clever way. Kostidis was once again the public hero, the tireless fighter against crime. He had succeeded in portraying Vitali as a ruthless real-estate speculator without explicitly attacking him, and he didn't even mention that Cesare Vitali was dead. Things had gone from bad to worse. De Lancie felt sick, and a stomach ulcer caused him stabbing pain.

"Isn't this great news?" his assistant asked. "It looks like we finally caught hold of solid evidence against Vitali!"

For decades, Sergio Vitali had been considered the archenemy of the US Attorney's Office, with mountains of files piled up in its basement.

"Don't you have anything better to do than stand around here," de Lancie snarled at her. His assistant threw him a surprised look. She'd assumed that her boss would be happy, but the exact opposite appeared to be the case.

"Get out of here!" De Lancie pressed his hand against his abdomen. After she closed the door behind her, he staggered over to his desk and sank into his chair. These goddamn stomach pains were going to tear him apart. The telephone rang. John de Lancie picked it up with a sigh.

"That's your idea of help?" The sound of Massimo Vitali's cold voice reverberated in his ear. "You were really great. The only thing I can say is that my father made a bad investment in you."

"Listen!" de Lancie yelled. "I'm sorry. Kostidis was already there when I arrived. There was nothing I could do. I tried everything, but—"

"You screwed up," Massimo Vitali interrupted him coolly. "I only hope that you know what you have to do now. There could be unpleasant consequences for you if you don't at least control the damage you caused."

"But—"

The line was dead. This arrogant bastard had just hung up on him! De Lancie buried his face in his hands. He understood the threat all too well. Once it became public knowledge that he'd accepted money from Vitali, he would be finished forever. He would have no choice but to put a revolver in his mouth and pull the trigger. What demon had possessed him—who had never before had any trouble with the law—to get involved with Sergio Vitali? He had risked everything he had worked so hard for.

He raised his head and stared into the mayor's face on the screen. What could he even do with this situation? Kostidis made the headlines of the day, and as the US attorney, he could hardly side with a man who had been chased by his own agency for years. Above all, de Lancie couldn't afford to raise any suspicions with his staff. He needed to play the role that everyone expected of him, whether he liked it or not—a role into which

Nick Kostidis had forced him. Had the mayor really seen right through him last night? *Sometimes I wonder which side you're on...*

How could he let his guard down in front of Kostidis, of all people! He was in a tight spot now. He had to help Vitali or he was finished. But this help mustn't be too obvious. There had to be a way to save face and still do Vitali a favor. Vitali was not his biggest problem. It was Nick Kostidis—the mayor of New York.

Alex also had a sleepless night. She had been pacing the halls of her apartment ever since Sergio's driver dropped her off at home. Her whole body trembled, and she only managed to calm down somewhat after three glasses of straight vodka. She wasn't shocked by the gunshots fired in her direction from the moving car, but rather the crystal-clear realization that she had gotten herself into a situation she couldn't get out of. If she went to Kostidis to tell him what he wanted to know, Sergio would find out and have her killed just as he did with David Zuckerman. Quitting her job and leaving the country seemed like the only solution. Maybe she could find a new job in Singapore or Japan, as far away as possible from Sergio and the menacing men she saw in that dark Brooklyn warehouse. But how could she move on knowing that Sergio was free and ordering others killed with impunity? Wasn't it her civic duty to try and prevent this? She thought about Kostidis's words on Christmas Day at the Downeys' house. *I had the impression that you would have the courage to do the right thing...*

She flinched as she saw Nick Kostidis come onto the screen. He stood in front of a police station surrounded by reporters, and his dark eyes seemed to being looking directly at her. Pleading. Demanding. Compelling. This man was just as hard to read as Sergio. Alex didn't trust him. There were so many secrets, and the truth behind these secrets seemed far more complex and dangerous than Alex had ever imagined. Alex was so lost in thought that she didn't even hear what Kostidis was talking about. Now she turned up the volume. Sergio's son Cesare had been arrested last night.

"We've suspected for a long time that Mr. Vitali was involved in the numerous raids on Bronx apartment buildings," the mayor said, *"and the participation by his son Cesare in last night's events offers conclusive evidence."*

Alex groped for her pack of cigarettes. When she realized that it was empty, she crumpled it impatiently. One of the reporters asked Kostidis whether he believed that there was a connection between the assassination attempt on Vitali and the drug bust at the Brooklyn port.

"I was informed that Mr. Vitali was apparently involved in a shooting incident last night," Kostidis said—it seemed to Alex that he was looking straight at her. *"Eyewitnesses reported that someone shot at Vitali and his companions from a moving vehicle outside a restaurant on Fifty-First Street. However, we don't know anything about the perpetrators or their motives. We don't even know if Vitali was injured or if he is even alive."*

"Oh my God," Alex murmured, wrapping her arms around her knees. If she hadn't reacted so fast, Sergio would probably be dead now. Mayor Kostidis certainly wouldn't be too sad about that.

Nelson and Massimo were waiting outside the clinic room door to speak with Sergio. Anxiety was etched across their faces.

"Doctor, when can I speak to my father?" Massimo asked Dr. Sutton.

"It'll take a little more time," the doctor said. "He needs plenty of rest after the operation and his extreme blood loss."

"I can't wait!" Massimo struggled to keep his voice down. "My brother killed himself last night. My father is the only person who can tell me what I should do now."

"Martin," Nelson van Mieren interjected, "the situation is really very serious."

The doctor gave in, and Massimo opened the door of the clinic room, with Nelson in tow.

"Papa!" The young man stepped to Sergio's bed; he was terrified when he saw how bad his father looked. The injury hadn't looked that serious to him on Saturday night. Now, all the machines and tubes made Massimo even more nervous. Until yesterday he hadn't the slightest idea what his father actually did all day, and was only vaguely familiar with the fatal consequences of one wrong decision. Massimo had been confident that it would be no big deal if his father were sidelined for a few days. But the events of the last forty-eight hours had proved the young man wrong. He felt like a listless sailor on a ship lost at sea with no captain. His younger brother's arrest and sudden death had such broad implications that Massimo was frightened. There was public speculation connecting his father with the illegal eviction campaigns and the drug seizure at the port. The reporters were talking about an underworld war with the Colombian drug cartel, and Massimo didn't know what to do. Three men who worked for his father were shot at the port last night. The situation was spinning out of control.

"Massimo," Sergio said in a fragile voice.

"Yes, Papa, it's me. How are you feeling?"

"Like shit," Sergio replied. "Where's Nelson?"

"I'm here!"

"You were right," Sergio murmured. "Ortega didn't hesitate long."

The lawyer saw how bad Sergio's condition actually was and hesitated to report on the new problems that had emerged.

"Massimo, did you tell your mother what happened?"

"Yes, I did. But…" He fell silent and quickly exchanged a look with Nelson.

"But what?" Sergio's gaze wandered from Massimo to Nelson and back to his eldest son. He saw their gray faces and knew that something was wrong.

"What happened?" he asked in a flat voice.

"Cesare's dead," Massimo responded. He and Nelson took turns as they described what had transpired, beginning with Cesare's arrest, the scene with Kostidis and de Lancie at the police station, Cesare's suicide, the three men shot down at the port, and the wild media speculations.

Sergio was silent as they told him everything. He needed time to put the pieces together. For a moment, he was tempted to give in to the feeling of weakness inside him. Cesare didn't commit suicide. There was no way that he would do that, he was too much of a coward. *He* was responsible for the boy's death, because he'd given Luca the unmistakable order to ensure that Cesare never spilled the beans. How could he have known that this situation would actually arise? He had been annoyed with his youngest son many times; it was painful for him to accept that Cesare was a good-for-nothing. But despite everything, Cesare was his own flesh and blood—his son—and now he was dead.

"What should we do now, Papa?" Massimo asked, verging on desperation.

"Above all, you need to maintain your composure," Sergio replied, "no matter what else happens. Take cover and wait. No rash actions. What about de Lancie? Is he still on our side?"

"I think so," Massimo replied.

"But Kostidis is running wild," Nelson remarked. "He senses his chance to finally get to you."

"Yes, I can imagine that." Sergio frowned in thought. He needed to reassert his control as quickly as possible before any irreversible damage was done.

"Does Constanzia already know about Cesare?"

"Yes," Massimo nodded, "it's all over the TV. Domenico's with her. She completely collapsed. She says that…"

He stopped and looked down to the ground, ill at ease. Sergio knew that Constanzia had loved the youngest and weakest of their sons more than the other two. He could easily imagine what kind of scene was unfolding at his house.

"What does she say?" he asked harshly.

"She says," Massimo inhaled deeply and struggled to look into his father's eyes, "that you had him killed."

Sergio's fingers seized the bedcovers. Constanzia knew him better than he realized.

"That's nonsense," Nelson said. "Your father has been in this clinic since Saturday night!"

"Papa, I know that you never thought much of Cesare," Massimo said, his voice pleading, "but I told Mama that you'd never do such a thing. That's the truth, isn't it, Papa?"

"Of course, I've done nothing of the sort."

Massimo seemed relieved, but Nelson still had something on his mind.

"Before Cesare hung himself," he said, "he told the cops that they raided the building on Silvio's order. They arrested him yesterday."

Sergio closed his eyes. Cesare really didn't understand anything, not even the most important law that they lived by—the code of silence, *omertà*.

"They won't be able to use his confession," Nelson continued, "because it was made under coercion."

"It's too late now anyway," Sergio answered in a rough voice. "Cesare's dead and nothing will change that. We need to approach things differently."

Thinking clearly was an incredible strain for him.

"Find someone to claim that he shot at me," he said hoarsely, "and think about a plausible reason. We need to publicly announce that the shots fired at me have nothing to do with Ortega. Nelson, bail Silvio out of jail."

He was exhausted, and he paused for a moment. The shadows under his eyes darkened, and his throat hurt from speaking. Sergio cursed the drugs that paralyzed his brain.

"Nelson," he murmured, "think of something we can use to distract the press. We've already talked about a scenario, do you remember?"

The lawyer nodded. Dr. Sutton entered after knocking on the door.

"Gentlemen, I urge you," he insisted, "Mr. Vitali really needs to rest now."

"Nelson!" Sergio whispered, and the lawyer leaned over closer toward him. "Please call Alex. Tell her…"

I was ready to love you, Sergio. If you'd been honest with me, I would have accepted the truth, no matter how bad it might be.

He saw the rejection flare up in Nelson's eyes. No, she shouldn't see him this way, so weak and helpless, with all these tubes in his body.

"Never mind," he said, shaking his head, "don't call her. But please make sure that Domenico takes care of his mother. She mustn't be left alone now."

"I will." Nelson pressed his friend's hand with compassion. "We'll get everything under control again. Don't worry."

The phones had been ringing off the hook at city hall since early morning. Nick Kostidis didn't feel fatigued, even though he hadn't gotten a wink of sleep over the past few nights. Cesare Vitali's arrest and suicide and the attempt on his father's life were the top story in every news outlet—he had made sure of it. But Sergio Vitali had disappeared off the face of the earth.

He was either dead or so severely injured that he couldn't defend himself publicly, which was counter to Nick's expectations. In any case, his late-night appearance on television in the Bronx prevented the matter from simply being swept under the rug. De Lancie was forced to investigate the case.

There was a knock at the door.

"Mr. Harding is here, sir," Allie said. The police commissioner didn't wait. He pushed the secretary aside and charged into the mayor's office with a bright-red face.

"What the hell, Nick. Who do you think you are?" he screamed. "I'm out of town for two days, and then I hear something like this!"

He was so enraged that Nick thought for a moment he might assault him.

"What are you talking about, Jerome?" He pretended to be surprised.

"You're not a damn US attorney anymore!" Harding roared. "How dare you interfere with a police investigation? How could you claim in front of running cameras that Vitali was gunned down by the Colombian drug cartel?"

"That's not what I said—"

"Of course not!" Harding's voice almost cracked in his rage. "You only insinuated it, but that's bad enough! The governor called me. Even the secretary of state and the deputy attorney general from Washington want to know what's going on here. I'm standing out in the rain like a complete idiot, and people are asking me why the mayor is doing my job."

Nick suppressed a satisfied grin.

"Calm down, Jerome," he said. "I haven't done anything but point out some grievances in the Bronx. Wouldn't you agree that these raids on apartment buildings—"

"Spare me your PR speech," Harding interrupted him harshly. "You can't fool me! You're taking advantage of this situation to continue your crusade against Vitali. But you're obstructing the police and obstructing justice in the process."

"How is that?" Nick squinted at the police commissioner. "Because I prevented de Lancie from covering up this incident as quickly as possible?"

"That's not your job anymore," Harding replied vehemently. "Do you know what Vitali will do once he finds out that you've slandered him?"

Nick jumped up. "I don't give a damn what he does. I represent my city's interests, since nobody else cares to. The US attorney only cared about Cesare Vitali's well-being on Saturday night. He didn't say a single word about the injured police officer or the endangered citizens. It almost seemed he was trying to sweep these incidents under the rug, and I have to ask myself why. What interest would Mr. de Lancie have in protecting the reputation of someone like Vitali? I have the same question for you, Jerome. Why do you care what Vitali thinks?"

Harding's face turned a deeper shade of red, but Nick continued, unperturbed.

"There are stacks of files on Vitali in the basement of the US Attorney's Office. Everyone knows that, but we can't prove any wrongdoings. Now we have a tiny chance to convict him of a crime. I won't allow some corrupt bureaucrat to destroy this opportunity."

"Be careful, Mayor Kostidis." Harding's voice was reduced to a threatening whisper. "What are you trying to suggest with that comment?"

"What am I trying to suggest?" Nick stopped just a few inches before the gigantic police commissioner, who was at least a head taller than him. "I have the suspicion that there are many influential people on Vitali's payroll. Because of their silence, he's in a position to do what he wants. I won't tolerate the Mob ruling my city any longer, and I hope that you agree with me, Jerome."

Harding stared at him and took a deep breath. But then he ran his hand through his dense white hair and sighed. Suddenly, his anger seemed to have blown over.

"You're right," he finally said, and let himself fall into a leather chair at the conference table. "The city is as corrupt as it's ever been. We're tilting at windmills. But the way you're doing it won't work."

"Yes, it will," Nick disagreed. "It's the only way. We must publicly denounce this corruption. No politician will dare to side with a man like Vitali. His political network is paralyzed, at least for now."

The police commissioner was silent.

"Jerome!" Nick looked at him imploringly. "This is my job, my struggle. I won't capitulate because of convenience or fear and look the other way like so many others do. I want to put a stop to Sergio Vitali's game."

"When he's gone another man will take his place," Harding said, frowning. "It'll never end. You know that as well as I do."

Someone knocked on the door, and Frank Cohen entered the room.

"They caught the guy who tried to kill Vitali. It's on the news right now. He's even confessed."

Harding and the mayor jumped to their feet.

"They say he was a former bodyguard of Vitali's who wanted revenge."

"Not the Colombian drug cartel, Nick," Harding said disdainfully. "Just a frustrated ex-bodyguard."

Nick didn't answer and shook his head in silence.

"In case you should need me, I'll be at police headquarters," the police commissioner said. "I should take care of this matter personally before even more damage is done."

Harding had barely left the office when Nick turned on the television. He and Frank silently watched a report about the alleged perpetrator's arrest.

"Isn't it strange," Frank said, "that this guy turns himself in to the police and confesses even though they weren't even searching for him? That's too good to be true."

"Simple solutions always make me suspicious." Nick furrowed his brow in thought. "Four days after a sizeable amount of cocaine was seized due to an anonymous tip, someone makes an attempt on Vitali's life. We know from our informants that a war is in the making between the Colombian drug cartel and the local crime syndicate. Then three men are shot dead at the port—all of them Italian—who, if we dug deeper, would surely turn out to be Vitali's men."

He turned off the television.

"Vitali has disappeared. He must have been wounded, and that's why we haven't seen or heard from him. Damn it, all of this is related. But everyone else refuses to believe it."

"How could this guy drive the car and shoot a Kalashnikov through the open window at the same time?"

Frank shook his head.

"It seems to me that there are people who would prefer for all of this to simply disappear," Nick said. "This whole thing is—"

The telephone rang, and he pushed the button of the intercom system.

"It's Eugene Varelli," Allie said, "and he says it's urgent."

Eugene Varelli was the New York State commissioner of health.

"Hello, Nick," he said. "I'm sorry to bother you, but it looks like we have a serious problem on our hands."

"Great." Nick rolled his eyes. He put the telephone on speaker so that Frank could listen in. "What kind of problem is it this time?"

"The FBI tried calling but couldn't reach you. I said I'd call myself. We received an anonymous threat in the mail today, so my people didn't take it seriously," Varelli said, "but then I received a phone call about an hour ago. A man threatened to infect groceries with anthrax spores. He named the addresses of two stores in Queens and Morningside Heights. He allegedly infected some Freezo brand frozen hamburger patties. I've sent some people there to check all possibly affected products."

"Great."

"The FBI is taking this threat pretty seriously, Nick. The man didn't sound like a nutcase. Furthermore, he made precise demands and announced that he wanted to make it public."

"What are his demands?"

"Three million dollars to a numbered offshore account. And..."

"And what?"

"Your resignation."

"He doesn't want me to personally hand over the money, does he?"

"I don't think sarcasm is appropriate in this situation," Varelli replied stiffly. "How should we proceed?"

Nick threw a glance at Frank and then sighed.

"Inform the police and the US Department of Health."

"Okay."

"Oh, and Eugene," Nick said. "Keep me posted."

He hung up. It was silent for a moment, and then Nick leaped out of his chair.

"Sergio Vitali is calling in the cavalry," he said. "I'd bet my right hand that this act of terrorism is just a diversion to get Cesare's death and the assassination attempt out of the headlines."

Frank looked concerned.

"And what if this is a genuine terrorist?"

Nick grinned wearily. "Then I'll resign and spend the rest of my life playing golf and fly-fishing. And I won't turn around to look at Sodom and Gomorrah. That I swear to you, Frank."

Naturally, the anthrax story was leaked to the press in spite of being highly classified information. The public's reaction bordered on hysteria, and the media did its part to fuel the panic. The press focused on the anonymous terrorist and his strange demands. Old documentaries that had gathered dust in the TV station's archives were dug up showing people who had been infected with anthrax. There were reports about how dangerous anthrax was, and interviews with any obscure expert they could find confirming that the disease would lead to certain death within two to three days. All of the Freezo brand products in the city were confiscated, which in turn led to vehement protests by the company's management. The FBI checked laboratories across the country in order to find out where the pathogen could possibly have originated. The mayor established a crisis committee and a hotline where concerned citizens could get more information. The telephones rang off the hook, and many families decided that it would be better to visit distant relatives outside the city.

"That was good work," Sergio said, satisfied, as van Mieren reported on the operation's success.

"They have their assassin, and he's got nothing to do with any Colombians." Nelson smiled. "There won't be a gang war, and everybody calmed down."

"Your name is out of the headlines," Massimo affirmed. He was relieved that his father had recovered so quickly and was able to once again make decisions. On their way from Long Island to Mount Kisco, the helicopter flew over Queens. During the flight, Sergio dictated to Nelson a list of people he should contact. He needed to know who was still on his side and what Kostidis had up his sleeve. Sergio was completely sure that the mayor wouldn't believe the story of the self-confessed assassin. More than ever before, he had the feeling that Kostidis was a serious threat. It was late afternoon when Sergio entered his house near Mount Kisco. His second eldest son, Domenico, came to meet him with a concerned expression.

"Papa!" he called. "Thank God!"

Sergio hugged him clumsily with his right arm.

"How's your mother?"

"She refuses to take the sedatives. But she's somewhat composed. I still can't believe that Cesare is dead."

"Yes, it's terrible."

Sergio crossed the entrance hall, followed by his sons and Nelson van Mieren. He entered the grand living room. Constanzia was sitting on the massive leather couch with her daughters-in-law Victoria and Isabelle. Her sister Rosa and cousin Maria were also with her. Dressed in black, the five women had tearstained faces. Sergio's eyes fell on a large framed picture of Cesare that someone had decorated with a black ribbon, and his stomach cramped painfully for a moment.

"Good afternoon," Sergio said.

"Mr. Vitali"—a young doctor from Mount Kisco walked toward him with quick steps—"my condolences. It's a real tragedy."

"Yes, it is, indeed. Thank you." Sergio nodded. Constanzia caught sight of her husband at that moment and jumped up with surprising agility. Her face, swollen from nonstop crying, contorted into an enraged mask.

"Assassino!" she screamed and charged Sergio before anyone could stop her. *"L'hai ammazzato! Bestia! Assassino!* You had him killed! Your own son!"

The other women jumped up, appalled, and Massimo and Domenico rushed to embrace their rampaging mother. They were visibly shocked by the allegations she flung at their father. The doctor stared at the woman in shock.

"He annoyed you!" Constanzia screamed. "You always despised him because he wasn't as cold as you are! You had him killed, you cold-blooded bastard! Just like you sent my father to prison, when you knew it would be his certain death! You ordered the deaths of so many who were in your way, and now my baby, my darling. *Oh, dio mio!*"

She was reeling, and her tirade erupted into loud wailing. Her voice barely had anything human left in it.

"You're not in your right mind, Constanzia," Sergio said, extending his hand toward her.

"Don't touch me, you murderer!" she screeched.

"No one did anything to Cesare," he said in a calm voice. "He panicked and hung himself with his own belt. He was probably all coked up again."

He noticed the incredulous glances of the doctor and his daughters-in-law, he saw the doubt in Nelson's eyes, and he knew that even both his sons believed their mother in that moment.

"You never liked Cesare," Constanzia said in a quieter voice. "The only thing you cared about was your damn business! I hate you!"

"Please give her a sedative injection," Sergio said, turning to the doctor. "The pain of our son's death is too much for her nerves."

"Yes!" Constanzia laughed with utter hatred. "You just keep telling them that! But I know you, Sergio Vitali! I know exactly what you're capable of! You're as cold as ice!"

"Mama!" Domenico said in desperation. "Be quiet, please! Let's go upstairs. Papa just returned from the hospital. He's also grieving."

"No, he's not." Constanzia freed herself from their grip. "This man never grieves. He has no emotions because he has no heart."

Then she turned around and left the salon, followed by Victoria, Rosa, Maria, and the doctor. Sergio sat down awkwardly in an armchair.

"Bring me a whiskey, Massimo," he said. His son obeyed, while the others stood there, silent and ill at ease. Constanzia's uncontrolled fit of rage had profoundly shocked them because she was always calm and friendly.

"Why are you staring at me like that, Isabelle?" Sergio asked Massimo's wife. "Do you really believe that I ordered Cesare's death?"

"No," the young woman said quickly, shaking her head, "of course not. It's just terrible to see her suffer like this. She was very attached to Cesare."

"I know," Sergio replied. "It's hard for her. She refuses to accept death. She also blamed me for her father's death when he died of cancer. She'll calm down again."

Alex sat at her desk and read the *Times* article about Cesare Vitali's suicide. She shivered as she recalled her first and only encounter with Sergio's youngest son, which could very well have ended fatally for her. Her assistant Marcia peeked in through the door.

"Mr. Vitali's on the phone," she whispered dramatically, "and Mr. St. John wants you to call him back. It's urgent."

"Thanks." Alex picked up the receiver. She had been waiting three days to hear from Sergio. She was in deep and time was flying by. First the attempt on Sergio's life, then his son's death, and now—after the alleged assassin was arrested—a terrorist dominated the newspaper headlines. Alex was quite sure that the men in that car were not former bodyguards, but perhaps it was best that no one found out the truth. She for one had banished any thought of that terrible night from her mind.

"Sergio?" she said.

"No. This is Massimo Vitali."

"How's your father?"

"Better. He wants to see you, Alex. If you can arrange it, right now."

"I'm very busy," Alex said evasively. She didn't want to see Sergio.

"It's important. My father asked you to visit him at his Park Avenue apartment. I can send a car if you like."

"That won't be necessary. I'll take a taxi," Alex answered. "And Massimo—I'm sorry to hear about your brother. I read it in the newspaper today."

"Thank you," Sergio's son said in the same cold voice of his father. "So when will you be here?"

"In an hour."

Alex stood up without further ado. It was better to get this visit over and done with instead of procrastinating. Mark Ashton's desk on the trading floor was empty, but Alex ran into him in the hallway. He had just returned from lunch.

"Did you reach Oliver?"

"I'm meeting him this weekend," Mark responded. "He said that he would help me if he can."

Something else occurred to Alex.

"Did St. John ask you today about Syncrotron by chance?"

"Yes," Mark said, looking at his boss in surprise, "he sure did. Is that a new client?"

"No." Alex grinned and winked at him. "It's part of my plan. We'll lure St. John down a dead end and watch what happens next."

Sergio lay on the couch in his Park Avenue apartment. He'd made one phone call after another to ensure the loyalty of his "friends," but the result was devastating in almost every case. Most of them had someone make flimsy excuses on their behalf, and the ones to whom he spoke acted very reserved, or even turned him away.

"Fred Schumer's out of his office." Nelson hung up the telephone receiver. "His secretary doesn't know when he'll be back."

Sergio sighed. Fred Schumer was the powerful chairman of the House Oversight Committee, an influential man who usually didn't care about rumors. Sergio had known him for over twenty years. Schumer had been extremely helpful on several occasions.

"It doesn't look good." Nelson looked concerned.

"These goddamn cowards," Sergio growled. "Gutless opportunists. They can kiss my ass."

He was tired, and his injured shoulder was hurting, but at least his mind was functioning impeccably again.

"But we need them," Nelson said, voicing his concern.

"I know!" Sergio's anger flared. "But what the hell am I supposed to do?"

Massimo and Luca exchanged a telling look. The situation was serious. Sergio could lose his power if he lost the protection of his political connections. The television was on, and the newscast reported hourly about the latest developments in the anthrax case. Then Mayor Kostidis appeared on the screen. He stood on the city hall steps with dozens of reporters and TV cameras crowded around him. Sergio sat up straight. Massimo, Luca, and Nelson also fell silent and listened.

"Mayor Kostidis, what do you think about the terrorist demanding your resignation?" the NBC reporter asked.

"In my opinion, this is nothing but a clever diversion," Kostidis replied calmly.

He was filled with energy and seemed to be completely in control of the situation, although he had barely slept since Saturday.

"What kind of diversion?" another journalist yelled.

"There was an assassination attempt on Sergio Vitali on Saturday night," Kostidis said, *"after a large shipment of cocaine was seized by the customs authorities at the Brooklyn port on Tuesday. The drugs were discovered on a freighter coming from Costa Rica, which is the drug cartel's classic transportation route. The police and customs authorities received an anonymous tip. We've been monitoring Vitali's connection with the port for a long time."*

"That goddamn bastard," Sergio muttered with a stoic expression. The other men were silent.

"A gang war rages between Vitali and the Colombian drug cartel. Three men were shot dead at the port on Sunday evening—three Americans of

Italian origin—who likely worked for Vitali. It seems plausible to me that the attempt on Vitali's life was revenge for blowing the cover of a drug shipment."

"But the perpetrator has been caught," one of the reporters argued.

"That's rather unlikely, isn't it?" Kostidis smiled. *"I assume that the man who confessed to this crime has been paid off by Vitali. He'll be sentenced to two years in prison, and then he'll be released again after one year for good conduct. The public is reassured that this is just one lunatic instead of a gang war."*

"How do you know about all this, Mayor Kostidis?"

"I don't know anything," the mayor replied, *"but I suspect that the sole purpose of this scheme to poison groceries is to distract us from the assassination attempt on Vitali."*

"These are dangerous speculations, Mayor Kostidis," one reporter said. *"Do you have any evidence?"*

"Not yet. But I'll have it soon. I was a US attorney fighting against these criminals long enough to know their methods and ways of thinking."

"You can't call Mr. Vitali a criminal!"

"Really? I can't?" Kostidis's dark eyes sparkled. *"Well, I'm doing it! He may own many serious businesses and donate millions of dollars to charities, but if you could take a look behind his mask of altruism, you'd see that he's a criminal. Sergio Vitali is the godfather of New York City."*

Massimo, Luca, and Nelson threw covert glances at Sergio, but he kept a straight face.

"You've got to give it to this man," he said eventually. "He's pretty clever. It's a real shame that he's not on our side."

"He's dangerous," Nelson replied in concern, "extremely dangerous. He's seen through everything."

"But he has no evidence," Massimo objected. "He talks and talks, and that's all he does."

"Kostidis doesn't need evidence," Sergio answered grimly. "Every word he says rattles the people who are on our side. Not one of them will publicly side with us as long he utters such things on television. They can't afford to because they'd lose their jobs otherwise."

"Let's do something about him!" Massimo shouted passionately. "Why don't we sue him for libel and slander? How can he claim such things?"

Sergio threw a glance at his son and slowly shook his head. "We've got to do something," he said.

"But what do you suggest?" Nelson asked. "I could try to obtain a preliminary injunction that prohibits him from—"

"That's useless," Sergio snapped. "Kostidis doesn't give a crap about preliminary injunctions or libel actions. He's obsessed with being right. As a matter of fact—he is."

"We'll shut him up!" Massimo said.

"Unfortunately, it's not that easy," Sergio countered. "He is the mayor of this city. He's very influential and incredibly popular. There's only one solution in his case."

The room was dead silent. Each of the men understood what Sergio meant.

"No." Nelson broke the silence and stood up. "You can't kill the mayor."

"Who said anything about killing?" Sergio stared at the television screen with a gloomy face. "An accident—a tragic, regrettable accident. A human life is so fragile."

Nelson looked at his old friend and realized that he was serious. Sergio was in a precarious position: he was still recovering from the shooting, and he was distraught because of Cesare's death and Constanzia's violent reaction. Old friends were avoiding him, and the house of cards of sensitive relationships threatened to collapse. The trouble with Ortega and the port was the icing on the cake. Kostidis could cause severe damage. This crisis had come to a head. It was time for action. "He must disappear," Sergio said at that moment, "the faster, the better."

"We shouldn't plan on that option right away," Nelson objected carefully. "We could intimidate Kostidis and tell him clearly that it would be better for him to shut up."

"Intimidate him?" Sergio laughed and immediately grimaced in pain. "How do you plan to intimidate this man? Kostidis doesn't fear the devil himself!"

"We could...intimidate him physically."

Sergio snorted disdainfully and held his empty glass to Luca, who instantly refilled it with whiskey.

"He'd crawl in front of the cameras to proclaim his allegations if he was half dead." Sergio finished the glass with one gulp. "No, Nicholas Kostidis doesn't understand threats."

"But if he dies, they will immediately suspect you."

"Once he's gone, I'll finally have my peace. Remember that the men who will investigate his death are on our payroll."

Nelson van Mieren shook his head determinedly. He didn't care if Massimo and Luca witnessed his insubordination.

"I won't be a party to that," he finally said. "I've always been on your side, Sergio. I've fought quite a few battles and wars with you. We've built up all of this and managed to make it legal. I understood that we needed to get some people out of the way every now and then. But if you order the assassination of the mayor, then it will have far broader implications than we'll be able to handle. His death would drag all of us into the abyss!"

Sergio stared in surprise at his oldest and most loyal companion. He wasn't used to hearing such explicit opposition from him.

"I know you're not afraid of anything," Nelson implored "but we can also solve this problem. Right now it's important to come to an agreement with Ortega. Everything else will turn out all right."

"Kostidis is destroying everything I've built," Sergio said in a sinister tone. "He's tasted blood and won't let go anymore. You know that as well as I do!"

"If you plan on killing him, I want no part of it," Nelson repeated in a low voice as he looked away. Sergio raised himself up with difficulty, but he hadn't lost all of his strength.

"Nelson," he said softly, "you're my oldest friend. You're the only person on this planet I would call a friend. However, you know that I can't afford this. You understand that Kostidis has turned into an incalculable risk, don't you?"

"Yes," Nelson nodded, "but that doesn't mean you need to kill him!"

Sergio stared straight through him for a long time. After a while, Nelson bowed his head.

"If you'll excuse me now," he said, "I need to go to the medical examiner's office. The results of the autopsy should be available at one o'clock. I also need to post bail for Silvio."

Sergio sat down again after Nelson left the room. He looked around aimlessly, looking gloomy.

"Luca," he said eventually, "please prepare a plan for how we can silence Kostidis once and for all. I don't care how you do it. The most important thing is that it happens fast."

Luca nodded.

"And pick two of your best men. They should keep an eye on Nelson around the clock."

"Okay, boss." Luca bowed slightly and left.

"Papa," Massimo said, turning to his father after silently following this scene, "do you think that Nelson will betray us?"

"No," Sergio replied, sounding tired. "Nelson's sick. He's getting old. His nerves aren't the best anymore. He was different back in the day, but he's forgotten what it means to wage a war."

"But Ortega—" Massimo started to say.

"I'm not talking about Ortega," Sergio said. "I'm talking about Kostidis. His weapons are much more subtle than Ortega's, but no less effective. He takes advantage of every sign of weakness. He's clever, too."

When Alex arrived at Sergio's apartment, she had to admit that he seemed to be in control of his situation, although he was clearly still unwell. His face was leaner than usual, and his expression was more pronounced and colder. He looked like a general—proud, aware of his power. The apartment, which was usually deserted, was crowded with his men. Alex even had to put up with them searching her purse.

"I'm very sorry about your son," Alex said, stopping a few feet shy of him. She made no attempt to kiss him. She had not forgotten that he'd knowingly put her life at risk.

"Thank you," he replied, "it's hard for his mother."

"And for you?"

His eyes narrowed for a split second, and then he raised his shoulders.

"Cesare was a weak person," he said. "He was a drug addict, a frail man."

"But he was your son!" Alex was shocked by his indifference.

"And still, he didn't mean more to me than anyone else," Sergio countered. "Are you shocked now? Why should I pretend to be the grieving father if I'm not?"

Alex remained silent. If she thought that he needed comfort after all that had happened, then she was wrong. Sergio was miles away from any kind of human feelings.

"How are you, *cara*?" he asked.

Alex didn't respond to his question. "How are you?"

"Getting better. They removed the bullet."

Alex couldn't believe it. He acted as if this were all as trivial as an appendectomy.

"I'm wondering why you're keeping half an army of bodyguards in your apartment," she said coolly. "The television said that they arrested the shooter."

Sergio sat down on the sofa.

"Well, you never know." His expression was inscrutable.

"Maybe you vaguely remember that I was standing right next to you when you were shot," Alex countered harshly, "and without a bulletproof vest at that! It wasn't this guy. So who was it then?"

"I know who it was," countered Sergio, "but that doesn't matter. It wasn't meant personally."

"It wasn't meant personally?" Alex laughed in disbelief. "I think I'd take it personally if someone was trying to kill me!"

"I stepped on someone's toes." Sergio sipped his whiskey to numb the pain in his shoulder, at least a little bit. "And that was his response."

Alex stared at Sergio. He felt more like a stranger than ever before. The presence of the armed men triggered the same uneasy feeling she had at the warehouse in Brooklyn.

"Come, sit down next to me!" Sergio asked her. Alex hesitated. She complied with his request but sat at the far end of the couch.

"Why did you want to see me?" she asked stiffly. "I dropped everything because your son said it was urgent."

"I thought about our conversation," Sergio said. "You mentioned that you wanted to end our relationship."

Alex kept silent and waited for him to keep talking.

"I understand that you're angry with me," he continued in an unusually reasonable manner. "I've made some mistakes. But I don't want to lose you, and that's why I'd like to suggest something to you."

Alex didn't want to hear his suggestion. He leaned forward and grabbed her hand before she could get up.

"You don't have to give me an answer right away. Take your time and think about it." He didn't smile. His eyes were inscrutable. He looked at her for a while and then let go of her hand. He stood up.

"I'm divorcing Constanzia," he said to Alex's complete astonishment, "and I want you to be my wife."

Alex didn't think she had heard right. Marry Sergio? Just a year ago she would have thought about it, but she'd seen far too much of Sergio's world. The things that she'd witnessed had revolted her. Sergio turned toward her.

"So what do you think?"

Alex struggled to keep her composure. He had her cornered. She searched desperately for the right words.

"That...comes as quite a surprise."

"You could keep working or not. You could do whatever you want." His voice was rough. "I'll buy you a house and we could have children. Isn't that what you want?"

Alex cringed at the thought of her life married to Sergio and completely at his mercy. People died by his order, and the memory of the dark warehouse in Brooklyn made her wince.

"Promise me that you'll think about it?" He squatted down in front of her and grabbed her hands. The look in his blue eyes was serious, and something deep inside them alarmed Alex. Sergio was a man with many faces. There was a reason for everything he did. But why did he want to marry her all of a sudden? What had happened?

"I'll think about it," she replied to put him off. "I promise."

"Good." There was an irritating hint of triumph in his smile. She felt quite sure that this was part of a larger plan that she didn't understand. She was glad that he didn't try to kiss or sleep with her. Alex rejected his offer to be driven downtown. She just wanted to get out of this apartment, away from this man she couldn't figure out and who terrified her so much.

Thomas Ganelli, the police officer who was shot during the raid on the Bronx apartment building and who succumbed to his injuries a few days later, was buried at the Astoria Park Cemetery in Queens. The American flag was laid out on his casket, which was carried by his colleagues from the Forty-First Precinct. Accompanied by their spouses, rows of police officers wearing splendid dress uniforms were sweating in the sweltering heat of this July afternoon; they were in a state of shock and anger at the senseless death of their comrade. Of course, Police Commissioner Jerome Harding was also in attendance at this highly publicized funeral. Furthermore, officials from the Department of State, high-ranking officers of the NYPD, and the mayor of New York City were there. Harding delivered an emotional half-hour speech at the open grave, in which he demanded even tougher measures against every criminal. Nick Kostidis kept his speech short. He knew that Harding's tone was inappropriate in this situation, and therefore limited himself to words of consolation for the family and the colleagues of the deceased. In addition, he thanked all the police officers for their dangerous and important work.

Frank Cohen stood in the very back and once again admired his boss's talent to spontaneously find the right words in every situation. Frank was sincerely moved, even though he didn't know this young police officer. When the funeral was over, Nick gave his condolences to the parents and the young widow and promised genuine assistance on behalf of the city administration, not just empty gestures. Then the two men walked back to the waiting limousine in silence.

"It's a goddamn shame that so many young people must die," Nick said as they were on their way back to Manhattan. He stared gloomily at the passing apartment blocks. "It's completely senseless."

"Ganelli's parents were really consoled by your words," Frank remarked. "The people could feel that you honestly mean it."

"I wish that I could have said some honest words at his medal of valor ceremony instead of his funeral." Nick leaned back in fatigue.

The past weeks had been exhausting. The terrorist had disappeared, and the FBI couldn't figure out whether anthrax cultures had ever been stolen from a laboratory. There was a temporary cease-fire in the mutual mudslinging between Nick and Sergio Vitali. After Cesare Vitali's autopsy clearly confirmed suicide by hanging with a belt as the cause of death, the press turned to other topics. No evidence suggested foul play was involved in the young man's death.

Despite the superficial easing of the situation, it seemed like new threatening storm clouds were forming on the horizon. That very morning, Nick found a letter with no return address on his desk. This happened frequently, but this letter was neither postmarked nor did it have a postage stamp. Inside was a threat. *You will die if you don't shut up*. It was written on a simple white sheet—a normal piece of copy paper. The script was apparently from a laser printer. No one in the office had a clue how the letter had found its way to the mayor's desk. Nick had crumpled it up and thrown it into the wastepaper basket, shaking his head. But Frank had fished out the letter and put it in his pocket.

"Nick," he started carefully after they left the Midtown tunnel behind them and arrived in Manhattan, "I know that you don't want to hear it, but I'm very concerned about that letter."

"Good grief." Nick smiled indulgently. "You know how many threatening letters I've received in my life. That's just the way it is when you're holding political office. You're always unpopular with some people."

"No," Frank objected, "it's different this time. Especially in light of what has happened over the past weeks. I have the feeling that this is a serious threat. Maybe it's this terrorist; maybe Vitali is behind it. You've pushed him into a corner pretty hard with your public statements."

"Anonymous letters aren't really Vitali's style."

"Please, Nick. You need extra personal protection—at least until this whole fuss about Vitali has settled down a bit."

"I don't want strangers following me into the restroom," Nick said, warding off the idea. "Nothing will happen."

"I'd still prefer if at least your wife had—"

"Mary doesn't need to know about this," Nick replied. "It would only upset her. Anyway, she's going to her sister's in Montauk with Christopher and his fiancée in a few days to prepare for the wedding. I hope that this whole mess blows over by then."

Nick smiled at Frank reassuringly.

"Your nerves are overstrained, Frank. You haven't been getting enough sleep lately. Why don't you take a weekend off for a change?"

"Because I'm worried about you," Frank answered. "At least promise me that you'll stop riding the subway through the city by yourself?"

"Only if you don't force any bodyguards on me in return."

Nick closed the issue with a smile, but Frank didn't give up.

"How did this letter get on your desk? That's what gives me a headache."

"I don't want to hear another word about this ridiculous letter." Nick shook his head. "Anyone from the cleaning crew could have put it there!"

"Let's hope so," Frank sighed, shaking his head.

Raymond Howard was on the phone, preparing for the Fourth of July fireworks show in lower Manhattan. He sat in his office with a phone to each ear, and was trying to simultaneously calm down both the head of the festival, who was close to a nervous breakdown, and the raging chairman of the Veterans Association, when he saw Frank standing in the door. He signaled his colleague to wait and ended both conversations.

"For God's sake, these idiots," he fumed. "I can't take this annual jockeying anymore."

One of the telephones rang, but he ignored it.

"Good you're here," he said to Frank. "You could help me set the seating plan for the official gallery. The president's daughter is coming, and she's bringing a friend."

Then he noticed Frank's worried expression.

"What's wrong with you?"

"I don't know." Frank pulled the crumpled note out of his jacket pocket and handed it to Howard. "What do you think about this?"

Howard took the sheet and read the line with raised eyebrows. The second telephone started to ring.

"Hmm," he said and looked up, "sounds quite determined. What does Nick say about it?"

"He won't take it seriously," Frank said in a depressed voice, "as usual."

"And you?"

"I have this strange feeling. I've seen a few threatening letters addressed to him over the past years, but they never threatened to kill him."

Howard shrugged his shoulders.

"At least he promised not to take the subway for the next few weeks." Frank folded the sheet and put it into his pocket. "Lhota should earn his wages for a change."

"Well, that seems like a pretty good idea to me." Raymond Howard nodded and put his hand on the telephone receiver.

"I hope you're right." Frank managed a forced smile. He wondered whether he was the only one who thought that this letter was threatening enough to take seriously.

Just as Alex stepped out of the shower, she heard the telephone ring. The answering machine was turned on as usual, but she listened to hear whose voice would speak after the tone. She hadn't contacted Sergio since his proposal and was happy that he wasn't calling to ask for her answer.

"Alex!"

It was Mark, and he sounded unusually agitated.

"Please answer if you're there! It's urgent!"

Alex quickly wrapped a towel around herself and grabbed the phone.

"Hey, Mark. What's so important?"

"Can we meet for dinner tonight?" Mark asked. "We've figured out a way to—"

"Hold on!" Alex interrupted. She still feared that Sergio had tapped her telephone line.

"I'll call you back on my cell phone in a second." Punching Mark's number into her cell phone, she stepped out on to the terrace. She'd been invited to Gracie Mansion that evening. Just as Kostidis had promised, she'd received a written invitation. She accepted it after some consideration and also because of Madeleine's insistence.

"What's up?" she asked when Mark answered.

"Maybe it would be better not to discuss this over the telephone." Mark spoke hastily. "Could you fly to Boston with me tonight?"

"No, I'm invited to Gracie Mansion this evening," Alex replied. "Come on, Mark, tell me. What's going on?"

"Oliver thinks that it's virtually impossible to get legal access to the registration documents of an offshore company," Mark said, "but he had an idea yesterday. We know someone from our college days who works at MIT in Boston. This guy is a real computer geek."

"Slow down." Alex shook her head in confusion. "What does this guy have to do with offshore companies?"

"Nothing. But he's a professional hacker. He works as a programmer at MIT, where he tests the security of software. Oliver's talked to him over the phone and discussed the problem—without mentioning any names, of course. Our friend knows how to infiltrate computers." Mark lowered his voice to an excited whisper.

Alex began to understand.

"That sounds pretty illegal."

"It's also illegal to trade on insider information."

Alex contemplated this for a moment. It seemed like this could work. And if it failed, then they'd at least have given it a try.

"We could fly to Boston tomorrow morning," Mark pushed. Alex felt her heart beating in excitement. She needed to know who was behind these rotten deals. On the other hand, she was afraid of what she might uncover. But her curiosity was ultimately stronger than her fear.

"Book an early flight to Boston," she said after a short pause. "Leave me a message on my cell phone about when I need to be at the airport. Will Oliver come with us?"

"I think so. If you're okay with that."

"For heaven's sake, yes!" Alex was worried about spending time with Oliver, but she still looked forward to seeing him again.

"I'll stay in touch. Have fun tonight."

Alex drove with Trevor and Madeleine to the mayor's reception. Security guards checked their invitations and then let them pass through the gate. The colonial-style mansion was in a magnificent park at the East River, nestled between tall, old trees. Since Mayor Fiorello LaGuardia chose this house as his residence in 1942, it had become a tradition for every successor to live here. Alex felt her heart pounding when she entered the house. She wasn't quite sure whether or not she liked Nick Kostidis, and she also didn't know whether it was a good idea to accept his invitation. In the foyer, Kostidis rushed toward them with open arms and a hearty smile.

"My wife and I are extremely happy that you're our guest tonight, Alex," he said with sincere cordiality.

"It's an honor and pleasure for me," she replied politely.

Through the wide-open glass doors, they stepped out onto a large terrace that offered a magnificent view of the East River. Alex met Christopher—Nick and Mary Kostidis's son—and his fiancée Britney Edwards. Then Kostidis introduced other guests such as Canadian ambassador Jacques Toussaint and his wife Véronique; Patrick Grimford, the legendary publisher of the *New York Times;* Hollywood actor Michael Campione, who lived in Tribeca; fashion czar Kevin Lang; and Francis Dulong, who was a senior partner of the prestigious law firm Dulong & Kirschbaum.

Alex enjoyed lively conversation. It was wonderful to talk with interesting people and forget about her worries for a while. There were champagne cocktails and Japanese hors d'oeuvres offered to the guests by a liveried waiter. After the sticky July day, the mild evening air added to Alex's good mood.

Mary Kostidis was an unobtrusive and courteous host. Alex liked her right away. They talked for a long time, and Alex sensed the trust and deep connection between her and Nick that can only result from true love, similar to that shared by the Downeys. She shivered, imagining what it would be like to actually marry Sergio Vitali. At the very least, she would stop receiving invitations to Gracie Mansion. During dinner—which was served in one of the splendid salons, with wide-open terrace doors—Alex sat between Kevin Lang and Michael Campione.

Around eleven, the Canadian ambassador and his wife said their good-byes, which lightened the atmosphere, making it less formal and more sociable. All of the people present seemed to know each other fairly well, and the party moved to a different salon with comfortable sofas and armchairs. Alex was talking to Trevor, Madeleine, Michael Campione, Francis Dulong, and his wife when Nick Kostidis joined them.

"The only possible reason for me to consider running for mayor of New York would be this house," Trevor said jokingly.

"Really?" Nick replied. "Actually, to be honest with you, it was an important reason for me. And hey, you don't have to mow your own lawn."

Everyone laughed. Alex found the mayor was downright likable when he was relaxed like this.

"I hope you're having a good time."

"I really am. It's a highly enjoyable evening." She smiled.

"Would you like a drink?"

"Yes, I'd love another."

Nick waved a waiter over to fill Alex's glass with champagne.

"Let's go outside for a moment to get some fresh air," Nick suggested, and Alex agreed. They stepped out onto the terrace. It was a mild, warm night. It almost felt like being in the countryside. The city's lights sparkled on the river's ink-black water, and there was a scent of lilac and sweet fading flowers in the air.

"Wonderful." Alex stepped toward the railing of the terrace, taking a deep breath. "It's hard to believe that we're in the middle of New York City."

"Do you sometimes miss your homeland?" Nick Kostidis asked as he stood behind her. She turned around. He had one hand in his pocket and held his glass with the other, observing her with friendly interest.

"Sometimes I miss certain places where I spent my childhood." She smiled. "Have you ever been to Germany?"

"Unfortunately not," Nick replied with regret. "Actually, I've never even been to Europe."

"I spent almost all of my holidays with relatives in France or Ticino," Alex told him. "My family is large. We have uncles, aunts, and cousins everywhere. I especially liked to go to the mountains in the winter. They're…one of a kind. Just before the first snow falls, the air is as clear as glass. And when you get up in the morning, the entire countryside is white. And the icy winds really push the snow around on the ground. You don't really feel the seasons in the city."

She looked pensively into the park's darkness.

"I miss the smell of fall—the scent of the moist earth and decaying leaves and the fire. Sometimes in Germany the sky is high and wide, and then it's all foggy again. In the spring, I clearly remember the feeling I had the first time I could go horseback riding outside and gallop across the meadows after a dark winter. I was so happy."

Caught in her memories, she paused for a moment without noticing the enraptured way Nick Kostidis looked at her.

"In nature," Alex continued, "I feel small and unimportant. It puts everything in the right perspective."

The smile vanished from Nick's face.

"We take ourselves so seriously," Alex went on, "our lives, our problems, and everyday worries. Only in the face of nature do we realize how insignificant we really are."

"Is that what we are? Insignificant?"

Alex looked at him. His question was sincere.

"In comparison to nature—yes. Just think about how many millions of years it took for our earth to form. What's a human life in comparison to that? And who really cares what you do or what you strive for when you're gone all of a sudden?"

"Those are frightening thoughts."

"I don't know. I think that the steady course of nature is very comforting."

"You're a real philosopher," Nick said. Alex tried to detect if she heard a hint of mockery in his voice, but he was sincere.

"No." She laughed self-consciously. "I just got a bit carried away."

She was surprised at how openly she could talk to Nick Kostidis.

"In any case, you've sparked my interest about Europe," Nick said. They looked at each other in silence, and then Alex turned away. She didn't want this conversation to get too personal.

"I couldn't believe that I was seated next to Michael Campione, of all people. I had a huge crush on him when I was younger," she said, smiling.

"Really?" Nick also seemed happy to talk about a harmless subject again. "Mike's an old friend of mine. We grew up in the same neighborhood and had similarly ambitious dreams."

"Did you realize your dreams?" Alex asked.

"I've reached many of my goals," Nick said, looking at her seriously, "but it's a strange thing…"

"You don't dream about the dark side," she said, and he nodded.

They stood together in silence.

"Which one of Mike's films is your favorite?"

Alex looked at him for a moment, and then she laughed in embarrassment.

"If I tell you, then you'll probably think, *Of course, what else*."

"Why?"

The intensity of his dark eyes made her nervous, but she had to admit deep inside that she had misjudged Nick Kostidis. He seemed so likable and authentic now.

"It's *Murder, Inc.*"

Voices and laughter could be heard from the house.

"Why should I think that?" Nick asked quietly.

"Well, that could explain my fascination with a man like Vitali, don't you think?"

Nick shook his head slightly.

"I don't think that you're fascinated by him anymore."

Alex stopped breathing. How could he know that?

"You got angry when I asked you about him on Christmas Day," Nick said. "But I think you were insecure, and you got mad at me because I saw that."

Alex laughed insecurely now.

"Did you study psychology?"

"Something like that." He smiled, shrugging his shoulders. "I was a US attorney, and I think that I've developed a fairly good understanding of human behavior. I—"

Mary Kostidis stepped onto the terrace escorted by a young man. Alex recognized him as the one she'd seen with Nick that evening at the Plaza. But she also knew that she'd seen him somewhere else, and that she had a bad feeling about him.

"I don't mean to interrupt," Mary said. "Nick, Ray wants to talk to you for a second."

"Yes, of course." He turned toward Alex. "Would you excuse me please, Alex?"

She nodded, looking after him with a mixture of fascination and uncertainty as he disappeared into the house.

"Come in, Alex," Mary said in a friendly tone, "we still have a little dessert."

"What's so important?" Nick asked his assistant after he'd closed the door to his office.

"Another letter was dropped off for you," Raymond Howard replied, handing him the envelope with just his name written on it.

Nick ripped the envelope open. *You didn't shut up. You will die.*

"Bullshit!" He crumpled the paper indignantly. "Where did you get this?"

"It was dropped off with one of the security guards," Howard said. Nick shrugged his shoulders and sat down at his desk. He ran all ten fingers through his thick, dark hair and stared out the window into the nighttime blackness of the park.

"By the way, the US Attorney's Office has ordered a judicial investigation in the case of Cesare Vitali."

"Why would they do that?" Nick looked at his assistant in consternation. "I thought the autopsy confirmed that it was suicide."

"Vitali claims that his son was killed."

"That's utter nonsense! The kid was all coked up and lost his marbles!"

"Well," Howard said as he strolled through the room, "de Lancie wants to summon you for the investigation."

"Excuse me?" Nick sensed cold rage rising inside of him. "What's this all about? What do I have to do with it?"

"You stepped on de Lancie's toes," Howard explained. "You compromised him when you stepped in front of the television cameras that morning. And de Lancie is very sensitive."

"Call him. Now."

"It's after midnight."

"I don't care," Nick said abruptly. "I want to speak to him now."

Howard glanced at his boss and then grabbed the telephone receiver and dialed a number. It took a few seconds, which Nick spent pacing angrily across his office.

"John!" Nick yelled into the telephone, enraged. "I just heard that you're ordering a judicial investigation."

"Yes, that's correct," John de Lancie replied, not even mentioning the unusual time of this call. "There are a few inconsistencies that require clarification."

"What kind of inconsistencies? This kid raided an apartment building with some criminals known to the police under orders from his father. Two people were killed in the process. Vitali Junior was unstable, high on drugs, and then he committed suicide in a sudden panic!"

"He was pressured and physically abused," de Lancie countered. "The NYPD is currently investigating all officers of the Forty-First Precinct who were on duty that night."

"For what reason?"

"Cesare Vitale's body had signs of physical abuse all over it. He was beaten before he died."

"Well," Nick said. "And why am I being summoned? Do you think I did it?"

"I'm not obliged to inform you of the details," de Lancie answered, "but I'll tell you anyway. You were surprisingly fast showing up at the police station. You talked to officers, made a statement in front of the cameras, and put me in an uncomfortable position."

"You're summoning me because you're upset that I did your job?"

"You interfered with an ongoing police investigation," the US attorney replied coldly. "You shouldn't be surprised that now you're tangled up in this case."

"That's ridiculous. And you damn well know it!"

"The only thing I know is that the kid was abused in order to extract a confession. There's also a well-founded suspicion that it occurred at your instigation."

"That's unbelievable!" Nick jumped up in a rage. "Are you seriously insinuating that I solicited police officers to torture a detainee?"

"I'm not insinuating anything," de Lancie said. "The family of the deceased insists on an investigation of the events."

"Listen to me closely, John," Nick interrupted de Lancie in a low, threatening voice. "God knows that I have other things to take care of right now, but I won't stand idle and watch you trying to publicly discredit me."

"I don't have a choice—" de Lancie began, but Nick didn't let him finish his sentence.

"Oh yes you do!" he yelled. "I did the same job as you long enough to know that no one can put you under pressure—especially not the family of a man who was caught in the act of committing a crime—unless someone has leverage against you."

"What are you saying?" De Lancie's voice hardened.

"Should I express myself more clearly?" Nick was so enraged that he was about to call de Lancie one of Vitali's henchmen.

"I warn you, Kostidis," John de Lancie said, "don't interfere with things that are none of your business."

"You were surprisingly fast to show up at the police station yourself. Why didn't you just send someone from your staff like you usually do?"

De Lancie's voice became even frostier: "You may be the mayor of this city, and you may be incredibly popular, but I don't care. What you insinuated is incredibly insolent. I've summoned you before the investigation committee; I advise you to show up. Good night!"

"Can I tell you something, Ray?" Nick slammed down the receiver on the hook, grinning ferociously. "This bastard's scared. Someone is putting him under serious pressure, someone he's obligated to. I'm sure it's Vitali."

"You think that Vitali bought de Lancie?" Howard opened his eyes wide. "The US attorney?"

"Yes, that's what I think." Nick ran his hand through his hair. "The only reason he ordered an investigation is to crucify me. It's a joke! I didn't speak to a single police officer that night. Nobody but Vitali himself had an interest in this kid's death. He really would have been more useful alive."

"They will charge you with slander if you publicly claim that," Howard warned him.

"I don't need to do that," Nick countered. "De Lancie knows that I suspect him of corruption. But he's losing his nerve. He'll make a mistake one day. I'll find out who's behind this."

Someone knocked on the door, and Mary entered the office. She saw her husband standing at the window with a grim expression on his face and his hands linked behind his back. He stared out across the river.

"Some of the guests are ready to leave, Nick."

"I'll come in a second," he replied curtly.

"What are you going to do?" Howard asked.

"What do you think?" Nick looked at his assistant suspiciously.

Howard shrugged his shoulders. "You can't afford too much negative publicity. Will you tolerate their attempt to publicly discredit you?"

"I'm accountable to my constituents and myself." Nick turned around. "I won't let the Mob and its paid henchmen throw me off course! Not through an investigation committee, not through extortion, not through threatening letters! I've never let myself be intimidated. Vitali should know better than that."

His burning black eyes seemed to pierce Howard, and blood rushed into Howard's face.

"This is *my* city, Ray. Do you understand?"

Howard turned his gaze away. He had mistaken Nick's aggressive response for weakness, but Nicholas Kostidis was courageous, and he was tough. Tough as steel. He was the best mayor this city had ever had, but he was too straightforward for this job, too stubborn and unwilling to compromise. He stood in the way of influential men—some of whom didn't care about human life.

"I need to go back to my guests," Nick said. "Go home, Ray. I'll see you here tomorrow morning at nine. And then we'll devise a strategy."

Howard responded with a smile, but it vanished after the mayor left the room. It was a shame. There were very few men like Nick Kostidis. But now he had really stepped on Vitali's toes. He had no future; perhaps it would be better to side with someone who did. The letters warned that the mayor of New York didn't have long to live.

A bright-blue sky arched across the city's skyline with the promise of another hot day as Alex took a taxi to LaGuardia Airport. The party had left her with a strange feeling. She had long suspected that Nick Kostidis only wanted to use her for his own purposes, but now she wasn't so sure. Last night, she had gotten to know his likable side, which made her both curious and insecure. She regretted that she couldn't continue the conversation with Nick; he was certainly more concerned about her than she'd thought. He wasn't the obsessed fanatic that Sergio claimed he was. He was natural, human. People in New York tended to look at their fellow human beings from the perspective of usefulness. Nick Kostidis was different, and Alex had to admit that she'd gotten him all wrong.

The taxi stopped in front of the airport terminal, and she paid and got out. Her heart tensed up when she saw Oliver standing at the Delta counter. More than a year had passed since she last saw him. Alex mustered all of her courage and walked over to him.

"Hi," she said.

"Hi, Alex." His gray eyes gazed at her through his round glasses. He seemed just as relaxed and steadfast as ever. All of a sudden, she realized how much she had missed him. She smiled shyly, and he smiled too. He opened his arms, and she flung her arms around his neck.

"Are we okay?" she whispered, and Oliver nodded his head silently. "I'm so sorry about what happened. I had no idea until Mark told me about it."

"I survived." Oliver held her tight for a moment, and then he observed her closely. "You look pretty stressed out."

"I wish I had listened to you," Alex said, exhaling deeply, "but now I'm in too deep in this mess. Thank you for helping me."

"I'm not going to let some Mafia thugs intimidate me," he said, and Alex didn't know whether to laugh or cry. The fear that had become her constant companion suddenly seemed a little bit more tolerable.

"I missed you, Alex," Oliver said quietly and cradled her face in his hands, "and I was very worried about you."

"I missed you, too." She felt a thick lump in her throat. She quickly wiped away the tears with the back of her hand as she saw Mark walking toward them in the terminal. Oliver grabbed her hand and pressed it firmly. They boarded the flight to Boston at a quarter to nine. During the flight, Oliver explained to Alex and Mark how the incorporation process of an international business worked on the British Virgin Islands and what he hoped to find out with his friend Justin's help.

At the Boston airport, they took a taxi to the Massachusetts Institute of Technology. Justin Savier was waiting for them at the Wiesner Building, a futuristic structure that housed the world-renowned MIT Media Lab. Justin wasn't the geeky computer nerd that Alex expected but a lean, sunburned man with an abundance of dark dreadlocks. He wore jeans, sneakers, and a washed-out T-shirt. The three men greeted each other, and after Alex was introduced, Justin handed out little plastic name tags. They passed through a turnstile at a security gate, and Alex was astonished to find herself in almost monastically simple corridors. There was no indication that scientists were working on the world's most advanced technologies behind these doors. They rode an elevator two stories underground; they reached a large anteroom with a steel door that looked like a vault.

"The hallowed halls are behind this door," Justin declared with reverence. Alex was amazed. "America's intellectual elite spends half of their lives here. The Western world's most powerful computers are here—supercomputers worth hundreds of millions of dollars. They're the heart and the brain of our modern technological world."

He positioned himself in front of a retina scanner, a green-lit windowpane that was embedded into the wall. It beeped, the steel door opened with a quiet clicking noise, and they entered an imposing hall.

"Welcome to the world of artificial intelligence," Justin said with a grin. Compared to the solemn silence of the upper stories, the large, fluorescent-lit room was almost shocking. Gray cabinets were lined up in long rows and made an unexpected amount of noise.

"These are air-conditioning units," Justin said, before Alex could even ask. "It would be unbearably hot in here without them. The computers need an enormous amount of electricity—almost as much as a small town."

Alex felt like a trespasser sneaking around in a restricted military bunker.

"We're working with the world's most advanced supercomputers," Justin continued. He stopped in front of one of the machines. It seemed practical and unimpressive and was housed in a plain gray cabinet. "For example, this is a Cray-2. With a memory of two terabytes, it can process about 1.6 million operations per second. That one over there is an ETA, which is already eight times more powerful. The SUPRENUM is even a little faster. It's connected to thirty-two parallel operating node computer systems and is capable of unbelievably complex processing. These contain the largest nonmilitary databases in the Western world."

Alex, Oliver, and Mark nodded in fascination. They continued walking.

"These supercomputers are quickly on their way to overcoming the limitations of the human brain. The future of our world belongs to machines like this," Justin said.

"Sounds like science fiction," Oliver remarked, and Justin grinned.

"Cool, isn't it?" he said. They had entered into a confusing labyrinth of hallways flanked by gigantic computers. After walking a while, they reached a row of offices—similar to the layout at LMI—separated only by glass walls. Justin entered the third glass box, its door bearing his name. As expected, the small room was stuffed to the gills with the most modern computer technology. An unimaginable array of computers and hardware components, drives, printers, monitors, and all kinds of other conceivable devices cluttered the room. An impressive tangle of cables disappeared into the floor. Justin sat down at his hopelessly overloaded desk, which had no fewer than five monitors on top of it. He leaned back and lit a cigarette. He simultaneously pushed a button, which started the exhaust fan in the ceiling.

Alex began briefing him on the PBA Steel matter and her suspicion that someone was transacting illegal business behind her back using her confidential information.

"Mark found out that there's a connection between the brokerage firm that purchased the stocks and LMI," she said, "and we'd love to know who's behind it."

Oliver explained to Justin about offshore companies and that it was virtually impossible to find out who founded them.

"Hmm." Justin scratched his head. "Your company created a corporation, which in turn is owned by another corporation that is involved in illegal business. Do I have that right?"

"Sort of." Alex was impressed by Justin's quick comprehension. "LMI has launched a fund that, among other things, is invested in a venture-capital company called SeaStarFriends, which in turn is registered on the British Virgin Islands."

Justin drummed his fingers on the desktop.

"Where should I start?" He looked at his visitors' faces.

"At LMI," Oliver decided.

"Can you get into LMI's central computer?" Mark inquired.

"That shouldn't be a problem." Justin nodded. "They're probably working with an industry-standard operating system."

"Are you familiar with that?" Alex wanted to know, and got an amused look.

"Just a little bit." Justin grinned.

He asked them for some information about LMI, and then his fingers whizzed around the keyboard. He raised his head with a smile after a few minutes.

"Welcome to LMI," he announced with a hint of pride and a touch of casual professionalism. "They're using BankManager 5.3. That's an old friend of mine, which makes things much easier."

Mark and Alex leaned forward in disbelief. Oliver grinned.

"LMI has an information security department," Alex said, voicing her concern. "They'll notice if someone invades the system from the outside."

"Sure"—Justin nodded—"BankManager 5.3 has a firewall, just like all the other corporate networks. But coincidentally, IBM gave us a contract for this system's security testing—something we frequently do for software companies. At that time, we installed a 'back door,' which allows us to circumvent the normal protections. We can gain access to the entire system at any given time."

"Does this mean," Mark asked, "that you can get into the central computer of any company that uses this software?"

"That's right." Justin leaned back with a satisfied smile on his face. "We're concerned with the system's security. We work on improving security to protect against attacks from lunatics who want to wreak havoc."

He turned his eyes back to the monitor and worked the keyboard relentlessly.

"Let's open the back door now and walk in," he said with a focused expression.

"BM 5.3 is protected by a secure-access firewall. This is a password-protected authentication method. Secure access works with Phazer, a fiber optic device that detects and defends against both internal and external attacks on the network."

Alex leaned forward and looked at the incomprehensible row of numbers and letters flashing by on the monitor.

"But if this thing recognizes every access," she asked, "how can you get into the system without anyone noticing?"

"Like I said, through the back door," Justin answered. "There's a command that gives me administrator's rights."

"Aha."

"Such a large and complex system as BM 5.3 naturally has strict access controls. The network administrator is the only authorized individual to read, modify, or delete any system files. He also assigns access rights to individual users and monitors them. BM 5.3 has a directory structure that we call Listing, with which the network administrator monitors access rights. Every user has his or her own identification code, the UIC. Based on this personal code, the computer recognizes which resources are available to the user after log-in."

"So those people who monitor everything can also snoop around in my files?" Alex asked in disbelief.

"Of course," Justin said.

"That's just unbelievable!" She shook her head in disgust. "I save tons of important things on my computer."

"If they are so secret that no one should know about them, then you shouldn't save them on your computer. I can show you a trick to set up a secret file even your administrator can't crack."

"You get full access with one simple command?" Mark was mightily impressed.

"Yes." Justin looked up and grinned. "Pretty easy, isn't it? You just need to know the command. If you tried to hack the passwords, it would attract attention right away. Most of the software for password hacking needs an incredible amount of capacity. We also happened to install Stealth into BM 5.3, a program that allows us to access the system unnoticed. It's named after the stealth bomber that enemy radar can't detect, and it makes the external user invisible to the network administrator."

"What's the secret command?" Mark asked curiously.

"I'll tell you," Justin answered with a smile, "because the command itself doesn't really get you very far."

He turned the monitor slightly to the right so that Alex, Oliver, and Mark could see the screen and typed a combination of numbers and letters on the keyboard.

RloginBM5.0LMINY.target.com-1-froot<

The screen turned black for a few seconds, and then the password prompt appeared.

"And now?" Mark asked.

"This system has an embedded command that circumvents the password. You have to think of it as a universal key."

>etx/passw/10pht.com.unix<

The computer hummed away busily. Then the monitor flickered and displayed a message that Justin obviously expected, but it took Alex and Mark's breathe away.

Welcome to Levy Manhattan Investments, New York City.

"Unbelievable," Alex murmured.

"Ingenious!" Mark said, visibly impressed.

"Now we have unrestricted access to the server." Justin licked his lips like a satisfied cat. "Let's see if we can solve your problem. What should I look for?"

"Private Equity Technology Partners," Alex said promptly.

"Fund management," Oliver added. It took a few minutes for Justin to find the securities department information after maneuvering through various LMI server interfaces.

"Holy cow," he said, "they've got hundreds of them!"

"Of course," Alex said, "investment funds are totally legal."

Oliver leaned forward and looked over Justin's shoulder.

"That's the one," he said. "May I?"

"Sure, go ahead." Justin moved aside obligingly. Alex marveled at Oliver's focus. She had never seen him at work before and noticed that he appeared to be on familiar ground. But after a while the hopeful tension in his face gave way to a look of resignation.

"This is the wrong place," he said, chewing pensively on his lower lip. "They only manage legal funds, and there's no indication of risky investments."

He gave Justin his seat back.

"We need to get into the database module where the offshore companies are managed," he said.

"Maybe they're not doing it from headquarters, but from a subsidiary in the Caymans or Switzerland."

"Okay," Justin said, "let me try a help command."

He typed in a combination of numbers and letters again.

"Ah, yes," he eventually said, "here it is. There are a number of limited partnerships that are owned by the company's subsidiaries. We have quite a big selection here: LMI in Los Angeles, Chicago, London, Frankfurt, Hong Kong, Cape Town, or Singapore; Banque Villiers Suisse in Geneva, Zurich, Monaco, and Liechtenstein; Levy & Villiers in Zurich, Nassau/ Bahamas, and Georgetown/Grand Cayman; LV Invest on Samoa and Labuan; SeViCo in Panama City, Gibraltar, Road Town/BVI..."

"Stop!" Oliver yelled; everyone looked at him in surprise.

"Let me see," he said. "They list SeViCo as a subsidiary of LMI? Unbelievable! I thought that only Vitali was behind this, but..."

His eyes met Alex's.

"SeViCo," she murmured, "could also be derived from Sergio and Vincent."

"Exactly," Oliver said, "and it would be the proof that the two of them are in it together."

Justin focused and worked silently for almost an hour, but then he shook his head.

"It's a dead end," he said. "I'm not getting anywhere with SeViCo. They do it differently; I don't get it."

The four of them were at a loss. How all of these companies were related to each other was too complex to figure out. Oliver jumped up and paced back and forth in the tiny office.

"Let's recap," he said. "Alex has a suspicion that someone conducts illegal business with her confidential information. Mark and Alex found out that MPM buys the stock of companies that are about to be acquired or merged. According to the commercial register, MPM is owned by Venture Capital SeaStarFriends Limited Partnership. In turn, a fund launched by LMI called Private Equity Technology Partners is invested in the latter. Correct?"

Alex and Mark nodded.

"SeaStarFriends is a partnership registered in the British Virgin Islands. All of this smells like money laundering." Oliver frowned and shook his head. "We need to approach this differently. Justin, can you try to get into the commercial registry on the British Virgin Islands?"

"Sure." Justin went back to work. Oliver, Mark, and Alex followed his efforts, tensely registering his every breath.

"I should work for the IRS," he said after about a half hour. "I'm in."

The three of them felt electrified.

"The safety measures are quite ridiculous." Justin pointed to his screen. "Here are the registration numbers of every company registered on the British Virgin Islands...Let's see..."

"Venture Capital SeaStarFriends Limited Partnership," Oliver said with a triumphant smile, "incorporated on May 25, 1998. The general partner is Vincent Isaac Levy, and the limited partner is Mr. Sergio Ignazio Vitali."

"My God," Alex whispered, "I can't believe it."

"MPM is owned by Levy and Vitali," Oliver said.

"Then Zack isn't working for himself. He's working for them." Alex felt miserable all of a sudden. Vincent Levy and Sergio Vitali made gigantic, risk-free profits through this fake company using insider information that *she* delivered to them! She didn't even have to look for the individual stock purchases—she was certain that MPM always bought before a merger or acquisition was publicly announced. Sergio must have made millions, if not billions, over the past few months! Rage rose within her. Sergio had been using her the whole time. Now she understood his attempt at reconciliation the night he was shot, as well as his marriage proposal: he was afraid that his golden goose would fly off if she left him. Worst of all, she didn't know what to do with this discovery. No one would believe that she hadn't a clue about MPM and SeaStarFriends. She was Sergio's lover. People would obviously think that she was an accomplice.

"That's exactly what Shanahan did," Oliver observed, but Alex didn't respond. He had been right the whole time!

"If there's one of these companies," Mark pointed out, "then there are probably more like it. And if LMI invests in them with its own funds, then that means Levy and Vitali profit. Tax free."

Alex felt a chill. Sergio and Levy started SeaStarFriends right when she joined LMI. They had profited from her deals from the very beginning. But in contrast to Shanahan, who knew what he was doing, she wasn't privy to the situation. Sergio had lied to her in every respect.

"What are they doing with all this dough?" Justin threw out. "I mean, what do you need all those millions for?"

"If you have one million, then you want two," Oliver replied. "If you have two, then you want ten; and if you have ten, you want a hundred. The greed of some people is virtually insatiable."

"This setup is almost perfect," Mark observed. "Really, we should admire anyone who could come up with this."

"That's true," Oliver said, "and it's absolutely safe for the people pulling the strings. If one of these companies goes bust, then you can hardly trace it back to whoever is behind it. The authorities are busy enough. If one of the trails leads to an offshore financial center, they'll simply drop it and keep going after little guys they can catch in their own country."

"Nevertheless," Alex said, trying to maintain her composure, although she was boiling inside, "Justin's question is valid. I'd also love to find out what they're doing with all this money. Vitali already has everything that money can buy. There must be another reason why he's doing this."

"What do you mean?" Oliver cast her a probing glance, but Alex didn't answer. She suddenly remembered a conversation that she'd overheard during the charity event at the Plaza. The wife of New

York's building commissioner told Vincent Levy's wife that they had been vacationing in the Caymans at Sergio's expense. Did Sergio repay McIntyre for a favor in this way?

"Justin," Alex asked, "could you get into the computer of Levy & Villiers in Georgetown on Grand Cayman?"

"I can try," he said.

"What do you expect to find?" Oliver asked in surprise.

"Maybe nothing," Alex said, "but maybe material that will secure your Pulitzer Prize."

Oliver grinned, but Justin's face turned grim after a few minutes.

"I need a specific password in order to get into the network on the Caymans," he said.

"Why's that? Do they use a different operating system?" Mark asked.

"It's an added safety feature." Justin shrugged his shoulders. "The computer isn't linked to the one in New York."

He went to work at a different computer.

Eventually, he said, "Let's grab some food. If we're lucky, CryptCrack will hack the password by the time we're back."

"What the hell is that?" Mark wanted to know.

"CryptCrack," Justin said, "is a password-hacking program that I recently developed. Now I can test it in real circumstances."

They left the computer alone with this Herculean task and went to the MIT cafeteria, located in a different building on the campus. They were starving after so many tense hours in the basement.

Mary Kostidis sighed. Even though he didn't say anything, more and more she could feel the enormous pressure weighing on her husband. Vitali Junior's death, the hostilities in the press, and this strange terrorist—all of this strained his nerves. At last night's dinner for the Canadian ambassador, Nick was his old entertaining, charming, and relaxed self for a while. However, when Mary later went into his office—where he had disappeared with Ray Howard—she could tell from his expression that something else had happened. She asked him about it afterward, but he simply dismissed her question.

In the past, Nick had involved her in his life. They discussed their problems with each other, and he'd asked for her opinion. But during the last few months, something had changed between them. For the first time in their long marriage, Mary Kostidis didn't know what her husband was dealing with. Why was he hiding important things from her? When she stepped out on the terrace last night, she had thought for a brief, crazy moment that there could possibly be another woman in his life. Mary noticed how her husband looked at Alex Sontheim, the beautiful and highly intelligent banker. The expression on his face caused a painful sting in her heart. For as long as she'd known him, he had never given her such an enraptured and fascinated look. Had Nick fallen in love with her? Without a doubt, Alex was an extraordinary woman: successful, independent, and exceptionally sharp. She was beautiful, but she was also Sergio Vitali's lover. Was that possibly the reason why he had invited her? Did Nick think that he could finally get to his archenemy through Alex? Or was there more behind it?

The morning was still fresh, but the heat would become unbearable in a few hours. The months of July and August were intolerable in the city, which is why many New Yorkers who could afford to spent their time in the countryside or near the ocean did so. Nick Kostidis sat in the office at Gracie Mansion with his assistants Frank Cohen and Ray Howard, something they often did on Sunday mornings. After a light breakfast, they discussed important issues for which they rarely had time otherwise. Frank read the agenda for the imminent visit of a Korean delegation, and Nick watched out the window as Christopher and Britney loaded their luggage into their black BMW. He was glad that they were taking Mary with them for a while. The way that things were developing here, it seemed better for to get her out of the city for a few days. Especially considering the second threatening letter. Frank vehemently insisted on getting Nick more security, but he didn't tell Mary any of this. There were some things he preferred to keep to himself to avoid unnecessarily upsetting his wife. Mary had been nervous, even depressed in recent months. Time and again, Nick caught her staring absentmindedly out the window. She was usually bursting with energy, but now she seemed to be collapsing like a withered flower. He feared that she was sick, but none of the doctors could explain her condition. They advised him to shield her from any worries and show her more attention. But he missed exchanging ideas with Mary. For so many years, she had accepted the idea that his work had priority without complaining. Now, in her weakened state, he decided not to bother her with his worries.

It had been difficult for him to maintain his fearless and strong demeanor recently, because he felt increasingly discouraged and depressed. Things had gotten worse because he secretly longed for a woman other than his own wife. Nick couldn't explain his fascination for Alex Sontheim, but there wasn't a single day that he didn't think about her. Yesterday evening, he'd noticed with a racing heart that her open aversion toward him had given way to a cautious sympathy. Maybe it would have been better not to invite her after all.

"I think they're having problems with the car," Frank observed and pulled Nick from his thoughts. "It looks like it's not starting."

"Let me take a look." Nick stood up. "I'll be back in a moment."

"The alternator is dead," Christopher Kostidis announced as his father stepped into the parking lot. Carey Lhota shrugged his shoulders and stepped back from the open hood.

"Unfortunately, I can't do anything about it," the chauffeur apologized.

"Too bad," Mary said. "Now we have to postpone our departure for a few hours."

"We can't fix it that fast." Christopher was annoyed as he looked under the hood. "Especially on a Sunday."

"Well," Nick said with a grin, "if you drove a solid American car, then…"

"Then it'd also take time to get a new alternator," Christopher proudly defended his BMW.

"Why don't you take my car," Nick suggested. "Carey can bring the BMW to the repair shop tomorrow."

"But you still need the car," Mary objected.

"I can ride with Frank or Ray." Nick shook his head. "That's no problem."

"I hope you're not riding around town on the subway?" Mary looked at her husband with concern.

"No, I know you don't like when I do that." Nick laughed and put an arm around his wife's waist.

"I'd really like to leave before it occurs to the rest of New York to go to Long Island." Christopher looked at his watch.

"Come on!" Nick called. "Reload your luggage."

Mary took his hand.

"Can't you come with us for a few days?" she asked. Nick smiled and touched her face with both of his hands.

"You know what I was just thinking?" he said quietly. "I actually thought about coming out to Montauk on Friday."

"Really?" Mary looked at her husband incredulously. "And your work?"

"I'll arrange it somehow." He kissed her.

"You promise?" Mary suddenly seemed genuinely happy.

"Yes, I promise. I'm looking forward to it."

"We're ready to go, Mom!" Christopher called. Britney was already sitting in the limousine's passenger seat.

"I love you, Nick," Mary whispered. "Take good care of yourself!"

"What the heck are they doing?"

Raymond Howard looked out the window and saw Christopher Kostidis sitting behind the wheel of the limousine. His face suddenly turned as white as a sheet.

"What's going on?" Frank asked his colleague in surprise.

"My God, no. They must not under any circumstance…" Howard fell silent. Cold sweat broke out on his forehead. He saw Mary Kostidis kissing her husband good-bye. Christopher waved impatiently and called out something, while Britney Edwards sat in the passenger seat and smiled.

"Shit!" Howard cursed and charged out the door as if being chased by furies. Frank didn't understand what was happening. Howard ran down the long corridor as fast as he could. The limousine had just rolled out of the parking lot as he jumped down the stairs. Mary and Britney waved from the open windows. Howard saw Nick smile and wave. He saw the dark blue car and ran after it, without regard for what his boss thought about him.

"Stop!" he screamed, running after the car with wildly waving arms. "Stop! Stop at once! Get out of the car, right now!"

When Justin got back to his desk, he found that CryptCrack had actually done its job, and he laughed like a little boy. He rubbed his hands and turned his gaze toward the screen. For a while, he seemed to forget everything around him. Just Oliver and Alex returned to MIT's basement with Justin. During their meal, they'd decided that Mark should fly back to New York. Although Alex hadn't eaten anything since the evening at Gracie Mansion, she couldn't manage more than half a sandwich. Her stomach was tied in knots, and not just because of Oliver's probing glance, directed at her every now and then. What should she do if her suspicion was confirmed? How could she keep working at a firm that was involved in such illegal business? And how could she ever get rid of Sergio? She felt trapped, controlled by these people.

"There's a high security area in the Levy & Villiers computer," Justin said suddenly, startling Alex out of her thoughts. "There's nothing unusual here at first sight, but some files are ultrasecure."

"Can you get into them?" Oliver asked and Justin nodded. Except for the clicking of the keyboard, it was completely quiet in the office. Mark's presence had neutralized the tension between them, but now it was back again and any levity had disappeared.

"Weird," Justin said after a while, "these are just anonymous numbered accounts."

"Let me see," Oliver and Alex said at the same time, looking over Justin's shoulder.

Alex explained to Justin how people opened numbered accounts. Anywhere in the world, the client needed to present proof of identity to the bank. But after that, the account was given a number or fictitious name known only to the client and the bank's employee. Clients were protected from detection by the authorities—at least at banks in Switzerland, Liechtenstein, Luxembourg, or the Caribbean. These banks provided the utmost discretion and lured individuals with wealth of questionable origin. The Bahamas and the Caymans attracted many people who didn't want to travel as far as Europe to evade taxation or the judicial authorities.

"What are you hoping to find?" Oliver asked curiously.

"Some kind of evidence of what they do with the money," Alex replied. "MPM wasn't created for their personal enrichment. Neither Levy nor Vitali needs to make money from insider trading. They're wealthy enough already. There's another reason why they're doing this, and I want to find that out."

Nick Kostidis turned around in surprise as his assistant charged down the stairs, screaming and waving. Nick registered the expression of terror and panic on Howard's face, but he didn't understand why this man—who was usually casual, cynical—was behaving this way. Howard was completely beside himself, chasing after the dark-blue car. Christopher seemed to have spotted him in the rearview mirror because he slowed down the car.

All of a sudden, Nick was overcome by a terrible premonition, and he instinctively also started to run. He saw Mary's confused face through the car window as her smile vanished. Howard had just touched the door handle when a bright darting flame sparked from the limousine's front hood; the car's hood catapulted several yards into the air like a toy. Just a split second later, an enormous explosion shocked the car and ripped it to pieces.

Not comprehending what was happening in front of his eyes, Nick saw the explosive flame. The shock wave of the explosion, which even shattered some of the house windows, blew him off his feet and tossed him against the wall. Dazed and shocked, Nick crawled on all fours toward the burning inferno that the bomb had left behind on this peaceful Sunday morning.

"Mary!" he screamed. "Oh my God, no! Mary! Mary!"

Frank Cohen appeared in the door and stared uncomprehendingly at this horrific image. Nick had crawled to within a few yards of the burning car, and Frank ran after him without thinking about his own safety.

At that moment, the fuel tank exploded, and Frank jumped on his boss, who screamed as if he'd lost his mind. Nick hardly noticed Frank holding him back. He struggled, kicked his legs, and screamed like a mortally wounded animal. He was close to jumping into the flames, although it was too late to save anyone. The three people in the car were long dead. Nick saw Howard stumbling around the burning lawn like a living torch, and white flames were hurling up from the glowing red car wreck into the branches of an old chestnut tree.

"Mary!" he screamed madly. "Mary! Mary! *Oh my God, NO!*"

Nick didn't feel the scorching heat burning his skin. He didn't notice that a glowing piece of metal had pierced his arm. He felt no pain, only horror—abysmally cruel horror. The blast of the two explosions had startled the security officers. Devastated, they gazed at the burning pile that had just been an armored limousine. One of the men had the presence of mind to aim a fire extinguisher at Howard as he collapsed on the charred grass, his body jerking and curling up into a ball.

Carey Lhota lay unconscious at the bottom of the stairs—the blast had thrown him and smashed his head against the steps. The air was filled with dense smoke and the smell of gasoline and burned flesh. The glowing firestorm had burned all the flowers, and the branches of the massive chestnut were now ablaze. Wreckage was scattered everywhere, and the grass on the lawn had turned to gray ash.

The staff of Gracie Mansion ran outside and looked in shock at this horrible scene that resembled a plane crash. Nick had stopped fighting. He lay on the ground, sobbing, with his burned fingers clawed into the ground; he kept stammering his wife's and son's names. Blood ran over his face and poured out of a deep wound on his left arm. He couldn't take his gaze off the burning wreck in which his entire family had died before his eyes.

"Get him away from here!" Frank yelled at the security officers. "Move it! Take him inside the house!"

Someone had called the fire department, and several fire trucks with loudly wailing sirens now sped through the park ahead of police cars and an ambulance. Frank Cohen's entire body shook. He was incapable of comprehending what had just taken place. The threatening letters were serious. Someone had just tried to kill Nick Kostidis, but they got his family instead.

And Ray…Frank's gaze was filled with terror as it wandered to the burned figure. Ray had known it! He was the mole that Nick was looking for. Frank's legs caved beneath him. He sank to the ground and groped for his broken glasses as mayhem broke out around him. Firefighters, police, paramedics, and security officers screamed at each other. The water hoses were unrolled, but it was too late—much too late—after the water and foam finally extinguished the flames.

"According to the latest report, Nick Kostidis was not in the vehicle when the bomb exploded at ten after eleven this morning at Gracie Mansion," the visibly shocked TV reporter said. *"Although there are no official reports yet, it appears that at least three individuals have lost their lives in the explosion. According to unconfirmed sources, the victims are the mayor's wife, his son, and his son's fiancée. An unidentified man with serious burns was rushed to the burn unit at Columbia Presbyterian…"*

Sergio stared at the TV with a straight face. He slowly turned to the two men standing silently behind him.

"You screwed it up." His voice was as cold as a glacier, and there was a deep crease of displeasure between his eyes. "What good is it to us if his wife and son are dead?"

Luca and Silvio looked down at the ground in embarrassment.

"Fucking hell!" Sergio suddenly screamed. "Am I surrounded by amateurs? Who had this idiotic idea of a car bomb?"

"Howard called us," Luca eventually said. "First we planned to kill him on his way to the subway, but then Howard told us that he would take the limousine from now on for security reasons. A car bomb seemed to be the safest bet."

"The safest thing would have been to put a bullet into this bastard's head," Sergio interrupted him angrily. "God damn it!"

"But then it wouldn't have looked like an accident," Silvio countered. "And you said—"

The telephone rang.

"I know what I said!" Sergio snarled at him. "A bomb doesn't exactly look like an accident either!"

He signaled Luca to pick up the telephone.

"It's Mr. van Mieren," Luca said, and Sergio grabbed the phone. Nelson had been in Las Vegas since yesterday.

"I'm watching the news right now," Nelson said, not wasting time to say hello. "I hope you've got nothing to do with this."

"With what?"

"The bomb attack on the mayor."

"Why would you think I had something to do with it?" Sergio controlled his anger, acting surprised.

"Because you just recently talked about getting Kostidis out of the way."

"He's got a lot of enemies in this city besides me."

"I wish I believed you, Sergio." Nelson sighed. "I've never questioned anything that you've done before. But this time I'll only ask you once, and for our long friendship's sake, I'm asking you to tell me the truth."

"Is there someone with you?" Sergio asked warily.

Nelson was speechless for a moment. How could he be suspicious?

"Of course not," he replied in irritation. "I'm calling from a secure telephone, and I'm alone. So?"

Sergio didn't hesitate to take advantage of his oldest friend's trust.

"I had nothing to do with the attack," he said in a calm voice. "When I said to get Kostidis out of the way, I didn't think about anything like this."

Nelson wasn't quite convinced, but he also had a hard time believing that Sergio would lie to him. After their conversation, Sergio turned to Luca and Silvio.

"Nelson mustn't find out that we were involved in this. And it's better if Massimo doesn't know about it either."

The two men nodded silently. They were relieved that their boss had seemed to come to terms with the botched operation.

"Okay," Sergio said, "this one went wrong. The next time we'll be more successful."

The telephone rang again, and Luca picked up.

"It's St. John," he said. Sergio took the call. His face darkened noticeably while he listened, and then he hung up. Raymond Howard was dead. The loss of this important informer was more painful to Sergio than the failed assassination. Howard had been supplying him with invaluable information straight from the mayor's office over the past several years. But Sergio Vitali tended not to worry about what he couldn't change. Kostidis's days were numbered anyway. Once the mayor was dead, he wouldn't need a mole to spy on him anymore.

It was ten at night when Justin succeeded in penetrating the secret numbered accounts file at Levy & Villiers on Grand Cayman. Alex, Oliver, and Justin looked through countless accounts. Although many of them would have been interesting for the US tax authorities, the ones that Alex hoped to find were not among them. Justin eventually came across an extremely secure file that instantly aroused his curiosity. It took him almost an hour and a half to successfully hack it. The silence in the small room was thick enough to cut with a knife. The ashtray overflowed. Soda cans, empty packs of chips, and chocolate bar wrappers gathered around Justin's revolving chair.

"Fucking hell," he said quietly. "I've actually done it! We're in!"

His eyes were glowing, and he grinned triumphantly. It was a tricky affair, yet he'd found a way to crack into the highly secure file.

"The guys in this joint really know their stuff when it comes to data security," he said with honest admiration for his counterparts.

Alex and Oliver, who were about to fall asleep after several long hours in the cold fluorescent light of the basement office, jerked to attention.

"I think I found what you're looking for," said Justin, and Alex moved her chair next to his. She stared at the screen and couldn't believe her eyes. The bankers on Grand Cayman had meticulously listed the account numbers and code names together with the dates the accounts were opened. These were followed by the name of the account holder and the address.

"What's this?" Oliver asked. Alex didn't answer.

"Is it normal to list addresses and names?" Justin asked.

"It's not unusual," Alex said, "because the bank is bound to secrecy by law. As you can see, it's impossible to stumble upon this data. It seems pretty secure to me."

She scanned an account statement with the code name "Amazed" that listed Mr. Frederick P. Hoffman as its owner. To her surprise, there were no investment funds or stock portfolios, just regular cash deposits in staggering amounts.

"What's this?" Oliver urged curiously.

"Exactly what I was afraid to find." Alex looked at him. "Bribes paid to numbered accounts."

Oliver's eyes widened and Alex turned toward the screen again.

"Senator Fred Hoffman," she said. "I know him!"

His account had a balance of 1.8 million dollars. Tax free, illegal, paid in cash.

"Anyone else?" Justin asked as his fingers hovered over the keyboard.

"Zachary St. John," Alex replied and nervously rubbed the moist palms of her hands together. Justin typed in his name, and seconds later the account statement appeared.

"Code name: Goldfinger." Justin grinned.

"Typical," Alex said in a mocking tone. She was astonished to see how much Zack had amassed over the years. The staggering cash deposits took away Alex's breath. Zack didn't fool around! The balance of his account was a respectable twenty-two million dollars.

"Unbelievable." She shook her head. For the next two hours, they worked through all fifty-four of the secret accounts at Levy & Villiers in Georgetown, Grand Cayman. And what they found pointed to one of the biggest corruption cases of all time. They came across the names of Governor Robert Landford Rhodes; John de Lancie, the US Attorney for the Southern District of New York; David Norman, a board member of the NYSE; and Jerome Harding, New York's police commissioner. Greg Tarrance was a high-ranking administrator at the SEC's enforcement division. Alex knew his name because it had appeared time and again in connection with investigations. Senator Hoffman was only one of many politicians who helped themselves to tax-free additional income. The deposits to all the accounts always occurred on the same day and were always in cash.

Alex slowly started to understand what was going on. She couldn't help but admire whoever had come up with this simple yet ingenious system. Every time Alex told St. John about an imminent deal, he ordered the broker Jack Lang to buy stock of the company that was subject to a merger or acquisition for MPM. Once the stock price skyrocketed due to the public announcement of the deal, Lang sold the stock, and the proceeds of the sale were transported to Grand Cayman in cash, probably by St. John himself. With one of Vitali's private jets, they could easily circumvent customs. This method of raising funds was highly illegal, but they were protected by high-ranking judges, US attorneys, SEC administrators, and

NYSE board members on their bribery payroll. If there were transgressions, no one was interested in investigating any further.

Alex vividly remembered PBA Steel. No wonder Sergio didn't worry about the SEC. The investigation had fizzled out after just two days, with no resolution. Sergio had bribed the most influential men of the city and state, his connections reaching as far as Washington DC. His "friends" were in Congress, the Senate, the Department of Justice, the Department of the Treasury, and the Department of Defense. With these accounts, he had wonderful leverage against them. Passive corruption by itself was ruinous for a politician or public officer, but not paying taxes on this income was highly punishable as tax fraud.

"Some of them get ten grand a month." Justin was amazed. "This one doesn't seem to be as important. He only gets three."

Alex's eyes fell on the name, and she froze. *Raymond Howard.* Alex remembered the man with the thin blond hair whom she'd seen at the Plaza for the first time and then at Gracie Mansion last night. He was the man Nick Kostidis was looking for! Nick suspected that there was an informer on his staff, but he had no idea that it was one of his most trusted employees. And then she remembered where else she had seen him. He was with Zack at Luna Luna that evening when she'd celebrated the Maxxam deal with her staff. Raymond Howard knew Zack! Now that she was aware of it, she needed to tell Nick. She couldn't possibly leave him in the dark any longer.

"What are you going to do now?" Justin asked as they left the Media Lab building feeling drained sixteen hours after their arrival. Outside it was dawn, and the birds chirped in the trees. Justin had printed the entire dossier, and Alex carried it in her briefcase. She felt like she had pure explosives under her arm.

"I don't know," she replied, "but I don't feel like making myself a target. If Vitali finds out that I know about these secret accounts, he'll kill me."

Justin stared at her.

"You can't be serious."

"Absolutely," Alex said, nodding, "this isn't petty embezzlement. This is an elaborate web of bribes, and I'm in the middle of it. As of today, I can't claim that I don't know anything about this."

They reached the nearly empty parking lot and squeezed into Justin's dusty Nissan. Justin dropped them off at the airport a half hour later. Oliver and Alex thanked him for his incredibly helpful work and promised to keep him posted. Without saying a word, they entered the departure terminal and inquired about the next flight to New York. They reserved two seats for the 6:20 a.m. flight and then walked to the coffee shop, where only a few early travelers and the crew of a Far East airline were passing the time.

Alex realized that Oliver would have liked to talk about something entirely different, but she couldn't get her thoughts off the findings of the past few hours. She no longer had a future in New York. They silently drank their coffee and chewed on doughnuts while Alex stared at the TV, which was tuned to CNN. Suddenly, she dropped her coffee cup. The blood drained from her face when she realized what the reporter was talking about. She jumped up and ran to the bar.

"Could you please turn it up a little?" she asked the waitress. The woman grabbed the remote control and turned up the volume. Aghast, Alex listened to the reporter.

"Initial investigations by the FBI's explosives experts indicate that the bomb was placed under the hood of the mayor's armored limousine. Kostidis's wife Mary, his son Christopher, and his son's fiancée Britney Edwards were killed in this attack. Another man who attempted to save the three individuals from the flames suffered severe burns and succumbed to his injuries

one hour later at Columbia Presbyterian. Mayor Kostidis, the alleged target of this assassination attempt, was admitted to Mount Sinai Hospital. No details have yet been disclosed about his condition."

"Oh my God!" Alex whispered. Her heart was pounding in her chest, and she felt sick. It couldn't be true! She had just talked to Mary and Christopher Kostidis so recently. And now they were dead? Oliver stood up and put his arm around her shoulders.

"I was at Gracie Mansion on Saturday evening," Alex said, her whole body shaking, "and now they're dead! I can't believe it!"

Oliver held her a little tighter in his arms. The television showed images from the lawn at Gracie Mansion, and Alex saw the smoldering remnants of the car. The power of the detonation had torn the heavy limousine into two pieces, making the lawn look like a battlefield.

"Excuse me." Alex freed herself from Oliver's arms and ran out to the restroom. Tears poured down her face as she sat sobbing on the floor of the closed bathroom stall. Nick Kostidis had publicly voiced dangerous allegations after Cesare's death and the attempt on Sergio. She admired him for his courage, but now she realized that this had to be the reason for the attack. The mayor had come too close to the truth and become a risk for Sergio Vitali.

Alex pressed her face into her hands. This brutal man had proposed marriage to her just a few days ago! She wiped the tears from her cheeks. Nick Kostidis had asked for her help a number of times, but she'd refused because she was afraid of the consequences. She'd been too big a coward, and now Nick's family had been cruelly annihilated. Alex closed her eyes. Wasn't she also to blame? She had known since last summer that David Zuckerman had been killed on Sergio's order. If she had told Nick at the time, everything might have turned out differently. Or not? She felt more miserable than she ever had in her life. She gradually realized the far-reaching consequences of her discovery, and she almost regretted her curiosity. This was no longer about lies and hurt pride. If she used her knowledge, undeniably triggering an enormous scandal, then more than just her job would be on the line. Sergio wouldn't sit idly by while his empire wavered, and she knew exactly what he was capable of. She was scared, terribly scared. And there was no one who could help her.

The flight from Boston landed at eight thirty. Oliver and Alex took a cab together to Manhattan.

"What are you going to do now?" Oliver asked in concern.

"I can't do anything," Alex replied. Fear had overcome her. She made sure that the dividing glass to the driver was closed, but she still whispered. "I know that Sergio had David Zuckerman killed last summer, and that he ordered the assassination attempt on Kostidis. If he finds out that I have the slightest idea, then I'm dead."

Oliver gave her a perplexed stare.

"I have to keep playing along and try to maneuver myself out of this mess by making bad deals. And I've got another idea."

"What are you going to do with these documents?"

"I'll put them in a safety-deposit box at some bank."

"Let me take care of that," Oliver said, grabbing her hand.

"No." She vehemently shook her head. "I don't want anything else to happen to you. I have to fight this war by myself."

They looked at each other in silence.

"Thanks," Alex whispered when the taxi stopped in front of her building.

"Please take care of yourself, Alex," Oliver said seriously, "and call me soon. We'll find a solution together."

She nodded and quickly kissed his cheek before she got out. Just the thought that Sergio owned the apartment in which she lived filled her with horror. After she took a shower and got dressed, she pushed the printouts of the numbered accounts beneath the TV.

On her way to the subway, she bought a paper and came across a small article on the fifth page while riding downtown. One of the journalists wondered why Syncrotron had filed for bankruptcy yesterday as there'd been noticeably active trading in Syncrotron shares recently. "*The question remains,*" Alex read with a grim smile, "*who would buy shares of a company such as Syncrotron that apparently had liquidity issues and no future. At the very least, this small manufacturer of circuit boards that became a total bust (due to incompetent management and lack of innovation) will turn into a nightmare today for these daring investors.*"

Alex folded the newspaper. Zack should know by now that MPM was sitting on a pile of worthless stock. She didn't think that the company would get into any serious trouble because the stock purchases were likely fully financed by LMI or even personally by Sergio. There would be no callback where the borrowed money would have to be returned, which is what happened every now and then when a speculator placed a wrong bet. Nevertheless, it was possible that the SEC would initiate an investigation. It was very unusual for someone to accumulate such a large position in a company known to be on the brink of bankruptcy. This absolutely smelled like insider trading. Alex wished that she could hole up somewhere. The lack of sleep and the terrible news about the bomb had her depressed, and she didn't feel up to the challenge of an imminent confrontation with Sergio or Zack. The clarity with which she saw her situation was frightening, paralyzing. Just one small mistake on her part could have fatal consequences.

At nine thirty, Alex paced through the blue-tiled Wall Street subway station to the escalators. She could hardly believe that life continued as if nothing had happened. In light of her discoveries and the tragedy, it seemed that everything should be different now. But in the bright Monday-morning sunlight, the city seemed as busy as ever. Alex saw her secretary standing near the glass door at the entrance of the trading floor. She'd been desperately waiting for her.

"Alex!" she called in relief and ran toward her. "Finally! The telephone's ringing off the hook! And Mr. St. John is waiting for you in your office. He's really pissed off!"

"Thanks, Marcia," Alex replied. The familiar environment helped her cope with her confusion. She crossed the trading floor and nodded to the traders, who were yelling and wildly gesticulating on the telephone as usual. She flung open the glass door to her office with élan. Zack, who'd been wandering around nervously, quickly turned around.

"Where the hell have you been all weekend?" he yelled furiously. "Why don't you answer your cell phone?"

"Good morning, Zack," Alex replied, pretending to be calm. "I was in the country. Did something happen?"

"What's going on with Syncrotron?"

"Syncrotron?" Alex feigned astonishment. Zack's face was as white as a ghost. He had dark circles under his eyes. There was nothing left of his arrogance and pride.

"Yes, damn it! Are you deaf?"

"Why are you so upset?" Alex sat down and began to look through the phone messages Marcia had placed neatly on her desk.

"Here!" Zack slammed the newspaper that she'd already read on the table, sending her notes flying. He poked his finger at the article about Syncrotron's bankruptcy so hard it seemed he wanted to pierce the tabletop. She shot a quick glance at the newspaper.

"What idiot would buy stock in this company?" she said calmly. Zack went speechless, and his face turned bright red.

"But…but…you…" he stammered, then gave her an uncomprehending look. Alex had never mentioned a single word about Syncrotron. He had just found a note on her desk and plans for an LBO in her computer.

"I what?" Alex looked at him with her eyebrows raised, but on the inside she felt triumphant. Zack had stepped right into her trap without even checking the facts about Syncrotron, as any proper banker should have done. He stared at her with a murderous rage.

"Why are you even upset?" Alex forced herself to smile. "We're in no way involved with Syncrotron."

That was too much for Zack. He was so full of anger that he couldn't even think straight anymore.

"You worked on an LBO for Syncrotron!" It burst out of him. "I know for sure! The numbers looked good, and it seemed like a safe bet!"

"Why would I have prepared an LBO for a company that was sure to go bankrupt soon? That would have been a total waste of time." Alex shook her head unsympathetically. "What makes you think that?"

"I…I've…I'm…" He wiped the sweat off his forehead with the back of his hands and then took a deep breath. "I saw the papers on your desk."

Alex couldn't believe that he actually admitted to it.

"If I understand you correctly, you snooped around in my desk," she said. "Apart from that blatant lack of respect, I have to tell you that…"

She paused and then slapped her hand against her forehead as if something had just occurred to her.

"Ahh, now I know what you're talking about!" she said. "I had a new potential client. It's already been a couple of months; I think that I even told you about it. I *did* actually prepare some numbers for them. I just replaced their real name with an alias. Maybe I picked Syncrotron."

Zack looked as if he would faint at any second.

"I do that frequently." Alex smiled. "After all, I don't want everyone to know right away what I'm working on."

Zack fell into the chair in front of her desk and ran all ten fingers through his hair.

"I can't believe you snooped around my desk—"

"Damn it!" Zack hissed, interrupting Alex. "Such stupid shit! You assign different names to your clients? That's the most fucked-up thing I've ever heard!"

"Why are you so upset?" Alex acted dismayed. "It's my decision how I code my projects."

Zack's gaze wandered through the office aimlessly. This is how desperate investors must have looked after the crash on Black Monday, when they heard that they'd become penniless overnight.

"I see." Alex looked at him closely. "Don't tell me that you've speculated on your own account? And you got smoked."

She leaned back.

"Did you actually invest in other deals I told you about? That's called insider trading."

"I could wring your neck," he hissed through his clenched teeth. Then he jumped up and left her office. The smile vanished from Alex's face. His fury removed any lingering doubts. Zack hadn't shied away from breaking into her computer and rifling through her desk in order to find out what she was working on. She was part of a huge scheme, and that was the irrevocable truth.

Alex gathered the messages and started to sort them. Sergio had tried to reach her. She had to call him now for tactical reasons, even though every part of her being opposed it. Since this morning, her aversion had turned to pure fear. She needed to pretend that she was outraged about Zack's illegal dealings and his breach of trust. She needed to act normally. Under any circumstances, she couldn't raise Sergio's suspicions.

After the bombing, a wave of compassion washed over the population—even those who didn't support Nick Kostidis and his policies sincerely grieved for the mayor's family. Countless people placed bouquets of flowers at the gate of Gracie Mansion and city hall. They lit candles and waited patiently in the sweltering summer heat to sign one of the condolence books. The bombing had been the feature story on TV and radio stations nationwide for the past ten days. Even the tiniest development was extensively covered. Wild speculation about the bombers' motives circulated in the media, but little progress was made in getting to the truth. Outside city hall and Mount Sinai Hospital, concerned citizens and reporters waited patiently for news about the mayor's health. All of the city's churches and synagogues held services for the victims of the attack.

Frank Cohen had lived through the worst ten days of his life. Since that fateful Sunday morning, he had been peppered with questions from all directions about the incident at Gracie Mansion. Although he wasn't an eyewitness, agents and officers of the FBI, the NYPD, and the Department of State asked him the same questions over and over. Did Nick Kostidis have enemies? Of course he did—what a stupid question! Any man in his position had enemies. With his blunt candor, Nick had inevitably stepped on some toes.

The worst thing about the endless questioning was that Frank actually knew who was behind this attack, but he couldn't say a word until he had spoken to Nick. Filled with horror, he recalled the sight of Raymond Howard. Every time he closed his eyes, he could see the man's badly burned face. The explosion had ripped off both of his hands. It would have been more merciful if he had died right away.

When the security officers rushed Nick into the house after the bomb went off, Frank rushed to Howard's side. Just five minutes before, Ray Howard had been a good-looking man with a fit body, but now he was a horrific sight. His hair, his eyebrows—everything was burned. His skin looked as if it had shrunk. Ray looked like a mummy, but he was still alive. Despite his disgust, Frank leaned over him as the paramedic carefully wrapped the burned body in aluminum foil. Ray had extended what was left of his arm toward him, and the eyes in this cruelly disfigured face looked up at him in desperation. He tried over and over to tell him something before Frank finally understood. Ray was telling him who was responsible for the attack, but that was no surprise. The really shattering insight was that Ray Howard—who had been Frank's colleague for six years and worked by his side almost every day—was the mole Nick had been so desperate to uncover.

Frank Cohen took on the difficult task of calling the relatives. He called Mary's sister Maureen, her parents, and the parents of Britney Edwards. He talked to the shocked and crying staff at Gracie Mansion, and then he drove to city hall to take on a responsibility that weighed heavily on his shoulders. All he wanted to do was hole up somewhere and cry. He worshiped Nick Kostidis like a father and it grieved Frank enormously that he couldn't help him. But he couldn't afford to collapse. He had to stay strong—unlike Allie Mitchell and many other members of the mayor's staff. Everyone at city hall was paralyzed in the days after the attack, wondering how they could possibly go on with their work. Official events were canceled, and all flags in New York City flew at half-mast. Hundreds of condolence calls and letters flooded into the mayor's office each day. It was a small consolation that there were kind-hearted people in this cold, monstrous city. Although he usually shunned public appearances, Frank rose to the challenge. He spoke to the press, helped the deputy mayor put a crisis team together, and kept a level head. He helped clean up the debris from the explosion after the police had concluded their investigation. Not a trace remained of Sunday's tragedy, which had wiped out four lives and possibly destroyed another one forever.

Vincent Levy and Sergio Vitali sat across from each other at La Côte Basque, a renowned French restaurant on West Fifty-Fifth Street. Levy felt the need to tell Sergio what went wrong with Syncotron after Alex clued him in. He would have preferred not to tell him, but new safety measures were in order that required discussion.

"Unfortunately, Zack acted the fool," Levy concluded his remarks.

"This man is a weak link," Sergio replied.

"Yes. Unfortunately. Especially when it comes to Alex Sontheim," Levy confirmed. "Sometimes it almost seems like he's jealous of her success."

Sergio furrowed his brow in thought. Alex had been outraged when she called him, and he had to force himself to listen calmly and not scream at her. She was at Gracie Mansion as the mayor's guest on Saturday night! Was she double-dealing? Why else hadn't she told him about this invitation? What did she talk about with Kostidis? Did she know he was behind this bombing? He couldn't afford to underestimate Alex under any circumstances. She was too clever. He couldn't afford any mistakes, but at the moment, it seemed like she was provoking him to do exactly that. Because of St. John's stupidity, she could be growing suspicious.

"We need something that we can use against her," Levy contemplated, "but what?"

Sergio cleared his throat. He had been thinking about that for days. He knew that Levy was right.

"We'll open an account in her name and deposit money from deals that she closes for LMI. We'll book a flight in her name to the Bahamas, send a woman who looks like her, and once the account is open we'll have leverage against her."

"Hmm." Levy pondered. "That sounds pretty good."

Sergio reached into his inner jacket pocket.

"Here's her passport," he said. "I have too many things to deal with right now. Take care of St. John and see to it that things calm down. I don't need any unnecessary problems right now."

"But...I..." Levy hesitated.

"Yes?"

"Umm...I know that you and Alex...well...umm..."

"I bang her every now and then." Sergio kept a straight face. "So what? That doesn't mean that I'm taking any business risk because of it. Do what you have to do. You have my blessing."

The hospital room was large and bright. It had a magnificent view across Central Park through the galvanized-steel wire mesh of the security windows, but Nick saw neither the green leaves nor the silvery shimmering lake. He sat slumped on a chair and stared aimlessly at the wall. His hands, with which he usually gestured so vividly, were bound and lay limply in his lap. The burn wounds on his face looked blood-red in comparison to the deathly pallor of his skin.

Frank Cohen fought back tears when he saw his boss. Whoever had killed Nick's family with the intention of getting to him had achieved his goal. The Nick Kostidis Frank knew had died the second they turned to ash. Frank wanted to say something to console him, something compassionate and understanding—something that Nick might have said in such a situation—but he couldn't think of anything.

"Hello," Frank said timidly. Nick turned around slowly. Frank was shocked to see the dull, lifeless look in his bloodshot eyes. The burns and flesh wounds on his body would heal, but no one could possibly imagine the psychological scars.

"Frank." Nick's voice sounded coarse and strange. The drugs had put him into a numb, deadened state. "Christopher's car wouldn't start," he suddenly said. "I suggested that they take my car. They didn't want to leave too late because of the heat."

Frank bit at his lip trying not to cry.

"I insisted. I couldn't possibly have known…" Nick stopped and took an agonized breath. "They're dead now. And it's my fault."

"No, it's not," Frank objected quietly.

"Yes, it is. I didn't take those letters seriously. I didn't listen to Mary. It's my fault that they had to die."

Nick's face was expressionless. He seemed neither desperate nor close to a nervous breakdown. He was completely devoid of emotion, which was terrifying.

"Ray was the mole I was looking for. He knew about the bomb in the car. He would have let me die, but he wanted to prevent my family from dying."

Frank swallowed and fought his tears.

"Why? Why did he do that? I knew him for such a long time, and I trusted him."

Frank didn't know how to respond. He'd asked himself this very same question over and over again.

After he was alone again, Nick stood up and walked to the window with heavy steps. He pressed his forehead against the cold glass and closed his eyes. If he had more strength, he would have tried to jump out the window. The strong sedatives prescribed by the doctors had put him in a semiconscious, trancelike state.

But the kind moment of numbness granted by the drugs seemed to be coming to a close. He was forced to face the brutal reality that slowly and frighteningly approached him like an all-encompassing black tidal wave. Mary was dead. Christopher was dead. His entire family had been extinguished in a few seconds, vanished forever. He didn't even have the chance to say good-bye to their lifeless bodies because there was nothing left of the two people who meant the most to him in this world. As if in an endless, slow-motion loop, Nick saw Mary's smile, her wave, and the look of panic in Raymond Howard's eyes. And then he saw the bright spark of the flame and felt the incredible force of the explosion that ripped the heavy armored car into two pieces like a toy.

Desperately, Nick pressed his burned hands over his ears and closed his eyes, but he couldn't dispel the noises and images in his head. And yet there was no sorrow in his heart, nor pain and anger—only emptiness and numbness. He could hear their voices when people talked to him. He saw their worry and compassion and knew that they wanted to help him, but what could they do? A torrential black river rushed between them, and this river was his guilt. There was no consolation, no salvation for him, because he was guilty of Mary's and Christopher's deaths. He'd gone too far with his obsession, and now he had to atone for it. He would have to live with this guilt for the rest of his life. Fate had spared him, but at what cost? Nick convulsed from the pain. His heart was as heavy as a rock, and he feared the day when he had to leave the protective walls of the hospital and look life in the eye again.

Frank burst into tears when he got into his car in the hospital's parking garage. He pressed his forehead against the steering wheel and sobbed. If only he could do something for Nick, something that would relieve his pain and suffering! But there was nothing, no chance, because Nick wouldn't allow it. He had shut down, he was lost inside of himself, and nothing, no one, could reach him. Suddenly, Frank stopped crying and lifted his head. Yes! There was someone who might be able to help! He remembered how much Nick admired his old friend, the Jesuit priest Kevin O'Shaughnessy of the St. Ignatius monastery in Brooklyn. The priest had once been a practicing doctor. Although Frank was completely exhausted, longing only for his bed after ten terrible days, he started the engine and drove out of the underground lot. He headed straight to Brooklyn. He knew he was grasping at straws, but perhaps this straw could save someone's life.

"Zack, you know as well as I do that we need Alex!" Vincent Levy yelled in annoyance. "So stop sulking like a baby and control the damage that you've caused!"

"How dare she give her clients false names?" St. John clenched his fist in anger.

"How dare you snoop around on her desk and her computer and then admit it to her?" Levy countered angrily. Through a mistake like this, the entire lucrative scheme could blow up. Alex was too smart; her suspicion could have dangerous consequences.

"That dumb bitch," Zack said. "I could—"

"You're acting like a jealous prima donna," Levy interrupted him harshly.

"I'm not jealous!" LMI's managing director disputed.

"Whatever." Levy glanced at his watch. "Given the circumstances, I think it's appropriate to get some leverage against Alex."

"Leverage?" Zack looked up in surprise.

"Yes." The voice of LMI's president sounded scornful. "Thanks to your hysterical reaction, she has cause for suspicion. And she's intelligent enough to see through all of this."

He opened his desk drawer, took out a German passport, and tossed it to Zack.

"That's her passport. This afternoon, you'll fly to Nassau with a young lady traveling under Alex's name. You'll help her open an account there at the local branch of the Teignier & Fils Swiss bank. Then you will deposit two hundred thousand dollars in cash and fly back again."

Zack's eyes widened, and then he grinned.

"That's one hell of a plan. It sounds like something I'd come up with!"

Levy shrugged his shoulders and handed him two airline tickets.

"Perfect. That's a great idea, Vince." Zack rubbed his hands. His irritation was gone and felt back on top again.

"It wasn't my idea," Levy answered stiffly.

"I thought so." Zack gave his boss a mocking look and then grabbed the tickets and passport. "You don't have that much imagination."

"Don't forget why you are on LMI's board. Another faux pas like this and you'll be working in the mail room," Levy said.

Zack's face turned grim, and a hateful twinkle appeared in his eyes.

"By the way, Zack," Levy said without a smile, "you're flying to LA on Monday and will stay there until the dust has settled around here. We can't afford to upset Alex."

"As you wish, sir." Zack faked a submissive bow. "I've heard that our esteemed M&A head has a meeting with Michael Whithers of Whithers Computers in Dallas next Thursday. This could turn out to be a huge deal if she doesn't screw it up."

"The only person screwing things up here," Levy said coolly, "is you."

Zack grimaced. Alex was in for the shock of her life, and so was this arrogant idiot Levy if he kept treating him in this demeaning manner. He had enough information to take them all down.

Father Kevin O'Shaughnessy didn't hesitate for a second when Frank Cohen asked him for help. He had just returned from Europe the day before and had been thinking of paying his old friend a visit. At Mount Sinai, he learned that the doctors considered his visit the last attempt before they admitted their most prominent patient to the psychiatric unit. Nick sat on a chair by the window staring at his hands.

"Good evening, Nicholas," Father Kevin said. Nick raised his head, and a spark of interest glimmered in his eyes, but it disappeared again at once.

"Good evening, Father," he replied indifferently. The Jesuit priest's heart grew heavy with sympathy when he realized what fate had done to this human being who had once been so fearless, so full of energy. A broken man sat in front of him. Horror and shock were visible in his dark eyes. Kevin O'Shaughnessy knew this expression all too well. He had seen it in the eyes of the many soldiers he's seen return from Vietnam. Some of them were never able to overcome the trauma of war. They couldn't forget the dead, the atrocities that they had witnessed. How much more terrible it must be to witness your own family's death. What could he possibly say to a person who'd just suffered such a loss?

"Nicholas." Father Kevin put his hand on the mayor's shoulder, "Words can not express the deep sympathy that I feel for you, and how much I grieve for Mary and Christopher."

Nick sighed.

"I want to help you. Tell me what I can do for you."

"You can't help me, Father." Nick shook his head. "No one can."

"God works in mysterious ways. Nothing happens without a reason on His earth."

"What reason could there be to let three innocent people die?" Nick responded bitterly.

"Not one of us knows in the hour of death," Father Kevin countered softly. "God has taken Mary and Christopher to His side because He thought it was right. Now they are with Him. But you must live on."

"Must I?" Nick turned his face to the side. "It's no consolation for me that they may be in heaven. I wonder whether there's a God at all if He allows things like this to happen. Mary never harmed anyone, and still God allowed that she…that she…"

He stopped and wiped his bandaged hand across his face.

"Jesus Christ doubted in His hours of fear and hopelessness," Father Kevin replied. "It's human nature to have doubts. Everyone has them. If you don't doubt, you can't believe."

"I don't know if all of that is true. I don't know anything. None of this makes sense anymore." Nick looked at his old friend. "I wish that I had the courage to kill myself."

Father Kevin looked at him seriously and then placed his hands on his shoulders.

"I remember this little boy," he said in a low voice, "a boy I respected because he had courage. He had a grand vision that shone above his path like a bright star. This boy didn't have an easy life. He had to witness the death of his mother, his father, and his brothers. But he never gave up. He never understood why his father gave up on himself. This boy fought for all of his life."

Nick frowned.

"It's not the same anymore," he whispered. "I don't have any strength left."

"God will give you the strength to endure what He imposes on you. Even if you don't understand at this moment how He let it happen that Mary and Christopher had to die."

"No! There's no consolation for this!" Nick replied vehemently. "Not for me! It's my fault."

"You should allow others to help you." Father Kevin let him go and sat on the edge of the bed.

"They want me to talk about it," Nick said, sounding agonized, "but I can't. I don't want to talk."

"The doctors are very worried. And not only them. The entire city is grieving with you. The people waiting outside the hospital want you to get better because they love and trust you. You've become their role model, their guiding light."

"No, no. I don't want to hear that. I don't want other people to expect something of me. I want…I…"

"They want to help you."

"Damn it! What do they expect? Should I cry and scream and pull out my hair?"

"Yes." Father Kevin nodded slowly. "I think that they expect something like that. They're waiting for a reaction from you so they can see that you've overcome your shock."

"I'm not in shock. I simply can't cry! Everything is cold and dead inside of me."

"Because you're not allowing it. You're afraid to lose control."

Nick stood up and stepped toward the window.

"That may be," he said, shrugging his shoulders. "Maybe I'm afraid of going crazy."

Both men were silent. The blood-red sun set over the other side of the park, behind the apartment buildings on the west side. Nick breathed heavily. What good would it do to talk about the horror that he experienced over and over again? It wouldn't change anything. No one could help him—not even God. How should he continue to live with the thought that he was solely responsible for the death of these three people? Why hadn't he listened to Mary's plea that he simply forget Vitali? He had achieved so much and celebrated many successes, but that wasn't enough for him. Filled with arrogance, he thought he was invincible. Now fate had taught him otherwise. Vitali had taken from him what he had loved most in his life. And the punishment for his guilt was agony and loneliness. No, there was no solace. Not for him. But no one understood.

"I love the Lord," Father Kevin said in a low voice, quoting the Bible, "who listened to my voice. Who turned an ear to me on the day I called. I was caught by the cords of death, the snares of hell had seized me; I felt agony and dread. Then I called on the name of the Lord: 'O Lord, save my life!' Gracious is the Lord and righteous; our God is merciful. The Lord protects the simple hearts."

Nick heard the springs squeak as the old man raised himself from the edge of the bed. The Jesuit priest's gaze was full of compassion, and he put his hand on Nick's shoulder once again.

"You can come to me whenever you need to," he said, "but don't allow your heart to harden against God in anger."

Nick remained silent.

"Don't judge yourself more harshly than God would judge you," the Father raised himself up again, "and the sun will also shine for you again. The Lord will help you in His mercy if you ask Him to."

The head physician and his team were eagerly awaiting the Jesuit priest as he left the room.

"Did he speak to you?" Dr. Simmons asked.

"Yes," Father Kevin O'Shaughnessy replied, "but don't expect him to talk about the things that torment him. He's never been one to speak of his feelings, not in all the forty years I've known him. It's pointless to keep him here."

"Are you suggesting we simply release him, even though he's still in shock?"

"Yes." Father Kevin nodded. "He's going to be okay. I'm also a medical doctor with many years of experience treating traumatized people, especially soldiers returning from Vietnam. Nicholas Kostidis reminds me of those men. His behavior shows every symptom of post-traumatic stress disorder: a disturbed affect and a seeming lack of feeling. But just because he cannot express it does not mean grief is not roiling inside of him."

The doctors looked at the priest in astonishment.

"But what about the suicide risk?" another senior physician said. "He mentioned several times that he wished he had the courage to kill himself."

"He said that to me," Father Kevin confirmed, "but I don't take it seriously. A man like Nick Kostidis doesn't tend to commit suicide. Although he's still incapable of grieving, he couldn't force himself to do that. But he blames himself for his family's death. We won't be able to talk him out of believing it."

"Maybe it would be best to admit him to a—"

"For heaven's sake!" Father Kevin interrupted the senior physician. "He's not crazy! Give him time to accept his family's death. The only thing that can help him now is time. He'll come to terms with it one day. I'm sure of it."

The three senior physicians were perplexed as they looked at each other.

"Okay, Father," the head physician finally said. "We'll release Mr. Kostidis on Tuesday. We should respect that he doesn't want to talk about something that's still so fresh and painful. Maybe you're right, and time will heal his wounds."

Frank Cohen and Michael Page invited all the people Nick himself would have if he had been up to the task. They waited at the old, tree-filled cemetery of the St. Ignatius monastery in Brooklyn. Francis Dulong and his wife, Trevor and Madeleine Downey, Michael Campione and his wife Sally, and Christopher Kostidis's best friends were among the group of about eighty mourners. The grounds of the monastery were sealed off by over a hundred police officers. No one without a permit was allowed near the cemetery. Countless reporters, camera teams, and also citizens of the city, who wanted to support their mayor in this hardest hour of his life, crowded behind the police barriers.

Nick's face looked as if it were set in stone as he walked along the cemetery's winding paths between his in-laws. He stared straight ahead and seated himself in the first row of chairs at the open grave into which the urns had been placed. Piles of funeral wreaths and flower arrangements, which had been diligently checked by FBI and NYPD explosives experts, were piled around the open grave. The mourners took their seats. No one uttered a word. The tragic deaths of Mary, Christopher, and Britney Edwards had shocked them, but the sight of Nick Kostidis had them speechless in dismay. They'd come because they wanted to stand by him and express their compassion and deep sorrow, but he didn't give them a chance to do so. He sat stiffly on his chair, as white as a sheet, without expressing the slightest emotion, without even once averting his gaze from the urns. When Father Kevin stepped over to the grave with a procession of four altar boys, everyone except Nick stood up. It was as if he hadn't even noticed them.

"Out of the depths I call to you, O Lord," the priest began in a low voice that still carried to the last row. "Hear my voice, O Lord! Let your ears be attentive to my voice in supplication. If you, O Lord, mark iniquities, who can stand? But with you is forgiveness, that you may be revered. I trust in the Lord; my soul trusts his word. My soul waits for the Lord, more than sentinels wait for the dawn."

The Jesuit priest sprinkled holy water over the urns. The words he spoke were simple but full of compassion, and few mourners were able to hold back their tears.

Mary's mother sobbed and blew her nose loudly. Father Kevin said the first words of the Lord's Prayer aloud, and then he continued to pray in silence, sprinkling the urns with holy water again and swinging small incense censers back and forth. "And lead us not into temptation, but deliver us from evil. O Lord, save their souls from the gates of hell! Let them rest in peace."

The church bell of the abbey chimed. Mourners continued sobbing quietly, but Nick sat motionless with a frozen face.

"I am the resurrection and the life," Father Kevin said. "Whoever believes in Me will live, even though he dies; whoever lives and believes in Me will never die."

In conclusion, the Jesuit priest took some soil from the bowl standing next to the grave and threw in three handfuls.

"For you are dust and to dust you shall return. The Lord will raise you up on the last day."

By request, the mourners refrained from giving their condolences to Nick after paying their last respects to the deceased. They exited in silence, until he was the last one left sitting in the first row of chairs. Despite the oppressive heat, he didn't seem to sweat in his black suit and hadn't moved once since he sat down an hour ago.

Frank watched his boss with an uncertain look. Did he even realize that the funeral was over? The gravediggers arrived and started to shovel dirt onto the grave and pile the flowers and wreaths on top of it. They were used to grieving relatives and performed their duty quickly and quietly. Frank and the bodyguards waited patiently a few yards away in the heat of the July afternoon.

Only now did Nick stand up and step toward the grave where his parents and brothers had been buried. He swayed slightly, but then he managed to straighten his shoulders and take a deep breath. He didn't feel the heat that had built up between the old cemetery's ivy-covered walls. He didn't see the clear blue sky, which arched brightly over the city despite his sorrow. He couldn't hear the birds singing in the crown of the dense old trees. The sun was setting in the west by the time Nick Kostidis finished his silent dialogue with all those whom he'd accompanied to this place. He left the cemetery with a lowered head, the epitome of grief and despair.

PART THREE

Early October 2000

Zack disappeared to California for a few weeks after the Syncrotron debacle. The official story was that he had to organize the restructuring of LMI's West Coast office. But Alex knew better. Levy had sent Zack to LA until the dust settled and she had calmed down. Even Sergio left the city for a while in August, and she was happy that there was no follow-up on his marriage proposal. She was also relieved that he hadn't asked her to see him, since the sheer thought of seeing him caused her physical discomfort.

Oliver had helped her find a new place, because she could no longer stand living in Sergio's apartment. The converted loft was in Tribeca, in a secure complex that had residential units, offices, and a film company headquarters. Alex liked the underground parking garage the best. In case Sergio was still watching her, it had exits to two streets so she could escape from possible pursuers.

Over the past few months, she had often considered calling Nick Kostidis, but she simply didn't have the courage. She had sent him a condolence card and received a printed thank-you note soon thereafter, which he had signed personally.

The entire financial world seemed to be on vacation in August. But with the start of September, Wall Street was once again flooded with new transactions, and—thanks to Alex—LMI was involved in the biggest and most profitable deals.

On October 1, she ran into Zack in the LMI Building lobby. He was leaner and seemed relaxed.

"Let's bury the hatchet, Alex," he said in a friendly tone. "I made a silly mistake and got roasted because of it."

Alex trusted him as little as before, but she shook his hand for tactical reasons.

"Truce?" Zack asked.

"Truce," she replied.

She wasn't surprised when Sergio called her that very same afternoon, right after Levy had ordered her into his office to request a meeting Saturday morning. It was clear they feared that she would resign because Zack was back in town. Their game was annoyingly transparent to Alex. She would have simply loved to tell Sergio to go to hell and leave her alone, but she couldn't do it just like that. Instead, because of his persistence, she reluctantly accepted an invitation for dinner at his apartment on Park Avenue that coming Friday.

Sergio was suntanned, and his blue eyes were gleaming. The bullet wound and his son's death—all of it seemed to have passed him by without a trace. But for the first time since she had known him, Alex wasn't taken by his handsome looks; she saw that his beauty was as cold and empty as that of an antique statue. The smile didn't shine in his eyes, and his charming exterior was like a thin layer of varnish over what she knew was a ruthless and brutal core. The moment Alex saw him, she realized that there had never been anything more between them than pure physical attraction.

They entered one of the apartment's huge salons where a table was set for two. During the multicourse dinner, Alex had to muster all her strength to pretend that she was happy to see him again after such a long time. But really, she wanted to tell him that she knew he was a murderer. She longed for this arduous evening to end, but the time passed so painfully slowly. They finally made it to the digestif, and Sergio led her to a different salon.

"I also have a little gift for you, *cara*," he announced with a smile and handed her a small package. "Open it. I'm sure that you'll like it."

Alex obeyed and froze when she opened the jewelry box. A diamond-studded white gold necklace lay on black velvet. She would not allow herself to be bought by this gift. Thirty pieces of silver for her silence. Sergio took the necklace and placed it around her neck. She shivered when the cool metal touched her skin. "Wonderful," he said, satisfied. "I knew that it would look magnificent on you."

"I can't accept this," Alex refused. "It's much too valuable."

"Yes, you can." Sergio leaned toward her and kissed her. "You can. The most beautiful jewelry for the most beautiful woman I know."

"Sergio, I…" Alex felt more uncomfortable by the minute, but he put his index finger on her lips, smiling.

"This past year has been difficult for my business," he said, "but now I've solved all the problems and come to the conclusion that it's time to change my life."

Alex felt a chill. She thought about Nick Kostidis, David Zuckerman, and the assassination attempt by the Colombian drug cartel. Oh yes, Sergio had definitely solved his problems in his own way.

"I think," he continued, "that you should live here. With me. I'll file for a divorce from Constanzia, and then we can get married."

Alex had hoped that he would never mention this topic again. She didn't know how to react. His hand was resting on her knee and wandered up her thigh. Then he leaned her head back and kissed her.

"I love you, *cara*," he murmured. "I've longed for you so much in the past weeks."

Alex cursed herself for accepting Sergio's invitation. She didn't want his gift, and she couldn't stand his touch. The mere thought of being married to this ice-cold killer filled her with horror.

"We'll have a wedding that people will still talk about fifty years from now." His hands slid beneath her blouse, and he started breathing heavily. "And then we'll cruise on the *Stella Maris* for our honeymoon—just you and I. For as long as you want. Wouldn't that be wonderful?"

Sergio pulled her on top of him, and she was filled with disgust when she felt his erection. But what could she do in this situation other than play along with him?

"I wish we could get married tomorrow," she lied, responding to his kiss. She felt like bursting into tears. "It was always my dream to live on Park Avenue. I'm curious what Trevor and Madeleine will say. Maybe you can buy a house on Long Island. Perhaps I'll resign my position at LMI."

Sergio paused for a split second.

"If that's what you want, *cara*," he whispered hoarsely. "You can do whatever you like."

On Saturday morning, Alex arrived at eleven o'clock on the nose at Vincent Levy's office. Levy led her to his office and offered her some coffee.

"Alex," LMI's president began, "I'd like to talk to you about St. John."

He crossed his legs and waited for a reaction, but Alex had no intention of accommodating him. This conversation had been long overdue and should have occurred three months ago, but he had probably been too cowardly.

"Well," he continued, "St. John has come to his senses recently. It's a terrible thing that he snooped around in your desk. I was very angry about that and clearly expressed that to him. But I'm pretty sure that he has learned his lesson. He lost a lot of money using the information that he found to speculate on his own account."

Liar, Alex thought. Zack hadn't lost a penny because it wasn't his money. But she knew that she also needed to play along with Levy's game.

"St. John used an outside brokerage account for his…hmm…personal trades so that no harm was done to LMI."

That was also a lie.

"Vincent," Alex said, leaning forward, "I suspect that Zack has done this before. I've informed him about every imminent deal, as you asked me to, although that violates all kinds of rules. LMI still has an impeccable reputation, but I seriously fear that St. John is threatening it with his insider trading."

"I agree." Levy seemed embarrassed. "This certainly is serious, and I've warned St. John never to violate the law again so blatantly."

Alex would have burst out laughing if Levy's farce didn't have such serious consequences. How stupid did he think she was?

"I don't want to work with him anymore," she said with determination. "He's betrayed my confidence. I don't want to be subject to an SEC investigation. I won't pass on any information to him, and I demand that you prohibit him from entering my office."

Alex noticed the thin layer of sweat on Levy's forehead despite the cool temperature in his office. She had him backed in to a corner. Levy and Vitali needed both her and Zack equally to continue their fraudulent conspiracy.

"I understand that you feel betrayed." Levy cleared his throat and forced himself to smile. "I also understand that you're angry, but we'll find a way to continue together."

"Not with St. John!" She shook her head emphatically. "Vince, I have to tell you, I keep getting interesting offers from other firms that I've so far declined because I'm happy at LMI and enjoy working here. But if there's another incident like this, I'll feel compelled to resign on the spot."

"Calm down, Alex! It won't happen again. I promise you."

"Will St. John leave the company?"

"He's on the board." Levy shifted back and forth in his chair. "His dismissal would cause a lot of talk and unrest."

“Put yourself in my shoes. Would you like to work with someone who digs around in your desk behind your back?”

Alex could see how uncomfortable Levy felt.

“From now on, you will just report to me personally, Alex. You won’t have to deal with St. John anymore.”

“He’ll boycott all of my deals.” She looked at her boss coolly. “He has already threatened me with that. That’s not particularly fertile ground for a successful future, is it?”

Levy desperately tried to justify keeping St. John with the firm. He normally would have been fired for insider trading and reported to the authorities—board member or not—but Alex knew that Levy couldn’t exactly do that.

“Since I can’t trust the information flow in this company anymore,” she said, “I’ll strictly adhere to the Chinese wall principle and keep all of the information to myself until it’s made public.”

“You’re right.” Levy leaned forward. It almost seemed like there was a hint of panic in his eyes. “You should do it exactly that way. Maybe it was my mistake to involve St. John too much with the M&A department. From now on, you just report to me personally.”

Alex looked at him closely, and then she stood up.

“I don’t have a good feeling about this, Vincent. I’ll stay until you find a suitable successor for my position.”

She knew that Levy would immediately tell Sergio about this conversation. Yesterday, she had told him that she would like to resign at LMI. Everything was working out perfectly. It wouldn’t be hard for her to move on from LMI; she really would have no problem finding a new job. She’d just recently had an interesting conversation with Carter Ringwood from First Boston, where he had offered her a position. Levy also stood up.

“I understand your anger,” he said, “but please don’t make any rash decisions. We’re extremely pleased with your performance and would be happy to offer you a contract with a higher fixed salary. Think about it.”

"It's not about the money," Alex replied. "I just don't want to be put behind bars."

"I'll arrange everything so you're happy," Levy promised. "Okay?"

"Do what you can."

She shook her boss's hand and left his office.

Right after the door closed behind her, Levy sank into the chair behind his desk. He felt like wringing St. John's neck! Everything was going smoothly, but the man had acted like an absolute rookie. If St. John hadn't told Alex that he'd rummaged around in her papers, then nothing would have happened. Damn his greed and pathological narcissism! Someone in his position had to be able to keep it together. Nevertheless, it was obvious the man couldn't bear the fact that Alex's star was shining brighter than ever.

Levy sighed as he grabbed the telephone and dialed Sergio Vitali's number. He had hoped that Alex would calm down after three months, but this apparently wasn't the case. If she stuck to her threat and left LMI, it would put an end to these lucrative side earnings for quite a while. Finding someone as good as she was would be difficult, if not impossible.

On the other end of the line, Sergio personally answered the phone.

"I'm afraid that she's suspicious," Levy said. "She demands that I fire Zack. If not, she's threatening to quit LMI."

Sergio replied calmly. "Just take it easy. We've opened an account for her, and we'll tell her about it when the time is right. I bet that she'll become agreeable by then."

"I don't know. It's not easy to intimidate her. She's really clever."

Sergio knew that. He smiled slightly. Although he still couldn't figure her out, she had seemed sincere with him last night. She had seemed pleased with the necklace and the prospect of living on Park Avenue. They made plans for their future together. She had even confided in him about her mistrust of St. John and her desire to leave LMI. She even told him that she'd been at Gracie Mansion, and how shocked she was about the attack on the mayor. Never before had Alex talked this openly to him.

"She'll be reasonable, Vince," he reassured his business partner. "Don't worry about her."

"I hope you're right."

Levy wasn't so convinced.

"I will be, as usual," Sergio countered. "I have Alex under control."

Alex left her office after sitting at her desk for a few hours. She hadn't accomplished anything. She was preoccupied with Sergio's behavior and all of the things that she had uncovered. It was obvious that Levy wasn't about to fire Zack—after all, he was the man for his dirty work. Furthermore, he knew too much. But despite all of this, *she* was also indispensable to this elaborate scheme to generate dirty money. This was obviously why Sergio and Levy wouldn't let her leave LMI. Sergio's renewed marriage proposal could have been earnest, but Alex wasn't sure whether his primary motive was to tie her to him and to LMI. It would be a lie to claim she wasn't afraid of Sergio. He terrified her.

Alex sighed and closed her eyes. Last night she had decided to call Nick Kostidis. She needed to talk to him. He was the only person who could tell her what to do with the information she had. From a phone booth, she dialed the number that Nick had given to her. A man named Frank Cohen answered.

"This is Alex Sontheim," she said. "I need to speak to Mayor Kostidis. It's important."

"Mayor Kostidis is unavailable at the moment," he replied.

"I was a guest at Gracie Mansion in July. Mayor Kostidis knows me."

Cohen hesitated.

"Listen," Alex said emphatically, "I know that this might be a bad time, but I have information that could shed light on the bombing."

"Mayor Kostidis is in no condition to talk about this. I hope you understand."

"Of course," Alex replied. "But when can I speak to him?"

"I can't help you. I'm sorry. Try his office again in a few weeks."

In a few weeks! This guy must be joking! Alex thanked him and hung up. It occurred to her that she'd read somewhere that Nick's family had been buried at the St. Ignatius cemetery in Brooklyn. It was too late now, but she planned to drive there the next morning. Maybe she'd be lucky and find Nick there.

The St. Ignatius cemetery was so old it almost felt medieval. With its tall old trees and ivy-covered walls, it seemed like a film set for a historical movie.

In the taxi to Brooklyn, Alex kept looking through the rear window, but her fear of being followed seemed unfounded. The air was cool for early October, and morning fog made the cemetery even darker than it already was.

Alex walked slowly through the rows of graves. Weeds were sprouting from the cracks in the veined, bulging stone slabs. The lettering on the gravestones was faded from the wind and weather. Mold-covered marble angels stared stoically into the distance with unfocused eyes.

Although the aura of mortality was oppressive, she was fascinated by this cemetery—a peaceful, surreal oasis in the middle of this restless city. Alex had no clue where the graves of Mary and Christopher Kostidis were, and she seemed to be the only living person there. She wandered among the graves until she finally saw Nick Kostidis. He was sitting on a bench with his back hunched and his head lowered. He seemed so lonely, so unhappy, that her heart constricted in sympathy. How could she even consider bothering him with her problems? Who was she to disturb him in his grieving? It was far too late to help him.

Alex hesitated and was about to turn around when the church bells started chiming. Kostidis looked up, and their eyes met. She walked over to him.

She looked down at the grave. Reading the names etched into the granite gravestone, she realized that Nick Kostidis's entire family was buried here: his parents, his brothers, and now also his wife and son. Suddenly, she felt his pain and fought back tears while folding her hands and murmuring the only prayer that she could remember from her childhood—the Lord's Prayer.

How terrible and senseless these deaths were. She slowly turned her gaze toward the dark eyes of this man she had met that night at the Plaza almost two years ago. He had warned her at the time, but she didn't listen to him. Alex remembered the intensity of his eyes and his laugh. He had aged years during the past few months.

She suddenly couldn't remember why she had come here. Without saying a word, she sat down next to him on the bench. The bells stopped chiming, and the quiet sound of an organ seeped through the thick walls of the church, its silhouette visible in the morning fog.

"For almost three months now, I've been sitting here for hours every day," Nick said quietly after a while. "I'm waiting for the moment when I can finally cry."

He ran a hand through his hair, which had turned increasingly gray.

"I suggested that they take my car because Christopher's car wouldn't start, and now they're dead."

Alex was deeply touched by his trust. She could feel Nick's need to talk in order not to suffocate. He stared off into the distance.

"I'd love to be able to cry. But I can't. Everything is dead inside of me. I keep asking myself *why*? Why Mary? Why my son? Why the girl? It's not their fault that I…I…that I refused to listen to the warnings. It's my fault because I thought of nothing else but chasing Vitali, even though Mary kept asking—no, *begging*—me to stop."

He fell silent, and Alex heard him take a deep breath before continuing.

"How can I live with this? How can I ever fix what I've caused?"

"But you didn't do anything. *He* did."

"No," Nick said, shaking his head. "I was obsessed by the thought of stopping him. I shouldn't have provoked him."

He grimaced.

"What difference would it make if he were in prison today? With his connections, he'd be out in no time, and nothing would have changed. If I'd stopped chasing him and attacking him in public, they would still be alive today."

Nick hid his face in his hands. Alex hardly understood a single word he said.

"I was arrogant. Fanatical. But I was wrong. It almost seems as if God wanted to punish me for my pride and arrogance.

"No," Alex objected quietly, "you only tried to speak the truth. That was courageous of you."

"Courageous?" His voice sounded bitter. "It wasn't courageous. It was stupid."

"You warned me about Vitali," Alex said. "I refused to believe you at the time, but now I see that you were right."

He looked at her with bloodshot eyes.

"No one can get to him. He's stronger because he's unscrupulous and brutal."

"That's not true," Alex answered. "It is possible to get to him. I've unearthed things about him that could ruin him."

"A few months ago, I would have been happy to hear that," Nick said and sighed. "Now I just don't care anymore. That won't bring my family back to life."

Alex remained silent. She understood how he felt.

"Why did you come here, Alex?" Nick looked at her with torment and self-reproach in his eyes. Alex felt like holding him in her arms and consoling him.

"I didn't know your wife very well," Alex whispered, fighting her tears, "but I respected her very much. And I also like you, Nick. It kills me to see you suffer like this."

A tear ran down her cheek, and she noticed how Nick's lips quivered.

"It's strange." He gave her a hopeless and penetrating gaze. "Of all the people I thought were my friends, no one has said that to me. They only had empty words. 'Life goes on' and 'time heals all wounds.' They stay away from me as if I had leprosy. I can sense it. But really, what I needed was someone to talk to."

"Most people are afraid of being confronted with death," Alex replied.

"But you, Alex, you hardly know me, and still you aren't afraid to come here and talk to me."

"I grew up in the country," she answered. "The cycle of life and death is normal there. People here remain silent, as if death didn't exist."

"I could accept death, even though it would be difficult," Nick said, "but the thought that it's my fault..."

"As long as you tell yourself that you're at fault for your family's death, you'll never be able to cope with what happened."

"What do you mean?" Nick looked at Alex with a somewhat surprised expression.

"Forgive me, Nick," she replied, "but I don't think you're even trying to process what happened. You're running away by tormenting yourself with this self-reproach."

Nick was silent for a moment. Alex was afraid she had offended him.

"Vitali must have tried to kill you because you stepped on his toes. You didn't do it out of vanity, but conviction," she said emphatically. "You were convinced that you were doing the right thing. How can that be a mistake? It was a tragic chain of unfortunate events that your family was hit instead of you. If you and your chauffeur had taken the car, then you'd be dead now."

Nick stared at her, and she returned his look.

"When I was ten," she said quietly, "my grandfather gave me a foal. I raised it, broke it in myself, and loved it more than anything else in the world. It was a magnificent horse. A few years later, a thunderstorm approached. My grandfather called to me and said that I should bring the horse into the stable. I didn't do it because I was reading an exciting book. Thunderstorms were nothing unusual. So I left my horse outside."

Nick looked at Alex steadily.

"The next morning," she continued, "I wanted go riding, but my horse wasn't there. I searched the entire paddock and finally found it. It had been struck by lightning out in the meadow. I was beside myself with grief and blamed myself. I knew that it was my fault because I hadn't listened to my grandfather. Of all the horses, *my* horse was dead. I thought I'd die from grief, and my feelings of guilt were so intense. I wished that I could turn back time and undo my mistake, but I couldn't."

She sighed, remembering.

"I blamed myself. That was the first time in my life that I realized how many things just happen in life, and we can't change them after the fact. This may sound fatalistic, but that's simply the way it is. My girlfriend's father was struck dead by a falling tree, my younger brother died while walking home from school when a truck driver lost control of his vehicle, and a friend of mine from school died at fifteen from leukemia. Aren't these cases just as senseless as your family's death? And who's at fault?"

Nick's face was twitching. Alex detected a glimmer of hope in his eyes. Impulsively, she grabbed his hand, which was scarred from the burns.

"It's not your fault, Nick." Her voice trembled. "And your wife certainly wouldn't want you to sit here and torment yourself with all this guilt."

"No," Nick said, his voice gruff, "she wouldn't want that. She…had steadfast belief in God and always found comfort in the Bible."

Alex sensed him trembling.

"The Lord is my shepherd," he whispered, "I shall not want. He makes me lie down in green pastures. He leads me beside still waters. He restores my soul. He leads me in paths of righteousness for His name's sake. Even though I walk through the valley of the shadow of death, I fear no evil; for You are with me. Your rod and Your staff, they comfort me. You prepare a table before me in the presence of my enemies. You anoint my head with oil; my cup overflows. Surely goodness and mercy shall follow me all the days of my life; and I shall dwell in the House of the Lord forever."

Pools of tears formed in Alex's eyes.

"Psalm 23. It was her favorite verse. I keep repeating these words, hoping to understand what Mary found comforting in them."

Nick's voice failed him, and his hand clamped around Alex's.

"My God," he exclaimed, "I miss them so much! I always thought that we had an infinite amount of time together, but now I see there's no time left at all!"

Nick saw Alex's tears and sensed her sincere sympathy. Maybe it was this certainty that he was no longer alone, that another person understood his pain, that let the dam inside of him burst all at once. His long-suppressed tears suddenly ran down his face, and he didn't feel ashamed. The powerful, fearless Nicholas Kostidis allowed himself to be weak and discouraged. He cried unlike anyone Alex had ever seen cry before. It was the terrible sobbing of a desperate man. She took him into her arms.

He slipped off the bench, fell to his knees, and crying desperately, he pressed his face into Alex's lap. She simply held him tight, stroked his hair, and let him cry the cathartic tears. His abysmal grief shook her to the core, but she admired him for showing his real emotions. After a while, Nick's crying abated. He clung to Alex like a child looking for comfort and security.

"Everything will be all right," she murmured. "Everything will be all right."

"Really?" Nick raised his tearstained face to look at her. His eyes were red from crying.

"Yes," she nodded, "I'm sure of it. All wounds heal, and what remains are the memories of the beautiful things that you experienced together. There won't be any forgetting, but there will be understanding."

"How can you be so sure, Alex?"

Nick was still kneeling in front of her, and she held both of his hands.

"Because that's the way it is. Because I've experienced it myself."

Nick leaned his head on her knee again and took a trembling breath.

"I'm sorry that I lost my composure like this," he whispered.

"You don't need to apologize," Alex answered softly. "It makes me happy to know that I could help you even the smallest bit. There are times when we need someone to listen and try to understand."

"Do you?" Nick looked at her again. "Do you understand me?"

"I think I do." Alex observed his tormented and hopeless face pensively. She reached out and stroked his unshaven cheek, which was moist with tears. A bond of trust had formed between them.

"If you need someone to talk to, I'm here for you, Nick," Alex said in a throaty voice. "And you don't have to worry that I'll tell anyone."

"Thank you." He managed to smile slightly and rose to his feet with some effort. "I'm so grateful to you."

They sat next to each other for a while before Alex realized that she was still holding Nick's hand. She let go of it with a sense of embarrassment.

"I...I have to go now. Are you okay?"

"Yes," he replied, and it seemed to Alex as if a tiny glimpse of his old energy had returned. "I'm much better now."

Before she could leave, he grabbed her hand again. "Why did you really come here, Alex?"

She looked at him, and then she stood up.

"It doesn't matter anymore," she replied.

Lost in her thoughts, she walked along the cemetery's winding paths. The sun had penetrated the dense clouds in some areas; its warm rays had melted the fog away. The Mass was over, and churchgoers visited their relatives' graves. Alex was still dazed by the unexpected trust that Nick Kostidis had placed in her, and she felt a deep affection for him. He wasn't hard and ruthless. He was completely different than she ever imagined.

As Alex turned a corner, she almost collided with a man. She murmured an apology, but an ice-cold shock struck her when she saw this man's face. Never again would she forget those cold, yellowish eyes. It was the man she had seen at Sergio's birthday party—the man who killed David Zuckerman. And there could only be one reason why he was here at this cemetery: he'd come to finish a job that failed a few weeks ago. Sergio had sent him here to kill Nick Kostidis.

Alex didn't consider the fact that she was also in danger, that the man possibly recognized her and might tell Sergio she was here. She worried only for Nick as he sat unsuspectingly at his family's grave. Luckily, the man with the yellow eyes didn't know exactly where Nick was. He walked slowly around the cemetery's paths with a searching look, but trying not to attract any attention.

Alex broke into a run with a pounding heart and reached the bench where she had sat next to Nick just moments earlier. But the bench was empty. Panic raced through her, and she started to run again. Finally she saw him. He was walking toward the church with his head down and his hands buried deep in his coat pockets.

Apparently the man with the yellow eyes had spotted him that very same moment. Protected by a massive yew tree, he raised his rifle and took aim. Alex stumbled across the graves. She didn't care that people were looking at her angrily.

"Nick!" Her voice cracked. "Watch out!"

Nick Kostidis turned around in surprise, but she had already reached him and thrown her body against his. They both lost their balance and fell to the ground. The bullet that was meant for Nick hit the gravestone right behind them, smashing the stone slab and breaking it into two pieces.

"What…what…what was that?" he asked in confusion. Alex carefully turned her head to look for the shooter. He was gone. Then the floodgates burst, and she started to cry. A few passersby came closer and stared curiously at them.

"Somebody shot at me, right?" Nick whispered.

"Yes." Alex got up, sobbing, wiping her tears. Nick also stood up. He was very pale, yet surprisingly calm.

"You saved my life," he said and grabbed her hand. Alex flung her arms around his neck and buried her face in his shoulder.

"I recognized this man by chance when he walked past me," she said, her voice wavering hysterically. "I've seen him at Vitali's house. I was at his birthday party and got lost in the house when suddenly this man was standing right in front of me."

Her knees turned to rubber, and she needed to sit down. Nick knelt next to her, looking at her in concern.

"I followed him. The door to the library was slightly ajar, and then I heard…I…I heard this man say to Sergio: It is done. Zuckerman won't utter another word. Do you understand, Nick? This man shot David Zuckerman, and now he tried to kill you!"

"Are you sure it was the same man?" Nick observed her closely.

"Yes, yes, definitely." She nodded vehemently. "I'll never forget his face. He's one of Vitali's henchmen. Oh my God, this is terrible!"

She couldn't stop the tears flowing down her face, and this time it was Nick's turn to console her.

"Come on, Alex." He grabbed her hand and pulled her up gently. "Let's get out of here."

"And what if he tries again?"

"He won't." Nick was surprised by his own coldness. Alex's panic sobered him, and suddenly he was able to think more clearly than he had in months. Just this morning, he would have preferred to die so that he wouldn't have to endure this pain and his terrible feelings of guilt. He thought he would never feel anything again, but he was mistaken. He'd clearly felt fear just now, and he was worried about Alex—who had just saved his life by risking her own. They entered the church though a hidden side door, but even the thick walls couldn't make Alex feel safe. She looked back repeatedly and almost expected to see the man with the rifle reappear. Nick held her hand while she walked beside him as if in trance. They left the church and turned into a cloister that had a green courtyard at its center. Nick knew his way around surprisingly well in this maze of corridors and hallways.

Ten minutes later, they were on the third floor of this fortresslike monastery. He stopped in front of one of the doors and knocked.

"Come in!" someone called, and Nick opened the door. The whitewashed room had dark oak beams on the high ceilings and was modestly furnished. Beside the massive, dark wooden desk were floor-to-ceiling bookcases, and the only wall decorations were a wooden cross and a framed picture of Pope John Paul II. A lean, white-haired Jesuit priest sitting at the desk looked up in surprise.

"Nick!" the priest exclaimed, and a warm smile spread across his face. "How nice to see you!"

"Hello, Father," Nick replied.

"How are you?" The priest took Nick's hands in his and looked at him with total sympathy. Alex figured he was older than he looked, for she had never before seen such wisdom as in his kind eyes.

"I'm doing better," Nick replied. "Thank you."

"Inscrutable are the ways of God."

"Yes. It's difficult, but I think I'll make it."

"You are always in our prayers."

"I know. Thank you."

Only then did he seem to remember that he wasn't alone.

"Father, allow me to introduce Ms. Alex Sontheim. She's a friend of... Mary's and mine. Alex, this is Father Kevin O'Shaughnessy."

"Hello." Father Kevin extended his hand toward Alex, and his firm handshake surprised her.

"Father Kevin is an old friend of mine," Nick explained. "I was an altar boy in his church."

"Sit down, please," the Jesuit offered. Alex, whose knees were still soft as butter, smiled gratefully. She sat down on one of the simple wooden chairs, which was as uncomfortable as it looked.

"Someone just tried to shoot me here in the cemetery," Nick said, and Father Kevin turned pale.

"*Shoot you?* In our cemetery?" He made the sign of the cross.

Nick told him briefly what had happened and then grabbed the telephone. Alex, whose body was still shaking, noticed that his voice sounded almost as firm and energetic as when she knew him before. He called his assistant—this Frank Cohen who'd brushed her off so determinedly yesterday—and repeated the whole story. Then Nick turned to Alex.

"How are you?" he asked, sincerely concerned, and grabbed her hand.

"That's what I should ask you." She tried to smile but hardly managed it. "You're the one who was shot at, after all."

Nick gave her a friendly look. The desperation had vanished from his dark eyes.

"I owe very much to you, Alex," he said quietly. "You brought me back to life today and saved it shortly thereafter. As of this morning, I felt like I'd rather be dead, but now I realize that I'm still clinging to my life."

Father Kevin, who had been listening silently, cleared his throat.

"Can I help in any way, Nick?"

"I'm sorry that something like this had to happen here of all places," he responded. "The police will be here any minute."

Father Kevin looked worried.

"The main thing is that no one got hurt. Do you have any idea who this was?"

Nick's face darkened, and he swallowed slowly. Alex slightly squeezed his hand, which she was still holding.

"I'm afraid," he said in a strained voice, "that it was the same people who tried to kill me with the car bomb."

A half hour later, the otherwise peaceful cemetery was filled with people. The police searched every corner for evidence that could point to the perpetrator. Officers of the NYPD Crime Scene Unit examined the broken tombstone and the bullet, which had been fired by a precision rifle with a silencer. They crawled under the yew tree in search of footprints and talked to other cemetery visitors.

Nick introduced Alex to his assistant, who had rushed over from city hall. She had pictured him completely differently—much older and less pleasant—after their phone conversation the previous day. Frank Cohen was actually hardly older than she was, and he had a serious, narrow face and short dark hair. Behind his thick glasses, she detected an emotion in his eyes she was all too familiar with: fear.

"Nick," she said quietly, "I can't tell the police where I know this man from."

He looked at her.

"Before I talk to the police, I'd like to tell you everything. Please."

"Of course," he said. "We'll tell the police that you're a random visitor at the cemetery. Okay?"

Alex nodded in relief.

"Come with me," he said as he put his arm around her shoulders. "Let's go to my office. They don't need us here anymore."

This was Alex's first time at city hall. She was impressed when she looked around the office of New York City's mayor. During the past few hours, she had completely forgotten Nick's position. She knew many powerful and influential men, but Nick Kostidis was the first to show her that even a powerful man could experience emotions.

Frank Cohen brewed some coffee. Alex initially thought that she couldn't eat anything, but then suddenly felt as hungry as a wolf. After two cups of coffee and a sandwich, she felt much better. She eased into telling her story. She briefly explained to them what she did at LMI and then talked about Sergio. She was astonished how easy it was for her to talk to the mayor and his assistant about all the things that she had been keeping completely secret. It almost felt like a confession, and she was relieved. She told them about the conversation she had overheard at Sergio's birthday party last year, about the assassination attempt she had witnessed, about the warehouse in Brooklyn, and her suspicion that Sergio and Levy were exploiting her information for insider trading. Then she shared with them what she'd discovered about the secret slush-fund accounts on Grand Cayman. Both men listened to her with growing consternation. Nick stared at her, leaning forward with his elbows resting on his knees.

"What do you think about that, Nick?" Frank said. "De Lancie, McIntyre, Whitewater, Rhodes, Senator Hoffman, even Jerome Harding."

"I can't believe it." Nick leaned back and ran his hand through his hair. "If that's actually true, then..."

Frank Cohen jumped up excitedly.

"This scheme goes even deeper than we ever suspected!"

Nick suddenly looked tired and very depressed.

"Now I understand why I never had a chance against this man," he said in a low voice. "Howard informed them about all of my actions. And all the others covered his back no matter what he did."

"We might be able to get all of them." Frank's eyes gleamed. "We could finally drain this swamp of corruption! Nick! This is what you've always been fighting for!"

Nick stood up and stepped to the window. He looked out pensively.

"No," he said after a while.

"But why not?" Alex asked in surprise. He turned around and met her gaze.

"I can't do this," he said, shaking his head. "Vitali will find out where we got our information from."

"How could he find out?" Frank protested.

"You must do this, Nick." Alex made herself heard. "Frank's right. You could free the city from this terrible corruption with a single blow."

"No," Nick repeated, "I can't take responsibility for this."

"But—"

"I don't want anything to happen to you, Alex," Nick interrupted her. "Too many people have died on Vitali's orders. He tried to have me killed again today. If he finds out that you've given me this information, then he'll also kill you. And that…no…I don't want that to happen."

He took a deep breath and straightened his shoulders.

"I may need to resign as mayor."

Nelson van Mieren made himself comfortable in first class on the United flight from Chicago O'Hare to La Guardia. He had gone to Chicago for the weekend for business, but the talks went nowhere. He was frustrated that these three days had been nothing but wasted time. On top of that, he had missed his eldest grandson's birthday party. While passengers boarded the airplane, Nelson opened the newspaper he had picked up in the departures lounge. One headline caught his eye immediately, and he froze when he caught sight of the drawing that was placed directly below the bold caption.

Shots Fired at Mayor Kostidis

Early Sunday morning, less than three months after his wife and son were killed by a car bomb, another assassination attempt was committed against New York City's mayor, Nick Kostidis, at St. Ignatius cemetery in Brooklyn. Several eyewitnesses observed a man aiming at Kostidis with a precision rifle from a distance of about forty yards. It was one cemetery visitor's presence of mind that saved the mayor's life. The shooter was able to flee the scene, but police artists created this sketch based on eyewitness descriptions.

Nelson van Mieren turned pale. His heart was racing, and he realized that he was breaking into a cold sweat. The drawing of the alleged shooter—whom Nelson knew all too well—was alarmingly accurate. There was no doubt that this was Natale Torrinio, called "the Neapolitan." Nelson closed his eyes. His heart was pounding in his head. He realized that Sergio had sent him to Chicago under false pretense so that he could take his time and set the Neapolitan on the mayor. Sergio had lied to him when he reassured him that he had nothing to do with the bombing of the mayor's car. The realization that his oldest friend had lied to him was the most painful feeling Nelson had experienced in his life.

Sergio thought it was a bad joke when the butler from Mount Kisco called his office to say that Constanzia had left early in the morning by taxi—with four large suitcases and a few bags. She hadn't announced where she was going. Although it didn't fit into today's schedule at all, he ordered his sons to go to Mount Kisco. Then he took his helicopter there to determine what had happened.

Sergio was in a murderously bad mood after his best man Natale had botched the job yesterday. There hadn't been an opening to get to Kostidis for weeks. He'd been constantly surrounded by a line of bodyguards. It was Natale's idea to kill him at the cemetery because he found out that Kostidis didn't let his security follow him to his family's grave. It seemed like an easy enough operation. He could generally rely one hundred percent on Natale, but this time he'd not only missed his mark but had also been seen. Sergio could have dealt with that, but Natale also claimed that he saw Alex together with Kostidis at the cemetery.

Sergio had unsuccessfully tried to call her at home and on her cell phone, so finally he sent his people over to her apartment. They confirmed that she wasn't there. She only appeared again at six that evening. Someone with a blue Honda had dropped her off at home, and Sergio was close to going on a rampage when he heard about that.

Then he found a letter addressed to him on his desk in his Mount Kisco house. He tore it open impatiently and read the few lines Constanzia had written in her sweeping handwriting:

Sergio,
I'm leaving you today. I thought long and hard about this decision, but after Cesare's death I no longer see any possibility of continuing my life as it has been up to now. My sons don't need me anymore. And you don't need me either, if you ever have. I can't stand the house and the loneliness anymore.
Constanzia

He stared at the letter in his hands silently. Fury consumed him. How dare Constanzia? She had packed her bags and disappeared like a thief in the night without even uttering a word. He crumpled the paper angrily and threw it away. Silvio and his sons stood in front of the desk with embarrassed faces while Sergio paced up and down the large room furiously.

"How could she do this?" he roared. "How dare she? Didn't I give her everything that a woman dreams of? Didn't I buy her everything she wanted? She has countless servants. Three cars!"

"Mama was very unhappy," Domenico said carefully. "And after Cesare's death—"

"Unhappy, ha!" Sergio cut him off. "She made him into what he was! A good-for-nothing, spoiled, and ungrateful brat! He was cowardly and dumb to boot!"

He felt like killing someone with his bare hands, which is why these three men who knew him well prudently remained silent.

"Domenico," Sergio ordered, "bring all of the domestic workers here, right now. I want to know where she went. The last thing I can afford right now is the headline that my wife…"

He fell silent. He couldn't bring himself to say his wife had left him out loud. How could Constanzia humiliate him like this? If he'd wanted to get divorced, then it was up to him to do so, but the fact that she'd run away was more than his vanity could take.

"I told you to get them!" he yelled at his younger son. "*Pronto!*"

Domenico shot him an upset look and disappeared.

"How could she do this to me?" Sergio continued his restless pacing like a predator in a cage. "How could she expose me like this?"

"But, Papa," Massimo tried to argue, "she didn't expose you at all. No one but us knows about this."

"Soon everyone will know!" Sergio yelled. "Everyone will make fun of me!"

"Ahh, I don't believe that."

"Shut up!" Sergio snarled at his son. His face was pale with anger. "She makes me look like an idiot in front of my people. I'll never forgive her for that! Sergio Vitali left by his wife! That's unheard of!"

Sergio's anger wasn't really about his wife. What really made him furious was the fact that Alex had lied to him. She had told him that she was with the Downeys on Long Island. But instead, she'd snuck behind his back to see Kostidis!

"Silvio," Sergio said after a while, calming down, "make sure that Constanzia comes back here. I don't care how you do it. But if I read a single line about it in the newspaper, you're fired! *Capito?*"

Silvio nodded calmly. He had gotten used to his boss's temper tantrums years ago.

"Hold on!" There was a cruel smile on Sergio's face.

"Call Luca. I have a special job for him."

Silvio nodded and left the room.

"What's your plan, Papa?" Massimo asked, concerned. "What will you do with Mama?"

"Nothing." Sergio waved his hand dismissively and walked to the bar to pour himself a whiskey. "I just want her to return to this house."

"What about this special job?"

"It has nothing to do with your mother." He downed the whiskey in one gulp. That damn bitch Alex was about to really get to know him! First she'd pretended that she couldn't wait to get married and live with him, and then she met secretly with his archenemy!

Alex looked around her now-empty apartment as she waited for the movers to arrive. Maybe it was naive of her to think that she could escape from Sergio, but at least she no longer owed him anything. Alex checked her watch and lit a cigarette. Her thoughts drifted back to last Sunday. She was deeply touched that Nick put her safety ahead of her information against Sergio. She had assumed that he'd do anything to avenge the murder of his wife and his son, but the bombing and the shooting at the cemetery had changed his mind. When he called her late Monday afternoon, they talked for nearly fifteen minutes. But he didn't utter a single word about what Alex had told him on Sunday.

The doorbell rang right at that moment. Alex walked across her apartment, opened the door, and froze. Constanzia Vitali was standing in front of her.

"Excuse me for showing up unannounced," Sergio's wife said. "May I come in?"

"Umm…of course." Alex was astonished and embarrassed at the same time. Had Sergio actually filed for divorce? Did his wife come here to make a scene? Constanzia Vitali stepped into the foyer.

Alex had only seen Sergio's wife once before, and that was a year and a half ago. The woman had visibly aged since then. Deep wrinkles had settled into her face, and she had bags under her brown eyes. She couldn't hide her unhappiness. She had lost her son, and Alex suspected Sergio did little to comfort his wife during this difficult time.

"You won't be surprised to hear that I don't want to see your husband anymore," Alex said.

"You're leaving him?" Constanzia raised her eyebrows in surprise.

"That's my intention," Alex replied.

"Well," Constanzia said, smiling with wicked amusement, "then Sergio has been left by his wife and his lover on the same day. That'll be a big blow for his ego and his pride."

"You…*left him*?" Alex asked in disbelief.

"Yes." Constanzia nodded and gave her a probing look.

Constanzia sat down in one of the rattan chairs and observed Alex, who was her absolute opposite in terms of appearance. She was silent for a while as she considered how to phrase her question.

"I have known Sergio since we were small children," she began. "We grew up in Little Italy. Everyone knew everyone there. Ignazio Vitali sent

Sergio to a boarding school when he was six years old, shortly after his brother Aldo was killed by a rival gang."

Alex was astonished because Sergio told her that his brother died of an illness, but she wasn't surprised to learn he had kept the truth from her.

"Sergio only returned to the city after his father's death," Constanzia continued. "Ignazio, who was the *padrino* of the Genovese family, was essentially executed because he was in the way. My father was his successor. I didn't understand the intricacies of the power structure among the city's families back then. I fell head over heels in love with Sergio when I saw him at a girlfriend's wedding, and I could hardly believe it when we got married just a short time later. I was deaf and blind with love and didn't listen to my father's warnings. However, I realized very quickly that Sergio didn't love me."

Constanzia's face hardened when she remembered the humiliation that Sergio had caused her.

"When I was pregnant my husband cheated on me with every cheap whore on Mulberry Street, but I didn't say a word, just like any good Italian wife. Sergio was much too busy becoming rich and powerful to be interested in what I was doing. He married me for just one reason—because I was Carlo Gambino's daughter."

Constanzia looked inquiringly at Alex.

"You're not surprised to hear that Sergio comes from one of the city's most powerful Mafia families, are you?"

"He told me that his father was a known killer," Alex replied hesitantly.

"Pah!" Constanzia exclaimed. "Ignazio Vitali wasn't just a killer. He was the feared enforcer of Lucky Luciano and Dutch Schultz—both of whom he later shot, by the way. But this is old stuff. They're all long dead. Sergio bought the house in Mount Kisco after he made his first millions. It was terrible for me to live so far away from my family and friends, but Sergio thought it would be beneath his dignity to keep living on Mulberry Street. He bought the apartment on Park Avenue and only came home to me every now and then. He's always been an inconsiderate egomaniac, and our marriage was never worth more than the paper it was written on. Sergio always did what he wanted, and I knew from the very first day that he couldn't resist a beautiful young woman."

Alex blushed, but Constanzia didn't seem to notice.

"As the years passed, our sons grew up and left the house. All of them, except Cesare." Constanzia sighed heavily. "Sergio always despised Cesare. He was different from his brothers, weaker and not as intelligent. He was in trouble all the time, and I lived in constant fear of Sergio's temper tantrums when Cesare got himself into hot water."

She smiled sadly, and the tears shone in her big eyes.

"It happened on the day of Sergio's birthday party last year, as you probably remember. Sergio threw Cesare out of the house, and he never came back. He called me every now and then, but I didn't know where he lived or what he was doing. I was terribly worried about him. Whenever I tried to talk to Sergio about the boy, he got angry. A few days after the party, I heard that David Zuckerman had been shot. He and his wife were good friends with my eldest son and often came over to visit. I knew right away that Sergio was responsible for his death."

Alex held her breath.

"Then came the day Sergio was shot. I wasn't shocked when Massimo called to tell me that his father was injured. No, I wasn't hysterical. I laughed. May God forgive me, but for a second I hoped that he was dead."

She smiled briefly at her own ridiculousness, but quickly her expression turned grim.

"Cesare was arrested that very same night. When I learned that he was…dead, I almost lost it. I was sure that Sergio had something to do with his death. I accused him of it a few days later when he came home from the hospital. I screamed and said all kinds of hideous things to him. Everything that had accumulated inside of me over the years burst out, and I finally realized that it was the truth that I never wanted to see."

Alex saw Constanzia's tears, and she understood how this woman felt. Wasn't she in a similar situation?

"On that day it became clear to me that I hated Sergio. I wished him dead. I decided to leave him right then, but I lacked the courage. Then I heard about the assassination attempt on the mayor that killed his wife and son. I know how much Sergio despises Mayor Kostidis. Even though he never talked to me about business, I witnessed enough in thirty years to put two and two together." Constanzia shrugged her shoulders. "Sergio orders people who stand in his way killed. Ever since childhood, I've been used to people around me dying—but not from old age in their bed. My father was a Mafioso, just like my brothers and uncles, but my husband Sergio is the worst of them all—more brutal and ruthless than even Lucky Luciano or Al Capone ever were. He's a criminal, and I know it. I've endured all of this for my boys through all these years. But now that Cesare is dead, I can't go on like this anymore. All of the blood, violence, and death—it's too much for my conscience."

Alex felt as if a cold hand had grabbed her by the neck. All of the color vanished from her face.

"Sergio killed his own son?" she whispered, terrified.

"Yes," Constanzia said, nodding, "not with his own hands, of course. He wouldn't, because he has people for that. But I know he did. He was afraid that, under pressure in prison, Cesare would start talking. My son had to die for the same reason as David Zuckerman or the man at LMI who was supposedly run over."

Alex swallowed frantically.

"Gilbert Shanahan?"

"Yes, I think that was his name. His wife told the truth. The poor woman would have been better off keeping her mouth shut. They put her into a psychiatric clinic, and now she's wasting away in a padded cell."

Alex's mouth was dry as cotton. Once she took it all in, she was overcome with terror. Oliver was right. Gilbert Shanahan had been killed because he didn't want to play the game anymore and tried to get out.

"Why are you telling me all this, Mrs. Vitali?" she whispered.

Constanzia looked at her.

"I came here to warn you and to ask you for something," she said. "I overheard a conversation last Sunday evening. Natale Torrinio, one of the killers who works for Sergio, told him that he saw you at the cemetery with Mayor Kostidis."

Alex tried to control her panic. Natale Torrinio—the man with the yellow eyes.

"Alex," Constanzia said emphatically, "Sergio has caused enough grief and sorrow. I wish that I had the courage to stab a kitchen knife through his cold heart, but I'm too much of a coward for that. I want someone to put an end to his crimes. I want revenge for my dead son and for everything that this monster has done to me and my family."

She leaned forward and grabbed Alex's hand.

"I have an ally," she said, lowering her voice, "but he and I won't be able to do it on our own, although we could destroy Sergio with our knowledge. I need contact with someone who is powerful and fearless enough to support me with what I must do. I can't simply go to the police or the US Attorney's Office. Sergio would find out about it right away and have me silenced."

She paused for a moment.

"Alex, you know the right people. You know the mayor. You can help me!"

Alex jumped up and desperately wrapped her arms around herself. Of all people, Constanzia Vitali had come to her for help! She felt miserable. If Sergio hadn't even batted an eye at the murder of his own son, he certainly wouldn't hesitate to kill her. What had she gotten herself into? And all of this because of her damned ambition, her arrogance, her insatiable drive to belong in high society. She was a gangster's whore, just what Oliver had accused her of being. All her work, her education—everything had been in vain! At thirty-seven, when others were getting their careers in high gear, her future was already over. She'd never be safe from Sergio again. Fear sprang to her eyes, and she turned around to face Constanzia Vitali. And somehow the woman was looking at her, full of hope.

"I'm afraid that I can't help you, Mrs. Vitali," she said, struggling to keep her composure. She thought about Nick's words. *A few months ago, I would have been happy to hear that. Now I just don't care anymore. That won't bring my family back to life.*

No, she wouldn't be able to help either.

Constanzia stood up.

"I don't mean to pressure you." She rummaged around in her purse until she found what she was looking for. "This is my phone number. You can reach me at any time."

Once Sergio's wife left, Alex sank down to the ground, sobbing and burying her face in her hands. The bitter truth was that she had irrevocably botched her future. Her entire life was ruined.

Sergio stood silently in the penthouse apartment where Alex used to live. She had moved out. The closets were empty, the refrigerator was unplugged, and all of her books and CDs were gone. Sergio felt his insides contract as a wave of disappointment rolled through him; he couldn't deny how skillfully she had deceived him. She had been acting for the past few days, and he—being somewhat serious with his marriage proposal—had let her lead him by his nose like a little boy. It was an ironic twist of fate that Alex had left him on the same day as Constanzia. He had been so close to trusting her, and now this! This rejection was too humiliating, and at the same time he was overcome with a feeling of emptiness that was foreign and threatening to him.

His first impulse was to call her, but then his reason took hold. He breathed heavily and closed his eyes for a moment. Alex hadn't gone to the Downeys last Sunday. Natale was right: She had met that bastard Kostidis at the cemetery in Brooklyn. She was the one who saved him. Of all people, it was because of Alex that this miserable son of a bitch was still alive.

"What should we do now, boss?" Luca asked.

"Nothing," said Sergio, unaffected on the surface. "Remove the microphones and cameras and renovate the apartment. And give me her passport. I'll return it to her personally."

He clenched his hands into fists. His disappointment had turned into cold rage.

It was eight fifteen when Frank Cohen entered his boss's office. Nick Kostidis was behind his desk, staring at a framed picture of his deceased wife, as he had done so many times recently.

"I thought you left already," Nick said.

"I revised the press release for the planned welfare reform again," Frank replied, "and jotted down a couple of arguments that could be helpful for your meeting with Paul Inishan of the Coalition for the Homeless."

"Ah, yes." Nick removed his reading glasses and rubbed his tired eyes. "I'll go over it tomorrow morning."

"Yes, of course."

"What's on my schedule for tomorrow?"

"Paul Inishan at nine. Coalition for the Homeless complained about your planned work program. After that, the delegation from Oman from ten until about one. Then you have a meeting with Lucie

McMillan of WCBS, who will accompany you to Fresh Kills, broadcast live. You have an appointment in Queens at three to see the new orphanage. Then, there's the ceremony honoring those firefighters who rescued the kids from that burning house in Morningside Heights last August—at five."

Frank looked at his boss. Nick appeared exhausted, but it was no wonder. Since his family's funeral, he'd recklessly thrown himself into his work. He had one appointment after another, from early morning until late at night. Nick rushed through the city, escorted by the police and security guards, and some staff members started complaining that the mayor forgot some people had lives outside of work. Frank wondered how much longer Nick could sustain this tempo. He'd created set an inhuman pace, but there was no one to slow him down. Frank had a feeling that Nick was doing this to escape his loneliness and his thoughts. He seemed just like his old self on the outside. But whenever he found himself alone, he virtually collapsed. On more than one occasion, Frank had caught him staring aimlessly into space or at his wife's picture.

"Have you thought about what Alex Sontheim told us?" Frank asked carefully.

"I can't think of anything else," Nick admitted. "Every day when I speak with these people, I realize how phony and devious they are. It may very well be that corruption has always been the order of the day in New York, but I just can't believe that even the police commissioner and the US attorney let themselves be bought by a criminal like Vitali."

"Maybe we can actually do something about it," Frank said. "How much of this story is true in your opinion?"

"Probably all of it. Why should she make such things up?"

"Then we shouldn't hesitate any longer. We could pass on that information to the US Attorney's Office." Frank sat down at the desk across from Nick. "You finally have the opportunity to hold Vitali accountable for everything he has done!"

"Frank, I've told you before," Nick answered with unusual patience. "My family had to die because I chased after Vitali like a maniac. With his latest attempt, he made it very clear that he still intends to kill me. He's dead serious. I won't risk the life of the woman who saved me."

"Alex Sontheim knows exactly what she's doing. She gave you this information so you'd something with it."

"Damn it!" Nick's voice turned harsh. "I take sleeping pills every night so I can sleep for at least a few hours. I immerse myself in my work to distract myself from these terrible images. My heart is filled with anger and lust for revenge. How could I possibly burden my conscience with even more guilt? Do you think that Vitali would hesitate to kill Alex once he found out what she knows?"

"She was, or still is, his lover after all," Frank replied. "Can we even be sure she was honest with us?"

Nick took a deep breath.

"I've considered that. But somehow I think she's being honest. Why else would she come to meet me at the cemetery? Why would she risk her life to save mine? That shot could have easily hit her!"

"Maybe it's all part of a plan so you believe exactly that."

"You're distrustful, Frank."

"I've learned that from you, Nick." Frank smiled mildly. "It was you who always questioned everything a hundred times before you believed it. And often enough you were right."

"Yes," Nick sighed bleakly, "I've always been proud of my knowledge of human nature, but it apparently leaves much to be desired. I never thought Ray capable of such betrayal."

"We should talk to Alex again," Frank suggested, "and ask her for documented evidence."

"Yes, maybe." Nick leaned back. Frank Cohen knew his boss well enough to know he didn't want to delve into this any deeper. Before leaving, he turned around one more time.

"Oh, Nick?"

"What else is there?"

"Have you eaten anything today?"

Nick smiled briefly, and then he nodded.

"I think I had a doughnut for breakfast. Go on, get out of here. Good night."

"Good night, boss. See you tomorrow."

Nick waited as his assistant closed the door behind him. Then he opened his desk drawer and took out an old issue of *People*. He flipped to the story about Alex Sontheim and stared at the large photograph of her. With a pensive smile on his face, he thought about that morning on Montauk Beach when he saw her galloping on that horse. He was suddenly sure that she had been honest with him.

On Tuesday afternoon, Alex had a meeting with Vincent Levy, Michael Friedman, and Hugh Weinberg. The three men were excited about the deal she was working on, in which LMI was to represent Whithers, the computer manufacturer from Texas, in its merger with Database Inc., earning a handsome fee for its services. The deal was as good as closed. The details would be ironed out over the next few weeks, followed by several meetings with the management teams from Whithers and Database.

Alex stared vacantly at her computer screen after she got back to her desk. She had spoken with Carter Ringwood at First Boston on the phone right before the meeting, and what she told him was a serious violation of securities law. If Levy found out what she had done, he wouldn't just fire her, he'd sue her in court—and rightfully so. Alex had learned that First Boston represented Softland Corporation, a competitor of Whithers. Softland was just as interested in Database as Whithers was. She mentioned in passing how much her offer was worth. Alex sighed and rested her chin in her hand. The deal would blow up for sure because Ringwood would certainly use her information to the advantage of his client. Alex didn't care. She was already planning to quit LMI this month and leave the city. She could go to Chicago, San Francisco, Europe, Asia. M&A specialists were in demand everywhere. Alex grinned bitterly as she thought about what was happening right now a few stories above her. Without a doubt, Levy was informing his managing director about the planned Whithers deal, and it was just as certain that Zack was building a position in Whithers stock. She expected that the imminent public announcement of the Database acquisition would catapult Whithers stock to new heights. What a pity for Zack if a white knight called Softland Corporation unexpectedly appeared out of nowhere on the merger battlefield! Alex's thoughts were elsewhere when her phone buzzed.

"Hello, Alex. This is Nick."

"Nick!" she exclaimed in surprise, her heart pounding. "How are you? I thought that something had happened because you didn't call."

"Oh no! I'm sorry. I've been very busy the past few days. I was also thinking about things."

"Aha."

He hesitated for a moment.

"Do you have time for dinner tonight?"

Alex swallowed. She had no plans.

"I'd love to," she said. "When and where?"

"There's a small Greek restaurant in an alley near the corner of Chambers Street and Hudson in Tribeca. It's called Alexis Sorbas. It's practically hidden. I'll see you at nine?"

"I'll find it," Alex replied.

She hung up and chewed pensively on her lower lip. Had Nick changed his mind? His voice sounded almost as determined as before the tragedy, but Alex no longer felt the urge to convince him. He had won her deep respect after the vulnerability he'd shown her at the cemetery. Sergio wouldn't hesitate a second if someone offered him information like this. He'd have precious little interest whether a life was put in danger, as long as he gained an advantage. Nick let go of his desire for revenge because he was worried about her safety. She found that simply incredible.

Someone knocked on the door, and Mark entered the room.

"I just received the quarterly results of Database," he announced. "Do you want to take a look at them?"

"Later. Thanks."

Mark put the folder on her desk. He was about to leave again when Alex asked him to stay.

"Sit down for a moment, please," she said. Mark did as he was told. He had become a very good friend over the past few months.

"I'm going to meet Mayor Kostidis this evening," she said.

"Aha."

"Ever since our trip to Boston, I've been thinking," Alex continued, not mentioning to Mark what she had already told the mayor. "I've come to the conclusion that I should tell him everything and give him the documents Justin printed out for us."

"Are you sure that's a good idea?"

"I don't know," Alex sighed, "but I can't go on like this. I know enough about Vitali to be seriously frightened of him. This man is capable of anything."

Suddenly, she had to fight her rising tears.

"Mark, I'm in deeper than you can imagine. This is no longer about right and wrong, or a betrayal of trust—it's about my life!" She bit her lip. "If Vitali finds out what I know, I'm as good as dead! He had Gilbert Shanahan killed because he wanted to get out, too."

"My God," Mark whispered in terror, "did you tell Oliver?"

"He suspected it the whole time," Alex replied in resignation. "He insinuated it when we first met at Battery Park. I should have believed him and left LMI."

Her office, guarded by thick glass panels that muted any noise from the trading floor, was silent.

"I'm resigning," Alex said. "That's actually what I wanted to tell you. I want to thank you for all of your hard work, and especially for your loyalty. I could always trust you."

"It was my pleasure." A sad smile flitted across Mark's face. "You're definitely the best boss I've ever had. If you're looking for an assistant at your new job, let me know."

Alex attempted a smile, then she wondered whether she should tell Mark about her conversation with Carter Ringwood. He deserved to know the truth because he had worked as hard on the Whithers deal as she had. She pulled herself together and told him what she had done.

Mark didn't seem shocked. "I hope you know what you're doing. If this comes out, then you're done."

Alex nodded. "I'm not sure if I did the right thing."

"You're going to blow up the deal in order to pull one over on Vitali, Levy, and St. John, right?"

Alex nodded again. Then Mark leaned across the desk and grabbed her hand.

"No matter what happens, Alex, I'm on your side. I also think that I've spent enough time in this joint. Maybe I'll quit, too."

"Don't make any rash decisions. I'm in deep trouble, but you're not. You still have a future."

"There probably won't be any M&A department left." He smiled and stood up. "I've somehow already gotten used to the idea."

After he left her office, Alex closed her eyes and sighed. There was nothing left of her ambition, and she suddenly longed for an average life, with a small family, a nice house with a yard, and someone who loved her.

Alex left her apartment through one of the back exits. Her blonde hair was hidden under a baseball cap. She was wearing a worn-out leather jacket, blue jeans, and heavy Doc Martens. She was unrecognizable.

Alex walked past the Dumpsters in the courtyard and entered the neighboring building. She and Oliver had identified all of the possible escape routes when she moved in, and she used them to remain undetected by Sergio's people. She had already noticed people waiting for her and tailing her from the LMI Building, and she recognized most of them. Perhaps Sergio hadn't yet found out where she lived.

Alex turned onto the lively Greenwich Street with its row of restaurants. New businesses were opening on an almost daily basis ever since an affluent crowd discovered this part of the city. It was just before nine, and the sidewalks were still filled with people. Indian summer had been unusually warm this year, and the bars set their tables and chairs on the sidewalks.

Alex turned onto Chambers Street. In small side alley, she finally found the inconspicuous restaurant Nick had invited her to. She heard muted Greek folk music as she entered a large room. Its ceiling and walls were decorated with realistic-looking plastic vines, creating a pergola-like effect. Its many cheap replicas of famous statues, pictures of the Acropolis, and photographs of the blue Mediterranean Sea with dazzling white houses hinted at the owner's homesickness.

Most of the tables were still empty, and the waiter led her to the corner. Alex ordered a glass of white wine. Shortly after nine, two men entered the restaurant—looking around and inspecting it suspiciously. Nick came in shortly thereafter. He smiled at Alex, but stopped to exchange a few words with the chef before walking over to her table.

"Good evening, Alex."

"Hello, Nick." She smiled somewhat nervously.

"I hope you're hungry," he said. "I ordered two saganaki as appetizers and souvlaki after that."

He winked at her, grinning slightly.

"It's not exactly Le Cirque, but Konstantinos makes the city's best souvlaki."

"Whatever that is, I believe you."

They looked at each other for a moment without saying a word. Alex noticed that Nick looked exhausted and that his face had become thinner. His hair was longer than usual, and a bluish five o'clock shadow covered his cheeks.

"Do you speak Greek?" she asked, just to make conversation.

"A little bit. My mother never learned to speak English properly. People in Greece would immediately identify me as a foreigner, but Konstantinos likes it when I speak Greek with him."

"But you're Catholic, right? I thought people in Greece are usually..."

"Greek Orthodox," he said, nodding. "My parents weren't religious. They didn't care what I did. There was a young priest in our neighborhood who looked after the street kids—Father Kevin, you met him the other day. He gave me books to read and took me to church, where I became an altar boy. I think I liked Catholicism's simple dogmatism of good and evil as a child, and that's how I've felt ever since."

Nick folded his hands and rested his chin on them. She looked at him closely for the first time. Alex noticed that his eyes weren't black but rather a very dark brown. They were beautiful and expressive, filled with warmth and a hint of melancholy.

"I believe that there is a certain period in everyone's life where their character is set for the rest of their days," he said pensively. "For me it was the time when I discovered the world of education and faith through the Jesuit priest. Good and evil, black and white—that was my perspective of life for forty years. But now I see that this isn't quite accurate. There are other colors as well."

The waiter served them an appetizer of baked feta cheese, with tomatoes and cucumber. They clinked their wine glasses and ate in silence.

"Are things going well for you, Nick?" Alex asked after she had finished. A shadow flitted across his face, and he waited until the waiter had cleared the table.

"No," he replied and sighed. "I'm not doing very well. I immerse myself in my work during the day, and sometimes I even manage not to think about Mary and Chris. But when I come home at night, it feels like I'm standing before an abyss. Mary had always been there—for thirty years."

His gaze was empty and hollow-eyed. Alex suspected that something was gnawing at him somewhere deep inside; a wild cry waiting to erupt, just as it had at the cemetery.

"I often think about asking her opinion about this and that, and then I realize that she's not there anymore. It's terrible."

Alex looked at him sympathetically. She really wanted to grab his hand and say something consoling, but she couldn't—not here in public, with his bodyguards watching from the neighboring table.

"People treat me like a monster." He shook his head in helpless desperation. "Most of the people who I thought were my friends have distanced themselves from me. No one dares to speak to me about Mary, and that's why they don't invite me out anymore. Maybe they're afraid I might burst into tears at the table and embarrass them."

"They're not real friends then," Alex replied. "I wouldn't be embarrassed if you cried here and now."

Nick looked at her, and for a moment she thought that he would actually break down.

"I know," he said, his voice gruff, "and believe it or not, that's a great comfort to me. It's strange that even though we hardly know each other, I don't feel the need to pretend when I'm with you."

He took a sip of wine. They remained silent for a moment, but it wasn't an uncomfortable silence.

"Are you really considering resigning?" Alex asked.

"I don't know," he answered. "Everything I do seems pointless now. But whenever I'm about to give up, I feel I have a great and important duty to perform on behalf of my constituents. I gave them my word, and they trust me. How can I just give up on everything?"

He smiled slightly.

"I have the bank statements for you," Alex said abruptly. "I thought that was why you wanted to meet with me."

The smile vanished from Nick's face.

"You're still suspicious," he said, "and I can't blame you for it. I admit that I actually tried to get information about Vitali from you last Christmas at the Downeys'. But then…"

Alex's heart started pounding again when she felt his gaze. It was as penetrating as it had been at the Lands End House.

"Then I learned that you're friends with the Downeys, and I thought that this woman couldn't possibly be on Vitali's side if she also spends her weekends with Trevor and Maddy."

She turned and pulled the rolled-up printouts from her jacket. She had taken them from the bank safe-deposit box that afternoon. Nick stared blankly at the sheets, but then he put on his reading glasses, spread out the papers, and started to read with an expressionless face.

"Unbelievable," he murmured after a while. "McIntyre…and here, Alan Milkwood from the Department of Buildings and Jerome Harding—those corrupt bastards."

"Did anyone ever try to bribe you?"

"More than once," Nick said, looking up, "over and over again. Not only with money. They also offered trades: a kindergarten in return for a building permit, a donation to the NYPD widows and orphans fund in return for dropping criminal charges. That's how things go in New York City."

He sighed.

"I've always resisted. It's difficult; at times the temptation is strong. The city has no money to build new schools, and who really cares whether a skyscraper turns out to be three stories taller if hundreds of kids in Harlem or the Bronx enjoy a state-of-the-art kindergarten in return? I've stood in my own way many times."

"Can you use these bank statements for something?" Alex wanted to know.

"If they're real, then definitely." Nick smiled grimly and looked at the next page. "I would have been ecstatic if I had gotten my hands on something like this during my days as a US attorney. This is more than just the tip of the iceberg—this is the whole conspiracy."

"Why don't you pass it on to the US Attorney's Office?"

"Alex!" He put the papers down and looked at her seriously. "This is pure dynamite! This is more than just a few headlines in the newspaper. These names and numbers will shake this city's power structure to the core, and none of these people will simply put up with being accused of corruption. There will be extensive legal proceedings, libel actions, allegations, possibly even deaths. I've seen it happen before: in the seventies and eighties with the Mafia, and with Wall Street after that."

He stared at the stack of papers, shuffled them nervously, and then looked up again.

"Believe me. I know how this goes, how much work is involved, how often the accused manage to squirm their way out with the help of their clever lawyers."

"But a US attorney, a judge, or even a governor is finished when the public finds out he's corrupt, right?"

"Yes, that's true," Nick admitted, "but do you know what power-hungry people are capable of when they realize they've been cornered?"

The waiter served the entrées, and Nick fell silent. They waited until the food was laid out.

"I'm not interested in all those people." Alex lowered her voice. "This is about Vitali."

"Because of personal vengeance or hurt vanity?"

"No! This man kills people who stand in his way. I know it! With my own ears, I heard someone tell him that David Zuckerman had been silenced."

Nick looked at her pensively; then he put his cutlery down.

"Okay," he said in a sober voice, "let me explain to you how this would work. I hand this material over to the US Attorney's Office or the FBI. They investigate and possibly conclude that there's something to it. Vitali is arrested, but thanks to his connections, he's most likely released on bail. If charges are actually brought against him, then you'd be the main witness for the prosecution."

Alex swallowed nervously.

"This would not be the first time we thought we had enough evidence to take down Vitali. But our witnesses always failed us. Some of them lost their memory overnight, and others disappeared without a trace. Sometimes they were found again in a landfill or floating in the river. Vitali is merciless. Would you want to live with a new identity somewhere in the Midwest for the rest of your life, constantly in fear that one day they'll find you?"

He shook his head.

"In the past, I would have done anything to get to Vitali. Today, I doubt whether something could be right if it costs a person's life."

Alex licked her dry lips.

"What would you do in my position, Nick?" she whispered. "I can't go on like this. I'm scared of him, but I still want him to be brought to justice."

Nick stared at her.

"You're very brave. And intelligent. I admire that about you."

"No I'm not. Otherwise, I wouldn't have fallen for Vitali."

"Many other women would fall for him, too," Nick said. "He's good looking, charming, and incredibly rich."

"Oh yes," she said and laughed bitterly. "He reserved the entire Crows Nest at the Water Club for one evening—the whole staff, and a band."

"Did you love him?"

Alex hesitated, surprised by this very personal question.

"No," she said slowly, "it wasn't love. I was impressed and flattered that such a powerful, famous man was courting me. I aspired to become one of the city's famous and powerful people, and I thought that I could accomplish that through him. How could I have known that I was only a small cog in the wheel of his dirty business?"

"Are you still in contact with him?"

"Do you mean, do I still sleep with him?"

"No." Nick blushed slightly. "I…I didn't mean it that way."

"He asked me to marry him the last time I saw him." Alex's face hardened. "Most likely because he's afraid he won't be able to bring in those lucrative deals anymore. I moved out of the apartment he rented to me. A friend signed a new lease for me in his name, and since then, I have been afraid that Vitali will find out where I live. I change trains three times in the subway and sneak out of the building through the back. He knows that I was with you at the cemetery. The man who tried to shoot you recognized me."

Nick looked alarmed. "Did he tell you that?"

"His wife came over to my place to warn me," she replied. "She left him because she's convinced that Vitali ordered the death of his own son."

"Vitali's wife came to you?" Nick asked in disbelief.

"Yes. She hates him and wants revenge. And she'd like to talk to you, Nick."

"You're in great danger, Alex."

"I know. But he won't touch me as long as I'm coordinating his dirty business. But once he no longer needs me…" She fell silent.

"I can arrange personal security for you," Nick offered. "Where do you live now?"

"On Reade Street. Just around the corner." Alex ate a bite from her already cold kabob, although her stomach felt sealed shut. "Personal protection is unnecessary; I work at a company that he largely owns."

When the waiter came to clear the table, Nick had hardly eaten anything. He handled a piece of bread, lost in thought.

"Do you know why I don't want to pass on this information?" he asked in a throaty voice. "I'm afraid that Vitali will hurt you."

On their way out, they saw that the restaurant had filled up since their arrival. The four bodyguards were waiting for them at the street corner.

"Isn't it better if I have someone drive you home?" Nick asked, and Alex detected true concern in his eyes.

"No, it's okay. It's so close."

"Are you sure?"

"Yes. It's better if I use my secret paths."

"I'm worried about you, Alex."

"I'm really in hot water, aren't I?"

Nick looked at her with a grave expression.

"Yes, I'm afraid so."

She dug both her hands into her jacket pockets. "Would you pass the information against Vitali on to the US Attorney's Office if I quit my job and leave the city?"

"Is that what you're planning to do?"

"I hardly have a choice." Alex felt a painful lump in her throat. She was more aware of the hopelessness of her situation than ever before.

"Maybe you're right," Nick said and sighed. "I toyed with the idea of packing it all in myself. No one could blame you for it. Who the hell cares."

Still standing outside the restaurant, they gazed at each other under the lantern's dim light.

"I have to go," she said. "Thank you, Nick, for the lovely evening."

Nick extended his hand and she took it. Alex remembered how she had held him in her arms as he cried, and she fervently wished that she could stay with him a little longer. She didn't care who he was, although it would have been much easier if he hadn't been—of all people—the mayor of New York.

Alex let go of his hand, but he didn't seem ready to leave either. Then she impulsively flung her arms around him and nestled her face against his rough cheek. They remained in a comforting embrace for a brief moment until another customer came out of the restaurant.

"Take care of yourself, Alex," Nick whispered gruffly. She nodded silently and then turned around and disappeared with quick steps.

Wednesday, December 1, 2000

Vincent Levy's face was grim as he hung up the phone. LMI's board was anxiously awaiting their president's explanation of just what had interrupted their extraordinary meeting on this rainy December afternoon. Levy looked around the group, and then he walked over to the large window. Everything seemed to shift in the hazy air. The Verrazano Bridge was just visible in the distance, and even the Statue of Liberty seemed farther away than usual. There was complete silence in the room as Levy turned around.

"Gentlemen," he said, clearing his throat, "I've just learned that the acquisition of Database Inc. by Whithers Computers is off. Database has agreed to a friendly takeover by Softland Corporation. First Boston made the cut. We're out."

Everyone in the room was speechless as they stared at the president. The deal, worth almost two billion dollars—one of the biggest ever in the technology sector—seemed signed, sealed, and delivered long ago. The M&A department had been working on little else for weeks. St. John finally broke his board colleagues' numb silence.

"That stupid bitch screwed it up!" he yelled. He banged his fist on the table with such force that the glasses and bottles rattled. "I could wring her neck!"

"What do you mean, Zack?" Hugh Weinberg asked in surprise.

"Just like I said!" Zack's face turned bright red, and beads of sweat appeared on his forehead. "This was a surefire deal, but she was too stupid to seal it!"

"Zack, I beg your pardon!" Levy interrupted. "You can't blame Alex for the Database shareholders' decision."

"What the hell!" Zack jumped up and laughed derisively. "You're all blind because she closed a few good transactions! But she just screwed up the year's biggest deal in the technology sector!"

"That's not true!" Michael Friedman objected. "She did the best she could. She made a solid offer. Database stock was to be acquired for forty dollars a share—"

"I don't give a shit how good that damned offer was." Zack cut him off harshly. "It wasn't good enough. Why are we paying her all of this money if she can't even keep an eye on the market properly?"

"That's not fair, Zack," John Kwai said. "Alex has closed a lot of good deals for us. We can't condemn her just because one of them goes sour!"

"Come with me, Zack." Levy threw an imploring look at his managing director. He was the only one who knew why Zack was overreacting like this. Since Alex had told them about the planned deal, MPM had established a large position in Whithers shares—causing their stock price to skyrocket accordingly. Levy guided the incensed man to an adjacent office and closed the door.

"We're ruined, Vince!" Zack exclaimed in agitation. "Jack and I bought a shitload of Whithers stock for thirty-eight a share, fucking hell! We'll never get rid of them at this price!"

"Calm down, Zack," Levy said in a conciliatory tone. "We can handle a loss of a few dollars per share."

"No, we can't!" Sweat was running down Zack's face. "I invested a fucking *hundred million dollars*!"

"Excuse me?" Levy went pale. "Are you crazy?"

"It was a sure thing! According to Weinberg's forecast, the stock would have gone up thirty points after the announcement of the takeover."

Zack's body shook. His face flashed red and paled again.

"I financed the hundred million through LMI."

"You're joking." Levy couldn't believe his ears. "How could you do such a thing? We talked about buying for ten million, maybe fifteen—but one hundred million...That can't be true!"

"I'm not joking, damn it!" Zack roared at him. "Fucking hell, I still can't believe it!"

"We have to get rid of these shares immediately," Levy said, struggling to stay calm. "Call our broker on the West Coast. The exchange is still open there. Tell him to sell at any price!"

Zack didn't hesitate. While Zack was on the phone, Levy paced, looking panicked.

"Whithers is trading down to thirty-one at the Pacific Stock Exchange and thirty and seven-eighths on the OTC market," Zack said in a sepulchral tone. "Koons will try to sell as much as possible, but it doesn't look good."

Levy shook his head with a sense of helplessness. Because of Zack's greed, they were sitting on a pile of devalued stock that was on its way to hitting rock bottom.

"I have to talk to Vitali," Levy murmured. "This is a catastrophe."

"This is more than a catastrophe," Zack said grimly as he dialed another number. "MPM is ruined."

"How could you do this without discussing it with me in advance?"

Real horror scenarios played back like a film in Levy's mind's eye. He saw himself at the center of an SEC investigation, his name in the headlines, his firm on the brink of bankruptcy.

"Don't freak out!" Zack snarled at him. "Maybe there's a way to get us out of this mess unscathed."

"What do you mean?"

"As of now, no one knows about the Database shareholders' decision. I know a few people who would be thankful for a tip. I could sell the Whithers stock to them."

"No!" Levy said sharply. "Under no circumstances will you do that! No employee of LMI will pass on insider information with one hundred million dollars on the line. If that got out, we'd be ruined. No one would do business with us again."

Levy left the room and rushed into his office to call Vitali.

It was seven thirty when Sergio Vitali entered Levy's office.

"What's going on here?" The look on Zack and Levy's frozen faces soured his mood. Zack had four telephones in front of him, and an ashtray overflowed next to them.

"The Whithers deal is off," Levy said gloomily.

"So what?" Sergio looked back and forth between the two men.

"We were sure that the deal was sealed, so Zack bought one hundred million dollars' worth of Whithers through MPM. The share price has already fallen thirteen dollars since news broke that Database is merging with Softland Corporation. The hundred million was financed by LMI. We're done."

Zack turned around. His face was pale, and his voice sounded strained.

"I just managed to sell another hundred and fifty thousand shares at thirty-one dollars, but that was it."

"If Whithers opens below thirty dollars tomorrow, we're ruined," Levy said. "That will certainly happen. I even think they'll halt trading in Whithers altogether. Not a single soul will want to buy Whithers stock."

"How could this happen?" Sergio asked. He suddenly fully understood the consequences.

"That dumb bitch screwed it up," Zack said.

"Who is he talking about?" Sergio looked at Levy.

"Alex Sontheim," Levy replied, "but it's not her fault. She prepared a good offer. Everything went well and the lawyers agreed, but then this white knight appeared and made a better offer. That's business, it happens. It was unfortunate that Zack bought so much of it."

"This is the second time in a very short time span." Sergio turned toward Zack. "What was that other deal?"

Zack threw him an angry look.

"Syncrotron." He clenched his teeth in anger.

"What can we do now?" Sergio asked. "It's pointless to sit around and wait for the exchange to open in the morning."

"There's nothing more we can do." Levy poured himself a double shot of whiskey. "We're sitting on a pile of shares that no one will take off our hands. MPM needs to liquidate its position tomorrow and raise a hundred million dollars. LMI is financially solid, but we can't write off such a large sum just like that."

"Tell Lang to sell other shares…of something…what do I know!" Sergio suggested.

"We already considered all the scenarios." Levy shook his head. "Even if MPM liquidates all of its assets, we have a maximum of fifty million. MPM will be in violation of capital requirements tomorrow morning, and therefore insolvent."

"And what does that mean?" Sergio asked in irritation. "Can you please explain it to me in plain English?"

"It means," Levy said in an annoyed voice, "that MPM is bankrupt."

"Never has a company of mine gone bankrupt!" Sergio said, struggling to keep his voice down. "Get Alex here immediately, and also Friedman, Weinberg, and Fitzgerald."

"We can't do that," Levy reminded him, "because they don't know that MPM belongs to us. They didn't understand why Zack was freaking out. For them it's just a lucrative deal that slipped through our fingers."

Sergio sat down and began deliberating feverishly. If that was the case, then it would inevitably become public who was behind MPM and SeaStarFriends. His name would be tied to a bankrupt company in all the newspapers. And not only that: if the press caught wind of the fact that he and Levy—as the president and a board member of LMI—were involved in insider trading through their own brokerage firm, they would be ruined. It would have unforeseeable consequences for all of his businesses. Sergio knew how sensitively his business partners reacted to negative headlines. If he were charged with serious violations of securities law, it would even be worse. He needed to prevent this at all costs.

Suddenly, he had an idea. If SeaStarFriends—which was the owner of MPM—didn't belong to him and Levy but rather to someone else, then it was possible their names would never come into play.

"I'll be in my office," Zack said with a sullen expression and walked toward the door. "I'll try to make something happen in Europe or Asia."

"Good," Levy replied, "but stay in the building. I might need you later on."

"Sure, Vince." Zack put out his cigarette and shuffled out. Sergio waited until he left.

"Vince," he said slowly, "is it possible to change the owners of a partnership?"

"Officially no," Levy replied, "but maybe..."

He understood, and a hopeful smile flitted across his face. He snapped out of his lethargy and quickly dialed a telephone number.

"Monaghan?" he said after a while, and his voice sounded as businesslike as usual. "This is Vincent Levy speaking. Could you please come to my office immediately?"

"What can Monaghan do?" Sergio asked.

"He'll be able to tell us whether his people can change the MPM registration," Levy replied and smiled. "Because if that's possible, then we can let MPM go bankrupt without worrying."

The smile vanished from his face, and he rubbed his neck pensively.

"Now," Levy said, biting his lower lip, "someone needs to be the new owner."

"Yes, of course." Sergio grinned coldly. "That someone is Zack."

Vincent Levy nodded slowly.

"We need to get rid of him," Sergio said. "He's lost his nerve."

"But he knows too much!" Levy said. "He knows the names, the accounts, and—"

"Don't worry about that," Sergio said. "You take care of changing MPM's ownership and removing SeaStarFriends from the commercial registry. I'll take care of the rest."

Vincent Levy nodded. Without a doubt, this was the best solution. They would shift all the blame on Zack and come out of this mess clean. Sergio walked to the other side of the room and called Silvio Bacchiocchi.

"Take your two best men and come to LMI," he ordered, adding quietly, "I have a job for you. Bring an unregistered gun."

Henry Monaghan was at the door. Levy quickly explained to him what had to be done. LMI's head of security listened impassively and then glanced at his watch.

"I'll see what I can do. We can get into the commercial registry's central computer and make a change. But if any registration certificates are filed, we're out of luck."

"So be it," Sergio interjected. "If there's an investigation they'll look at the current printout instead of older documents."

"Good point," Monaghan said with a nod. "I'll work on it."

"Whew." Vincent Levy loosened his tie. "This could have blown up in our faces. I can't understand how Zack could do such a thing."

"I can," Sergio countered. "He wanted to make up for his recent mistake. And he's envious of Alex's success."

"I have the same impression," Levy said. "The jealousy of a spurned lover."

Sergio turned around quickly. "What did you just say?"

"If I understood St. John correctly, there was something going on between them some time ago." Levy poured himself another whiskey. "They were colleagues at Franklin Myers, after all."

Blood rushed into Sergio's face. He banged his fist on the table with such ferocity that Levy winced. How could he be so stupid? Alex and St. John!

"You didn't know that?" Levy asked in surprise.

"No," Sergio growled, "and I don't care."

His cell phone vibrated again, and he felt like throwing it against the wall. It was Luca.

"Boss," he said, "we're cleaning up the penthouse apartment."

"Why should I care? You want me to tell you where the vacuum cleaner is?"

"We found something," Luca continued unfazed, "under the TV. It's a computer printout of a bank statement."

"A bank statement?"

"It's a statement in the name of Levy & Villiers, dated July of this year," Luca said, "and the name of the account holder is Bruce Wellington."

Sergio froze. His nerves tingled. Bruce Wellington was the chairman of the city council and one of the more important people on his bribery payroll. How did his bank statement end up in Alex's apartment? No one had statements from these secret accounts. Not even he or Levy had seen them. He hadn't needed them in order to remind his "friends" that they owed him a favor. These highly confidential statements had never left the bank building.

"I want to see them," Sergio said in a gruff tone. "Come here immediately."

He hung up the phone and stared silently into space. St. John was the only one who could get to these statements. Were he and Alex secretly in cahoots together, and only pretending to hate each other?

"What's the matter?" Levy asked. After solving the MPM problem and drinking some whiskey, he was in a good mood again.

"Alex Sontheim," Sergio said without looking at him, "had bank statements from Levy & Villiers in her apartment."

"That can't be true!" Levy turned pale. "Not more bad news!"

"Maybe the two of them were working together," murmured Sergio. He frantically tried to put everything together, but he simply didn't get it. Alex had been in touch with Kostidis. The statement that Luca found was dated July. Had Alex already informed that bastard of a mayor in the meantime? No, that was impossible! Kostidis would never keep such a thing to himself.

"Pour me a whiskey!" Sergio said, and Levy handed him a glass. Sergio flushed in anger when he noticed that his hands were shaking.

It was shortly after eleven when St. John entered Levy's office. His pale face looked extremely frustrated.

"I managed to sell some more stock," he announced, letting himself fall into an armchair, "but that was it."

"MPM will go bankrupt tomorrow," Levy said.

"Yes, it looks like it," Zack replied grimly. "Nothing will happen, right?"

"No." Sergio stood up. He had himself under control after three double whiskeys, even though wild rage was boiling inside of him like a volcano.

"Nothing will happen. A brief investigation, some arrests...two, three years in prison—that's all you'll get."

"What?" Zack stared at him in disbelief. "What do I have to do with this?"

"Oh," Sergio said with a sardonic smile, "we just checked in our computer and discovered that you and Alex Sontheim are the owners of a small but mighty investment firm called MPM."

Zack sat up.

"That's a bad joke," he whispered hoarsely.

"Not at all," Sergio said, "but we won't forget about you, Zack, if you act prudently and keep your mouth shut. Once the commotion blows over, you'll receive a tidy sum. Early retirement at forty—that's a great thing."

"No," Zack whispered as he slowly realized what was going on. Vitali and Levy wanted to ditch him and blame him for everything. He didn't give a damn about Alex.

"Pull yourself together, Zack. What difference can two years make anyway?"

"No!" Zachary St. John jumped to his feet. Helpless, furious, he stared at both men with bloodshot eyes. "If I do that, then I'm done on Wall Street. And this is all because of the bullshit you talked me into!"

"You've also made a pretty penny," Levy noted coolly.

"You used me!" Zack shouted. "This is just a game for you, a damn chess game! And now you want to sacrifice a pawn to save the king!"

He laughed shrilly.

"That's quite a plan you came up with! But not for me!"

"Have you seen this before, Zack?" Sergio showed him the piece of paper that Luca had found in Alex's apartment. Zack glanced at it briefly and then shrugged his shoulders.

"No, I haven't," he answered.

"We found this in Alex Sontheim's apartment."

Hatred flared in Zack's eyes.

"Alex," he said, grinding his teeth angrily, "that miserable bitch."

"Can you explain how she got her hands on a bank statement from Levy & Villiers?"

"No, I can't," Zack snapped. "I've got nothing to do with her. That backstabbing snake fucked me over! Ever since she arrived, I've played the fool!"

"You're not in league with her behind our backs by chance?"

This question bewildered Zack even further.

"Never in a million years!" he exclaimed. "I hate that woman!"

"Okay." Sergio folded the paper and put it in his pocket.

Zack sank down in the chair and buried his face in his hands. "No one will ever talk to me again," he said despondently. "They'll all point their fingers at me and whisper to each other when they see me. I'll be a pariah."

"Stop pitying yourself!" Levy snarled at him. "You put us in this situation in the first place!"

"No!" Zack roared. "She provoked me to do it! And you left me high and dry! Now you want me to put my neck on the line so that you can keep your names out of this! But I won't accept it!"

"Think about it," Sergio said with an almost pitying smile. "It's not the end of the world. You'll forget all of this when you're under a palm tree somewhere in the Caribbean with a beautiful girl in your arms, contemplating how long you'll have to live to spend all your money."

Zack stared at him silently and was about to respond, but then he changed his mind and shrugged his shoulders.

"Okay," he mumbled quietly. "Okay. Okay."

He turned around and left the office. Sergio stepped to the window and stared out into the night. What kind of game was Alex playing? He believed St. John when he said he wasn't collaborating with her. His hatred was genuine. Alex must have gotten her hands on those secret bank statements some other way. How could he have underestimated her so? Chaos reigned in Sergio's head. Had he mentioned something to her himself? Different possibilities presented themselves, only to quickly fall apart again.

He turned to Levy. "Can you check whether any bank statements have been accessed in Georgetown?"

"I don't know," he replied. "I'll have to ask Monaghan."

"Do that. Call him." Sergio sat down again.

When Levy reached his head of security, he turned on the speakerphone so Sergio could listen to the conversation.

"The commercial registry has been changed," Monaghan said. "The new owners are Mr. Zachary George St. John and Ms.—"

"Okay, okay," Levy cut him off, and explained the next looming catastrophe. "Henry, is it possible to get into a computer from the outside to print out bank statements?"

"Theoretically, yes," LMI's head of security said pensively. "A clever hacker could access the server, but we'd notice such an intrusion. We put very strict security systems in place."

"Could you find out whether someone hacked into the server at Levy & Villiers on July 6?"

"I can try," Monaghan answered.

After the conversation ended, Sergio fell into a deep brooding silence. He had found a clean solution for St. John's screw-up. He wasn't worried about that anymore. It was far more important to find out how much Alex actually knew. He had to speak to her immediately. He knew that she had met that dumb journalist just two weeks ago. A cruel smile played on Sergio's lips. He knew Skerritt's address and decided that it was time to pay the man a visit.

Oliver winced when his cell phone rang and answered the call immediately.

"Hey, buddy," Justin said, "I found out a few things. It looks like the shit has hit the fan on Wall Street."

Alex leaned forward. She, Oliver, and Mark had called Justin and asked for information about MPM's activities in Whithers stock. For two hours, they'd been waiting for his call back at the Italian trattoria across from Oliver's apartment building. The three of them had deliberated all evening over how to proceed. Oliver handed his phone to Alex.

"MPM bought 2.6 million shares of Whithers Computers over the past six weeks," Justin said, "at an average price of thirty-eight dollars a share."

Alex quickly estimated the sum in her head. She had assumed that Zack would buy ten million dollars of stock, but it seemed that he'd bought ten times that amount.

"Just like you said," Justin continued, "the deal is off and Whithers stock has crashed over the last few hours. It closed at twenty-nine and a quarter, which means that MPM has lost thirty million so far. It looks like it'll be much more."

Oliver and Mark looked at Alex expectantly.

"No one will touch Whithers tomorrow," Alex said slowly. "The stock crashed and MPM must regain its position in the morning. They won't be able to get it done. There's no way that they'll get a hundred million together."

"Which means what?"

"MPM is bankrupt. There'll be an SEC investigation. And they'll find out who's behind MPM."

"Levy and Vitali…"

"Exactly," Alex said. "I can't imagine that they'll risk it. Levy will go to jail for ten years."

"What could they do to prevent that?"

"Not much." Alex pondered his question. "Maybe change the owners."

Suddenly, she sensed something disastrous brewing behind her back. Zack would blame her alone for the Whithers deal blowing up. Sergio wasn't on her side. It was two to one against her at the very least. Because no one knew yet how much she had found out, their best solution was to pin all the blame on her. Then she would be in for insider trading—big time.

"I'll check it out," Justin said and hung up. Alex briefly reported to Mark and Oliver what Justin had told her. While the two of them discussed the news, Alex was thinking intensely. Then she sat upright.

"I need to talk to Zack immediately," she said.

"But why?" Mark asked. "He hates you like the plague since the Syncrotron deal."

"I don't care how much of an asshole he is," Alex said as she stood up. "The pressure's on him too. I had no idea he would buy that much stock."

"Okay," Oliver said, "but you won't go alone. We'll come with you."

Mark signaled for the waiter and paid, and then they left the restaurant.

"Let me get my wallet. I left it in my apartment," Oliver said.

While Oliver went inside, Alex and Mark waited at the building's entrance.

"Zack will be absolutely furious," Mark said. "I'm not sure that it's a good idea to speak with him. What are you trying to get out of it?"

"Damn it, Mark, I thought that he'd lose five or ten million, but a hundred million is—" The sentence caught in Alex's throat as she watched a black limousine drive up the street.

"What is it?" Mark asked.

"Come inside, quick!" Alex pulled him into the hallway.

The limousine stopped directly in front of the building.

"What's wrong?" Mark didn't understand what was going on, but he followed her up the stairs. They ran into Oliver in front of his apartment.

"Sergio is here!" Alex exclaimed. Oliver immediately opened the door, and they sought refuge inside the apartment. Seconds later, the doorbell started buzzing like crazy. The three of them looked helplessly at one another.

"Police, open the door!" they heard a voice shout, and then someone banged a fist on the door. "Open the door or we'll break it down!"

"Shit," Mark whispered, scared. "What are we going to do?"

Alex was sobered by the fear.

"He's coming after me," she whispered. "Can I get out of here somehow?"

"You can get onto the roof of the adjacent warehouse from the balcony," Oliver said nervously, "but it's at least ten feet down."

"It doesn't matter. He'll kill me if he finds me here. And you too."

Mark turned as white as a ghost. The banging on the door grew louder. Alex ran into the living room and tore open the balcony door.

"Alex," Oliver hissed. He grabbed her arm as she raised her leg over the balcony railing. "You can't…Alex!"

"I have no choice," she replied. "I don't want to get you into trouble. Take care of yourselves. I'll be in touch!"

Before Oliver could say another word, she jumped ten feet from the balustrade down onto the warehouse roof and disappeared in the darkness like a shadow.

Sergio stood in the hallway outside Oliver Skerritt's door, his hands deep in the pockets of his cashmere coat. He was dead certain that Alex was sitting next to this guy right behind the door. He even thought he could smell her. Armando and Freddy looked at their boss and waited for his orders.

"Break down the door!" Sergio ordered. "I want to get into this damned apartment."

Then the door opened. A dark-haired man with glasses looked at them, displeased. Sergio recognized his face from the countless photos that his people had taken of him and Alex. He even knew what he looked like during sex. He used all his might to repress his fury, pushing past him into the loft before Oliver could say a word. Although it was fairly large, it was could fit into a single salon of Sergio's Park Avenue apartment.

"Hey!" The journalist ran after him. "What the hell is going on here? Why are you invading my apartment? Who are you?"

"Where is she?" Sergio looked everywhere, even the bathroom. He shoved Oliver, who looked terrified. He encountered Mark in the living room and ignored him. Then Sergio tore open the bedroom door expecting to find Alex in bed with wide-open, frightened eyes. The blood rushed in his ears. He'd beaten her down to the point that she couldn't let herself be seen in public for three weeks. But the bed was empty. Sergio charged into the room, pulled open the closet doors, and even got down on his knees to look under the bed. There was no trace of her. Did he get it all wrong?

"Where are you, you little whore?" He angrily ground his teeth and walked back to the living room. There, his men watched in silence as Sergio grabbed Oliver by his hair.

"Where the hell is she?"

"Who are you looking for anyway?" Oliver wheezed.

"Alex Sontheim." The urge to kill shone in Sergio's eyes.

"Why would she be here?"

"Haven't you learned your lesson yet?" His anger exploded inside of him, and he rammed his fist into Oliver's face; he felt a cruel sense of satisfaction when Oliver's glasses cracked and the blood splattered from his nose.

"Alex hasn't been here in months," Oliver mumbled. "I don't know where she is."

Sergio stared at him for a few seconds. "If you are lying to me," he hissed, "you're dead!"

Just minutes later, the nightmare was over and Oliver and Mark found themselves locked in the windowless bathroom. Oliver sat down on the edge of the bathtub, breathing heavily, and Mark let himself slide onto the floor. His whole body shook in fear. He had always been horrified by any kind of physical violence.

"What kind of an animal is this guy," he muttered. Oliver's cell phone rang again. He rummaged through his jacket pocket until he found it.

"I checked the commercial registry," Justin shouted. "You remember that a company was the owner of MPM, this SeaStar thing, right?"

"Yeah, sure." Oliver nodded and grimaced because his nose hurt like hell. "We printed out the certificates."

"But now MPM is listed as owned by Alex and Zachary St. John."

"Holy shit." Oliver rubbed his sore wrists, trying to take in what this meant.

Alex really was in grave danger—and she had no idea.

Alex's heart pounded furiously against her ribs as she darted toward Sixth Avenue under the protection of the building walls. A police siren was howling somewhere, but the street was deserted. She managed to finally hail a cab at West Houston Street.

"Battery Park City," she said to the taxi driver, leaning back in relief when the young Puerto Rican hit the pedal. She hoped that Sergio wouldn't harm Oliver and Mark. Her thoughts were racing as the cab drove south through nighttime Manhattan. She still couldn't believe that Zack had been so foolish as to buy so many shares. Even if the deal had gone through, it would have triggered the SEC's curiosity. But then it occurred to her that Sergio also had SEC officials and NYSE board members on his bribery payroll. It was likely nothing would have happened.

Fifteen minutes later, Alex reached Zack's building. She asked the cab driver to wait and walked in, but the doorman said Zach was away. She climbed back into the taxi and told the driver to take her to the financial district. Maybe Zack was still in his office. Alex frowned. She wasn't quite sure what to tell him, but she no matter what it couldn't wait. Tomorrow morning, they'd throw her and Zack to the wolves. Maybe she could convince Zack that it was time to take action together against Levy and Sergio. It was clear in her mind that neither of them would shy away from sacrificing her.

She got out of the cab at Broadway and Wall Street then walked the rest of the way to the LMI Building. The main entrance was closed at this time of night, and she hesitated to use her badge to get in. She knew that every swipe of the card was registered in the central computer. She glanced quickly at her watch. It was just after two thirty in the morning, and she couldn't wait any longer. She opened the door to the delivery entrance with her badge, and then stopped when she spotted the night porter strolling toward the restrooms. Alex snuck into the lobby and reached the open door to the stairwell. She couldn't take the elevator because it would have instantly alarmed the security guards. She prided herself on being in good shape, but she still needed to stop and catch her breath on the tenth and fourteenth floors.

Alex trembled with anxiety as she opened the fire door leading to the executive offices. Zack's office was the fourth on the left. A narrow strip of light escaped through a crack in the door. He was actually still here. Alex took a deep breath and then knocked at the door. When she entered the office, what she saw in the dim light of the desk lamp made her blood freeze. She wanted to run away, screaming her head off, but she stood there petrified. She couldn't tear her eyes away.

"Damn it," Oliver cursed, "she's not answering!"

It was the tenth time he reached Alex's voice mail.

"We've got to do something," he said as he rubbed his sore arm. Where could he find Alex to inform her about the outrageous information

Justin had just delivered? MPM would be bankrupt tomorrow. The press would jump on it as soon as they learned that LMI's managing director and head of M&A were jointly running a company making millions through insider trading. Alex was done for, even if it could eventually be proven in court that she had nothing to do with MPM. Her reputation on Wall Street would be ruined once and for all. Oliver's first—and hopefully last—personal encounter with Sergio Vitali confirmed everything that he had unearthed about him over the years. He shuddered again at the memory of the ice-cold look in his blue eyes.

"We'll never get this door open," Mark said despondently. Oliver rummaged around in the drawers of the bathroom cabinet for any object he could use to unscrew the door's hinges. He didn't care if he broke something. He needed to warn Alex. Immediately.

Zack sat dead in the chair behind his desk. This was without a doubt the worst sight Alex had ever seen. Half his face was missing, and his remaining eye was wide open and seemed to look at her reproachfully. The blood running from his mouth had already congealed, and he held a gun in his left hand that hung down limply. Both the wall behind him and the light-colored carpet were splattered with blood.

Alex's knees were as soft as butter, and her stomach lurched. She had triggered a catastrophe by tipping off Ringwood. She had just wanted to pull one over on Zack, Levy, and Sergio, but now she was responsible for Zack's death! Sure the deal was as good as sealed, he had bought Whithers stock. When he heard that the deal was off, it seemed he saw no way out besides suicide. Alex fought her rising panic, overcame her disgust and horror, and looked around his desk—which, to her surprise, had been cleared out. The glass tabletop, which was usually covered in yellow post-it notes, was spick-and-span. Zack hadn't left a suicide note, and

Alex noticed that the briefcase he always carried around with him was nowhere to be found.

Then her gaze fell on the computer. There was a yellow light blinking, indicating that something was downloading. She forced herself not to look at the corpse, leaning over him to move the mouse. The computer started to rumble, and the cloudy sky desktop wallpaper appeared seconds later. Alex held her breath. A rotating *E* at the upper right corner of the screen indicated that there were unread e-mails on the server. She clicked on the icon to have a look.

The computer showed four unread messages. She quickly opened the e-mails and read through them. One was from a broker in San Francisco, one from a lawyer's office in Los Angeles, and two from travel agencies in New York. Alex printed all of the messages so that she could read them later. Then she checked his outbox and sent folders.

"Bingo," she murmured. Zack had written three e-mails tonight, but he only sent one of them. She opened the first e-mail, which was addressed to Ken Matsumo at the California Savings & Loan Bank in Los Angeles. Her eyes grew ever larger when she read what Zack had written.

Hello Ken,
I just wired the amount of $50 million to my account at your bank. Please transfer these funds first thing in the morning to account number A/CH/334677810 at Bankhaus Ruetli & Hartmann in Zurich, Switzerland. I must leave the city tonight.
Thanks for your help.
Zack

"Unbelievable," Alex whispered in amazement. That certainly didn't sound like Zack had any plans of putting a bullet through his head. Did he suspect what Levy and Sergio were up to, and therefore embezzled fifty million dollars into his account at California Savings & Loan? He was certainly trying to make a run for it with this money. Clever boy! Sergio and Levy had clearly overestimated Zack's loyalty.

The second e-mail was in French, addressed to Cécile d'Aubray in Geneva.

Cécile,
This is our last night apart. We'll leave for Geneva at midday tomorrow and we will be immensely rich.
With love,
ZStJ

Zack wanted to leave the country and go to Geneva—with fifty million dollars in his luggage. Not too shabby. A third e-mail was addressed to a lawyer named John Sturgess in LA, asking him to forward a drafted document immediately to the US Attorney's Office in New York, as discussed. Alex printed all the e-mails. Swissair had confirmed two flights for Mr. John Fallino and Ms. Cécile d'Aubray to Geneva, and there was also confirmation of an Air Canada flight to Vancouver for Zachary St. John.

Zack's third unread message was by far the most interesting. The lawyer, John Sturgess, had sent him a three-page document in which Zack confessed to all of the illegal deals that he administered on behalf of Levy and Vitali, including the dates and amounts of transfers. This document directly threatened those who wanted to sacrifice him.

Alex slowly put two and two together and it all became clear as day. A chill ran down her spine when she realized what it meant. There was no way that Zack had committed suicide. Someone making such elaborate plans for his future wouldn't put a .38 to his head and pull the trigger. Zack was planning to disappear in a few hours with fifty million dollars. Leaving behind a hundred million dollar debt and a ruined investment firm and wreaking havoc by sending his written confession to the US attorney.

But someone had spoiled his plan—someone with no interest in the value of a human life. Alex didn't doubt for a second that Sergio had gotten rid of this dangerous accomplice, disguising the act as a suicide. It was a clever ploy; it seemed quite reasonable that someone in Zack's situation would prefer death over prison.

Alex suddenly remembered that she was standing next to a dead body. With shaking hands, she collected the pages spewed out by the printer. On impulse, she deleted all the e-mails and emptied the trash. Her heart pounded frantically. If Sergio found out what she knew, she was as dead as Zack.

As Alex turned around, she knocked the swivel chair in which Zack's corpse was dangling. The pages slipped out of her hands, and when she bent over to pick them up, her hand brushed against an object. She knelt down on the blood-splattered floor and grabbed a cell phone. She snuck it inside her jacket and left the office as quickly as possible. She'd nearly reached the fire door when she heard the elevator swoosh up. The red light next to the elevator door lit up. Someone was coming up! Alex looked around in utter panic and then opened the door to the ladies' bathroom and slipped inside. Through a small crack in the door, she watched someone coming out of the elevator. She thought her heart would stop beating when she saw Sergio and Henry Monaghan.

"The computer's on," Henry Monaghan observed.

"My guys probably forgot to turn it off," Sergio replied.

"Yes, apparently they did. But the screen is turned on and the printer is still warm." Monaghan shook his head. "It can't be more than fifteen minutes since someone used it. Otherwise the screensaver would have come up or the computer would have switched into sleep mode."

With a stony expression, Sergio watched this stocky man with a bushy moustache move the mouse back and forth while staring grimly at the screen.

"This someone has deleted all of the e-mails," he announced after a while. "There's nothing left."

A message on St. John's answering machine explained why the two men would risk being surprised alongside Zack's body at four in the morning. A lawyer by the name of John Sturgess had left a message saying that he'd recorded his statements and sent them to Zack's office via e-mail. Maybe it was important, maybe not. The phone call from California had come in at ten thirty, right after Sergio had informed Zack that he and Alex were the new owners of MPM. Zack had died at around a quarter past eleven, and no one knew what he'd been doing in his office for these forty-five minutes. The word *statements* sounded dangerous to Monaghan, and Sergio completely agreed with him. Did Zack call the lawyer to tell him about the dilemma he was in? And now it seemed as if someone else had intercepted John Sturgess's e-mail. Monaghan turned off the computer.

"We'll know in a second who was here," he said. "We just need to look at the surveillance tapes. Maybe this person is still in the building, and we can get to him before there's even more damage."

Alex crouched on the floor of the women's restroom, her back against the tiles and hardly daring to breathe. Sergio and Monaghan clearly weren't surprised by the sight of Zack. She felt sick when she realized how much danger she was in. The two of them had been in Zack's office for about five minutes, when they went back out to the hallway. Alex heard the elevator coming up.

"Luca," she heard Sergio say, "wait for my call. Search every room. It's possible that the person we're looking for is still here."

Alex froze. How could she get out of the building without being discovered? She crawled into one of the stalls, locked the door, and cowered on the toilet seat. There was no escape. Sergio's guys would find her, and she would be as dead as a doornail. A wave of panic rushed over her, and she wished for the thousandth time that she had never met Sergio Vitali.

The image on the screen was grainy at first, but then the thirtieth floor hallway—from the elevators to the reception desk—became clearly visible. Sergio stared at the screen. He was furious that he hadn't heard from Nelson for more than four days. Ever since Sergio had returned from Chicago, Nelson seemed different. And now he got the impression that his wife was making excuses for him on the telephone. He knew that Nelson was seriously ill, but he realized that he could no longer trust his oldest comrade-in-arms. And that's why he'd told Silvio to send two men to Long Island to keep an eye on him.

Furthermore, Sergio was angry that he couldn't find Constanzia. And to make matters worse, he had to deal with this nonsense with St. John and the possibility that Alex knew about the secret accounts! Sacrificing MPM didn't bother him. They could incorporate a new company tomorrow morning to carry on with their business. They would easily find a suitable replacement for St. John. Alex was the problem. He worried that he'd demeaned himself, invading the journalist's apartment in the middle of the night like a jealous lover. He hated her for making him look like a fool. Sergio chewed pensively on his lower lip. Why was all of this happening now, of all times? He had an important meeting tomorrow morning, and he'd been planning to fly to Costa Rica on Friday to meet with Ortega.

His charity event at the St. Regis for the Saturday before Christmas was just three weeks away. He would have loved to call the whole thing off, but canceling the party would only result in negative publicity.

Alex peeked into the hallway through the narrow crack. One of Sergio's guys was searching the offices, but Luca di Varese was standing directly in front of the door, languidly smoking a cigarette. They called out to each other every now and then, but Alex couldn't understand a word. It hadn't occurred to them to look in the bathrooms yet, but they would certainly do so very soon. Alex forced herself to think. Sergio and Monaghan suspected that someone was still in the building, but they didn't know where—and that was her lucky break. She folded the printouts and put them into the waistband of her jeans. She needed to get out of the bathroom somehow without anyone noticing. She scanned the room, and realized in desperation that there was no escape route. It wasn't hard to guess what Sergio would do to her once he captured her.

"Three minutes past eleven," Henry Monaghan said quietly. They watched three men walk along the hallway and disappear into St. John's office. The men came out carrying several bags about twenty minutes later. They had taken everything in the desk as ordered, but they had apparently neglected to check the computer. Sergio and Levy could be seen walking toward the elevator just before midnight. The time of the next recording was 3:16. Sergio and Monaghan stared at the screen spellbound when a person with a baseball cap and a dark hooded sweatshirt stepped from the staircase into the hallway and looked around.

"Alex," Sergio said in a hushed voice and automatically clenched his hands into fists. His own words sounded like derisive laughter in his ears. *Don't worry. I have Alex under control.* Alex knew about the secret accounts, and she was in possession of those damned e-mails from St. John's computer. She was one step ahead of him, and she might take everything to Kostidis if he didn't get to her in time.

"She was in his office for seventeen minutes." Monaghan lit a cigarette and exhaled the blue smoke. "We must have missed her by just a few seconds."

He stared at the screen. Alex stopped, looked around, and then turned left.

"Hey," Monaghan said with a grin, "she's still here!"

Sergio reached for his cell phone.

"I'm going to kill her," he said flatly, dialing Luca's number. "I'm going to kill that whore with my own hands."

Henry Monaghan flung open the door to the women's restroom and flipped the light switch. The room was immediately drenched in bright fluorescent light. Luca di Varese and the other guy walked past him and searched each of the eight stalls while Sergio waited in the hallway. One of the doors was locked, and Monaghan bent down to look beneath it. The stall was empty. His gaze wandered upward, and he was furious. Alex Sontheim had led them by the nose like fools! She'd climbed up the stall wall and lifted a panel in the ceiling. It was fairly easy for a somewhat fit person to crawl to a different room through the heating and ventilation shafts. It was pointless to send someone after her. She had probably escaped to a different floor. Monaghan turned around and walked out.

"Nothing?" Sergio asked.

"She escaped through the ceiling. But we'll get her."

"How?" Sergio's eyes were as cold as ice. "It's almost four thirty! I don't feel like being seen with a corpse."

Monaghan chewed angrily on his cigar, but then broke into a grin.

"It would be best for you to go home now," he said. "I have a perfect solution to our problem."

"And what would that would be?"

"I'm going to call the police now," Monaghan countered in a good mood. "I'll cut the surveillance tape and—voilà—we have evidence that Sontheim shot St. John between 3:16 and 3:36."

Sergio stared at the stocky man, and then he nodded slowly.

"Yes," he said, "that's a great idea. In addition to my guys, the cops will also be after her. No one will care about MPM's bankruptcy in all of the confusion. But I want to get to her first, you understand?"

The NYPD received a phone call at 6:14 a.m. A dead body had been found at investment firm LMI. Just a few minutes later, the first patrol cars arrived at the scene. By six forty-five, the entire building was buzzing with police officers and detectives. They examined Zachary St. John's disfigured corpse and watched the surveillance tape that showed Alex entering St. John's office at 3:16 a.m. and leaving it again twenty minutes later.

"Do you have any idea who this woman could be?" Detective Munroe asked the company's head of security.

"I'm not sure," Monaghan replied and scratched his head, "but she reminds me of Alex Sontheim, the head of our M&A department."

John Munroe jotted something on his notepad. He was tall, red-faced, and had thick, reddish-blond hair. He had been working in the NYPD's homicide department for fourteen years and had seen his share of corpses. At first glance, it looked like suicide, as the man on the top floor had the weapon in his hand. But could that woman have shot him and put the gun on him to make it look like a suicide? Vincent Levy, LMI's president, arrived in the meantime. He was shocked, but composed, and he easily identified the person on tape.

"Yes," he said, his bewilderment and horror genuine, "that's her. Alex Sontheim."

"Was it common for Mr. St. John to spend time at his office late at night?" the detective asked.

"Yes, that's not unusual," Levy confirmed. "We had some trouble with an important deal yesterday. It must have kept him late in his office."

The officer grabbed the telephone. He told his people to search for Alex Sontheim, that she was the main suspect, and then he turned to Monaghan.

"Do you have a picture of this woman?" he asked.

"I'll get you one," Monaghan replied, "and Detective, you should search the building. It's possible that she's still inside."

Munroe shot him an unfriendly look.

"You could have told me that right away," he snarled, rushing out to his colleagues.

"No, I couldn't have," Henry Monaghan muttered. Vitali had left no doubt that he wanted to get his hands on Alex before the police could question her.

Alex was surprised to see the police. Every corridor and hallway was swarming with them, along with LMI's security staff. Escape seemed impossible. She cowered in a heating shaft above an office, still on the thirtieth floor, and waited for an opportunity to get out. Her cell phone battery was dead, and she had no way of contacting Oliver or Mark. She was frightened, exhausted, and hungry, but she couldn't afford to make any mistakes. It was seven thirty already, which meant that she had been crawling around these dusty shafts for almost three hours. Alex kept feeling her way forward until she suddenly heard voices beneath her. She carefully moved one of the panels half an inch and peeked inside an office through the crack. Her heart jumped when she caught sight of Vincent Levy.

"I don't understand anything anymore! What's going on here?"

"We caught Sontheim on our surveillance tape," another man said, who was not visible to Alex. That must be Henry Monaghan's voice.

"She was in St. John's office and retrieved e-mails from his computer that possibly contain questionable information."

They certainly do, Alex thought.

"Are you sure that Alex killed St. John?" Levy asked.

"I have no idea," Monaghan replied, "but if the police believe it, then they'll do anything to catch her. Vitali wants to get his hands on her first. We need to wait for the cops to leave, and then we'll find her."

Alex felt her throat constricting in fear. She was trapped. She might get out of here, but only to run straight into the arms of Sergio's henchmen.

"Oh my God, this is terrible," Levy whined below her. "The damage to LMI is incalculable! A dead body in my firm and a manager as a murderer."

"There's no need to panic," Monaghan said harshly. "I have everything under control. Schedule a meeting at nine o'clock for all of the employees on the trading floor and tell them that St. John has been shot at his desk—most likely by Sontheim."

"Ahh, how awful, how awful."

"Pull yourself together," Monaghan growled. "Nothing will happen to you! The story's great, and the press will jump on it. St. John and Sontheim were in it together and executed insider trades through their small company, MPM. Then they fell out of favor with one another when they bit off more than they could chew with their last deal. As a result, Sontheim kills her partner in crime."

Alex could hardly believe her ears. She and Zack in cahoots?

"The police will interrogate me," Levy whimpered, and Alex wondered how she could ever have felt respect for this man. His spinelessness and his cowardice were shocking.

"Of course," Monaghan impatiently cut him off, "you'll tell them that, after serious contemplation, you already suspected that they were involved in some secret side deals together. After the deal blew up yesterday, they were sure to be discovered. They got into an argument, and then she killed him. That sounds great."

Alex felt compelled to agree with them. It certainly sounded plausible. She and St. John as accomplices, insider trading, millions lost, a fight, and one dead. They'd charge her with murder, as well as insider trading, fraud, embezzlement, and several other crimes. Levy and Vitali were clean, in any case.

"We need to go," Monaghan said.

"What about the bank statements?" Levy asked. "Did you find anything?"

"My people in Georgetown are working on it," Monaghan replied.

Alex waited until the two men had left Levy's office, pushed a ceiling panel aside, and then slid down gently. She would be done for if anyone saw her trying to escape the building. She wouldn't survive a single day in prison—just like Cesare Vitali. It was shortly before eight. She grabbed the telephone determinedly and dialed Mark's extension. He must be at work by this hour. With trembling hands, she waited, and she almost hung up right before he answered.

"Mark!" she whispered.

"Alex," he answered, sounding relieved, "where are you? We've been trying to reach you all night long. We even went to LMI, but I couldn't open the door with my badge. There's a rumor going around that you shot Zack!"

"None of it is true," she said. "Listen to me, Mark!"

She quickly recounted what had happened and what she had just witnessed.

"They want to pin this murder on me to cover everything up," she whispered quickly, "and they know I have evidence that could ruin them."

"They registered you and Zack as the owners of MPM," Mark reported. "Justin found out about it. Where are you?"

"I'm still on the thirtieth floor. I have to get out and see Kostidis." Alex hoped that the mayor would believe her, but she wasn't sure.

"What can I do to help?"

"Nothing," Alex replied after thinking a minute. "Get up, leave your desk as is, and get out of the building immediately."

"But—"

"Mark, do as I say, please," Alex whispered. "I'll get out of here somehow."

"Okay." Mark hesitated. "Should Oliver and I pick you up somewhere?"

Alex bit her lip. As appealing it seemed to get some help, it would be irresponsible to drag Oliver or Mark even deeper into this mess. This situation was no longer clear to her.

"No, absolutely not," she said quickly. "I'll get it done by myself."

"Alex, please, let us help you!"

"No." She remained steadfast. "Get up and get out of the office. Right now. I'll contact you as soon as I can."

Alex hung up. She hoped that it wasn't too late already for Mark. She closed her eyes for a moment and sorted her thoughts. She and Zack were the owners of MPM. Zack had liquidated all of the MPM holdings last night and wired fifty million dollars to his private account. Alex opened her eyes, and her gaze fell on Levy's computer screen. She suddenly had an idea. With a grim smile, she sat down at his desk and pulled the keyboard and the mouse closer. She would make sure that Sergio and Levy had plenty more to be angry about.

"Mr. Ashton?"

Mark still had the telephone receiver in his hand when two men stepped up to his desk. His heart stopped for a moment. "Detective John Munroe, NYPD," the taller one said, holding his police badge in Mark's face, "and this is my colleague, Detective Connolly. We have a few questions that we'd like to ask you."

Mark's heartbeat went back to normal when he realized that these men were police officers and not Vitali's bloodhounds. He sensed his colleagues' curious looks behind him. All of the chatter in the large, open office—solely about last night's incidents—fell silent.

"You work closely with Ms. Sontheim, is that correct?" the red-haired detective continued. "When did you last speak to her?"

"I…umm…" Mark's thoughts were racing. "I think it was yesterday afternoon."

Unprepared as he was, he gave the first response that came to mind. He didn't even know why he lied to the police. He was a lousy liar.

"Are you sure?" the red-haired detective asked suspiciously.

"I…I don't remember exactly anymore," Mark stammered. "I'm totally confused."

"Maybe we should continue this conversation at the precinct," Detective Munroe said.

"If you like," Mark started to say, but he fell silent when he saw two men heading toward him. He recognized Henry Monaghan, the fat security head at LMI, but he had never seen the other man before. Something inside of him told him that these two men were dangerous and that he would be much safer at the precinct.

"Hello, Mr. Ashton," Monaghan greeted him; the look in his small piggish eyes anything but friendly. "Mr. Levy would like to talk to you for a second."

Mark began to mumble. "I...umm...the detective has..." He shook with fear and secretly prayed that the detectives would take him with them. But nothing of the sort happened.

"I'll bring him back in a second," Monaghan reassured the two detectives with a congenial smile as false as his teeth. "It won't take very long. You can interview Ms. Sontheim's other employees in the meantime."

Munroe considered this for a moment, and then he shrugged his shoulders.

"Okay," he said, "but quickly. I don't have much time."

Mark felt a layer of sweat forming on his forehead. His first impulse was to run off screaming for help.

"Come with me, Ashton," Monaghan said, and Mark stood up stiffly. He left the office flanked by Monaghan and the other man, followed by many curious eyes. Right after the elevator door closed, all the friendliness in Monaghan's face disappeared and his expression turned threatening.

"We're going down?" Mark asked.

"Imagine that, fat boy," Monaghan growled. "Levy doesn't want to speak to you. But I need to know a few things."

As the elevator whooshed down to the lower basement, a thousand thoughts raced through Mark's head. Where was Alex? Had they caught her? All he felt right now was pure, naked fear. The men led him into a small, empty room. The ceiling's fluorescent lights radiated an uncomfortable glow, and it was unbearably hot. Monaghan closed the thick steel door behind him. Then he turned around quickly and grabbed Mark by his tie.

"Where's Sontheim?" he hissed.

"I...I don't know," Mark whispered.

"When was the last time you talked to her?" the dark-haired man with the acne scars wanted to know.

"Yesterday. I haven't seen her today."

"Enough with these lies," Monaghan cut him off harshly. "You tried to enter the building with your badge at 3:57 this morning. Sontheim entered the building just shortly before that. Her badge has access rights and yours doesn't. What did you want here this morning? You knew that Sontheim was here, didn't you?"

Mark remained silent. He felt sick.

"Come on, fatso," Monaghan said, clenching his teeth impatiently, "or should I jog your memory a little?"

He was boiling with fury because precious time was wasting that he would rather spend on finding the woman.

"I get claustrophobic in small rooms," Mark whispered with a dry mouth. "I can't think straight."

"Hurry up then." Monaghan's voice was cold as ice. "If you tell us what we want to know, we'll let you go back to your desk."

"I really don't know where Alex is," Mark mumbled. A punch hit him in the stomach. He stumbled, and his glasses fell to the ground. Desperate, increasingly fearful, Mark groped around the cold tiles. Monaghan seized him by the collar again and slammed his head against the wall several times. Mark felt his nose break and tasted blood.

"Open your trap!" Monaghan hissed. Mark was terrified. Alex had told him that these people wouldn't waste time getting serious. He had already experienced Sergio Vitali in action yesterday. His goons had killed St. John. They didn't care whether he lived or died. A few more punches pushed him past his limit.

"She just called me," he whispered. "She's still in the building. But she wants to go to Kostidis..."

"There you go," Monaghan said, letting go of him. "What were you waiting for?"

Mark felt more miserable than he ever had in his life. He had betrayed Alex to the enemy because he was frightened for himself. He was a wretched, spineless coward.

"Will you let me go now?" he asked pleadingly.

"Do I look like an idiot?" Monahan's voice was full of sarcasm. "You stay here until we find that woman. Pray that we find her quickly. Otherwise, this might turn out to be an extended stay for you."

The heavy steel door closed behind the two men, and Mark heard the key turn. He sank to the ground and broke out in tears. If they caught Alex, it would be his fault. How could he be so easily intimidated?

The hallway was deserted as Alex stepped out of Levy's office. She couldn't wait any longer. LMI security and the police were searching the entire building, and it was just a matter of time until they found her. She quickly dashed across the hall a few yards to the staircase and was relieved to find the door unlocked. She rushed down the stairs as quickly as possible, praying that no one would see her. She was completely out of breath when she reached the ground floor, but its glass door was locked. Alex stopped for a split second and glanced into the large lobby, which was buzzing with activity. Suddenly, she was standing face-to-face with a security guard, with just a glass panel separating them. He raised his walkie-talkie, and Alex turned on her heel. She rushed down the stairs to the basement and threw herself against a heavy metal door that led into the underground parking garage. Then she crouched down and ran along the parked cars.

Alex's heart was racing, and sweat poured down her face; she approached a rolling gate that was just opening at that second. She pressed her back against the wall. A silver-colored limousine rolled past her, just a few inches away. She started to run without a moment's hesitation, darting beneath the rolling gate as it came down, and dashing up the ramp to the street. The rain drenched through her clothes instantly, but at least she had managed to escape the building. There were police cars everywhere, lights flashing, and a crowd of people surrounding them just a few yards away at the main entrance. She saw a coroner's van approach. No one noticed her as she turned around and walked quickly along Wall Street toward Broadway.

"You're drinking whiskey again," Sergio remarked disapprovingly when he entered Levy's office. "Stop that!"

On the spur of the moment, he had decided to cancel the interview he had scheduled. Although Monaghan was right in suggesting he stay out of this matter, his brilliant plan had one major flaw: Alex was still on the run, and she was a significant risk. Sergio didn't appear one second too soon. He realized on arrival that Levy was quite obviously falling apart.

"That's easy for you to say!" Levy flared up. "The scene here is complete chaos! The building is filled with police, and on top of it, SEC agents and the US Attorney's Office arrested Jack Lang."

"I know." Sergio shrugged his shoulders. "I called Tarrance myself."

"You did what? Have you lost your mind?" Levy—whose face was as white as a sheet to begin with—turned even whiter.

"It's better to tip them off so they don't have to snoop around everywhere," Sergio countered. "It's more important for us to catch Alex."

Levy's eyes looked like they'd pop out of his head. He emptied his glass, but his hands were still trembling. He had just told LMI's employees about Zack's murder as they assembled on the trading floor, and their emotional reaction unsettled him. After all, he didn't know what was really going on. But Sergio looked the same as usual. His facial expression revealed no emotion. Someone knocked at the door, and Levy flinched.

Luca di Varese entered the room.

"We've just grilled one of Alex's employees," he said. "He claimed that she's still in the building and wants to go to the mayor."

"Send your guys to city hall right away," Sergio quickly decided. "Put two men at each entrance and put a few patrol cars in the area."

Luca nodded and left again.

"We have to find her before she causes more damage," Sergio said in a sinister tone.

"The damage is already done," Levy countered gloomily. "How could Zack be so stupid?"

"He was getting too brazen anyway." Sergio waved his hand dismissively. "We've got to organize this whole thing differently in the future."

"There's no future!" Levy said sharply. "Zack is dead, and Alex…"

She will be dead soon too, Sergio thought grimly. He would get her sooner or later. His men were at city hall. They were listening to the police radio to find out if the cops had caught her. There was no escape for Alex. Sergio's anger grew by the hour, and she'd pay dearly for it. The telephone rang, and it was Monaghan.

"My guy from Georgetown just called," he said. "He checked the computer systems of LMI and all its subsidiaries. Some confidential files were in fact accessed on July 6. However, it didn't come through as a hacker because that person had access rights."

He paused briefly.

"What does that mean?" Levy asked impatiently.

"Whoever accessed these files has the authority to do so or somehow got authorization. However, the system at Levy & Villiers recorded unusually high activity on that day, which indicates that a program was used to hack the password."

"Zack," Sergio muttered, "that little bastard."

"These files were accessed a total of fourteen times from an external computer."

"Fourteen times?" Levy swallowed.

"The last time was last night at nine thirty."

"Great." Sergio exchanged a glance with Levy.

"Who could this possibly be?" Levy was at a loss. "Only three people have universal access rights: Monaghan, Fox, and me. You can exclude me because I have no idea about this stuff."

"I don't have a clue either," Sergio said, "but didn't Monaghan mention something about an external computer? My layman's mind thinks that maybe it was neither Fox nor Monaghan but someone from the outside. I vaguely remember you telling me how secure this computer system is."

"And I remember you told me that you have Sontheim under control," LMI's president countered. Sergio stared at him angrily: 1-0, Levy.

Nick Kostidis was in a meeting with representatives from the health department when Frank Cohen came in. His usually calm face was strained as he signaled his boss to step outside.

"What's the matter?" he asked at the door.

"You should take a look at this," Frank replied. "They're reporting on TV about the murder of an investment banker. They say that Alex Sontheim shot the man in his office last night."

"She did what?" Nick asked in disbelief.

"Yes," Frank nodded, "she's on the run. The police and FBI are looking for her."

Nick turned around without saying a word. Frank followed him to his office and turned on the TV.

"Security officers found Zachary St. John, managing director of the investment firm Levy Manhattan Investments, shot dead at his desk," a female reporter announced, standing in front of a high-rise on Wall Street. The yellow crime scene tape fluttered in the wind behind her, and several police cars were parked in front of the entrance.

"A police spokesperson disclosed that the head of the mergers and acquisitions department, Alex Sontheim, is the main suspect in St. John's murder and has disappeared. There are rumors that St. John and Sontheim illegally acquired millions of dollars through insider trading conducted through a front organization. Following yesterday's failed takeover of Database Inc. by Whithers Computers, which was handled by Sontheim, this front organization is said to be close to bankruptcy. I'm Moira Roberts with NBC News."

"That can't be," Nick murmured in disbelief. "No, she didn't shoot anyone. I don't believe it. She wasn't involved in any illegal business. Otherwise she wouldn't have—"

He paused and then walked to a small safe behind his desk. He opened it and took out the papers that Alex had given him that evening at Alexis Sorbas. He paged quickly through the statements until he found the one that he was looking for.

"What's this?" Frank asked curiously.

"Statements from a bank on the Cayman Islands," Nick replied. "Alex gave them to me a few weeks ago."

"You never even told me." Frank threw his boss a hurt look.

"Here," he said, handing one of the pages to Frank, "Zachary St. John, code name Goldfinger. I'm pretty sure that he was involved in dirty business."

"What if Alex Sontheim was involved?"

"Then why would she point it out to me?" He handed the whole stack of papers to Frank. "Here, look at all these names. Look—John de Lancie, and over here Paul McIntyre..."

Frank shook his head, reading it out loud.

"I don't understand this whole thing. Why did she disappear if she's got nothing to do with the murder?"

Nick took a deep breath. He shrugged his shoulders.

Alex walked briskly up Broadway. Everyone on the street was focused on getting to their destination quickly in this stormy weather, so no one paid attention to the woman wearing a baseball hat and jeans. After what had happened last night, she had no other choice but to leave the city straight away. She had no time to go to her apartment to get clean clothes or her car. If she could get Zack's e-mails she'd retrieved from his computer to Nick, then he would believe her. It took her about fifteen minutes to walk to city hall; she didn't dare to hail a cab. She was completely soaked as she crossed Park Row and entered City Hall Park. The feeling of relief made her knees weak. Only a few hundred yards and she would be safe. She turned on the path leading to the main entrance of city hall and had almost reached the steps when a man stepped in her way.

"Excuse me," he said, and Alex stared at him.

The young man held a map in his hand, "Umm, could you tell me how to get to…"

Alex looked past him. She saw a dark-haired man standing at the door whose face looked familiar. He punched a number into his cell phone and glanced at her inconspicuously.

Shit, Alex thought.

"…the Empire State Building from here?"

"I can't help you," she said. "I'm not from here."

She looked around and saw a second man heading directly toward her. He walked fast and also held a cell phone to his ear. Before the young tourist's baffled eyes, Alex turned on her heel and jumped over the rosebushes. The two men dashed after her. As fast as she could, Alex ran across the lawn, wet grass squishing beneath her feet. She could have gone faster on the path, but she didn't look back. She focused on not slipping or falling down—because then she'd be a goner.

Alex rushed past the Tweed Courthouse toward Foley Square. She didn't pay any attention to the astonished looks of the few passersby as she raced past the US Court of International Trade. When she glanced over her shoulder, she saw that her pursuers were closer on her heels than she'd realized. She turned right onto Leonard Street, where, near the corner, a group of Japanese tourists stood in the pouring rain, wearing raincoats and posing for photos. Without slowing down, she cut through the group and bumped into a Japanese man, who lost his balance and fell to the ground. The tourists cursed at her with flailing arms, which forced Alex's pursuers to sidestep them.

This move cost them valuable seconds while Alex crossed Centre Street. Cars stopped with screeching tires as she ran across the street. Her strength was dwindling, and she was completely out of breath, but she could see Columbus Park ahead of her, barely a block away. Suddenly, a dark car turned in front of her and three men jumped out. Alex felt like a deer in headlights as she looked around. Three men blocked her way with grimly determined faces. The other two pursuers came running up behind her, gasping for air.

"Stop!" one of the three men yelled and spread his arms as if he could really stop her. Right at that moment, a silver Dodge turned from Baxter Street onto Hogan Place as a bicycle messenger sped down the street. He tried to evade the Dodge, but his tire slipped on the wet pavement. The young man fell on the ground, and his bicycle was hurled in front of Alex's feet. She didn't hesitate for a second. She grabbed the bike and swung herself onto the seat.

One of the men tried to grab her arm. With the strength of adrenaline triggered by her fear, she kicked him in the balls with all her might. He let go of her arm and yelled out in pain. Alex pedaled through Columbus Park faster than she'd ever ridden a bike before, thinking her lungs might explode any second. After a few minutes, she was at the very center of Chinatown—which was still bustling despite the rain. She ditched the bike on a street corner, vanishing into a maze of alleys between stalls and Chinese restaurants.

"She slipped through our fingers," Silvio Bacchiocchi reported to his boss, leaning on the Dodge's fender while grimacing in pain. The other men standing around him were irritated and soaked to the bone. No one laughed about Silvio's mishap. This woman was infuriating. It was pointless to continue the chase because they couldn't find someone hiding in Chinatown. The Chinese didn't like it at all when people were chased through their neighborhood. They sided with anyone on the run, and they would certainly provide protection and shelter for a distraught woman.

"Are you too stupid to catch a woman?" Sergio yelled into the phone. "That's unbelievable!"

"My guys saw her at city hall. But she ran like the devil, and then she snatched a messenger's bike and disappeared into Chinatown."

Silvio omitted the fact that Alex had kicked him in the balls.

"If she's not standing here in front of me by this afternoon," Sergio replied, "then I'll hold you personally responsible, *capito*?"

"Understood." Silvio hung up the phone.

Sergio closed his eyes for a moment. Alex was a clever bitch. Under different circumstances, he would have admired her for her courage and cleverness—but there was simply too much on the line in this case. Sergio hated her, yet there was also something inside of him that painfully longed for her. There was no question in his mind that she had been the first woman for whom he felt more than mere physical desire. However, she was also the first to betray and lie to him like this. Once he got a hold of her, he would beat her until she begged for mercy. She would bitterly regret the humiliation she had caused him!

"And?" Levy asked when Sergio had put away his cell phone. Sergio turned around quickly.

"And what?"

"Did they get her?"

"No," Sergio answered grimly. The telephone on Levy's desk rang.

"What is it?" LMI's president answered in an irritated voice. "I'm in an important meeting…Excuse me?"

Sergio could hear the agitated voice coming through the receiver. Levy listened silently, finally thanking his caller.

"Who was that?" Sergio asked. Levy, who had been under enormous pressure and was drinking much more than he could handle, looked bleary-eyed at Sergio.

"That was Lester Roman, our manager of strategic partnerships. He noticed a large transaction coming through one of our accounts this morning. Someone electronically requested the liquidation of MPM's account in the amount of fifty million dollars."

Sergio stared at him without comprehending. "How can that be? Doesn't that require the approval of the account holders?"

"Yes, it does," Levy confirmed, "but it happened. Everything was processed properly. No one thought it was suspicious because our employees routinely process very large transactions. Roman only got suspicious when he saw the name of the account holder during a routine check."

He paused and wiped the sweat off his forehead with a handkerchief.

"St. John entered the request, and Sontheim must have confirmed it. According to the account list, they were the sole owners of the MPM account and therefore were authorized to move the funds."

"Where did the money go?" Sergio asked after recovering from the initial shock.

"To an account at California S&L in Beverley Hills, Los Angeles."

"Who entered the transaction? Zack was already dead last night!"

"The request appeared on the computer this morning. It was approved at 8:31, originating from my computer. Everything was handled properly, and the password was correct. The responsible account manager compared the name of the person making the request with the account holder and approved it."

"From your computer?" Sergio was stunned and let himself sink into a chair. "That means that Alex was in this office an hour ago and sat calmly at your desk while hundreds of people were looking for her!"

"Fifty million dollars," Levy whispered, "and we can't even announce it publicly!"

Sergio stared blankly at the wall. Alex was even more audacious than he could have imagined. While they were searching for her in the building, she had stolen fifty million dollars from him outright. "I'm going to kill her," he growled. The thought that she had fooled him again tore him up inside. He—Sergio Vitali, who was so smart and cunning that his profitable businesses had operated unimpeded for decades—had been double-crossed by this bitch! Sergio briefly contemplated calling Nelson, but then he dismissed the idea. He grabbed Levy's telephone.

"What are you going to do?" Levy was nothing more than a frightened bundle of nerves.

"I'll finish her off." A cruel smile swirled around Sergio's lips. "She and her accomplices. Every cop in this country is chasing her now. She's going to pay for what she did to me."

He dialed a number that he knew by heart.

"This is Sergio Vitali speaking," he said when someone answered. "Please put me through to Mr. Harding."

Alex watched the news at a small joint in Chinatown. The police were looking for her because of Zack's murder. It was pointless to go to an airport because the risk of getting stopped was too great. She left the restaurant and walked in the rain to Canal Street, where she hailed a cab.

"Where to?" the cab driver asked.

"Port Authority," Alex replied. Neither Sergio nor the police would check all the buses that left the city. On her way to Forty-Second Street, she managed to calm herself down some. She had escaped Sergio's men by a whisker, but she certainly wouldn't be so lucky again. These men were dead serious. Things had been snapping quickly into place over the past forty-eight hours, and she had triggered it all. Alex leaned her forehead against the taxi's window. Would she have blown the Whithers deal if she had known what would happen? Zack was dead—murdered by the same men who were after her now. She shuddered when she realized that her life as she knew it was over. The thought that she was on the run, without a clue as to how and when it might end, was so frightening that she wanted to cry.

Oliver had been waiting for a phone call from Alex or Mark for three hours. He could hardly stand sitting in his apartment any longer, condemned to idleness and watching TV as it broadcast incredible cock-and-bull stories about Alex and St. John. Where was Alex? Why didn't she contact him?

The buzz of the doorbell tore him from his thoughts. But instead of Alex, two police officers with weapons drawn and two plainclothesmen were standing in the doorway. His first reflex was to slam the door shut, but the men were already in his apartment. They brutally pushed his face against the wall and twisted his arms behind his back.

"Are you Oliver Skerritt?" one of the men asked.

"Yes," Oliver said, wheezing in pain, "what do you want from me?"

"NYPD." The first man presented his badge while the other searched him for weapons. "We just want to ask you some questions. Please come with us."

"Do you have an arrest warrant?" Oliver's heart was pounding.

"We just want to ask you a few questions."

"About what?"

"About Alex Sontheim."

"And what exactly would you like to know?"

"You'll find out soon enough. Come on, let's go."

They dragged him from his apartment, and Oliver saw the flabbergasted faces of the couple living below him as the police escorted him downstairs. His fear that Sergio Vitali must be behind this arrest grew inside of him.

As Alex waited for the departure of her Greyhound to Boston, she remembered the cell phone she had found under Zack's desk and took it out of the pocket of her wet down jacket. It was set on silent, but still turned on. She dialed Mark's extension, but he didn't answer. Then she tried to reach Oliver. He also didn't pick up the phone. Determined, she called the operator to connect her with city hall. It took a while to get through to the mayor, but at last she had Nick on the line.

"Alex!" Nick's voice sounded tense. "Where are you?"

Alex closed her eyes with a sense of relief. The bus would leave in ten minutes.

"I don't have much time," she said quickly. "Please, listen to me! Nothing they claim on TV is true!"

"Alex—"

"No, please listen," she cut him off. "An important deal went sour yesterday. St. John bought a hundred million dollars' worth of shares for MPM whose value was cut in half overnight. Do you remember that partnership called SeaStarFriends that I told you about?"

"Yes."

"This partnership was originally founded by Levy and Vitali to operate an investment firm called MPM. But since last night, St. John and I are listed as the sole owners. They wanted to blame the whole disaster on us and be done with it."

"Hold on! I don't quite understand—"

"Because of St. John, MPM is sitting on a huge pile of unsellable shares. The firm will file for bankruptcy today for failure to meet net capital requirements. Vitali and Levy obviously didn't want to risk exposing their involvement with this dirty business, which is why they made St. John and me the owners. Zack probably found out and fought against it. That's why he was killed."

"Alex," Nick said emphatically, "they say that you killed him. The police and the FBI are after you. Can't you come here?"

"I've tried." Alex looked around, but no one in the Port Authority waiting area seemed to take any interest in a woman wearing a baseball hat. "I ran into Sergio's men at city hall and barely managed to escape. Nick, these guys want to kill me because I've discovered things that'll surely put Sergio behind bars. I haven't killed anyone. I went to St. John's office last night because I wanted to talk to him about everything, and then I found his dead body."

"Alex, for heaven's sake. Tell me where you are. I'll send someone over right away."

"No," she said, shaking her head. "I can't do that. I don't trust anyone anymore. There are too many people on Sergio's side."

"Then I'll come myself."

"Vitali is scouring the city for me. Nick, you must use the information that I've given you before Levy and Vitali manage to cover their tracks! Please!"

"Alex, let me come to you!"

"No. I'll skip town for a while, but I'll contact you again as soon as I can."

There was a click on the line, and the call ended. Nick stared at the receiver in his hand and slowly put it down. Her voice sounded desperate, but the things she told him sounded plausible. It wouldn't be the first time Vitali got rid of an inconvenient accomplice. And now he tried to blame the murder on Alex to discredit her. US Attorney John de Lancie appeared on TV. The reporter asked what kind of evidence the US Attorney's Office had to prove that Alex Sontheim committed the murder of Zachary St. John.

"Ms. Sontheim was in Mr. St. John's office," de Lancie said in a serious tone. With perfectly parted hair and steel-framed glasses, he seemed authoritative and determined. *"We checked the surveillance tapes numerous times, and there is no doubt that just Ms. Sontheim entered the office after St. John. He was killed by a shot to the head from a close distance. St. John held the weapon in his hand, which indicates that the crime was intended to be disguised as a suicide. Further evidence shows that Ms. Sontheim's fingerprints were all over the desk, the computer's keyboard, and the mouse. As we have learned in the meantime, she used her victim's computer to transfer a large sum of money from a company account to her personal account. We assume that she planned to flee the country with the money after she learned that the front organization she had used in her large-scale illegal insider trading scheme was doomed to bankruptcy. In all likelihood, a fight erupted, during which she shot her accomplice in order to seize all of the remaining money for herself."*

"Where's Ms. Sontheim at the moment?" a reporter asked.

"We don't know. She's still on the run. But since we issued a federal warrant for her arrest for the murder of Zachary St. John, she's not only wanted by the police but also the FBI and the US Marshals Service. I'm optimistic that we will capture her by the end of the day."

Nick stared at his successor's face. The alleged evidence against Alex was overwhelming: fingerprints, surveillance tapes, and now also embezzlement! And on top of it, she was a fugitive. If she were innocent, she could turn herself in to the police—at least an outside observer would believe. Nick wished that he could trust Alex, but he started to doubt her innocence. He realized he hardly knew her, and he wondered if his past sympathy for her may have influenced his objectivity. Maybe Alex hadn't accessed those bank statements by accident after all. It was certainly possible that she was not only in league with St. John, but maybe even with Vitali himself—until she had fallen out of favor with them.

Suspicion arose inside Nick, and he started to feel sick. Did Alex possibly just call on him to uncover the alleged bribery scandal to distract from her crime? How could he know whether these bank statements were real? It wasn't difficult for a banker to falsify such statements. Nick felt miserable. What if Alex had planned all of this long ago? It was conceivable that she had just visited him at the cemetery that Sunday to trick him into trusting her. Maybe she got into a lover's quarrel with Vitali and conjured up this perfidious plan to put one over on him. Who would make a more suitable ally than Nick Kostidis? But Alex's compassion and her fear of Vitali had seemed so genuine. He had believed her unconditionally.

"It almost seems this lady has led us by the nose," Frank said, voicing Nick's fears.

"I refuse to believe that," he said quietly. He remembered how she'd snuggled against his arm when they met on that evening in Tribeca. He was proud of his ability to read people. But suddenly he remembered Raymond Howard. He had let himself be deceived before. Could he have really deluded himself so tragically a second time?

"She asked me to use the information that she gave us immediately," Nick said.

"That would put an end to the headlines about this guy's murder for a while," Frank said, nodding. "In the meantime, she can bolt undisturbed."

Nick stared silently into space.

"That's a clever plan," Frank said. "I believed everything she said. She's a great actress."

"I have a feeling that this is yet another cover-up," Nick countered. "Just like that anthrax thing."

"Possibly," Frank replied skeptically, "but the question remains who wants to cover what up? It seems to me that Sontheim is trying to use this bribery scandal as a distraction from her dirty dealings."

"Please leave me alone for a moment," Nick asked. "I need to think about this. Tell Allie not to put any calls through, except…"

"Yes?"

"Except if it's Alex Sontheim."

"Nick! You're making a huge mistake! This woman is wanted for murder!"

"Frank, please!"

Frank Cohen threw his boss a doubtful look and left the office. Nick closed his eyes. He was bitterly disappointed. He would never trust a person in his life again if Alex had really deceived him so badly. He owed his life to her. Now she had asked him for help, and he was too much of a coward to act, too afraid to make a mistake. He had never been hesitant or timid in the past—back in the old days, before Vitali had succeeded in destroying him. Nick sighed in agony, wishing that he had someone to ask for advice. As a politician, he needed to be reelected every four years. Handing over dubious evidence could risk his reputation. His intuition told him that they were real, but what if they weren't? He turned on the television. He had never let himself be influenced by what other people thought before. If any decision he made was highly unpopular, then he would make it quickly to get it over with. Why didn't he just do what Alex had asked him to do? Did he really care about reelection? Sergio Vitali—who had humiliated and mocked him for years—had already taken everything he loved and cherished. He had nothing to lose.

Police Commissioner Harding appeared on the TV screen, and Nick turned up the volume. They were still talking about the murder. Harding spoke with exaggerated pathos, as if Alex had shot the president himself. And it was this minor detail that caught Nick's attention. This St. John character was just one of thousands of investment bankers on Wall Street. His death was certainly tragic, but did this really constitute a threat to national security requiring the involvement of the FBI? A murder case wasn't the responsibility of New York City's police commissioner but that of the homicide department. Nick had a feeling that his intuition was right. This whole thing was fishy. It was downright strange to make such a mountain out of a molehill. Did the involvement of both Harding and de Lancie, and the media hype around the murder of a relatively unknown investment banker, actually indicate that Vitali was involved? If that was the case, then Alex was right. The more Nick thought about it, the more plausible her admittedly wild story seemed. Assuming that they were real, the documents that she had given him were explosive. Vitali was certainly also aware of that.

"Blood-covered gloves were found in a trash can," Harding said, *"and the crime scene unit believes that the suspect wore these gloves when she committed the murder of her former accomplice."*

Gloves? Nick hesitated. De Lancie had just said that her fingerprints were clear proof of her guilt. Nick made his decision that very second. He could never look at himself in the mirror again if something happened to Alex because of his cowardice. His idle time was over. He would find out soon enough whether his decision was right or wrong. But doing nothing would only help Vitali.

"The confirmation arrived," Justin Savier said, turning toward Alex. "Fifty million dollars has been credited to your account at Bank of America."

Alex exhaled with a deep sigh and clenched her fists. It was three thirty, and she was wide awake and dead tired at the same time. She glanced at the muted TV. The manhunt for her in connection with Zack's murder was the top story on all the channels. She could hardly believe what was happening to her.

"Thanks, Justin," she said. "I don't know how I can ever repay you for all this."

"Don't worry about it." Justin smiled. For him it was all an exciting game. "What's next?"

"The money is wired to a numbered account at Gérard Frères in Zurich," Alex replied, "and then it'll vanish."

Justin nodded.

"By the way, that hair color looks really good on you." He grinned. Alex smiled in fatigue. She'd dyed her hair darker and wore blue contact lenses. Justin had taken pictures of her two hours ago and e-mailed them to an acquaintance. Her new American passport in the name of Emily Chambers would be ready an hour later. Justin's shady acquaintance had asked for a thousand dollars, which felt like nothing considering the passport could get her out of the country unscathed. The Swissair flight to Zurich Justin booked under this false name was scheduled to depart at ten o'clock. If everything went smoothly, she would be in Switzerland seven hours later, where Gerhard Etzbach—a fellow Stanford alumnus—would be waiting for her. He hadn't hesitated for a second when she called him and asked for help. Ten minutes later, he'd called her back to give her the details for the account he had opened in her name.

"I'm worried about Mark and Oliver." She couldn't bear sitting still despite her fatigue, so she paced back and forth through Justin's apartment. "I can only hope that Kostidis takes action."

"If we don't hear from him by nine, I'll fly straight to New York to see Kostidis," Justin offered. "I'll convince him that everything you told him is true. Then he's got no choice but to act."

"I hope it won't be too late by then." Alex couldn't fend off these dark premonitions. She had a feeling that the worst was yet to come.

It was ten thirty when Lloyd Connors—the deputy US attorney for the Southern District of New York—entered the mayor's office.

"What kind of crazy story is this, Nick?" he asked. "I hope that this really is important, because my wife was pretty mad when I told her that I had to leave the house again."

"Thank you for coming right away." Nick extended his hand to the younger man. They sat down at the table in his office. Connors had started at the US Attorney's Office straight out of law school when Nick was still the head of the agency. He had perseverance and was clever and ambitious. Nick wasn't one bit surprised that he had climbed the career ladder so quickly.

"You said on the telephone that de Lancie must not hear about this meeting. That had me wondering. So what's this all about?" Connors crossed his legs and watched Nick closely with a friendly smile. His adversaries had frequently underestimated him because he looked so harmless, but an alert intelligence lurked behind his boyish face.

"It's a complicated matter and highly explosive," Nick started out. "I finally got my hands on evidence against Vitali."

"Vitali again?" Connors said mildly. "You still haven't given up on him, have you?"

"I've always been right, and you know it. I simply couldn't prove anything."

"And now you can?" Connors raised his eyebrows.

"Yes," Nick said, nodding slowly, "I think so. However, this is really big. It'll have major consequences, affecting many powerful men in the city."

"You're making me curious."

"What would you say if I had a list of names of people who've been receiving bribes from Vitali for years?"

"Interesting. How credible is this…list?"

"They're bank statements from numbered bank accounts on Grand Cayman," Nick said. "It looks like a very sophisticated bribery system."

"Written evidence of paid bribes?"

"I think it's leverage against the people receiving the bribes. They're not aware of it."

"Now you really have my attention." Connors leaned back, sharply eyeing Nick.

"Somebody came to me a few weeks ago. This person works at a major investment firm on Wall Street. She told me that she'd stumbled upon a large-scale fraud scheme and unwittingly got tangled up in it. I got curious when she mentioned Vitali. It appears that Vitali had a front organization through which he bought large blocks of shares based on information obtained from insiders. The profits from these transactions were paid to these secret accounts in cash. This firm seems to serve the sole purpose of generating dirty money to bribe high-ranking officials and politicians. It's clearly evident where the money originated when you look at the deposits. Furthermore, I believe that Vitali has been laundering drug money through this front organization."

"What kind of money are we talking about?"

"Upward of fifty thousand dollars a month, for a period of at least three years."

"How reliable is this information?"

"I have the account statements."

"Is the person who passed this information to you willing to testify in court?"

Nick shrugged his shoulders. "To be honest with you, I don't know."

"Can you give me some names on the list?"

"Lloyd," Nick said as he stood up and looked at the deputy US attorney, "this is a life-threatening situation. The man who performed these transactions for Vitali was found dead today."

"You're talking about St. John at LMI."

"Exactly. St. John bought a large amount of stock in a company represented by his firm in a takeover deal. As you know, the deal went bust. The company through which St. John bought this stock filed for bankruptcy today."

"Manhattan Portfolio Management?" Connors looked at Nick in surprise.

"That's right. MPM itself is owned by a partnership. Vitali and Levy, LMI's president, are behind it."

"No, no, you're mistaken." Connors shook his head. "I've read the reports. This St. John and his accomplice, the head of the M&A department, were the owners of the firm. They got into a fight or panicked, and then the woman killed him and escaped."

"That's the official version," Nick objected, "but it's not true."

"How could that be? There's evidence—and an arrest warrant."

"Just a minute." Nick walked over to his desk and took out the papers that Alex had given him.

"This," Nick said as he handed Connors a sheet of paper, "is a computer printout from July sixth of this year. It comes from the Department of Commerce on the British Virgin Islands and clearly states the owners of the partnership SeaStarFriends. And this is a copy from the commercial registry stating that SeaStarFriends itself is the sole owner of MPM."

Connors studied the two pieces of paper and shook his head again.

"You're right," he admitted, "that's unbelievable."

"Yes, it is. The names of the owners were amended electronically after Vitali and Levy were in danger of being exposed through this firm's bankruptcy filing."

"That would be something!"

"Indeed," Nick confirmed. "It's illegal for the president or a board member of an investment firm to own a brokerage company dealing in shares of the firm's clients."

"Correct. That's a serious violation of securities law."

Connors frowned and stared at the papers.

"Where did you get this?"

Nick took a deep breath.

"From the woman you suspect of being St. John's murderer."

"Alex Sontheim?" Connors asked in disbelief.

"Yes," Nick replied. "She was afraid that Vitali had found out what she knew and went to discuss next steps with St. John. But she was too late—St. John was dead when she found him."

"And you believe her story?" Connors raised his eyebrows. "Come on, Nick! Where's your sense of reality? This woman embezzled fifty million dollars and is on the run! If she was innocent, she could turn herself in to the authorities."

"No, she can't," Nick countered. "Vitali would kill her."

Connors didn't seem convinced.

"She called me today," Nick said calmly. "I've heard many people lie before. She's not lying. I believe her—without a doubt."

"She called you?" Connors's eyes widened. "Fifty US marshals, the police, and the FBI are tracking her down for murder, and you tell me with a straight face that you had a phone conversation with this woman?"

"For God's sake, Lloyd, she didn't do it!" Nick replied vehemently. "I know something is seriously fishy here, and my instincts have rarely failed me. De Lancie and Harding are contradicting each other when it comes to the evidence. And why would the police commissioner get personally involved in a homicide investigation? He didn't even step in when Roddy Burillo, quarterback for the Giants, was killed—and that was a truly newsworthy case!"

"What are you insinuating?"

"Harding is Vitali's man. Just like de Lancie and Governor Rhodes."

"Come on, Nick! That's ridiculous!"

"Absolutely not." Nick handed the bank statements to the deputy US attorney. "Look at them closely and then tell me whether or not we have a case here."

He crossed his arms. Connors's face was first filled with astonishment, then with shock.

"For God's sake," Connors said, lowering the papers, "if all of this is true, then…then…"

"It's true. Raymond Howard's name is on the list. He was one of my closest employees for eight years. I often wondered why many of my secret plans were already known before they were officially made public. Howard was Vitali's mole in my office."

He paused for a moment and remembered Raymond Howard's terror when Mary and Christopher got into the limousine. He had known that there was a bomb in the car. A bomb that was meant for Nick.

"It was Howard who informed Vitali about Zuckerman's hideout. He was also the one who shared redevelopment plans for certain neighborhoods in the South Bronx. And as a result, Vitali purchased entire apartment blocks and sent his people there to intimidate the tenants. Vitali's son was arrested during one of those raids."

Connors stared at Nick with his mouth wide open.

"Alex Sontheim personally overheard the same man who shot at me at the cemetery in Brooklyn reporting Zuckerman's murder to Vitali. Vitali had Zuckerman killed because he was afraid he would reveal to the grand jury how he secured the contract to build the World Financial Center. By the way, you can ask Paul McIntyre about this. He's also on the list."

"But de Lancie…"

"Do you remember the incidents at the Forty-First Precinct in the Bronx the night of Cesare Vitali's arrest? Did you ever wonder why de Lancie personally showed up there?"

"Yes, I did."

"There you go. He had to show up because he's obligated to Vitali. I was also there, which he didn't like at all. He was acting strange for a US attorney. I told him straight to his face that I questioned his loyalty."

Connors nodded slowly.

"It was also strange that they captured the guy who allegedly shot at Vitali within just a few hours. Furthermore, there was this obscure terrorist case that—in my opinion—served to distract from Vitali and his son's death."

"So who actually shot at him?"

"I suspect that it was the Colombian drug cartel. Vitali tipped off customs, which in turn busted a huge cocaine shipment. The shots at Vitali were the Colombian's revenge. I saw through it, but I made the mistake of publicly announcing it. The attempt on my life was the final proof of how dangerously close I got to the truth."

"Good Lord. Nick, do you know what all of this means?"

"Yes," Nick said, frowning, "I know very well."

"But how does Sontheim fit into this? Why did she disappear?"

"She's understandably frightened after everything that's happened."

Connors started pacing. He frowned, chewing on his lower lip.

"I hope you get this, Lloyd," Nick said. "I'm pretty sure Vitali spread the rumor that Alex killed St. John to create a distraction. A murder suspect is useless as a witness in court."

The deputy US attorney stopped.

"Looking at it that way, it doesn't sound as absurd anymore." He took a deep breath and exhaled again. "But I can't rush things. A case like this must be prepared carefully."

"We don't have much time left. With every passing hour, Vitali has more opportunity to destroy the evidence."

And he could find Alex. And kill her...

No, he mustn't think about that now. Above all else, he had to make sure that no one caught on to his feelings for this woman, who was the key witness in one of the biggest corruption scandals in New York's history. Connors leaned forward, his hands braced on the tabletop; he stared at the papers spread out in front of him.

"I don't know what kind of avalanche we may trigger here," he said to Nick's relief, "but we'll get to the bottom of this."

"We have a lead," Luca announced. "She bought something at a department store in Boston this morning with her credit card."

Sergio had been lying on the sofa with his eyes closed; he jumped up. Alex had gotten out of the city. Did she make a purchase with her credit card on purpose, or was it just poor judgment? She must know that credit cards could be traced.

"The FBI is watching every international airport," Massimo said. "She won't be able to leave the country."

"Of course she can," Sergio replied, annoyed. "She probably has new papers and a different appearance by now. Alex is damn clever."

Massimo, Luca, and Silvio looked at each other. They had never seen Sergio Vitali admit to a mistake.

"We have to catch her before the cops do," Sergio said, more to himself than the other three men. "Luca, send two guys to the airport in Boston. And Silvio, what about this lawyer in LA?"

"We've got all the documents," Silvio responded. "Our man is already on a plane back to New York. His tracks have been covered up carefully."

"Will the lawyer keep his mouth shut?"

"Yes, he will," Silvio confirmed. "He swallowed a bit too much water."

Sergio nodded in satisfaction. Levy would fly to Georgetown tomorrow morning to close all of the secret accounts. He hadn't heard anything yet, but there was still the possibility that Alex had told someone about these accounts. It was better to temporarily close them. The US Attorney's Office seemed to have swallowed the bait. The television news reports were all about the fugitive Alex Sontheim. The evidence against her was overwhelming. The FBI's involvement in the search had blown St. John's murder so out of proportion that MPM's bankruptcy had become a side issue. Exactly as planned. Sergio's friends at the SEC and the US Attorney's Office would pursue the investigation in their usual superficial way, and in two weeks no one would give a damn about it anymore. Oliver Skerritt was in a single cell at the police department. Alex's closest employee, Mark Ashton, was in a basement at LMI. All they could do now was wait.

The telephone rang shortly before midnight.

"The money was wired from California S&L to an account at Bank of America at eleven this morning," Levy announced. "A few hours later, it was transferred out of the country. This was all done electronically."

"Do you know where it was sent?"

"Of course," Levy replied with a hint of sarcasm in his voice. "That's one of the advantages of modern data communication. It was wired to Switzerland."

"There are hundreds of banks in Switzerland."

"Exactly. And this is where we lose the trail. It was transferred to an anonymous numbered account. Alex knows what she's doing. We'd better just accept it: that money is gone."

Tracy Taylor and Jason Bennett—Lloyd Connors's two closest staff members—arrived at city hall just after midnight. Frank had ordered some pizza and brewed a pot of coffee, and now they were sitting at the conference table with all of the papers spread out in front of them as they worked through a strategy. It was almost like old times, when Nick was still a US attorney planning the takedowns of Mafia bosses. But in contrast to those days, they needed to proceed with extreme caution because they could not discern friend from enemy. They couldn't trust a soul. Anyone working in the city could be on Vitali's payroll.

"We have to keep de Lancie out of this," Nick said. "He's one of Vitali's most important connections at the moment."

"We still don't know how bulletproof this evidence is," Connors said. "Where did this woman get these statements? Who obtained them?"

"That doesn't matter."

"Yes," the deputy US attorney objected, "it does. We must prove without a doubt that these people actually used this money. We also need to prove how they accessed these accounts. They may be totally unaware of it. In that case, we'd have a case of attempted bribery, but no criminal offense."

"Above all, we need the woman," Jason Bennett spoke up. "She's the only one who understands all the connections."

Nick leaned back in exhaustion. If they confronted the people on this list with the bank statements, then they'd willingly testify just to save their own skin—he had no doubt about that. He didn't care whether or not Alex was the key witness, but he was still seriously worried about her. There was no doubt Vitali had ordered his people to track her down.

"We need to bring in the FBI," Connors added. "This thing is too big for us alone. Imagine what will happen when we arrest Governor Rhodes..."

"So what?" Nick walked back and forth restlessly. "He accepted money from a criminal."

"Did he really?"

Someone knocked at the door, and Allie Mitchell peeked in. She had come back to the office when Frank called her at home.

"There's a gentleman here by the name of Justin Savier," she said. "He claims to be a friend of Alex Sontheim."

"Send him in!" Nick exclaimed.

A skinny man in his midthirties with shoulder-length dreadlocks entered the office of New York City's mayor. "Excuse me for interrupting, but Alex Sontheim asked me to come here."

Nick looked at the man suspiciously. Was he really one of Vitali's spies just pretending to be Alex's friend?

"How do I know you are who you claim you are?"

"Do you want to see my ID?" the man asked. "I can prove to you that all of the documents Alex gave you are real."

Connors interrupted: "Then show us your evidence."

"Who are you, if I may ask?" Justin Savier challenged with raised eyebrows. Nick quickly introduced the US attorneys and offered him a seat and a cup of coffee. Justin accepted both. Then he explained that he was a college friend of Oliver Skerritt's and Alex's trusted employee Mark Ashton, and that he worked at MIT in Boston. He reported that Mark, Alex, and Oliver had approached him last summer because they wanted to find out more about the dirty dealings that she'd uncovered at LMI. Nick and Connors exchanged a glance.

"Where is Alex Sontheim now?" the deputy US attorney inquired.

"On an airplane to Europe," Justin replied.

"Impossible. All airports are under surveillance."

"I got her a fake passport," Justin admitted in front of the assembled US attorneys. "You've got to believe her. I have the e-mail that Alex printed from St. John's computer last night. Mark Ashton and Oliver Skerritt disappeared because this monster's already got a hold of them."

"Not so fast," Connors cut him off. "What do you have to do with this whole thing?"

Justin told them how he managed to get the information that Alex had handed over to Kostidis. Then he recounted what he had learned last night about the ownership structure of the SeaStarFriends partnership.

"Whew," Connors exhaled, running his hands through his hair.

"You don't believe me?" Justin asked.

"We've questioned the authenticity of the statements," Nick answered on Connors's behalf, "but they do appear to be real."

"They definitely are," Justin confirmed. "We were totally shocked when we realized the magnitude of this conspiracy."

"What makes you so sure that it wasn't Alex Sontheim who killed St. John?" Connors asked.

"She had absolutely no reason to kill him," Justin replied. "After all, he could have testified to what actually went down at LMI. After reading St. John's e-mails, you'll see that he had no intention of blowing his brains out. Alex believes that Vitali's thugs killed Zack, and now they're blaming her for the murder in order to divert attention."

Nick and Connors again exchanged a brief glance.

"Alex didn't kill St. John," Justin said emphatically. "I'm sure that you've noticed the police contradicting themselves on TV, right? First, they found fingerprints everywhere and then the gloves. That's totally contradictory!"

"Show us the e-mails," Connors requested.

Justin grabbed his backpack and pulled out a few pages. He placed them on the table. The deputy US attorney took the pages and read through them.

"Wow," he exclaimed and passed them on to Nick. "Incredible."

"Don't you believe Alex is telling the truth?" Justin asked.

Connors looked up.

"Yes," he said grimly. "Yes, now I believe her. Oh, this is going to be one hell of a ride."

Sergio spent half a day checking in with his connections at the US Attorney's Office and the police department. No one doubted that Alex had killed St. John out of greed and to cover her tracks. No one he talked to seemed nervous, which could only mean that Alex hadn't shared any evidence against him. Sergio still had no plausible explanation for how she had accessed a bank statement from Levy & Villiers, but even if she had run to Kostidis, there was no direct link leading to him. There was no way in hell that the people he bribed would admit to anything because then they'd be finished. There was no evidence. Zack—the only person besides him and Levy who knew the score—was dead. All of the documents that the lawyer from California had in his possession had been destroyed, and he was dead as a doornail.

A sinister smile appeared on Sergio's face. Zack thought he was smart, trying to cover his ass, but Sergio was smarter. Then his smile vanished. Yes, he was smarter than Zack, but Alex had him fooled. But even she couldn't hide from him forever. She'd trip up at some point, and he would pounce on her and show no mercy.

Silvio stopped the car at van Mieren's mansion at the edge of Hempstead on Long Island. Nelson hadn't left his house for the past three weeks. Sergio knew that his closest confidant was seriously ill, but he'd had enough of Nelson's wife's excuses to keep him off the phone. He wanted to hear Nelson explain himself. The situation had turned incredibly complex, and Sergio urgently needed the advice of his friend and lawyer. Carmen van Mieren opened the door.

"Sergio! Come in," she greeted him warmly and let him kiss her on the cheek. "I'll tell Nelson you're here. He's in bed."

"Thank you. I won't disturb him for too long."

Sergio walked into a comfortably furnished salon with a magnificent view of the lake. A thick fog hung like a cloud over the water. He gazed out at the leafless yard and down to the pier, unable to fend off memories of happier days. They had often sat in this yard and on the jetty, forging their ambitious plans. The children had played in the yard while Carmen and Constanzia prepared meals. Sergio remembered Nelson's son William's wedding, which they had celebrated here just one week after the magnificent opening ceremony of the VITAL Building, the steel-and-concrete manifestation of his success. Sergio remembered his sons as children and reminisced about the many years that he and Nelson had known each other. He and Nelson had been so successful in their work together. They had built an empire that generated billions. Sergio sighed. Nelson was the rock on which he always relied. His loyalty had been unshakable for forty years. Now they were old—older than their fathers ever were. It was time to sit back and enjoy the fruits of their hard labor, but instead everything had fallen apart. Constanzia had left him, Cesare was dead, and—because of Alex—his empire was shaken to its core. Sergio dug his hands into his pants pockets. He stiffened as he thought about her. Alex had humiliated him, wounded his pride, and now had also lied and stolen from him. She'd caused him a crushing defeat. But one lost battle didn't lose the war.

"Hello, Sergio."

He flinched and turned around quickly. Sergio was terrified at the sight of his old friend. Nelson must have lost forty-five pounds during the past few weeks. His complexion was unhealthy and gray, and he had dark circles under his eyes.

"Nelson, my dear friend." He walked toward Nelson and grabbed his hand heartily. "How are you?"

"It probably won't get any better," Nelson replied in a hoarse voice. "The doctors tell me to do chemotherapy, but I don't want it. I won't get healthy again doing that."

He walked over to an armchair and sat down clumsily.

"Why are you avoiding me?" Sergio suddenly asked.

"Do I give you that impression?"

"Yes, you do."

"Maybe you're right," Nelson said with a sigh. "I guess I probably owe you an apology."

Sergio sat down in another armchair across from him.

"I told you once before that I was out if you had the mayor killed. Do you remember that?"

"Yes, you said something along those lines." Sergio nodded impatiently. "Kostidis is alive and kicking. What else do you want?"

"You had a car bomb planted in his car that killed four people," Nelson said, "and you lied to me when you said that you had nothing to do with it. I believed you."

Sergio didn't bat an eye.

"Since Kostidis was still alive, you sent Natale to the cemetery," Nelson continued. "I'm also sure that you gave the order to have your own son killed, even though you also denied that to my face."

He fell silent.

In all of the long years they'd worked together, Nelson van Mieren had admired Sergio's intelligence, his energy, and his incredible willpower. He had never questioned Sergio's decisions, even though human beings died because of them. But now he couldn't do it anymore.

Now that his own death was imminent, perhaps Nelson realized he had chosen the wrong path in life. Their sprawling empire was built on blood and fear. Blinded by success and power, Nelson had gotten used to this. He had never taken anyone's life personally; he had no blood on his hands. It was merely a means to an end. This was simply part of business, and he never really thought about it—until the night that someone shot at Sergio. That night, he saw both Sergio's and his own future with shocking clarity. Like the big Mafia families a few decades ago, they were doomed to fail—if they weren't able to put an end to their dangerous and illegal business dealings. Nelson had tried to convince Sergio, but he was deaf to any argument. Doubts had suddenly crept in, and with those doubts came fear. The Kostidis business ultimately tilted the scales. Sergio still underestimated this man. And that would have disastrous consequences.

"I don't know whether my nerves got weaker or my conscience louder," Nelson continued. "I only know that I can't trust you anymore. You lied to me, and now you even have Luca's people watching me. That's not a basis for mutual trust and cooperation, and this is why I've decided not to work for you anymore. I want to spend my last remaining months in peace."

Sergio remained calm on the outside.

"We've walked a long way together and built a successful business," Nelson said. "I assumed that the times of killing were over, and we succeeded in doing things legally. That was always my goal. But now I'm forced to realize that the past can't be purged that easily."

He smiled sadly.

"You can't do this!" Sergio jumped up. "You can't just quit like some employee in a supermarket. I need you, Nelson. I can't do it without you!"

"But you'll have to in the future." Nelson shrugged his shoulders. "You know plenty of clever young lawyers who are more ruthless and ambitious than I am now. You'll find a successor for me."

Sergio stared at his oldest friend in disbelief. Up to now, he'd thought that he could appease Nelson somehow, but he suddenly realized that his companion had made an irrevocable decision. He was no longer on his side. Sergio's anger was mixed with serious concern. Nelson knew everything—all of the correlations, all the contacts and cover-ups—as well as he did. Nelson was his strongest support. People like St. John or Alex were replaceable—but not Nelson.

"What are you going to do now? Go to the police?" Sergio forced himself to speak in a disdainful tone. "Will you make your great confession and write a book about your life? Where does this sudden guilty conscience come from? What's suddenly so different? You've become rich and powerful because of me, Nelson. Your family is taken care of. You better than anyone know why I had to do all of this! It's a jungle out there: eat or be eaten. I'm not suitable prey! I've always fought and worked hard. I can't let some random idiot ruin everything that I've accomplished."

He stared at Nelson with fiery eyes.

"I understand," Nelson replied in a tired voice, "but I can't accept the way that you defend yourself anymore. I'm longing for peace and quiet.

I can't take all the tension anymore. I feel old, burned out. I'm afraid I'll make mistakes now."

"You don't make mistakes."

"Yes I do! I've already made one! I should have forced you to keep your hands off of Kostidis. You felt too secure, Sergio. You never listened to my warnings, and now Kostidis is not only your adversary but your sworn enemy. Believe me, he's a very dangerous man."

"I'm not afraid of Kostidis," Sergio said, waving his hand dismissively.

"You should be," Nelson replied, "and you know all too well that most of your allies are on your side against their will. As soon as you're under attack, they'll quickly forget their loyalty and turn their backs on you. Do you think that Levy will be at your side when you get into trouble?"

"You talk about trouble and problems, but everything's going great," Sergio said irritably.

"You're arrogant," Nelson said, slowly shaking his head. "Open your eyes for once! You've got problems at the port and also at LMI. Why don't you cut off the illegal parts of your business? How much richer do you want to be? Or are you afraid that someone else could become more powerful than you? Why are you putting everything at risk?"

"I'm not risking anything," Sergio countered coldly.

"Oh yes, you are. You think that you can move people around like chess pieces. But someone will come one day who's just as smart and ruthless as you are. You think that you're untouchable, but you're not. You're not above the law. You've just been lucky up to now."

"Who could get to me? Tell me! Who?"

"What's really going on with MPM?" Nelson sighed. "Who killed St. John? It wasn't Alex."

"Who cares as long as the police believe it?"

"You had him killed because he was a threat to you." Sergio thought he detected a hint of mockery in Nelson's eyes. "And then you blame your little girlfriend because she left you—just like Constanzia. Your pride couldn't take it."

"That's bullshit!" exclaimed Sergio, but the truth in Nelson's words stung.

"Does she know anything about you?"

"No," Sergio said, but he avoided looking at his friend. "Well, maybe… I don't know."

"You're about to lose control," Nelson said quietly, "and that's very dangerous."

Sergio breathed heavily, trying to control his rising anger. He had always hated asking anyone for anything, but now he was forced to.

"I'll do anything you say, Nelson," he said, humbly lowering his head. "I've made a few mistakes, but it won't happen again. You're right that the bloodshed must end. I beg you, for the sake of our long friendship, don't turn your back on me now."

Nelson gave Sergio a serious look. He knew too well how difficult it was for Sergio Vitali to utter such a plea. He felt compelled to reconsider his initial decision for a moment. But then Nelson stood up with a sigh. All he saw in Sergio's eyes was anger and coldness. Sergio wouldn't change a thing. His put-on humility was nothing but a tactic.

"Okay," Nelson said.

"Will you come to the office tomorrow?" Sergio asked. "At least for a few hours so we can talk things over?"

"Yes. I'll be there."

Relief washed over Sergio's face. He hugged Nelson quickly.

"See you tomorrow, my friend," he said.

Out the window, Nelson van Mieren watched Sergio walk to his limousine and get in.

"Is he gone?"

Nelson turned around. Constanzia Vitali and his wife Carmen stood in the doorway.

Nelson took the small recorder out of his robe pocket, pressed the stop button, and handed it to Constanzia.

"What will you do?" she asked. "Will you really return to him?"

"No"—Nelson sighed and shook his head—"I've made my decision. Nevertheless, I'm sorry that you—"

"You don't need to be sorry." Constanzia quickly cut him off and hugged him. "I've waited years for this opportunity. If it's the last thing I do, I'll get my revenge for everything that he's done to me. I'm not afraid of him."

Van Mieren smiled sadly.

"You're very brave, Connie."

"Someone has to do it," she said, tears sparkling in her eyes. "Sergio is responsible for so many deaths. And there's no end in sight."

Apart from the noise of the rain tapping against the window, it was completely silent.

"I should be the one to do what you're doing," Nelson said, his voice cracking, "but I'm a coward. I've been a coward all my life."

He turned toward his wife.

"Forgive me, my love," he murmured. "I'm sorry."

Then Nelsen turned around and walked to his office with wobbly steps. He closed the door behind him and sat down at his desk. There was no hope left that he would ever be healthy again. The cancer had been eating away at his body silently and now it was too late. Nelson had prepared himself for death over the past weeks, and now he felt ready to go. The room was filled with the sweet smell of flowers standing in a vase on the mantel. He took a gun out of the top drawer of the desk and looked at it reverently. Sergio had given him the weapon many years ago, but he had never used it. Until today. Nelson's eyes wandered to the window. It was a drizzly, dark day. The rain outside had just turned to snow. It was sticking to the wet grass, leaving a thin white film. His thoughts raced back to the days of his youth. Would his life have taken the same course if he had known then what he knew now? He shrugged his shoulders. His decision was made. He slowly loaded a bullet into the chamber, closed his eyes, pressed the gun to his temple, and pulled the trigger.

Today the giant Christmas tree was lit at Rockefeller Center. It shone with thousands of little lights over the city, buzzing with a pre-Christmas bustle. The temperature had dropped, and the rain of the past days had turned into thick, wet snowflakes.

Nick Kostidis stood at his office window with a cup of coffee and stared into space. They had all worked through the night. Lloyd Connors had temporarily declared Nick's office an improvised command center for the planned operation. The preparations for the first strike were in full swing. Connors had ordered his most trusted staff members to city hall the very same night, and they started analyzing the documents that Alex had procured for them. Some of the names on the bank statements were unfamiliar, but it was clear that these people also held important positions. Nick and Connors agreed that they needed to act as quickly as possible so Vitali wouldn't gain any additional advantage. They called Attorney General Gordon Engels that same night and briefly explained the politically charged case to him. Nick knew Engels personally, and he had no doubts about his integrity. Engels intended to come to New York in person the very next morning with his best people. Since it was clear to Nick and Connors that they couldn't risk bringing in the NYPD due to Jerome Harding's involvement, they had turned to the FBI for assistance. FBI Deputy Director Tate Jenkins informed them that he would arrive in the city in the early morning, accompanied by two agents from a special division of the FBI dealing with investigations of public officials.

Nick drank the last sip of coffee and grimaced. He used to love days like this. He always found the tree-lighting one of his most pleasant duties, but he had a hard time focusing on the hundred-foot-tall Norway spruce in Rockefeller Center today. He had sent other city hall representatives to various events in the city's boroughs, and he would stop by Rockefeller Center in the late afternoon. He had caught himself thinking that he should have called Mary last night to tell her that he probably wouldn't make it home. During his stint as a US attorney, he'd had to do that more than once. But it stung when he realized that no one was waiting for him anymore. Nick let out a tormented sigh. He felt a permeating sense of inadequacy joined with his feelings of pain and loneliness. He knew how silly it was to imagine that Alex felt more for him than mere sympathy. At thirty-eight, she was sixteen years younger than he was. He had read a lot into her sympathy. He probably felt more affection for the young woman than she did for him, which disturbed him; he feared that his affection could cloud his sense of judgment.

"I still can't understand it," Connors said, interrupting Nick's train of thought. He had put his feet up on the table and rolled up his sleeves. Like all of the others in the room, he had bloodshot eyes and sipped at one of the countless cups of coffee that he had consumed over the course of the night.

"This could turn out to be the biggest scandal since Watergate."

"It certainly seems like it," Nick said as he turned away from the window. "I just hope it's enough to put Vitali behind bars once and for all."

"It will be, believe me! He'll never get out of prison!" Connors laughed grimly, but Nick just sighed.

He had thought the same thing many times before, but every time Vitali had managed to squirm free like a fish from the net. He had an army of highly paid and extremely smart lawyers who knew every loophole in the law. They'd probably succeed again in getting him off the hook. But it would damage his empire significantly if there were no more judges, senators, police commissioners, and state attorneys to cover his back. Nick was surprised to notice that it didn't mean as much to him to bring Vitali to court. It was much more important to him that Alex was safe.

Connors stood up and walked over to the large whiteboard where they had written the names of all the people who appeared to be involved in this scandal. His initial skepticism had turned into euphoria and excitement. He worked with total commitment. Looking at the younger man, Nick was briefly reminded of himself. He was exactly the same way back in the day! He had worked day and night for weeks on end to accomplish his goal. Similar to Connors, he could motivate his employees and get the best work out of them. Yes, Connors was certainly the right man for this operation. He wasn't influenced by personal emotion but proceeded with the logic and clear calculation of a US attorney.

"We'll paralyze half of the city," Connors continued. "It'll affect almost every administrative body. Vitali has pulled them all to his side. It's incredible! Engels and Jenkins will be shocked when they see this!"

"I hope so," Nick said.

"What do you mean?" Connors looked at him in surprise.

"What I mean is that I hope that hasn't also bought someone like Engels."

"You can't be serious!"

"Nothing surprises me anymore." Nick ran his hand though his hair. "Before, I would have put my hand in the fire for Harding or Judge Whitewater."

"Hmm," Connors said, scratching his chin pensively, "I'll definitely pay a visit to de Lancie with two US marshals today and let him know that we suspect him of corruption. My intuition tells me that he would do anything to save his ass. At the very least, he'll bow out of the Sontheim investigation."

He sat down again and took a bite of a bagel.

"We'll warn him that we're informing the attorney general. And we'll do the same thing with Judge Whitewater, Governor Rhodes, and the senators."

"What about Harding?" Nick asked. "He's dangerous. He'll vehemently defend himself."

"Harding is a driving force in the St. John homicide investigation," Connors said after thinking for a moment. "He can do some serious damage if we leave him unchecked."

"But Vitali could become suspicious if de Lancie and Harding suddenly get sick," Nick said. "You should leave him alone for a couple of days. I think it's more important to contact the SEC investigation unit. I could call Rob Dreyfus. We cooperated with him back when we investigated the Bahamian banks. Now he's the government representative for the SEC."

Connors's staff member Tracy Taylor entered the office.

"What's up, Tracy?" Connors asked. "Did you find anything about this lawyer from California?"

"Yes," the young woman said, frowning apologetically. "I'm afraid that someone else got to him before us. Someone set his house on fire two nights ago. The police found a burned body that was most likely that of Sturgess's girlfriend. They initiated a search for John Sturgess after he didn't show up at his office yesterday. A surfer found his body close to the pier in Newport Beach two hours ago."

"Oh shit," Connors said. Nick just raised his eyebrows. It wasn't the first time that he'd seen the silencing of a witness.

"Nick," Frank Cohen said as he entered the room, "Mr. Engels and Mr. Jenkins just arrived."

"Great," Connors said gleefully, rubbing his hands eagerly, "let's get this party started."

Justin had booked a double room with a view at a five-star hotel on Lake Zurich under the names of Frank and Emily Chambers. There was an international warrant out for German citizen Alex Sontheim for suspected homicide, but no one would care if an American couple booked a hotel room—even if the husband never showed up. Alex almost fell asleep in the taxi that drove her from Zurich's Kloten Airport. Throughout the flight, she was frightened that someone would discover she was traveling under a fake passport, but nothing happened. Furthermore, her transformation was perfect. When she caught her relection in the mirror, Alex could hardly believe that the woman with the short dark curls and blue eyes was her. After almost seventy-two hours without sleep, she longed for a hot bath and a comfortable bed.

There was complete silence as Lloyd Connors finished his report. Gordon Engels and Tate Jenkins had showed up with three US marshals, Deputy Thomas J. Spooner, Deputy Randy Khazaeli, and Deputy Joe Stewart; and three FBI agents, Samuel Ramirez, Jeffrey Quinn, and Steve O'Brien. Everyone, including Nick, Frank, and Connors's staff, sat at the mayor's conference table.

"So these are the facts that we've gathered so far," Connors said, looking around the table. "It appears that Vitali has been bribing almost every important man in New York City and Albany for years. We have everyone listed here: the governor, senators, the police commissioner of New York City, the US attorney of the Southern District, federal judges, city council members, officers of the Securities and Exchange Commission, and even officials from the Department of State, the Department of Justice, and the Department of Commerce in Washington."

"Unbelievable," Engels commented after a brief silence. He was a skinny, gray-haired man with alert eyes behind thick glasses.

Jenkins remained skeptical. "How credible is this information?" he wanted to know.

"Very credible," Connors replied.

"I'm afraid," Engels said with a frown, knocking his knuckles on the copies of the bank statements, "that this is going to be an enormous scandal. We don't know what might happen when the people find out that almost every high-ranking official in New York accepted bribes."

"Before I take concrete action," Jenkins added, "I still need to talk to Mr. Horner. I can't move ahead with a case this huge without his approval."

Nick and Connors exchanged a glance. Engels and Jenkins seemed to be anything but delighted about the prospect of uncovering such a huge corruption scandal.

"In my opinion, it's imperative to act with urgency." Connors sat down. "Vitali hasn't just bribed these people. We have the written testimony of a man who did the dirty work for him. This man was shot last Thursday night. The lawyer who recorded his statement was killed two days ago. If Vitali gets wind of the fact that we're on his heels, he'll cover up his tracks and more people may die."

"What was the name of the man who was shot?" Gordon Engels inquired.

"His name was Zachary St. John."

"Oh," Jenkins said, raising his eyebrows, "the investment banker who was killed by his accomplice?"

"He wasn't killed by Alex Sontheim, but by Vitali's people," Connors replied, hardly suppressing his impatience. "Alex Sontheim is a threat to Vitali. That's why he's trying to put the blame on her for this murder."

"Do you have any evidence, Connors?"

Jenkins leaned back. The deputy US attorney threw him a quick glance.

"Nick," he said, "could you please explain this?"

Nick cleared his throat and sat up straight. He hadn't said a word yet, but he observed the reactions of Engels and Jenkins closely. Jenkins was hard to read, just like most FBI people. His face remained emotionless. Nick knew he needed to convince Jenkins how dangerous Vitali was. Briefly, he explained why he seriously doubted that Alex Sontheim had committed St. John's murder. He repeated in summary what Justin Savier had told him the night before, and he finally voiced his suspicion that Vitali had been shot by Colombian drug dealers in July of last year.

"How do you know all of this, Nick?" Engels asked in astonishment.

"I've been dealing with Vitali for many years now," Nick replied, "and prosecuted him myself at least a dozen times for various crimes. He managed to squirm free every time. I know him. I know his methods. I know his business. In July, I was sure that I would finally get my hands on Vitali. The same night that someone shot at him, his son was arrested during an illegal raid to clear out a building in the Bronx. As soon as I heard about it, I went to the precinct and—to my surprise—Mr. de Lancie was already there, even though everyone knows he prefers office work. He acted strangely for a US attorney, and I asked him which side of the law he was on. Cesare Vitali was then found hanged in his cell. The next day, a mysterious terrorist appeared and threatened to contaminate groceries with anthrax spores. On top of that, the man who allegedly shot Vitali turned himself in to the police and immediately made a confession. Both of these stories pushed the shots fired at Vitali from the headlines. It was a classic red herring, and it almost would have worked if I hadn't voiced my suspicions publicly. I was so sure of myself, but my excitement caused me to disregard how ruthless and dangerous this man can be when threatened."

Nick paused for a moment and then continued in a quiet voice.

"I personally had to learn through painful experience how close I had come to the truth."

"No charges were brought against Vitali," Engels interjected. "How can you be so sure that he was behind the bombing?"

"One of my closest employees was also on Vitali's payroll." Nick shrugged his shoulders. "Raymond Howard informed him about everything. He also died in the bombing."

"But—" Jenkins started to speak, but Frank Cohen interrupted. He couldn't take his boss's agonized expression.

"Howard personally told me who was behind the bombing. Just before he died, he told me that Vitali ordered the assassination."

"What exactly did he say?" Jenkins asked.

Frank took a deep breath, haunted by the memory. "He said that Vitali wanted to kill Nick."

Everyone sitting around the conference table was stunned.

"Why didn't you tell me before, Nick?" Connors asked.

"Because it wouldn't have brought my family back to life," the mayor replied. "When Frank told me about it, Ray was long dead. There were no witnesses. I didn't have the strength to endure such an investigation."

"Did Ms. Sontheim know about this?"

"No," Nick said, shaking his head, "I don't think so."

"Why did she come to you, of all people, with this information?"

Nick didn't answer right away. He remembered the morning at the beach in Montauk and the sight of the young woman with her blonde hair flowing in the wind.

"Nick?" Gordon Engels asked, and Nick noticed that everyone was staring at him.

"I met Ms. Sontheim through mutual friends," he said. "She apparently trusted me because she knew that I'm an avowed opponent of Vitali."

"When did you hear about the secret accounts?" Jenkins asked.

"On the day when Ms. Sontheim came to me at the monastery," Nick replied. "She recognized the man who shot at me, and that had apparently finally convinced her that Vitali is a criminal."

"Why didn't you tell the US Attorney's Office or the FBI earlier?"

"Mr. Jenkins," Nick said and leaned forward, "I've told you already. I've been observing Sergio Vitali for fifteen years. I know who he is, what he's capable of. During my time as the US attorney of this district, I witnessed bulletproof charges dropped many times because key witnesses suddenly lost their memory or disappeared. Vitali is the godfather of New York City—the last *capo di tutti capi*—and he's more powerful than any Mafia boss before him. I didn't want to put Ms. Sontheim's life at risk."

"And why did you change your mind now?"

Nick sighed. What was all this? Why was Jenkins acting like he was cross-examining a defendant?

"In my opinion, Ms. Sontheim is incorrectly under suspicion of murder," he said in a firm voice, "and this is a diversionary tactic, just like the anthrax terrorist was."

"Why do you believe that?" Jenkins was proving to be extraordinarily suspicious.

"Vitali and Levy owned a front organization called MPM, through which they operated a large-scale insider trading scheme with the help of Mr. St. John. The proceeds from these illegal transactions were funneled to secret accounts in the Caymans and the Bahamas. Ms. Sontheim provided us with the necessary information."

Jenkins interrupted him. "So she—"

"If you could let me finish please," Nick replied harshly. They briefly measured each other with cold looks. Jenkins frowned and signaled for him to continue. Nick recounted the instructions that Alex had received from the board of directors to inform them about every detail of her work. He mentioned the discovery that SeaStarFriends was the owner of MPM, and the busted takeover deal of Database by Whithers Computers.

"Ms. Sontheim found out that the owners of MPM were changed the very same night that St. John was murdered. Vitali and Levy decided to sacrifice their accomplice St. John in order to save their own skins."

"But this is mere speculation!"

"I'm in possession of a commercial registry certificate dated April 14, 2000. At that time, Venture Capital SeaStarFriends LP was the sole owner of MPM. Another commercial registry certificate from the British Virgin Islands confirms that Mr. Vincent Levy and Mr. Sergio Vitali were the owners of this offshore company. According to electronic records, Mr. Zachary St. John and Ms. Alexandra Sontheim have been the registered owners for four days now."

He paused and took a gulp of water.

"I'm pretty sure that St. John was shot because he refused to be sacrificed. Maybe he threatened to blow everything up. Just the fact that he prepared a complete written testimony proves that he was unsure about his boss's loyalty. By blaming the murder on Ms. Sontheim, Vitali killed two birds with one stone. As a murder suspect, she's hardly a credible witness, and while the press jumped on this murder, no one noticed how quickly the investigation of MPM's bankruptcy fizzled out thanks to Vitali's connections at the SEC. That's pretty clever, isn't it?"

"If there's a case here," Jenkins noted coolly, "it constitutes a criminal offense, as a conscious and willful deceit of the FBI and the US Attorney's Office."

"Yes. That's exactly what it is, in my opinion," Nick affirmed.

"But the police commissioner himself involved the FBI in the investigation."

"Harding is also on Vitali's payroll," Connors reminded him. "It's also in his interest that these bribes don't become public."

"Nick, do you know where Ms. Sontheim is at the moment?" Engels interjected.

"Unfortunately, I don't." Nick shook his head. "I only know that Vitali has a lot of people searching for her. She won't live much longer if he manages to get his hands on her."

Everyone in the room fell silent. They needed some time to process the facts.

"If we keep ignoring the corruption in this city, then Vitali will continue his operations," Nick said emphatically. "We need to blow this scandal up. The public's reaction is completely secondary."

"I'd still like to check your witness's credibility before I take further action," Jenkins insisted.

"I don't know where she is," Nick replied in a harsh tone. "I don't even know whether she'll appear again. The only thing I know is that Vitali spends every minute we waste doing nothing covering his tracks further."

"The evidence that we have against him is sufficient," Connors said. "Once we confront these people with our suspicion of corruption, they'll certainly provide the evidence we need to nail Vitali."

All eyes were resting expectantly on the deputy director of the FBI, who finally stood up.

"I need to call Mr. Horner," he said and walked over to Nick's desk. Nick and Connors looked at each other. If the FBI didn't cooperate or if it even hindered their work, they had little chance of success, even if the Department of Justice, as represented by Attorney General Engels, was on their side. Vitali would find out they were after him and he'd slip away again. Their advantage was that he didn't know yet that a storm was brewing over him. They needed to act quickly. They had already wasted too much time.

"Mr. Kostidis," Jenkins said after being on the telephone for a while, "Mr. Horner wants to talk to you."

Nick took the phone. He repeated a short version of the story to the director of the FBI, who then asked him to pass the phone back to Jenkins. Nick felt his heart beating. He remembered this feeling from the courtroom, when he had presented his closing arguments and sat waiting for the jury's decision. Just as he had with the many criminal court proceedings he'd worked on as an attorney, he had done everything he could. The final decision was out of his hands. Nick walked over to his chair, sat down, and closed his eyes. It was dead silent in the room except for Jenkins's muted voice. As the deputy director of the FBI finished his call and put the receiver on the handle, Nick looked over at him. He instantly knew what decision he had made. The relief made him tremble inside. Horner had given his okay. The FBI would support them in their operation to take down Sergio Vitali. His years of experience had taught Nick how to read people's decisions in their faces.

"Mr. Horner will speak to the president," Jenkins announced, "but he ordered us to take every necessary step to investigate this matter. He emphasized that we need to proceed as discreetly as possible, without any major press exposure."

Connors could hardly suppress his triumphant grin.

"Mr. Connors," Jenkins continued, "pay a visit to Mr. de Lancie today and tell him that he is suspended from his duties until further notice."

Connors nodded.

"What's the scope of the cooperation?" Engels inquired.

"Mr. Connors will lead the investigation," Jenkins said. "Gordon, give him your best people. Increase your efforts to find Ms. Sontheim."

"What about the arrest warrant?" Nick asked. He had hoped that they would repeal the warrant immediately.

"I'm not convinced of her innocence yet," Jenkins replied curtly. "The arrest warrant won't be repealed until we know for certain that she wasn't involved in this man's murder. If she should contact you, Mr. Kostidis, tell her that her presence is extremely important, and that we'll take care of her protection."

"She won't return as long as she's wanted for murder," Nick replied.

"She'd better come back," Jenkins said, looking at Nick coolly, "because I want to talk to her."

Nick shrugged his shoulders. Then he threw a quick glance at his watch and stood up.

"If you'll excuse me now," he said, "I still have a few official events to attend."

While Nick drove to Rockefeller Center, trying to hide his anxiety, Lloyd Connors headed to Greenwich, Connecticut, with the two US marshals, Spooner and Khazaeli. The three men walked through the accumulating snow toward the large, white house. The house, with its wraparound porch, was surrounded by magnificent old trees and had an extensive lawn. Connors briefly wondered why no one else had become suspicious long ago. There was no way that de Lancie could afford a house like this on his salary. John de Lancie opened the front door himself, and he turned pale when he saw Connors accompanied by two men.

"Hello, John," Connors said in a calm voice, "these are Deputies Spooner and Khazaeli from the US Marshals Service. I apologize for disturbing you on a Sunday afternoon, but we'd like to ask you a few questions."

"What is this about?" de Lancie asked curtly. "You're coming here at a rather inopportune time. Can't we discuss this tomorrow morning at my office?"

"I'm afraid not," Deputy Spooner said, "unless you want everyone to hear about it."

"Hear about what?"

Spooner and Connors exchanged a glance.

"May we come in, John?" Connors asked politely.

"First, I'd like to know what this is all about."

"As you wish." Spooner shrugged his shoulders. "We have a reasonable suspicion that you've accepted bribes on multiple occasions."

All of the color disappeared from the US attorney's face. De Lancie stood there as if paralyzed, silently staring at the three men.

"May we come in?" Connors repeated.

"Yes…yes, of course," de Lancie whispered and took a step back. "Let's go to my study."

John de Lancie only tried to deny the allegations for a few minutes. When Connors presented him with a copy of the bank statement from

Levy & Villiers, he collapsed. With tears in his eyes, he admitted that he'd accepted bribes from Sergio Vitali. As quid pro quo, he had agreed to do Vitali a favor every now and then.

Lloyd Connors felt a dizzying sensation of triumph. Until this moment he'd feared that the mere existence of the bank statements wouldn't be enough to prove that Vitali was handing out bribes, but de Lancie's confession established the connection. Now everything was clear. The testimony of just a single person in court would cause a lot of trouble for Vitali, and there were plenty of others on the list who had been bought too. It was simply incredible. This seemed to be the first time that the US Attorney's Office really had an airtight case against Sergio Vitali. Connors thought about the mountains of evidence against this man and all of the witnesses who'd suddenly disappeared or lost their memory. He also remembered, with a quiet sense of guilt, that many people at the US Attorney's Office—himself included—had sneered at Nick Kostidis's futile efforts to prove Vitali's crimes. But Nick had been right all along.

De Lancie confessed to everything in a whimpering voice. It almost seemed as if he were relieved to have freed himself from this burden that had weighed on him for so many months.

"What's going to happen now?" he asked, trembling.

"That depends on you, John," Connors said, shaking his head. "It's your choice. If you resign from office and serve as a witness, then we could possibly refrain from charging you with corruption. Otherwise—"

"No, no," de Lancie interrupted him quickly. "I'll do it. I've made a mistake, a huge mistake. I didn't know what I was getting myself into, but I don't want my family to suffer from this."

"Your name will be in the headlines," Connors said. "You'll have to live with it. However, you won't be charged and sentenced. If you cooperate with us, then we might be able to prevent you from being disbarred."

De Lancie's face was as white as a sheet. Was he thinking that his ambitious plans for the future had been destroyed in a single blow?

Connors knew that the job as US attorney for the Southern District was just a stepping-stone for big politics, but this dream seemed to be over now.

Connors opened his briefcase.

"Here's a statement I've prepared for you. Read through it and sign if you agree with its content."

De Lancie swallowed as he read the document.

"If I sign this, then I'm done," he whispered. His hands were shaking.

"I can arrest you, John," Connors said, "if you prefer. You have the right to remain silent. With a clever lawyer you might be able to squirm your way free from this mess, but it'll take a long time and all the dirt will stick to you longer. You know what's going to happen. Apart from the criminal proceedings, the IRS will knock on your door. And I'm pretty sure that it won't be easy to explain to the IRS where you got the money to pay for this mansion and your children's expensive schools."

De Lancie broke into tears and covered his face with his hands. Without sympathy, the three men watched the US attorney sob like a little child.

"Will you sign it?"

"Yes…yes…" He slowly stood up and walked to his desk with wobbling steps. Without looking up, he signed the paper, admitting his guilt.

Connors waited for the ink to dry.

"You'll call in sick tomorrow. Please don't leave your house until further notice."

"I'm under house arrest?"

"Yes," Connors said as he stood up. "If Vitali contacts you, I advise you not to tell him anything about our conversation. We're not after you, John, but a much bigger fish. We've tapped your telephone so that you won't be tempted to stab us in the back."

"I won't do that," de Lancie said, as he sat back down.

"I hope not. I don't need to tell you what the consequences would be."

De Lancie silently stared after the three men as tears ran down his cheeks. When his wife entered the study with a frightened expression, he made no effort to hide them.

John de Lancie was just the first on a long list of men who were paid unexpected visits on this Sunday afternoon. Tracy Taylor and Royce Shepard traveled all over the state of New York accompanied by US marshals, just like their boss. As Nick Kostidis had anticipated, all of the accused turned out to be cooperative. Sergio Vitali's empire had started to shake, but he didn't notice the tremors that were headed for him.

PART FOUR

Monday, December 6, 2000—Zurich, Switzerland

Alex woke up after ten hours of sleep feeling better rested than she had in days. She called Justin, and he confirmed that he had managed to block the secret files at Levy & Villiers. No one could delete them now, unless they were willing to destroy the entire computer system. Alex hung up and treated herself to some champagne with her room service breakfast. Her successful escape and the excitement of the last few days had put her into a state of manic euphoria, and she felt so safe that she would have loved to call Sergio to mock him. Instead, she called Nick Kostidis at home. It was the middle of the night in New York, but it was only a few seconds before he picked up.

"Yes, hello?" Alex heard a sleepy voice. She felt her heart start pounding, and she hesitated.

"Hello? Who is this?"

"Nick, it's me. Alex," she said. "I'm sorry if I woke you up."

"Alex!" Nick sounded wide awake at once. "Don't worry about it! How are you?"

"Good, thank you. Did Justin give you the e-mails?"

"Yes, he did."

Nick told her about his meeting with Engels and Jenkins and that all of the men who were questioned about the corruption allegations had confessed to their crimes.

"The murder charges against you have been dropped unofficially," he said, "and things are moving. The US Attorney's Office is working at full speed."

"That's a start."

"Tate Jenkins urgently asks you to come back to New York. The FBI will protect you."

"That's hardly reassuring," countered Alex. "Just think about David Zuckerman."

She lay on the bed and stared at her hotel room ceiling. How would it feel to be frightened and in hiding for an entire lifetime? The thought of a life on the run sobered her. This wasn't an exhilarating game or an exciting movie with a happy ending—her situation was deadly serious. Her euphoria suddenly vanished, and the champagne tasted flat.

"Justin Savier is very worried about you," Nick said, although he really wanted to tell her that he was the one most worried.

"Tell him that I'm doing well," Alex replied. "Did Mark Ashton or Oliver Skerritt get in touch with you or Justin?"

"No," Nick replied, "unfortunately not."

Alex felt a chill. Mark and Oliver were probably in serious trouble, while she was safe in Switzerland sipping champagne. And although the idea to go into hiding somewhere and never return to New York was appealing, she also knew that she couldn't turn her back on her friends.

"Alex," Nick said emphatically, "you're in great danger. Vitali will try everything to get a hold of you."

"Are you worried about me?"

"Yes, I am," Nick replied in a hoarse voice. "Very worried. The fact that you've stolen money from Vitali will make him furious. I know what he's capable of, and I don't want to see anything happen to you."

These words affected Alex. She felt that they came from the heart. The mayor of New York, this powerful man, was worried about her! And rightfully so.

"I didn't steal the money," she said. "I'll give it back to him if he leaves me alone. I don't want to be on the run for the rest of my life. But he can't forgive me for leaving him and..."

"And what?"

"...and coming to you, of all people."

There was complete silence again for a moment. His voice felt so close, it was as if he were standing right next to her, without the entire Atlantic Ocean between them.

"You've saved my life once," Nick said softly. "At a time when I was struggling, you bolstered my spirit and helped me move on with my life. I'll never forget that. Whenever you need help, you can count on me."

Suddenly, she felt a lump in her throat and tears pushed into her eyes. "I...I've got to go now. I'll get in touch with you again, okay?"

Henry Monaghan was furious that Alex Sontheim had escaped. What's worse, someone had hacked into LMI's central computer without his noticing. It undermined his authority as the head of security, and it was his own fault. Of course, no one would ever tell him that to his face. He desperately needed to recover his tarnished self-confidence.

He sat with Phil Fox—his closest staff member—in the basement security control center of the LMI Building trying to figure out who had snooped around in their corporate network. Without a doubt this someone was clever, because nothing had been destroyed. They were dealing with a professional who was already familiar with the system, and that significantly limited the circle of potential suspects. The windowless room, filled with state-of-the-art security technology, was cloudy with Monaghan's incessant cigar smoke. There were fifteen cigar stubs in the ashtray already when he lit himself another one.

"And?" Fox asked after Monaghan hung up the phone.

He had called the company that had installed the system five years ago, but no one was familiar with the software.

"They think that only someone who programmed the system could hack into it. He said that software manufacturers leave a back door open so that they can enter the system unnoticed at any time."

"Sure," Fox said, nodding, "I know that. Where should we start searching?"

"Which operating system are we using?"

"BankManager 5.3 by IBM."

"Great," Monaghan said with a frown, chewing on his cigar pensively, "IBM's a pretty big organization."

"It is," replied Fox, "but there couldn't be too many people who worked on BM 5.3. There are just a handful of programmers at that level."

Monaghan looked at the IT specialist and then picked up the telephone. After four phone calls, he was speaking with the head of software development at IBM. Monaghan quickly described his problem. However, he carefully kept the reason for his call to himself.

"BankManager 5.3 was developed in-house," IBM's head of technology explained, "but the security testing of the program was performed by external specialists."

"And which specialists did the testing?"

"Usually a team from MIT. However, that was six years ago. It's likely none of the same people still work there."

"Right, this seems pretty hopeless to me," Monaghan replied.

"Massachusetts Institute of Technology," he said to Fox in a sinister tone. "I bet the little asshole we're looking for is there somewhere. I'm flying to Boston tomorrow. I'll find out who's behind this."

Monday, December 6, 2000—Offices of Levy & Villiers, Georgetown, Grand Cayman

The young man responsible for Levy & Villiers's computer system turned to Vincent Levy and Lance Godfrey, director of the branch in Georgetown on Grand Cayman.

"I'm sorry, I can't access those files at the moment."

"What do you mean?" Levy asked indignantly. He hadn't slept well for a number of nights. During the day he was forced to deal with the SEC and the police. In the evenings, his wife was giving him hell. She found it intolerable that LMI had become the subject of negative headlines, and this made his life even more difficult. Levy couldn't bear her whiny reproaches anymore. To make things worse, he had to fly to the Caymans to have all documents relating to the secret accounts deleted—as if he didn't already have enough work on his plate.

"Something's not right here," the young man said. "It refuses access to certain files and tells me that a fatal exception error occurred. I'll risk crashing the entire system if I try to fix this."

He pressed a few buttons, moved the mouse back and forth, and then pointed to the screen with a distressed expression.

"Look, sir. I can open and print these files without a problem, but whenever I try to delete them it says this every time:

"Invalid operation. The file is being closed."

The way this man talked about the computer as if it were a human being made Levy nervous. He was also annoyed about how relaxed Godfrey seemed.

"I don't understand your agitation, Vince," he said, casually crossing his feet on the desk's glass tabletop. "There's no trace leading here. The data is as secure as Fort Knox."

Levy didn't respond. He thought it was best to keep Godfrey in the dark. With his athletic, six-foot-four frame, deep tan, and light-colored suit, this man looked more like a nightclub owner than the director of a prestigious private bank. And Levy didn't appreciate it. Godfrey was clearly a capable man, but a little more professionalism seemed appropriate for a man in his position. But this wasn't the right time to voice his disapproval.

"You better get this thing working again," Levy snarled at the young man. "That's what you're getting paid for, after all."

Lance Godfrey just grinned and shrugged his shoulders.

"I expect the error to be fixed in an hour," Levy said as he turned around and marched out of the room. The young man returned to the computer again with a sigh.

It was easy enough for Henry Monaghan to get the names of the people who'd worked on testing the security of IBM's BankManager 5.3 six years ago. There were three men: one of them was now in Silicon Valley, California; the second lived somewhere in Southeast Asia; the third man was still there. His name was Justin Savier, and he'd worked as a programmer at MIT's world-renowned Media Lab after graduating with honors with a degree in computer science. Monaghan's instinct told him that he had found the right guy.

Savier didn't show up to work on Tuesday morning. Monaghan had been sitting in his small glass office for almost two days and nights. Unfortunately, Savier's boss didn't allow Monaghan to look around his office, so he left the MIT premises. He found Savier's address in the phone book and drove to his apartment with his two assistants. They rang the doorbell three times, but Savier didn't come to the door. Monaghan got them into the apartment without a problem.

"What the hell is this?" LMI's head of security shook his head in disgust as he saw the disorder surrounding them. The three rooms stuffed floor to ceiling with computers, parts, books, and computer magazines. Hidden beneath were fitness machines, a bicycle, a vacuum cleaner, and pieces of furniture that didn't belong together. Piles of clothes, shoes, jackets, and even a few motorcycle helmets were strewn everywhere. These computer geeks were all the same! As brilliant as they might be at their jobs, their personal lives were chaotic and messy.

Monaghan sat down at the desk, opened all of the drawers, and rummaged around in the trash cans. He didn't even try to start up one of the computers. This Savier character had certainly installed countless access restrictions on them. Then he checked the bathroom and the bedroom. It was the same everywhere: overflowing ashtrays on every surface, empty beer and soda cans, CDs, and a cardboard box with the remnants of a Quattro Staggioni pizza.

"Hey, Henry," one of his men said. "Take a look at this."

He pointed to a yellowed newspaper clipping hanging between other notes on a pinboard in the kitchen.

"Teenage Computer Whiz Fools Generals", read the almost twenty-year-old headline. The newspaper article was about Justin Savier, who had hacked the central computer of the US Space & Missile Defense Command at the age of sixteen, and almost triggered World War III as a result. The military commanders had made fools of themselves because they hadn't realized a teenager was pranking them. They had seriously believed that the Soviets were preparing for a nuclear strike.

"I heard about that," Monaghan nodded. "This fits the picture exactly."

Hacking into other people's computer systems was apparently one of Justin Savier's specialties. Monaghan's gaze wandered over the books on a wobbly shelf. In contrast to what Savier usually read, this wasn't computer literature but primarily mindless science-fiction novels. Among other things, there were photo albums and yearbooks. Monaghan pulled out one after the other, browsed through them, and then carelessly dropped them on the floor.

"Well, well, look at this," he said to himself after a while. "If that isn't the fat bastard who's sitting in my basement."

Three young men grinned into the camera, and they also appeared on the following pages. Harvard students. What an arrogant bunch. He was dead sure that the one with the piglet face was Mark Ashton. Monaghan grinned with satisfaction.

"Hey, boss." The other man appeared in the door. "The woman was here, no doubt about it. I found empty packages from dark-brown hair dye and disposable contact lenses in the bathroom wastebasket."

Monaghan nodded grimly. Alex Sontheim had been here. They were hot on her heels! He walked back into the living room to have a closer look at the telephone and the answering machine. The answering machine's tape didn't hold any important messages, but then Monaghan had the idea of pressing the telephone's redial button. He eagerly waited to hear who would answer the phone at the other end of the line.

"*Bankhaus Gérard Frères, guten morgen*," a friendly female voice answered in German.

A triumphant smile spread across Henry Monaghan's reddened face. He excused himself politely and then hung up. Alex Sontheim was in Europe. In Switzerland. She didn't have the slightest clue that he was right behind her. He pulled out his cell phone and called Sergio Vitali. A small army would be heading to Zurich in no less than an hour.

The intercom on the glass desk in Lance Godfrey's spacious office buzzed. The director of Levy & Villiers frowned. He'd gone to bed very late last night because he had treated himself to a few drinks after spending a horrible day with Vincent Levy. Levy had taken the last flight to New York before they could fix the computer system. Godfrey didn't understand what the fuss was all about. Sometimes these machines refused to work, which wasn't a big deal. LMI's president had picked out stacks of files from the bank's archives and personally fed them to the shredder. He was in a murderously bad mood when Godfrey drove him to the airport that evening.

"What is it, Sheila?" Godfrey asked.

"There are five gentlemen here who would like to talk to you, sir."

"Do they have an appointment?" Godfrey threw a glance at the calendar on his desk.

"No. But…"

"I'm busy at the moment. Schedule an appointment."

He leaned back again as the door opened and the five men entered. Godfrey immediately realized that they weren't bank clients.

"I'm sorry, Mr. Godfrey," the secretary said, waving her hands in desperation.

"Mr. Lance Godfrey?" A black-haired man with a thin moustache revealed his badge. "I'm Agent Samuel Ramirez from the FBI. This is Agent Quinn, Mr. Dennis Rosenthal from the SEC's investigation unit, Mr. Green from the US embassy, and another member of our team, Mr. Savier."

"Good day, everyone," Lance Godfrey said smoothly, standing up. "How can I help you?"

"We have a warrant to search your premises," Agent Ramirez said and handed an official-looking document to him.

Godfrey was trembling inside, but he remained calm and polite.

"And what's the reason for your search?"

"We have reasonable suspicion that you have money originating from illegal insider trades in various secret accounts," Dennis Rosenthal announced.

"We suspect that it is part of a large-scale corruption scandal," Agent Ramirez continued. "If you give us access to your server, we'll be gone in less than an hour."

"Our server is out of order," Godfrey muttered.

"Yes, we know that." Ramirez nodded. "That's why we brought a specialist with us."

Godfrey stared at the men for a moment without saying a word.

"And if you're smart enough not to report this incident to New York," Agent Quinn added with a friendly smile, "then the fact that you're involved in a criminal conspiracy won't have any punitive consequences for you."

Now even Lance Godfrey turned pale despite his suntanned skin.

"I'm not…involved in any conspiracy," he stuttered.

"Really? That should be easy enough for us to prove," Agent Ramirez said. "I suggest that you leave town for a few days and forget about our short visit. You won't hear from us again in that case. Otherwise…"

There was a telling pause before the agent continued.

"Otherwise, we'll have to arrest you."

Lance Godfrey swallowed. Now it dawned on him why Levy had been acting so strangely and why this walrus-mustached Monaghan had appeared with a computer expert last week. He had never trusted St. John, and he'd suspected that the regular cash deposits he'd been receiving for years weren't quite kosher. But it must be a really big deal if the FBI, the SEC, and someone from the embassy were here with a search warrant.

"I think that I urgently need to pay a visit to my parents in Idaho," Lance Godfrey said. "My mother's not doing so well."

"Of course. You're free to depart right away," Agent Ramirez responded with a friendly smile. "If you would be so kind as to grant us access to your central computer and answer a few questions before you leave."

Lance Godfrey was the picture of helpfulness. He had no desire whatsoever to go to the slammer for something that he didn't do. Maybe he should look for another job. It was high time he disappeared for a while.

When Paul McIntyre—the commissioner of the New York City Department of Buildings—returned to his office after lunch, he found a note on his desk telling him to call the mayor. He picked up the telephone and was only briefly surprised when he was immediately put through to Kostidis. It usually took a few tries to reach the ever-busy mayor.

"Hello, Paul," Kostidis said. "I hear that you just came back from vacation. Did you get some good rest?"

"Hi, Nick," McIntyre replied. "Yes I did, thank you. Unfortunately, it was much too short as usual."

"Where did you go this time?"

"Oh, we got a little sun," McIntyre said with a laugh. "I get depressed with the weather here. We went to the Caymans. Swimming, snorkeling, sunbathing."

The Caymans! That wasn't a coincidence.

"Listen, Paul, I don't have much time, but I really need to talk to you. Could you come by my office?

"Yes, of course," McIntyre said, surprised. "Right away?"

"Yes, if you could manage it."

"Of course. I'll be there in fifteen minutes."

McIntyre left the Department of Buildings. He was in an excellent mood. After returning from the Caribbean two days ago, he and his wife had looked at the house that Vitali procured for them, and Jenny was delighted. It was out on the dunes with a view of Fire Island—it was simply fantastic! Only four more years, and then he could fulfill his dream and finally retire. Maybe even earlier, if he could find a doctor who would prescribe early retirement for his high blood pressure. Jenny could lunch at the country club, and he could play golf or go sailing all day long. The children and grandchildren could visit them on the weekends, stroll on the beach, swim in the pool, play tennis, or pursue other leisure activities for which the city lacked the space. Yes, it was an alluring prospect indeed to live in their own oceanfront house, after sixty years of renting apartments in this damned loud and dirty city. McIntyre whistled as he ran up the steps to city hall.

"Hello, Allie," he said to Kostidis's secretary. "You're getting prettier every day!"

"Thanks, Paul." Allie said with a teasing frown. "You're one charming liar. The mayor's waiting for you. Go right in."

McIntyre grinned and opened the door to Nick's office.

"Hello, Nick!" he called out in a good mood, but then his gaze landed on the two men sitting at the large table and his smile vanished. He suddenly had a feeling that something was wrong.

"Paul," Nick Kostidis said as he approached him and extended his hand, "thank you for coming so quickly. You know Lloyd Connors and Royce Shepard from the US Attorney's Office."

"Yes, we know each other," McIntyre said carefully. "What's going on?"

"Please take a seat," Connors requested, and McIntyre obeyed. His uneasy feeling intensified when he spotted the audio recorder on the table and Shepard asked whether he had any objection to him recording the conversation.

"Let me cut to the chase," Connors began. He looked pretty worn out. "We have evidence that you hold an account at a bank called Levy & Villiers in the Caymans."

McIntyre turned as white as a sheet and started trembling.

"We suspect that you received the money in this account from Mr. Sergio Vitali and that you promised certain favors to him in return."

McIntyre's eyes locked with Nick's inquiring gaze, and a dark redness crawled from his throat up his face.

"Do you have anything to say about these allegations?"

"That…that must be some kind of misunderstanding…I…" McIntyre stammered and wet his lips with his tongue. Thick beads of sweat appeared on his brow, although it wasn't particularly warm in the large room. This damned high blood pressure would kill him one of these days.

"Paul," Nick said, "it's not you the US Attorney's Office is after, it's Vitali."

"We have account statements proving that you've regularly withdrawn and spent the money that was paid to you," Connors continued. "So?"

McIntyre stared at the shiny tabletop, and he felt as if a dark abyss had opened up in front of him. It was the moment that he had feared all these years. The dream of a house on Long Island was over, and so was the prospect of a carefree life. Everything was over! He would be lucky to get any pension at all. Corruption was a serious crime that went severely punished, not to mention the fact that his reputation would be ruined forever.

"It...it's true," he mumbled after a while, and his confidence crumbled to dust. Nick sighed. In a small corner of his heart, he had hoped that it wasn't true. He liked Paul McIntyre, trusted him, and worked well with him.

"When did it begin?" Connors asked.

"A few years ago." McIntyre lowered his head. He couldn't take Kostidis's disappointed and hurt look anymore. "It was the invitation to bid for the construction of the World Financial Center. David Zuckerman approached me at the time. That wasn't unusual, but when I personally met Vitali for the first time he offered me money."

"And you accepted?" Connors asked.

"I hesitated at first." McIntyre looked up, and tears actually shone in his eyes. "I was proud that I was incorruptible. But I had only been in office for a few months and was in debt up to my ears. Unfortunately, my wife likes to shop, and the banks were hassling me for repayment of a loan, and I couldn't afford the payments on my salary. I knew how bad it would look if people found out I was technically bankrupt, and Vitali's offer seemed simple and harmless enough at the time."

Nick wiped his hand across his face. He didn't want to hear another word, but McIntyre was talking his head off, as if he were happy to be relieved of the pressure of his guilty conscience. Connors and Shepard listened carefully, asking questions now and then as McIntyre indulged in verbose justifications for his actions.

"Everyone lines their own pockets," the commissioner of the Department of Buildings finally said. "That's the norm. Small gifts, large gifts, a vacation package, a new car, and…money. I wouldn't have stayed in office for very long if I hadn't played along."

"What do you mean by that?" Connors observed McIntyre sternly.

"Just like I said." The broad-shouldered man with his carefully styled snow-white hair shrugged his shoulders. "Vitali and his people left no doubt that they would finish me off if I refused their offer."

His gaze fell on the mayor.

"You don't understand, Nick." McIntyre smiled with a hint of bitterness. "I've always admired you for your idealism, but if you think that you can purge New York City of corruption, you're crazy. Every civil servant is part of it—every single one of them."

Nick looked at him for quite some time. Then he slowly nodded and lowered his head. He knew that McIntyre was right, but it hurt him nonetheless. His statement was proof that he had accomplished absolutely nothing in regard to corruption over the years. It was a declaration of his political bankruptcy.

"What's going to become of me now?" McIntyre asked. Connors repeated the words he had spoken to many men over the past few days. He also handed him a prepared admission of guilt, and just like all the men before him, Paul McIntyre also signed.

"You're going to act completely normally toward Vitali and your staff," Connors said. "Of course, you're also attending Vitali's gala just as if nothing had happened. We want to avoid raising his suspicions too soon. Should you choose to warn him, then your prospects will look bad. Corruption in office, acceptance of bribes by a public official, falsification of building and planning applications, price-fixing—all over an extended period of time—this means that you're going to breathe filtered air for the rest of your life on top of the IRS coming after you for tax evasion and tax fraud."

"I'll do exactly as you say," McIntyre quickly reassured him. "I promise you that."

"That's certainly the smartest thing you can do."

McIntyre threw a glance at Nick, who was staring out the window with a blank expression.

"Nick," McIntyre said quietly to his boss, "I'm truly sorry."

Then, with hanging shoulders and clumsy steps, he walked out the door. The three men sat at the table in silence until someone else knocked on the door and Frank entered the room.

"What's up?" Nick asked tiredly.

"There's a woman who'd like to talk to you," Frank said. "She's been waiting for over an hour."

"Did she tell you her name or what she wants?"

"No."

Connors and Shepard collected their documents.

"Tell her I only have ten minutes," Nick said, thinking a minute and walking to his desk. Frank returned, accompanied by a small, pear-shaped woman of about fifty. She wore a simple black dress, a pearl necklace, and a black headscarf. Her gray hair was cut fashionably short. Sorrow and tension were visible in her face, but fierce vengeance sparkled in her big brown eyes. She gripped the handle of her large crocodile-skin bag with both hands. She looked at the two US attorneys with uncertainty.

"Good afternoon." Nick's smile was somewhat forced as he extended his hand. Time and again someone managed to get through to his office, and then he had to listen to problems ranging from a lost job or marital troubles to neighbors' disputes.

"How can I help you?" he asked. The woman glanced again at Connors and Shepard.

"These gentlemen are from the US Attorney's Office," Nick explained politely, "but they were just about to leave."

"No, no," the woman replied, "they should stay. What I have to say will also interest them."

The three men looked at the woman in surprise. She opened her bag, pulled out ten videotapes, and placed them on Nick's desk. Lloyd Connors curiously moved close.

"What's that?" he asked. The woman looked into his eyes and then straightened her shoulders with determination.

"My name is Constanzia Vitali. And I'd like to testify against my husband."

Monaghan and his men were patiently awaiting Justin Savier's return in his apartment. He stayed out all night. The telephone rang repeatedly, but when the answering machine switched on the person on the other end hung up.

Someone unlocked the front door at two thirty the following afternoon. Justin Savier kicked the door shut with his heel and dropped his jacket on the floor. All he longed for right now was his bed. The plane from Georgetown had landed two hours ago in Newark, and then he'd been flown to Boston in a helicopter. Alex was right, and thankfully the US attorneys also believed their story. The evidence he had uncovered on the Levy & Villiers computers was truly powerful.

Justin yawned and pulled his sweater over his head, and then he suddenly felt something hard press into his back. He froze.

"Hello, Mr. Savier," someone said behind him.

"He…hello," Justin stuttered. "W…who are you, and what are you doing in my apartment?"

"We've been waiting for you," Henry Monaghan replied, and Justin turned around quickly. He stared at the heavyset man with the walrus moustache.

"Who are you?" he repeated his question.

"That's irrelevant." Monaghan raised himself with surprising agility for such a fat man.

"How dare you break into my apartment?" Without a doubt, these were the people Alex was fleeing from.

"Funny you should put it that way," Monaghan said with the last remnants of friendliness remaining in him after waiting for nineteen hours. "We suspect that you illegally broke into the central computer of a New York investment firm."

Justin swallowed nervously.

"What makes you think that?"

"You worked on the security testing for BankManager 5.3," Monaghan said casually, "and when your old buddy Mark Ashton asked you for help with a small computer problem, you complied."

"I don't know any Mark."

"Really? That's strange, because you went to Harvard together. I've seen the pictures of you two in your photo albums."

Monaghan tried hard to stay calm and friendly. He would have loved to grab this guy who'd made a fool out of him and beat him to a pulp.

"Listen, Savier, I don't have time for silly question-and-answer games. I want to know what—"

The telephone rang, and Monaghan fell silent. He detected panic flaring up in Savier's eyes.

"Answer it!" he ordered, and since Justin showed no intention of doing so, he grabbed the revolver from his colleague Joey's hand and pressed it to Savier's temple. Justin turned an even paler shade of white. He picked up the receiver with shaking fingers. Monaghan pressed the speakerphone button with his left hand, and a hot wave of triumph flowed though him as he heard Alex Sontheim's voice.

"Justin, thank God! Where have you been for so long? I've tried to reach you countless times!"

Monaghan grinned. Vitali would be delighted by his next call. His people were certainly already closing in on Sontheim in Zurich.

"I've taken care of everything in Zurich," Alex said. "I'll go to—"

"Alex!" Justin interrupted her, but Monaghan pressed the barrel of the revolver more firmly to his temple and looked at him threateningly.

"Yes?"

"I..."

"Did you hear anything from Mark or Oliver?"

"No," Justin said, closing his eyes, "I had a lot of work to do."

"Ask her where she is!" Monaghan hissed.

"Justin?" Alex asked with sudden suspicion. "Is there someone with you? You sound so strange."

"No, no. I think I'm getting a cold. A *bad* virus is going around."

"Oh. I see. Get well soon..."

The dial tone sounded, and Monaghan understood what Justin had done.

"A virus is going around, huh?" he snorted angrily and dealt Justin a ferocious blow with the revolver's grip. "You think you're so clever, warning her, huh?"

"Listen!" Justin raised his hands imploringly. "I participated, but I don't know to this day what this is all about. I've got no clue."

"I don't believe a word you're saying." Monaghan signaled his guys, and they grabbed Justin from the left and right.

"We're going on a little excursion," Monaghan said, "and you should come with us without a fuss. Otherwise, I'll put a neat little hole in the back of your head and you won't see your dear Alex or your friend Mark ever again."

Nick, Connors, and Shepard stared at the woman in astonishment.

"Are you surprised to see me?" asked Constanzia Vitali. For a moment she almost seemed amused. Nick remembered Alex telling him that Mrs. Vitali had separated from her husband and that she wanted to talk to him. He had completely forgotten.

"We surely are," Connors said. "What's on those videotapes?"

Constanzia Vitali put her meticulously manicured hand on the tapes and smiled sadly. The three men waited impatiently.

"This," she said after a while, "is the testimony of Nelson van Mieren, my husband's long-time lawyer and confidant."

Connors opened his eyes wide.

"Testimony? What kind of testimony?"

"Everything that you need to put Sergio Vitali behind bars for the rest of his life."

The three men looked at each other, bewildered. Connors was the first to regain his faculties.

"Is…is that true?" he asked.

"Yes. See for yourself. I think it'll be quite revealing."

"Excuse us for being surprised," Nick said slowly. "Might I ask what motivated Mr. van Mieren, and especially you, to take this step?"

Constanzia Vitali looked at him for quite some time and then asked to sit down.

"Nelson was diagnosed terminal cancer," she said. "He realized his wrongs. He might have kept his mouth shut if Sergio hadn't lied to him."

"Lied?"

"It's all on the tapes." She gestured vaguely with her hand.

"And what about you?" Connors asked. "Why do you want to testify against your husband?"

"Because I hate him," the woman exclaimed with unexpected vehemence. "He has humiliated me and lied to me for thirty long years. He only married me because Carlo Gambino was my father. Sergio wanted my father's connections, and as you can see, he succeeded."

She sighed.

"I had to endure so much sorrow. I've tried to ignore all the corpses my husband left behind on his way to the top. But they reappear in my nightmares. And still, I tried to live with it. Until the day when Sergio ordered the murder of my son."

"I knew it," Connors murmured. "I've always doubted it was suicide."

"My husband ordered one of his men to kill Cesare and make it look like suicide." Her lips were quivering. She shook her head impatiently. "My boy was killed by his own father."

Tears sparkled in her big brown eyes, but she straightened her shoulders and managed to suppress the pain that still haunted her.

"I left my husband because I could no longer bear to be married to someone who had his own son killed like a stray dog."

"Do you have any evidence that your husband is behind this?" Connors's voice was breathless with excitement.

"Yes," Constanzia Vitali said, nodding, "it's all on the tapes."

She was silent for a moment and then looked at Nick.

"Mr. Kostidis," she said quietly, "I know that Sergio Vitali is responsible for the deaths of your wife and son. I'm terribly sorry about it. Believe me—I know how horrible it is to bury your own child."

Nick stared at her and then nodded slowly. He struggled to remain calm and composed.

"Sergio is a monster," she continued, "an ice-cold beast without human emotions. He kills anyone who's in his way or could threaten him. But I'm not afraid of him anymore. He's taken from me what I loved the most. I have nothing left to lose. Before I die, I want revenge and retribution for what he did."

Lloyd Connors could hardly believe it. Never before in the history of legal action against the Mafia had there been a key witness this far up in the families' hierarchy. Nelson van Mieren was an insider—no, he was *the* insider of the Vitali clan. He alone could break Sergio Vitali's back and help them close countless unsolved murder cases.

"Mrs. Vitali," Connors asked, trembling with excitement and triumph, "will Mr. van Mieren be willing to testify against your husband in a court trial?"

"I afraid he can't do that," Constanzia Vitali answered, dashing Connors's hopes.

"Why not? He already recorded his testimony on video!"

"Nelson put a bullet through his head on Sunday afternoon," Constanzia Vitali replied. "He's not dead yet, but he's in a coma. Even if he survives, he won't be able to testify."

Alex had understood Justin's warning. It could only mean that Sergio's people had already found and captured him. She quickly packed her bags and left the hotel through a back exit. Without a moment's hesitation, she headed to Germany in her rental car. It had unsettled her very much that neither Justin nor Nick had heard from Mark or Oliver. She had called both of them repeatedly, and she had to use every bit of willpower to suppress the trembling that overcame her when she thought about Sergio. What would Sergio do to these three completely innocent men? The thought that someone could be harmed just for helping her caused her terrible feelings of guilt. What would happen if she returned to New York and went to the FBI? Would they believe that she was innocent? Her disappearance was still in the headlines of every American newspaper. Her picture was everywhere.

Alex chewed her lip. She had stepped on a hornet's nest, and now the hornets were swarming. Ever since she'd handed the bank statements to Nick, the situation had gotten out of control. He had passed them on to the US Attorney's Office. Sergio wouldn't rest until he got his revenge for this humiliation. She couldn't possibly be on the run from him for the rest of her life.

In Basel, she crossed the border into Germany without a problem. Just after Freiburg, she exited to fill up and buy cigarettes and a few phone cards; then she walked to a telephone booth. It was about noon in New York right now. Alex dialed Mark's extension at LMI with shaking fingers. Mark didn't answer, but an entirely different voice did.

"Hello," she said in a French accent, "this is Hélène Lelièvre from Prudential Securities. Mr. Ashton?"

"No, Mr. Ashton is away from his desk at the moment."

"Oh, when will he be back?" Alex realized that she was talking to her employee Tom Burns. "He asked me to call him right back, that it was urgent."

"I have no idea when he'll be back. He hasn't been in the office for the last four days."

Alex hung up. She leaned against the wall of the phone booth, her heart pounding. Mark had been gone for four days. That could not be good! She decided to try calling Oliver again. But he didn't answer. As she dialed Nick's number, she was close to tears. She needed to return to New York! Nick answered the phone right away, sounding very concerned.

"Alex," he said in a muted voice, "where are you? Are you all right?"

"Yes, I'm okay. Have you heard from Mark Ashton?" she asked.

"No, but I found out where Oliver Skerritt is," Nick replied. "He's been sitting in a cell at the police headquarters for four days."

"Why?" Alex almost dropped the telephone receiver. "Where is he now?"

"I managed to get him out. I had him brought to a safe place," Nick answered. "He's doing reasonably well."

Alex felt miserable.

"I'll never forgive myself that all of the people who were only trying to help me are in danger," she sobbed. "They nabbed Justin yesterday. Nick, what should I do? I can't just stand by and watch what this man is doing to my friends!"

"Come back to the city," Nick pleaded. "I'll pick you up from the airport and make sure that nothing happens to you."

"I won't drag you into this as well." Alex wiped away her tears. "Out of the question. Vitali would kill us both!"

The phone card was almost used up, but she had made a decision. If she hurried, she could be in Frankfurt in three hours and—with some luck—in New York City about eight hours later. Then she would call Sergio to propose a deal.

"I'll call you again," she told Nick.

"Please be careful, Alex." Nick's voice was strained with worry. And then he added something that deeply touched Alex, despite her fear and worries.

"I'm thinking of you day and night, Alex," he said softly. "I wouldn't be able to handle it if something happened to you…"

The credit on the phone card was used up. Alex stared blankly through the fogged-up window. Her heart pounded wildly. *I'm thinking of you day and night.* Good Lord, she was doing the same!

Sergio Vitali sat at his desk at the VITAL Building. He stared at a brief newspaper obituary stating that renowned criminal defense lawyer Nelson van Mieren had succumbed to severe injuries last night. It hit Sergio like a punch to the stomach: of all people, his closest friend and long-time brother-in-arms had turned his back on him. Nelson had blown his brains out late Sunday afternoon. In reality, he'd never intended to work with him again. His promise to return to the office was just a scam. And now he was dead.

Sergio felt a wild, hot rage come over him. He took Nelson's decision as a personal insult, and it angered him so much that he couldn't grieve over the loss of his most important colleague and friend. Sergio crumpled the newspaper impulsively and threw it into the wastebasket. Nelson was sick anyway, and Sergio had already looked around for a suitable replacement—and found one. Although no one would ever have such comprehensive knowledge of his business as Nelson, Dennis Bruyner was an ace in his field. He was one of the best and smartest criminal defense lawyers in the United States—ambitious, sharp-witted, and completely unscrupulous. In his career so far, Bruyner had won dozens of cases that at first seemed completely hopeless, and he certainly didn't mind helping murderers and rapists retain their freedom. Sergio didn't need Nelson anymore, and if he preferred to die, so be it. No one lived forever. Furthermore, Nelson had been far too hesitant and scared recently.

Sergio turned toward the window with a grim expression and looked at the skyline. He had weathered worse storms, and he always emerged from them unscathed, and even stronger. Things would settle down again this time. Although MPM was lost, as well as his trust in Vincent Levy, there would be new opportunities for Sergio to secure his influence in the city. The men who were obligated to him wouldn't admit to anything—Sergio was certain about that. It didn't matter whether Kostidis had those bank statements, if there were actually copies of them. John de Lancie, for one, would never endanger his own future. He was ambitious and solely viewed his job as a US attorney of New York as a stepping-stone to Washington DC. Jerome Harding was eyeing the position of deputy secretary of state, and he had a good chance at it; Governor Rhodes also wanted to move up the ladder. No, these men would remain silent. And if they didn't, it would be no big deal because there was no evidence connecting him to the Grand Cayman accounts.

His face turned sullen. Alex was still the main problem, although she was severely discredited by the murder allegations. But she was smart and had nothing to lose. As long as she was on the run, she was dangerous. In Switzerland, she had just slipped through his net, and now Monaghan claimed that she was headed back to the city. Sergio had ordered observation of all three airports as well as Penn Station, Grand Central Station, and the Port Authority bus terminal. Thanks to Monaghan, if she appeared in a public place, his men would nab her.

"This is absolutely crazy." Lloyd Connors grinned in excitement as Nick entered his office. The control center had been moved to the US Attorney's Office after de Lancie had called in sick. "Van Mieren gave twelve hours of testimony. Come here, Nick. Look at this!" The TV and VCR were centered on a large table.

"Check this out!" he exclaimed.

Nelson van Mieren's face appeared on the screen. Nick could see that this man he had countered in the courtroom so many times over the years was very sick. His condition had rapidly deteriorated since their encounter at the Forty-First Precinct last summer. Over the next fifteen minutes, Nick and Connors listened attentively to van Mieren's precise statements about the contract award for the construction of the World Financial Center. He spoke the names of the people involved in the scandal, never before uncovered due to Zuckerman's death. He confessed how much money had been exchanged and described Vitali's pitiless extortion methods.

"Unbelievable." Nick shook his head.

"You were right all along," Connors replied, "and we thought you were just obsessed. I'm sincerely sorry."

Nick waved his hand. It was far too late. Zuckerman was dead, and the complex deals were water under the bridge now. Of course, they could confront Vitali with it, but any mediocre lawyer could get him off. Some of the crimes already exceeded the statute of limitations, and a video testimony might not be enough for a conviction in court.

"We're in a position now to ask Vitali entirely different questions."

His eyes sparkled with the excitement of a predator spotting its prey at a close range.

Nick sighed. "I knew all of this before. But no one wanted to hear it."

"You had just a hunch," Connors corrected him. "Now we have evidence."

"That's great. But…" Nick fell silent.

"But? But what?" Connors stared at him. "I thought you would be happy!"

"Lloyd," Nick said, sounding agonized, "I've spent years of my life hunting this guy. I know I was ridiculed behind my back, and that now the same people who laughed at me are having this served to them on a silver platter. Please don't take offense if I can't quite share your excitement. This man has destroyed my life. He killed my wife and son. He stole my time from me, time that I could have spent with Mary and Chris."

Connors looked at Nick in consternation.

"We're going to stop Vitali. We'll bring him to justice for everything he's done."

For a moment, Nick felt envious of the young man's optimism and enthusiasm, his firm conviction that he would accomplish his task. He had been like Lloyd Connors once, but it seemed like an eternity had passed since then. Nick sighed again. He felt so tired, so incredibly tired. He'd lost his sense of élan and power. Vitali had robbed him of his convictions, of his faith in law and order.

"I wish…" he started and stood up. "I really wish you all luck."

"It will be your success, Nick," Connors said, placing a hand on his shoulder. "You made this happen."

"No," Nick said, shaking his head, "this is none of my business anymore."

"But you must be satisfied if…"

"Satisfied?" Nick looked at the young man pensively. "No. I don't feel anything. There's just emptiness. What good is it to me if Vitali is sentenced? It won't bring anyone back to life."

Monday, December 6, 2000—The US Attorney's Office in Manhattan

"Before granting immunity to Alex Sontheim, I want to talk to her."

Tate Jenkins's voice squawked through the telephone's speaker. Nick and Lloyd Connors exchanged a brief glance.

"Mr. Jenkins," Nick said with growing impatience, "she called me yesterday morning. She won't return as long as she has reason to fear being arrested and charged with murder."

"No one will arrest her. I already promised you that. But I won't grant her immunity before I'm personally convinced of this woman's innocence." Jenkins sounded impatient. "You understand that, Mr. Kostidis, don't you? She's not just suspected of murder! Don't forget that she also embezzled money. Tell her to contact me. The sooner, the better."

Nick shrugged his shoulders.

"There's one more thing, Mr. Kostidis," said the deputy director of the FBI. "We were able to seize significant incriminating evidence on Grand Cayman. With the confessions of the bribed men, it could be enough."

"Enough for what? What do you mean?"

"I mean that Ms. Sontheim shouldn't gamble too much. If she waits any longer, then her testimony might lose its value. In that case, I'd have no reason whatsoever to repeal the arrest warrant because it falls within the NYPD's jurisdiction."

Connors gasped for air. Nick struggled to suppress his anger. This arrogant bastard didn't give a damn that it was Alex who got the ball rolling on this case. She had put her life at risk to bring Vitali to justice.

Without her, the FBI would never even have uncovered this corruption scandal!

"But Ms. Sontheim is the only person capable of bringing Vitali before a court. She has detailed knowledge of the processes, the sequence of events, and—"

"Vitali is not my problem," Jenkins said, interrupting Nick. "I'll straighten this out with minimal collateral damage. If your witness is unwilling to cooperate, then she must bear the consequences on her own."

"If I understand you correctly, Mr. Jenkins," Nick said, hardly managing to control his voice, "you don't have the slightest interest in arresting Vitali."

"My job is to find out how far the net of corruption reaches within the State's agencies and the City of New York," Jenkins replied coolly.

"Then go ahead," Nick said. "But you can rest assured that Vitali won't hesitate to bribe the successors of every single person you remove from office. We need to tackle the evil at its root. Otherwise, your efforts will be in vain."

"You better leave that problem to me, Kostidis."

Connors signaled Nick, but Nick was truly enraged. His original intention was to get Jenkins to drop the charges against Alex, but this bureaucratic disinterest riled him up and reignited his passion for justice.

"Listen, Jenkins," he said sharply, "I'm not some petty civil servant. In case you've forgotten, I was a US attorney and the deputy attorney general of the United States. I won't allow you and your agency to sweep everything under the rug once again! I don't know why you're sparing Vitali, but this time I'll put an end to his game. I'm toying with the idea of contacting the attorney general and the president, both of whom I know personally."

Connors grimaced as if he had a toothache, but he couldn't help but admire Nick's blunt courage.

"This case is none of your business whatsoever!" Tate Jenkins barked angrily.

"It's very much my business!" Nick countered. "My city has been made ungovernable by men like Vitali. I will no longer allow the Mob to rule this city, intimidating honest citizens with murder and threats! I lost my family because I dared to challenge this guy. I'll fight this man with everything that I've got. If the FBI decides not to cooperate with me, then I'll do it without you."

"Mr. Kostidis, listen to me—"

"No, you listen to me! I'll clean house this time. This opportunity presented itself, and I'm taking advantage of it. I don't give a crap who you are, Jenkins. My job is to keep this city safe and livable. How is it possible that a man has become so powerful that even the FBI bows to his pressure!"

"Watch what you say, Kostidis." Jenkins hissed.

"I don't care. And do you know why?" Nick lowered his voice. "I'll tell you. I've got nothing to lose. Absolutely nothing. My wife and my son died in front of my eyes because it didn't suit someone that I was speaking the truth. I won't let anyone or anything intimidate me. If you want to stop me from cleaning up this dirty business, then it'll be over my dead body."

"This is not the Wild West!"

"Exactly. Those days are over."

There was a moment of silence on the other end of the line, and Connors held his breath anxiously. Had Nick gone too far?

"So what do you want, Kostidis?"

"I want you to guarantee immunity for Alex Sontheim once she returns to the city. She's the most important witness against Vitali. In return, I'll make sure that she talks to you and to the SEC. Furthermore, I promise to mitigate information leaking to the public if your agency helps us bring Vitali to justice for everything that he has done."

"That actually doesn't fall under the FBI's jurisdiction."

"Yes, it does. This is a matter of national security. Remember that Vitali does business with a Colombian drug cartel."

Tate Jenkins sighed and gave in.

"I'll talk to Mr. Horner."

There was a click on the line, and the conversation was over. Nick leaned back in his chair and wiped the sweat from his forehead.

"Holy cow," Lloyd Connors said and laughed quietly. "I can't believe I heard that with my own ears. I don't think anyone has ever spoken that way to Jenkins before."

"They have no interest in Vitali," Nick said. "They want to hang the little guys and let the big guys get away."

"Yes, I have the same fear," Connors said. He had stopped laughing. "But what are you going to do? You can't force the FBI to do anything."

"Oh yes, I can." Nick looked up. "I have good connections with the press. The scandal would be out in a few hours. I'd tell them everything I know. It would be a sensation, especially if I mentioned names or even leaked parts of van Mieren's statement to the TV stations. Then they'd have no choice but to act."

"You can't be serious," Connors said, concerned. "You would ruin yourself."

"I don't care. I've achieved more than I ever dreamed I would, but I've also lost all that was dear to me. I don't care if I make myself unpopular."

"Have you ever considered what consequences this could have for me?"

"Of course." Nick nodded. "For that reason, you'll need to distance yourself from me immediately. I won't hold it against you."

The sleet lashed against the windows, and an icy wind howled around the building of the US Attorney's Office.

Nick stood up.

"I'm sick and tired of maneuvering and waiting. With every passing hour, the risk increases that Vitali finds out what's going on. As soon as he does, he will evade us again."

The telephone rang, and Connors answered. He listened for a few seconds, taken aback, and then the expression on his face turned dark.

"I'm coming right away," he said and hung up.

"Did something happen?" Nick asked.

"Yep," Connors replied grimly. "Clarence Whitewater. His wife found him dead. He committed suicide in his garage with exhaust fumes."

Nick was shocked. He had known Judge Clarence Whitewater for many years and worked with him frequently. The old man had been a model of integrity throughout his career. He had helped fight New York's Mafia families in the 1980s. Even before that, Whitewater had won a reputation as an incorruptible and fair judge. What had motivated him to become corrupted by Vitali at the end of his brilliant career?

"I need to go there." Connors grabbed his coat that he'd thrown across one of the chairs. "I'll call you."

Sergio's initial anger about Alex gave way to a cold desire for vengeance. Time and again, he imagined what he would do once he finally had her in his hands. Dennis Bruyner thought it would be best if the police or the FBI captured Alex, but Sergio had a different opinion. She would bitterly regret what she had done! Alex Sontheim wouldn't testify in any court. She'd be dead by the time he was finished with her.

The telephone rang, and Sergio winced.

"Yes?"

"Sergio!" Levy yelled in a hysterical voice. "Godfrey disappeared! The FBI showed up at Levy & Villiers a few days ago. They had a search warrant, and they brought people from the SEC and the US embassy."

"So what?" Sergio replied in a bored voice. "Didn't you go down there to make sure that the accounts were deleted? Let them search for what they like."

"I tried!" Levy lowered his voice into a hiss. "The computer was locked up, and we couldn't do a thing."

Sergio was stunned.

"What a fucking mess! I thought Godfrey had taken care of everything and deleted the files, but now he's supposedly been visiting his sick mother in Idaho since Tuesday. His parents have been dead for years. That miserable son of a bitch!"

Sergio listened to Levy's rant while his brain worked in high gear. There must be something more going on here. Did the other side have information directly from the bank's database? Would people like de Lancie, Harding, Governor Rhodes, or Senator Hoffman react differently if the FBI rang the doorbell instead of the US Attorney's Office?

"What could they possibly find?" Sergio asked.

"I don't know," Levy replied, "I've never dealt with these matters—it was St. John's job. For God's sake, why did I ever get myself into this? My reputation will be ruined if this comes out!"

"Shut up," Sergio said. "It does no good for you to keep wailing like a fucking wimp."

His mind churned feverishly. If the FBI or the SEC had concrete evidence, they would have showed up at LMI to question Levy. Their appearance at the bank in the Caymans seemed more like a shot in the dark. If his name had been dropped in connection with this investigation, his friends at the SEC would have informed him by now. It couldn't be all that bad.

"Listen, Vince," Sergio said. "If they have found something and they ask you about it, then you claim you know nothing. Tell them that St. John was solely responsible for the LMI subsidiaries. They'll never be able to prove we had anything to do with it."

"Actually, I really don't have anything to do with it," Levy responded, and Sergio caught his breath. *Rotten bastard,* he thought to himself. It wasn't for nothing that Nelson had warned him about Levy. Nelson had called him an opportunist. How right he had been!

"Vincent," Sergio said, hardly managing to contain his anger, "it was only because of me and my money that you were able to turn LMI from a small-time outfit into what it is today. You've fulfilled your lifelong dream—and, if I might add, you've done it with an impressive criminal energy. You're in just as deep as anyone—if not even deeper. As the president and chairman of the board, you're responsible for everything that happens in your firm. You'll regret it if you decide to turn your back on me."

"Are you threatening me?"

"I'm only saying, in for a penny, in for a pound. You're part of this to the bitter end, and if you're smart and keep your nerve, then nothing will happen to you. I can promise you that. But if you don't, you'll go under just like MPM."

Sergio hung up and slammed his fist on the table. *You're about to lose control*...Nelson van Mieren's words echoed in his head, and suddenly Sergio felt an unfamiliar, frightening sensation of panic rising inside of him. Had he overlooked something? Did he make a mistake somewhere? There was no one left he could ask for advice. Nelson and Zack were dead, and Alex, whom he'd never deemed especially important, seemed to have become pivotal in this situation. Did he make a mistake not letting her in on his business and making her his confidant? He sighed and stood up. It was pointless to grapple with *ifs* and *buts*. Now it was important to keep a level head. He needed to cover his back as quickly as possible.

The Delta Airlines flight from Miami landed in Newark at nine thirty p.m. Alex picked up her luggage at the baggage claim. Before exiting to the arrival hall, she disappeared into the restroom. She had no desire to run into the arms of Sergio's henchmen, which is why she quickly undressed, slipped into a business shirt and gray suit, knotted a tie around her neck, and put on men's shoes that she had bought—along with everything else—at the airport in Miami. Then she pulled her hair back tight and stuffed it beneath a blond short-haired wig. A fake moustache completed her costume. Alex reviewed her work in the mirror. She looked like a man—at least at first glance. As she left the ladies' restroom, she caught a surprised and disapproving glare from a woman washing her hands at the sink. The disguise worked.

Alex spotted Sergio's people immediately. Two men were standing at opposite sides of the automatic doors and closely observing every person walking between them. She slipped past unnoticed, and her heart somersaulted in relief. It worked! She hailed a cab outside the terminal. An icy, stormy wind was blowing, whipping the sleet sideways across the highway.

"Pretty nasty out there, isn't it?" the taxi driver asked. "Where are you from, sir?"

"Florida," Alex replied. "It wasn't much warmer down there if you can believe it."

"Where are you headed?"

"Manhattan. Do you know a cheap hotel in the Theater District?"

"Let's see. On Forty-Seventh Street, between Sixth and Seventh Avenues. The Portland Square Hotel. It's cheap, but clean."

"Sounds good. Take me there."

The taxi drove off. Alex had carefully deliberated on where she should stay after returning to the city. She had first considered a large, anonymous luxury hotel, but it might raise suspicions if she paid in cash. She would be less conspicuous at a cheaper hotel.

Alex longed for a hot shower and a soft bed. In the past forty-eight hours, she had been on so many airplanes that she had completely lost her sense of time. She'd traveled through Switzerland, Germany, France, and then Miami. She was wide awake and dead tired at the same time. The news was on the radio, and suddenly Alex jerked to attention.

"Could you turn the radio up a bit?" she asked the driver.

"Whitewater, who had been the chief judge of the State of New York since 1982, was found dead in the garage of his house in Patchogue on Long Island this morning. Speculation as to whether the death was a suicide has not yet been confirmed or denied by the US Attorney's Office..."

The blood rushed in Alex's ears. Clarence Whitewater was one of the men Sergio had paid off. She had personally met the stately, white-haired man with an impeccable reputation at Sergio's house. Did the judge commit suicide because he feared his connection to Vitali would come to light? Nick had given the bank statements to the US Attorney's Office, and they had apparently already gotten to work.

The taxi passed through the Holland Tunnel to Manhattan. It was too late to turn back. Alex took a deep breath, hoping the avalanche she'd triggered wouldn't suffocate her.

Shortly after ten, Nick returned to Gracie Mansion. He had spent the evening at a charity gala at the Waldorf Astoria, which he left immediately after the official portion ended. He didn't feel like being around laughing revelers, listening to gossip. Clarence Whitewater's death was the main topic of conversation. Everyone knew something about it, but no one had anything concrete to say. Nick wished the security officers a good night and walked to the wing of the house where his private rooms were located. Just like every evening when he returned to the house, he contemplated finding himself an apartment somewhere in the city.

Nick undressed and took a hot shower to relax his tense neck. He had been waiting two days to hear from Alex. Tate Jenkins had actually agreed to an amnesty, but on the condition that Alex contact him immediately. Time was running out, but Nick had no way of reaching her. For a brief moment, he thought that she might never return to New York again. She had plenty of money and a new identity. It would be easiest and safest for her to never set foot in this city again. Nick understood that, but the sheer possibility of never seeing her again caused him a sharp pain. He didn't care whether he looked like a fool in front of Jenkins and Connors if Alex remained on the run. It would be much worse not to see her again, not even knowing where she was or how she was doing.

Nick slipped into his bathrobe, walked into the kitchen, and stared into the refrigerator. Although he'd had the opportunity to feast on an opulent buffet at the Waldorf Astoria, he had spurned the lobster, veal medallions, stuffed quail breasts, and Beluga caviar. Just as he pulled a bottle of milk from the fridge, the telephone rang. He almost dropped the bottle in shock. As he had so many times over the past few days, he hoped that it might be Alex on the other end of the phone. And this time it was really her.

"Hello, Nick," she said. "It's me."

"Alex!" he exclaimed in relief. "How are you? I thought something had happened to you!"

"I could hardly call you from the airplane."

From the airplane? Nick's heart started pounding.

"Where are you now?" he asked.

"Back in the city."

"I must speak to you, Alex. It's very important. It was not without a fight with the FBI, but I managed to convince them to repeal your arrest warrant. When can we meet?"

Alex hesitated for a moment, and Nick feared that she would hang up.

"It's already late," she said, but then she seemed to change her mind. "Do you know the Portland Square Hotel in the Theater District? On Forty-Seventh Street, between Sixth and Seventh Avenues? I'm in room 211."

"Okay," Nick replied, "I know where that is."

Nick hung up and took a deep breath. He should have called Lloyd Connors immediately, but he decided to go to Alex by himself. There would be enough time for all the interrogation in the coming days.

"Are we supposed to sit here all night?" Gino Tardelli complained. "It's almost eleven. This guy isn't gonna hit the road in this lousy weather."

"Shut up," Luca said. He had personally taken on the mayor's surveillance and was in constant contact with two groups of twenty men via his cell phone. They took turns standing guard so that the mayor's security wouldn't get suspicious. They had been following him all over town for the past four days, observing him during his countless public appearances, but they saw nothing suspicious. Unfortunately, they couldn't tap his highly secured phone line, but if he met with Alex, they would notice.

"We'll stay here until one o'clock, and then the next shift will take over."

Luca lit a cigarette.

"This is such bullshit," the other man grumbled. "This guy lies in bed while we have to sit here in the freaking cold."

The two men almost failed to notice the small side door of the mansion opening. A man stepped outside. He wore a leather jacket with a baseball cap and walked swiftly up East End Avenue.

"Look at that." Luca straightened himself up and started the car's engine. He dialed a number and let the car roll onto the street.

"It's me," he said a moment later. "There's a guy with a leather jacket and a baseball cap coming up the street. You should be able to see him by now. Follow him and call me once you find out where he's going."

"Who is that?" Tardelli asked.

"I reckon it's our Mayor Kostidis." Luca put the cell phone away. "I bet that even his bodyguards don't know that he snuck out of the house."

Alex took a long shower and shampooed her hair, which caused most of the dark color to wash out. Her exhaustion was gone, but her nerves made her hands shake and her heart pound. Nick was on his way to her! Was it right to meet him in a hotel room? She was wanted for murder, and he would be in serious trouble if someone caught wind of their meeting like this. But despite her doubts, she looked forward to seeing him. She had been thinking about him for days.

Alex looked at her face, without makeup, in the dimly lit bathroom mirror. She still had a chance to get out. No one except Nick knew that she was back in town. She could leave New York and never be seen again. But what kind of life would that be? She never could have imagined how awful it was to be on the run with a false passport. She had trembled with fear at every passport checkpoint. Were the immigration officers holding on to her passport longer than other people's? Were they examining it more closely than others? No, she wasn't made for such a life. She could only hope that this nightmare would end. For the thousandth time since discovering Zack's dead body, she found herself wishing that she had stayed away from this whole situation.

Alex walked back into the room and turned on the television. The hotel was simple and clean. No one had wanted to see her passport when she registered as Mr. Bernard Chambers from Tallahassee. She'd bought a bottle of champagne and some sodas from the nearby liquor store to accompany her two limp shrink-wrapped sandwiches and a bag of chips. She needed the alcohol to fall asleep. One or two glasses of champagne on an empty stomach calmed down her jittery nerves. She would be safe from Sergio here for at least one night.

Nick had a feeling that Vitali would have him watched: not because he wanted to know what he was doing all day, but because he hoped that Nick would lead them to Alex once she was back in town. For this reason, he had the taxi drop him in busy Times Square and accepted that he would get wet from the walk. He had to avoid putting Vitali on Alex's trail. She might be safe at the Portland Square for one night, but she would have to change locations tomorrow. If Vitali had the slightest suspicion that Alex was staying somewhere around here, he was capable of having his minions search all of Midtown Manhattan.

Nick entered the unimpressive lobby of the Portland Square Hotel. It was filled with people. The Broadway shows were over, and people were returning to their hotels to escape this terrible weather. The elevator was full, so he took the stairs up to the second floor. His heart hammered in his chest as he approached room 211. He took a deep breath and knocked on the door.

"Who's there?" he heard Alex's voice though the cheaply made door.

The door was ripped open seconds later, and she stood in front of him. Nick felt a cheerful, wild bounce in his heart when he saw her. She was pale, but beautiful as ever. The stress of the last days had left its mark on her face. She wasn't the ice-cold, hard-nosed person the press had described, and she most certainly wasn't a calculating murderer. The woman standing in front of him was frightened and confused and just as lonely as he was. She wouldn't have come back to the city if she had done what she was accused of. Alex was an innocent victim in this intrigue.

He stepped inside, and she locked the door behind him. Until this moment, he had not realized how much he longed for her. They looked at each other silently for a few seconds, searching for the right words. Neither could think of what to say.

"You're completely soaked," Alex said.

"It's snowing outside," Nick replied numbly.

"You…you need to take off those wet clothes or you'll get sick." She took off his wet leather jacket, and he let her. Their eyes locked, and Alex suddenly lost her composure. She started to cry, surrendering to her fear and desperation. Nick put his arms around her and pressed her close to his body. He murmured consoling words, her face nestled to his cheek, and he felt the warmth of her body. He had longed for this during the many nights he had lain awake in his bed. He had a guilty conscience because his longing for Alex had replaced his grief for Mary. But he felt more alive than he had in a long time. Alex stopped crying, but they still held each other tightly. There was a certain shyness in the way they looked at each other.

"I'm glad you're here," Nick whispered hoarsely.

"I'm happy, too," Alex replied. "Everything is so terrible, but I'm not afraid when you're with me."

She wrapped her arms around his neck and held back a moment before leaning in for a tentative kiss. His heart beat faster as he kissed her back. She clung to him and pressed herself against his body, slipping her hands under his shirt and gently stroking his back. Her touch felt strong and sweet as the sensation coursed through him. He held her face in his hands and studied her for a moment before kissing her again tenderly. He didn't care if what he did was right or wrong. He couldn't care less about what the media would do if it came out that he—the mayor of New York City—had slept with a woman wanted for murder. He desired Alex more than he had ever desired any woman in his life.

As they kissed, they rid themselves of their clothes and sank down on the saggy bed. The sleet turned to snowflakes outside and the wind shook the windows. They had no desire to talk, think, be reasonable. There would be plenty of time for that later. Their hearts beat in excitement as they kissed and caressed each other, exploring, becoming familiar. There was no wild frenzy, no crazy ecstasy, no raging lust, but something else: something infinitely tender that brought tears to both of their eyes. They made love passionately in a way that only two human beings who trust and respect each other could. Their eyes locked while their bodies responded to each other, like two magnets, bodies that belonged together and had been separated far too long by inexplicable circumstances.

Alex felt a pulsing deep in her belly and waves flowing through her body—an overwhelming sensation, a longing desire to unite and create something new. She moved with Nick, found his same rhythm, and felt a surge catapult them to climax together. They paused at the peak of passion and looked at each other, almost surprised by how their bodies and souls coalesced in this magnificent, breathless moment. A wonderful feeling of happiness surrounded them, and they weren't embarrassed by their tears. They lay on the bed in a close embrace, smiling breathlessly and waiting for their heartbeats to calm down. Alex could see in Nick's eyes that he felt the same way she did. From the moment he arrived in the doorway, she had realized she loved him. "Hold me tight," she whispered, and Nick closed his arms around her even tighter. She snuggled in close to him and sighed. Feeling that she was no longer alone made all the tension that had weighed on her fall away. A pleasant exhaustion spread throughout her body.

Nick listened closely to her breathing getting calmer. He admired her sleeping face. He was dazed by the intensity of his feelings for this woman he held in his arms. With a twinge of guilt, he thought about how he had never felt this way with Mary. He could barely believe how magnificent he felt. He'd loved Mary, but he'd never managed to completely and utterly open up to her the way he had with Alex. He would have never burst into tears in front of Mary or confessed his deepest doubts and fears to her. Nick sighed, carefully kissing Alex's neck. His exuberant feeling of happiness gave way to a calm, deep joy, clouded only by concern over whether his love for Alex had a future. Here and now, they were two human beings who needed each other because they were alone and in dire straits. But how could this continue? Tiredness defeated all of his doubts, and Nick drifted off, closely nestled against Alex's warm, sleeping body.

It was four in the morning when Luca called his boss at the Painted Cat.

"And?" Sergio asked. "I don't want to hear any bad news!"

He was in an aggressive mood because he had failed to find sexual relief with the girls at the nightclub. His repeated failure enraged him. He had almost emptied an entire bottle of scotch—which was very unusual for him. Time and again, he thought about Alex, and his anger and thirst for vengeance grew immeasurably. She had led him by the nose, stolen from him, and plunged one of his companies into bankruptcy. And now she had also left him impotent! That was more than he could take. He stared into the mirror behind the bar and was terrified by his appearance. His face was bloated, and he had new bags beneath his bloodshot eyes. It almost seemed like Alex leaving him had stolen his feelings of immortality. A man in his late fifties, inexorably going on sixty, stared back at him. Sergio hated this sight, and still he couldn't look away from the mirror.

"My guys lost track of Kostidis at Times Square," Luca reported, "but they checked all of the hotels between Forty-Fifth and Forty-Ninth Streets. It looks like Alex checked in at the Portland Square under a false name."

Sergio sat upright with a start, and his hand gripped the scotch glass even tighter. Was she really dumb enough to return to the city? His pulse raced involuntarily. His felt the adrenaline spike of a hunter anticipating his prey.

"Has anyone seen her?"

"Not yet, but I came across the name 'Chambers,'" Luca replied. "She checked in under the same name at the Marriott in Zurich."

A grim smile spread across Sergio's face. If it really was Alex hiding behind this name, then she had made a mistake despite her cleverness.

"And on top of that," Luca continued, "one of the staff at the Portland Square claimed to have seen Kostidis in a leather jacket and a baseball cap."

"Let's go there!" Sergio said.

"No, boss," Luca objected, "we should wait until Kostidis is gone and she's alone. I've positioned my guys in every hallway of the hotel. I'll know within ten seconds when he leaves the room."

Sergio thought for a moment. He really wanted to go there immediately. He would kill Alex on the spot if he surprised her and this bastard in the same room. And if he should find out that she—just the thought was incredible!—was sleeping with Kostidis, then—

"Boss?" Luca interrupted Sergio's violent thoughts.

"Yes, yes...you're right. Send me a car. I want to be there when you go in."

He hung up the phone and finished his drink. Revenge was near; he could feel it.

The sun rose over New York. The city was awakening to a dull gray dawn. A gusty northwest wind drove the drizzle—mixed with just a few snowflakes—before it like fog. Alex blinked sleepily. It took her a few seconds to remember last night's events and remember the situation that she was in. The few hours in which she had suppressed the danger were over, and her fear returned with the dawning day. She turned toward Nick and saw that he was awake, gazing at her.

"Hello," she whispered.

"Hello," he replied quietly. There was a sad expression in his deep, dark eyes. How long had he been watching her like this?

"Do you have to go?" Alex asked quietly.

"Yes," Nick said with a regretful smile, "it's almost five thirty. Otherwise, people will think that I'm missing."

"Please hold me in your arms one more time," Alex asked.

He nodded silently and pulled her closer toward him. Alex sighed and nestled her face against his cheek. She wanted to tell him how much he meant to her, how much she liked him. But in the dawning light of day, this man lying next to her in bed was once again Nicholas Kostidis, the mayor of New York, who had official duties and a public waiting for him. Last night, they had just been a man and a woman who found refuge in each other's arms. They had forgotten reality, but now reality had caught up with them again.

Alex knew that it would be fatal for Nick's reputation if anyone found out about their night together. People didn't care that the allegations against her weren't true; Nick's enemies would see it as a welcome opportunity to sling mud at him.

They looked at each other in silence, both wishing that they could make time stand still.

"What will happen now?" Alex asked.

"I'm going to tell Jenkins that you'll speak to him," Nick replied, "and then the arrest warrant will finally be revoked."

The noise of the awakening city came in through the opened window.

"Where's Oliver?"

"At the St. Ignatius monastery. He's doing well."

Nick looked at her face and stroked her cheek tenderly.

"Come with me right now, Alex. I feel uneasy leaving you here by yourself."

Alex hesitated. She would have loved to pack her bags right away and go with him.

"No, that's a bad idea," she responded. "It would not be good for you if people see you with me. I'm safe for now here at the hotel."

I don't give a damn, Nick thought to himself. He only reluctantly let go of her and went into the bathroom to take a shower and get dressed.

"I'll call you as soon as I've spoken to Connors," he said in a husky voice as he put on his leather jacket. "Then I'll send two US marshals to pick you up."

Alex felt a lump in her throat.

She was emotionally overwhelmed. Sadness over their imminent good-bye mixed with helpless anger at the situation she was in. Nothing would ever be the same again. The man she had fallen in love with was forced to secretly steal away from her because she had been branded a murderer.

"Thank you, Alex," Nick said.

"I'm the one who should thank you," she replied, "because you came to me and you believe me."

"You're an amazing woman," Nick said, his voice hoarse. "This night was wonderful."

And I love you, he thought. Alex watched him as he slowly walked toward the door, and she almost jumped up to hold him back. But she knew that he needed to go. After the lock clicked into place behind him, Alex buried her face in the pillow and began to cry.

"There he is," Luca said as a man wearing a leather jacket and baseball cap stepped out of the hotel. He was relieved to find Kostidis and hoped that the mayor had actually visited Alex—although maybe they were mistaken and he had just spent the night with another woman.

Sergio Vitali silently sat in the car's backseat. He hadn't said a word in two hours as they waited in the parked car across the street from the hotel. There was no expression on his face, but a volcanic rage boiled inside of him.

"Okay," Luca said, "we're going in."

Sergio nodded and got out. In just a few more minutes, he would know the truth.

Alex flinched when she heard a knock at the door. She had showered and dressed and was just about to pack her suitcase.

"Who's there?" she called out.

"It's me. Nick."

Alex felt her heart jump with joy. Nick had come back to her! She opened the door with a smile, ready to fling her arms around Nick's neck. But it wasn't Nick standing in the hallway. Ice-cold shock shot through Alex's body, and the smile died on her lips. Sergio Vitali was standing in front of her, a murderous rage glowing in his eyes.

There was a great commotion in Gracie Mansion when Nick returned at ten to seven. The security officers and his staff were standing in the foyer, and Lloyd Connors, Frank Cohen, and Michael Page were having an animated discussion in Nick's study. Nick went into the house through the staff entrance and was astonished when he saw all of these people here so early on a Sunday morning.

"Hello," he said. The three men spun around and stared at him as if they had seen a ghost.

"Nick! For heaven's sake!" Frank was pale and visibly worried.

"What's the matter?" Nick asked innocently. "Did something happen?"

"You're unbelievable!" Relief was written clearly on Connors's tired face. "We're going crazy here worrying about you, and then you stroll in as cool as a cucumber and ask us what's going on!"

Nick's looked around the room from Connors to Frank, and then to his chief of staff Michael Page.

"Where have you been, Nick?" Frank asked reproachfully. "The security service called me at one o'clock saying that you weren't at home. No one knew where you were."

"We wanted to inform the police," Page said.

"I wanted to ride around the city a little last night," Nick replied. "I wanted to be alone. I'm not a child, after all."

"No one said that," Connors said in a conciliatory tone, "but since the assassination attempts, we have safety protocols almost as stringent as those for the president. We were worried, Nick."

"I thought that they had kidnapped you."

Frank let himself sink into a chair and took off his glasses.

"The security people were losing it," Page said, shaking his head, "and I was, too! You can imagine how much hell they'd give me if something were to happen to you."

"I've been roaming around the city by myself all of my life," Nick countered. "I didn't feel like running around with five bodyguards in tow."

"The next time you feel the need to stroll through the city at night, please at least let us know," Connors said as he grabbed his coat and yawned. "I'm going home now to catch a few hours of sleep."

Nick sighed. He felt guilty that his team had stayed up all night worrying about him. He was so excited by Alex's call last night that it simply didn't occur to him that anyone would notice his absence.

"I'm sorry I caused such a commotion," he said. "It won't happen again."

"Let's hope so." Connors grinned tiredly.

"Alex Sontheim is back in town," Nick said, and the deputy US attorney turned around abruptly.

"Since when?"

"Since yesterday evening. She's ready to speak to you and Jenkins today."

"Well, that's pretty good news for a change."

Connors's exhaustion vanished.

"Bed will have to wait a little longer then. Where is she?"

Nick hesitated. He couldn't tell them that he knew.

"She gave me her cell phone number."

"Okay," the deputy US attorney said with a nod, "let's drive to my office. We'll call her from there and then send someone over to pick her up."

Alex stared at Sergio with wide-open eyes. Her first reflex was to try to slam the door shut, but one of the men accompanying him had blocked her. So now they were all standing in the small room: Sergio Vitali, Luca, and three other men with cold stares who apparently wouldn't mind killing her. Alex's entire body was shaking, and fear pumped though her veins.

"So our paths cross again," Sergio said in a chilly voice. His gaze scanned the small room, fixating on the rumpled bedding for a few seconds. His hands clenched into fists, but he managed to keep his composure.

"Nice little room." He didn't let Alex out of his sight. "Did you run out of money? You could rent a suite at the Plaza with the fifty million that you stole from me."

Alex couldn't say a word. She was paralyzed with fear.

"You're a sneaky little whore," Sergio continued. "I truly misjudged you. I thought you were smart, but apparently you're not. You're quite stupid, actually."

Without warning he punched her in the face. Alex stumbled onto the bed. Sergio reached her in one step and pulled her up again.

"Who was here with you last night?" he demanded. Alex just silently shook her head. His face looked distorted, and he rammed his fist right into her stomach. He pulled her up by her hair and hit her so hard that her lip burst open. Blood dripped down her chin.

The pain robbed Alex of her breath. She looked around at the four other men, who watched indifferently. She couldn't expect any help from them.

"I asked you to tell me who you were fucking last night, you whore!" Sergio grabbed her by the shoulder and shook her. "Was it Kostidis? Tell me! Did you let that miserable little bastard fuck you?"

Alex's body throbbed with fear. Sergio would kill her, and there was no one to help her. This realization brought her racing thoughts to a standstill. She didn't want to die. Not here, not today, and not before she saw Nick again to tell him that she loved him.

"I could forgive you for stealing my money," Sergio said, his voice gritty with anger, "and also that you ruined MPM and caused me all of this trouble. Even for the thing with the accounts on Grand Cayman I could forgive you, but one thing I'll never forgive you for is…"

He stepped very close to her, but she didn't back up an inch.

"That you went to Kostidis, of all people," his voice turned into a hiss, "and told him everything. I won't forgive you for that. You will die for that."

She saw insane fury in his eyes.

"But before that, you'll tell me everything that I want to know. My guys have some pretty nice methods for bringing out the best in people. Just like your friend from Boston. First he pretended not to know anything, but then he suddenly remembered."

Justin! What had they done to him?

"And your fat little friend from your office," Sergio laughed derisively. "He ratted you out by the way, the coward."

"What did you do to them?" Alex whispered.

"Nothing compared to what I'll do to you," Sergio countered. "You did it with the fat one, right?"

He grimaced again. Alex could hardly believe that such a powerful man was tormented by childish jealousy.

"You let all of these guys fuck you! That shaggy computer nerd and that dumb journalist—and now even *Kostidis*!" Sergio spat out his name in disgust. "I thought that you had good taste in men, but you're completely indiscriminate. It's a downright insult that my name is on a list with scum like Kostidis!"

Alex followed his every movement and backed slowly away from him. Sergio wasn't just a ruthless criminal. A crippling inferiority complex and ruthless contempt for humanity were concealed behind his charming facade. This man—whom she once thought she loved—was a psychopath.

He stood in front of her. She felt his breath on her face and saw the glint in his eyes.

"You'll pay for what you've done, you whore!"

Out of the corner of her eye, Alex saw the champagne bottle that she'd bought yesterday standing on the table. After all this tension of the past days, she decided to go all or nothing. She wouldn't surrender to Sergio without a fight.

"Boss," Luca urged, "we should get out of here."

"Yes, we will," Sergio replied. He issued a short order to his men. One of them pulled out a roll of duct tape, and at that moment Alex got ready to fight. She grabbed the bottle and smashed it on the head of the man standing closest to her. She saw his surprised look before he went down on his knees and collapsed. Then she spotted the revolver he wore in his waistband. Taking advantage of the moment, she bent down and grabbed the weapon. Alex felt more energy pulsing through her body than she knew she had. She aimed the weapon at Sergio.

"You won't get out of here," he whispered as his voice trembled with rage.

"Yes, I will. And you're coming with me," she replied. "You'll take me to Mark and Justin. If you don't try to trick me, I'll tell you everything you want to know once both of them are safe."

"You're not in a position to make demands," Sergio said, grinding his teeth.

"Yes, I am," Alex countered. "I'm the one with a gun."

"You won't shoot me."

"Maybe not," she said, not taking her eyes off his. She smashed the champagne bottle against the edge of the table and it burst with a hiss. "But I will cut your throat."

The broken bottle neck was at least as deadly as the loaded .38 caliber in her other hand, and Alex was resolved to defend herself down to the last drop of blood.

"Boss," Luca said emphatically, "you should do what she says."

"Never."

With a quickness that Alex didn't expect, Sergio charged her and grabbed her right wrist. From the impact, she lost her balance and fell to the ground. She had underestimated his hatred and vengefulness. Now it was clear to her that she might not have the slightest chance of escaping him alive. His fist hit her in the face, and stars exploded in front of her eyes as she heard an angry wheeze.

"Nobody leaves me," he whispered hoarsely, "nobody betrays me. And nobody makes a fool out of me. Do you understand?"

It was a vicious fight, and Alex had lost. Luca leaned over her and pressed a cloth drenched with an acrid smelling liquid over her nose and mouth. She felt them tie up her arms and legs. She heard Sergio's voice from a distance.

"I have an appointment in the city now," she heard him say. "Do with her whatever you want, but make sure that she doesn't die before she tells us everything."

Alex heard her cell phone ring. In desperation, she thought about Nick and then lost consciousness.

Nick called repeatedly but kept getting Alex's voice mail.

"Strange," he said as he hung up, "she's not answering."

"Maybe she's taking a shower," Lloyd Connors remarked.

"Yes, maybe. I'll try again in a minute."

The men sat in Connors's office at the US Attorney's Office building. Tate Jenkins and Alan Harper, the head of the SEC's investigation unit, would arrive from Washington DC in three hours to interview Alex. Nick longed to see Alex again. He should have told her this morning what she meant to him and what he felt for her. He didn't just like her. He had fallen in love with her a long time ago, but this had become absolutely clear to him after last night.

"Try again," Connors said, jerking him out of his thoughts, and Nick dialed Alex's cell phone number again. It rang and rang, and no one answered. An uneasy feeling crept up inside him.

"Maybe she changed her mind after all and took off again," Connors speculated. "That would be quite an embarrassment for us."

"No way," Nick said, shaking his head. "She promised me that she'd speak with Jenkins and the people from the SEC. After all, that's why she returned to the city."

"Try again," the deputy US attorney suggested.

"I think it would be better to go there." Nick's uneasy feelings were turning to fear.

"So you do know where she is." Connors threw him a sharp look.

"I had to promise her I wouldn't tell anyone."

"So?"

"The Portland Square Hotel on Forty-Seventh Street."

"Okay." Connors grabbed the telephone receiver and called Deputy Spooner. "They're leaving right now," he announced after a brief conversation.

"I'm coming with you." Nick jumped up. Connors sighed but let Nick follow him. Accompanied by two US marshals, they headed to Forty-Seventh Street. Nick's foreboding feeling increased as they got closer to the hotel. Something had happened. It had been a mistake to leave Alex behind at the hotel. He should have insisted she come with him. Suddenly, he wondered whether he had possibly put Vitali on Alex's trail. He knew that they were watching him, but he hadn't detected anything suspicious last night. Even after all he had done or experienced in his life up to now, Nick had never before felt so afraid. Fear was alien to him. He had been indifferent to every storm, no matter how strong or threatening. Maybe it was this fearlessness, his inability to accept the dark side that had helped him succeed. Mary could never understand that. She was always frightened when he prosecuted the Mafia families or drug dealers. She didn't understand that their threats were his motivation.

But since Mary's death, something had changed inside of Nick. In his many hours of loneliness, he had thought about his mistakes; doubt had crept up, and he started to recognize that his uncompromising stubbornness had created many enemies over the years. And these enemies were dangerous.

The car raced through the empty Sunday morning streets toward the Theater District. It was all his fault if something had happened to Alex! Connors gave Nick a strange look.

"What's wrong with you?" he asked.

"I have a feeling that something terrible has happened," Nick replied, mumbling, "and if that's the case, then it's my fault."

"Nonsense," Connors said, shaking his head, "what do you have to do with this?"

"I was with her last night," Nick said quietly. The deputy US attorney stared at him in disbelief.

"You went to see Sontheim?" he whispered so that the two deputies couldn't hear. "For God's sake, why didn't you tell me?"

"I wanted to talk to her first." Nick shrugged his shoulders. "She called me around ten thirty, and I went to see her immediately."

"How could you do that, Nick?" Connors whispered. "This woman is a wanted fugitive! She's still under suspicion of murder! You should have called me right away!"

Nick struggled to stay relaxed. If Connors found out that he'd had sex with her, then he'd be immediately excluded from the investigation.

"I didn't want to bother you in the middle of the night."

"Great." Connors rolled his eyes. "I'm torn from my bed for every trifle, but if something really important happens, I don't hear about it!"

"I'm sorry."

"What did she say? What happened to the money?"

"She didn't touch it," Nick replied. "She intends to use it as evidence against Vitali."

"Hmm." Connors stared pensively out the window. Nick was crazy with nervousness. They finally reached the hotel. Before Deputy Khazaeli could bring the car to a complete stop, Nick jumped out and charged into the hotel lobby. A few guests watched curiously as the four men charged into the elevator. Nick led them to room 211.

"Step aside!" Spooner ordered, and Deputy Khazaeli kicked the flimsy door so hard that it flew off the hinges, crashing down. He and his colleague charged the room with their guns drawn. They searched the bathroom and the closets.

"Nothing." Spooner secured his revolver and put it back into its holster. "The bird has left the nest."

Nick shook his head in disbelief. Alex had really disappeared. The bed, where they had made love last night, was still disheveled.

"It seems she changed her mind," Connors observed. There was a hint of sarcasm in his voice. "What a pile of shit! What am I supposed to tell the FBI? I'll look like a complete idiot!"

He let himself sink into a chair and rubbed his reddened eyes. Nick stood in the middle of the room, stunned. Then his gaze fell on the bed. He leaned over it and touched a spot on the sheet with his index finger.

"Oh my God," he murmured, and all of his strength left him. It was blood. Undoubtedly.

"What is it?" Connors asked.

"There's blood everywhere," Nick whispered. "And it's fresh."

Connors jumped up as if he had been stung, and both of the US marshals stepped closer. They hadn't noticed the spots on the flowered bedding and the dark carpet, or the broken glass from the bottle on the floor.

"She didn't just run away." Nick's voice failed him.

All of the color vanished from his face, and panic overcame him. He couldn't suppress his shaking.

"That's right," Khazaeli nodded, "because otherwise she would have taken the suitcase with her."

He bent over and pulled her suitcase from under the bed. Someone had carelessly thrown Alex's belongings into it to make it look like she had checked out. While Connors was on the phone ordering the crime scene unit to the Portland Square Hotel and the US marshals looked everywhere for revealing clues, Nick stood there as if paralyzed. Alex was in Vitali's clutches. He must have found out about her whereabouts and waited until Nick left the room to strike. Now there was no hope left. Vitali would never let Alex go alive. Nick clenched his fists in helpless anger. He wanted to scream and rage, throw himself on the bed and cry like a baby, but that wouldn't help matters any. It was too late.

The largest search operation New York City had ever seen was well underway an hour after the police radio reported Alex Sontheim's disappearance. Gordon Engels dispatched his best men to question every guest and the entire staff of the Portland Square Hotel. Entire squadrons of police combed through the warehouses at the Brooklyn, Jersey City, and Staten Island docks. Roadblocks were set up on the bridges and tunnels leaving Manhattan. Suspicious vehicles were searched. The crisis team headquarters was established at the US Attorney's Office. All of the information was synthesized there, although Police Commissioner Jerome Harding vehemently protested. Outraged, Harding marched into Connors's office around noon after one of his staff members apprised him of the situation following a Sunday brunch with Sergio Vitali.

"This case is the sole jurisdiction of the NYPD!" he yelled at the deputy US attorney. "Why are you interfering with our work?"

His face was red, and he was so angry that at first he didn't even notice the other men.

Tate Jenkins smiled thinly. "Why are you so upset, Jerome? Cooperation between the agencies usually works out well."

The police commissioner turned around abruptly and stared at the deputy director of the FBI in surprise.

"Jenkins," he said, "this looks like a bigger operation. What are you doing here?"

"It's big, all right." Jenkins pointed to one of the vacant chairs across from him. "Take a seat, Jerome."

The police commissioner, who normally projected confidence, suddenly seemed intimidated.

"Is there something I should know?" he asked. "Why is the FBI chasing this woman? Did she try to kill the president or something?"

"Take a seat, Jerome," Tate Jenkins repeated. Lloyd Connors shot a quick glance at Nick, but the mayor just stared hollow-eyed off into space. It seemed like he had been in shock ever since they entered the hotel room.

"Connors," Jenkins said, "please inform Mr. Harding about the situation."

"What's going on here?" A fine film of sweat had formed on Harding's forehead, and his eyes flitted nervously back and forth. Lloyd Connors cleared his voice and prepared himself for one of the police commissioner's fierce and almost legendary temper tantrums.

"We're not just looking for Alex Sontheim because of Mr. St. John's murder," he stated calmly. "We expect her to testify with regard to a large-scale corruption scandal."

"A corruption scandal?"

Harding may have seemed surprised to anyone else, but Connors detected a flicker of terror in the police commissioner's eyes.

"We have evidence," he continued, "that high-ranking officials of this city have regularly received large sums of money in exchange for certain favors. We have procured comprehensive evidence that includes names, amounts, and bank account numbers in the Cayman Islands, the Bahamas, and in Switzerland. Even if only a fraction of this turns out to be true, then this is certainly one of the largest bribery cases in the history of New York City, if not the United States."

Jerome Harding's face flashed red and pale in turns, but he didn't collapse like the other men to whom Connors had given this speech in the past few days. Nick was right when he said that Harding would be a hard nut to crack. The police commissioner wasn't intimidated that easily, and the fact that he had never withdrawn any money from the account in his name at Levy & Villiers made it unclear whether a corruption charge even applied to him.

"Unbelievable!" Harding managed to appear indignant. "Why am I just now hearing about this?"

Jenkins leaned forward. His pale eyes were as cold as a fish's.

"Because your name appears in our documents, Jerome."

"Excuse me?" The police commissioner turned around quickly. The incredulous expression on his face would have seemed real if not for the sheer fear in his eyes.

"That's a disgraceful accusation!" Harding was outraged. "And from whom—if I may ask—did I accept this money?"

"We'd like to know that," Jenkins replied with a friendly smile. He crossed his legs and folded his arms across his chest. There was complete silence, and only the muted noise of ringing telephones and hectic conversation could be heard from outside. Then Harding pushed back his chair with a jerk and stood up.

"This," he said in a threatening, quiet voice, "is a truly incredible allegation! I've never ever accepted money from anyone! I've been the police commissioner of this city for almost eleven years now. I've succeeded in making New York a safer place during my time in office. I despise criminals of any kind, no matter if they are white collar or dealing crack in the subway! I have an impeccable reputation far beyond this city. I won't let you depict me in public as someone who accepts bribes!"

He yelled out the last words, and his angry face was bright red. Jenkins listened to him with an impassive expression.

"So?" Harding put his arms on his hips and looked at the men in a challenging pose. "From whom did I supposedly accept money?"

Connors couldn't help but admire Harding's grit, and for a second he had doubts about his involvement in this affair.

"From Sergio Vitali," someone said.

Harding turned around abruptly.

"Oh, Vitali again," he said disdainfully and threw Nick a hostile look. "The ghost that has been haunting your sick brain for the last twenty years, Kostidis."

"No," Nick said, shaking his head, "it's not a ghost. Definitely not. You know that as well as I do, Jerome."

"I don't know anything."

"Really?" Nick stood up and walked around the table.

His face was extremely pale.

"In that case, you have a short memory. I still vividly remember our conversation in my office the morning after Cesare Vitali was arrested and murdered."

"He hung himself," Harding interrupted him harshly.

"No, he didn't," Nick replied. "His own father sent someone to the Forty-First Precinct who gave thousands of dollars to a police officer to make sure Cesare Vitali was murdered. It was supposed to look like suicide."

"You must be—" Harding started to say, but Nick continued undeterred.

"You were angry because I drew a connection between the shots fired at Vitali and the Colombian drug cartel and explained it to the press. I couldn't understand why you were so mad that day, but then it dawned on me: Vitali had not only lured de Lancie to his side, but also you—a fearless fighter against crime. I told you that right to your face. Do you remember now?"

The police commissioner stared at him angrily, but remained silent.

"For years you have turned a blind eye to Vitali and his henchmen. In exchange for that, Vitali filled your account in the Caymans. You were far too smart to touch the money, but you knew the exact balance. A nice addition to your retirement, wasn't it?"

"I never liked you, Kostidis," Harding whispered. "You're a self-righteous fanatic, a…a…damn it, stop staring at me like that!"

Nick was unmoved, but it almost made him sad to look at Harding.

"You were the biggest disappointment of them all," Nick whispered. "I couldn't believe it. I would have put both of my hands in the fire for you, Jerome."

Harding bit his lip and lowered his head.

"What do you have to say about these allegations?" Jenkins asked.

"I won't say anything without my lawyer!" the police commissioner snapped. "And if you'll excuse me now, I've got work to do."

Connors rummaged in his briefcase and pulled out a piece of paper. "I have an arrest warrant for you, Mr. Harding. You are under arrest for corruption, obstruction of justice, failure to report planned crimes, providing preferential treatment, and multiple counts of coercion."

"Kiss my ass, you punk." Harding laughed disdainfully. "I'll wipe my ass with your arrest warrant!"

"If you say so." Connors remained calm. "In that case, we can add resisting arrest to the list."

He walked across the room and opened the door to signal the two US marshals waiting outside.

"Mr. Harding?" one of the deputies said as he pulled out the handcuffs. "Come with me, please. You have the right to remain silent—"

"I know my rights!" Harding snapped at the man and turned toward Jenkins, Connors, and Engels. "You'll live to regret this! My lawyer will tear you apart—all of you and your ridiculous arrest warrant! There's going to be a hefty claim for damages!"

"I hope you can afford a good lawyer now that your foreign assets have been seized by the IRS." Connors smiled coolly. "I'm afraid that you'll also be prosecuted for tax evasion."

Harding's eyes narrowed as the handcuffs clicked shut.

Connors nodded. "Take him out through the basement. I don't want his arrest to be public. He's not allowed to make a phone call until further notice."

While the others discussed the next course of the operation, Nick once again lapsed into a state of dull brooding. He wanted to drive around the city with the police and personally search the warehouses, docks, and known gangster hangouts on the Lower East Side and in Little Italy. But instead, he sat in this office, extremely tense, as he waited for the sparse updates coming in. Unfortunately, all the leads that had looked so promising had come to nothing so far. Two staff members at the Portland Square Hotel remembered some men hanging around in the hallways, but the descriptions were so contradictory that the police artist gave up after a few minutes in complete exasperation.

Nick bitterly reproached himself for not being on the alert for possible pursuers as he rushed to Alex. He couldn't rid himself of the gnawing thought that he was the one who'd put Vitali on Alex's trail. Why hadn't he listened to his instincts and convinced her to come with him? If he had insisted, she would be safe now. Nick buried his face in his hands. Seeing the bloodstains all over the hotel room had triggered the same terrible feeling as the moment when the car exploded with Mary and Christopher in it.

"What do you think, Nick?" Connors asked, and Nick jerked up.

"W...what? About what?"

Lloyd Connors looked at the mayor with concern. He had a feeling that for Nick, there was more to this than uncovering a bribery scandal. Connors noticed the dark circles around Nick's eyes. He would have loved to say something encouraging to him, but there was unfortunately nothing to say. If the woman was actually in Vitali's clutches, then the odds were definitely against her.

Alex regained consciousness, but she had completely lost any sense of time and space. The hard mattress she was lying on smelled old and musty. She tried to open her eyes, but the men had blindfolded her. Her head buzzed from Sergio's blows, and her mouth was dry as a bone from the ether that they had used to knock her out. Her bound hands and feet were numb. The memory of what had transpired suddenly rushed back.

"Totally tame, the little wildcat," a man behind her said in Italian, and Alex barely dared to breathe.

"I've never banged such a fine lady before," she heard a second man say. "The boss said we can do whatever we want, didn't he?"

Alex swallowed frantically, and her body stiffened in fear. She couldn't expect any sympathy, especially after hitting one of the guys over the head with a bottle. But maybe they would leave her alone if they thought she was unconscious.

"We could have a little fun with her, right?"

"Why not? The boss won't be back for a few hours."

While the men talked to each other in hushed tones, Alex realized the utter hopelessness of her situation. No one knew where she was, and her arms and legs were bound. Why hadn't she listened to Nick this morning and gone with him? Her thoughts were racing, but there was no possibility of escape. She was completely and utterly at Sergio's mercy.

"Let's go," one of the men said. "I have to take a leak. And then we'll get the others. I'm sure they want to have some fun, too."

They moved away. A door opened and closed again with a faint squeak. The room had to be quite large. It smelled damp and unused, like an old basement.

"Hello?" Alex whispered hoarsely after a while, but no one answered. Apparently, both of her guards had left the room. As she moved her hands and feet, the numbness turned to a painful prickle.

She managed to sit up and lean against a tiled wall. She rubbed her head against her shoulders, rotating her arms until the duct tape around them slowly loosened. With her fingernails, she worked on the tape around her ankles. Sweat streamed from her pores from the exertion, and her heart pounded. The men could return at any moment, and then her efforts would be in vain.

Her blindfold loosened and she finally caught a glimpse of the room where she was being held. The room was completely empty, and there were circular tracks on the ceiling. It looked like a slaughterhouse, which meant that she was likely in Manhattan's Meatpacking District in Chelsea, between Ninth and Eleventh Avenues. She ripped the tape from her feet and stood up. Dizzy, she forced herself to walk across the room to a metal shelf. She ripped the tape around her wrists on a sharp edge, not caring whether she might cut herself.

Alex frantically looked for an escape route. She could reach the frosted glass skylights if the decrepit metal shelf would hold her weight. She had to at least give it a try. She climbed up the wobbly shelf as fast as she could. She could reach the edge of the window with her fingertips. Desperately, she shook the rusty window lever, and it moved a fraction of an inch at a time. Suddenly, the skylight popped open. Alex wanted to jump for joy.

At that moment, the door opened at the other end of the large room. The men knew immediately what was going on, and they hollered wildly at each other and ran toward her. Alex gripped the window ledge, mustered all of her strength, and pulled herself up. She kicked the shelf with her foot, and it came crashing down. Panting from exertion, she hurled her body through the open skylight and dangled outside. The drop on the other side was about twelve feet, but she didn't care. She kept slipping, let her feet slide down the wall, closed her eyes, and let go.

"The cops are searching the entire city," Luca said to his boss. "They're arresting anyone they don't like. I bet that every single prison cell within a radius of a hundred miles will be triple-booked by the end of the night."

"Hmm," Sergio said, glancing at his watch, "maybe we should get it over with now."

He wasn't particularly alarmed by the intense police response, because Jerome Harding had reassured him during brunch just a few hours ago that the investigation had nothing to do with him, that it was solely about solving the St. John murder. Harding promised to call him immediately if he found out something different. Sergio knew that he could rely on Harding. And the cops could search as much as they liked, because in three hours Alex would be dead.

"How's Maurizio doing?" Sergio inquired as they drove toward Chelsea.

"I had him taken to Sutton," Luca answered. "That crazed woman nearly smashed in his skull."

Sergio nodded grimly. Despite his anger at Alex, he felt a hint of admiration. This woman was truly courageous, an almost equal opponent. But after spending seven hours tied up and gagged in the cold storage room of an old meat factory, she'd get the picture that he always won, and that she had no chance against him.

While they were stuck in traffic, Sergio toyed with the idea of leaking a story to the press that the honorable mayor had banged a wanted murderer last night. As great as that sounded, he needed to wait until Alex's body was floating in the East River. Then he could focus on finishing off the mayor.

Sergio grinned bitterly. No one had drawn a line from MPM and LMI to him. And once Alex was gone, there'd be no one left who could. The storm would die down, and he would remain quiet until then. The preparations for his charity ball in a few days were in full swing. Not one person had sent regrets, which was a good sign. If the cops had already grilled any of his friends, there would have been mass cancellations long ago. New Yorkers were the quickest to notice when someone should be shunned in high society.

"A tempest in a teapot," Sergio muttered and shrugged his shoulders. It wasn't anything more than that.

Alex felt like the fall had broken every single bone in her body. Unable to move, she lay flat on her back, gasping for air. Tears of anger soaked her face as she heard hurried steps. She was surrounded by a half dozen angry-looking men who pulled her up roughly and dragged her back into the building. Despite her pain and fear, she kicked at them, bit the hand of one, and wriggled like a fish. Her attempt to escape made Sergio's men even angrier. Her situation had worsened significantly.

Alex fought against the terror and weakness with all her might. Things couldn't get worse. She was determined not to collapse in front of Sergio, begging for mercy. When she heard his voice, she closed her eyes.

"The bitch ran away from us," one man said. "We had to use a bit more force with her. I'm sorry, boss."

"Put her on her feet," Sergio said coldly. "I want to look her in the eyes. And then leave us alone."

They roughly pulled Alex up. She stumbled and leaned against the wall, suppressing a groan.

"Look at me," Sergio ordered, and Alex slowly raised her beaten face. She realized in surprise that her fear of dying had vanished, giving way to a strange serenity. She wasn't afraid anymore. Instead, she felt nothing at all.

"I'm going to ask you a few questions that you had better answer. You'll regret it if you don't."

Alex nodded.

"Nelson warned me about you from the very start." He stood directly in front of her, observing her with a cruel smile, his hands deep in his coat pockets. "He saw through you right away—what a devious bitch you are."

"You made the biggest mistake of your life listening to him." Alex's voice was hoarse. "He was afraid that I could have more influence over you than he ever had. I would have done anything for you if you hadn't lied to me from the start."

The smile vanished from Sergio's face.

"He betrayed you," Alex said. "He blew his brains out instead of continuing to work for you."

"Shut up!" Sergio snarled at her.

"They'll all turn their backs on you," Alex continued, "but I would have stayed by your side—"

"I told you to shut up!" he roared.

"You know it yourself." Alex didn't blink. "You know you trusted the wrong people. Even your wife ran away from you. Did you know that she came to me on the day that she left you?"

Sergio's face turned red. Her words hit a nerve. He struggled to keep his cool.

"Where did you get the bank statement that I found in your apartment?" he asked in a gravelly voice. Alex stared into his eyes and remained silent.

"Don't think that you can deceive me," he hissed. "I know you're trembling with fear."

"I'm not afraid anymore," Alex replied. "You've already decided to kill me. It makes no difference whether or not I talk."

"What grandiose words," Sergio mocked her, "but I will show you how small you are—how pathetically small!"

Alex detected a spark of insanity in his blue eyes. Sergio walked to the door and called his men. She waited as they took their places all around her.

"Comu si dici in sicilianu?" she said. "*Omertà.* Isn't that right? I won't say a word."

Sergio pressed his lips together.

"I thought you didn't understand Italian," he said, and Alex shrugged her shoulders. Sergio took off his coat and handed it to Luca.

"I won't say another word," she said. Sergio's fist flew at her face that same moment. She felt her lip burst again and her nose break. He brutally grabbed her by the hair, pulled her head back, and leaned over her. His face was so close to hers that she could see every single pore. Saliva pooled at the corners of his mouth.

"You'll beg me to kill you," he hissed. "Count on it! You damned little whore!"

Alex felt warm blood running across her chin, but she didn't bat an eye.

"Speak!" Sergio let her go. "I don't have all day."

Alex closed her eyes. Her head was about to explode.

"Where is the money that you stole from me?"

Alex shrugged her shoulders again, although every movement hurt like hell.

"Tell me where it is!"

"No."

Sergio stared at her in a raging fury.

"Okay," he said, taking a deep breath, "okay. I can handle losing fifty million dollars. I won't go bankrupt. You can't blackmail me with that. But what about the bank statement? What about the e-mails from St. John's computer? Who knows about them? Did you run to Kostidis?"

The thought that she'd spent the night with the hated mayor made him insane.

"What did you say to him when he fucked you?"

Alex grinned, although it hurt. Sergio had lost. His jealousy and vanity consumed him.

"I told him," she said, looking Sergio square in the eye, "that he fucked me better than you."

Sergio lost it. He beat her with both fists until Luca and another man grabbed his arms. Sergio breathed heavily. Alex lay crumpled on the floor, but not a single sob crossed her lips. Whatever Sergio had thought about the weakness of women, Alex proved him wrong. And he hated her even more for it.

"Go on," he said and massaged his sore knuckles, "give her the special treatment!"

They grabbed her, tore her clothes off, and tied her up on a metal table dressed in just her underwear. The blows with the leather strap split the skin on her thighs and chest. Her agony took her breath away, but she suppressed any cry of pain. She became dizzy and almost blacked out, but they brutally kept her from losing consciousness.

"Talk!" Sergio hissed, clenching his hands in his pockets. He had been quite certain that it wouldn't take long to get her talking, but now it turned out to be a problem. He particularly feared losing face in front of his men.

"What will you do if I die before that?" Alex mumbled through her swollen lips. Any sign of arrogance had vanished from Sergio's face. In the bright fluorescent light, she noticed the bags under his eyes and the increasingly sagging skin on his neck. She realized that even Sergio Vitali had to capitulate to her stubbornness. The pain in her body was like a dull droning. Alex could no longer distinguish which body part hurt the most, but her triumph over Sergio in his rage and helplessness eased the pain.

"I'll have all of my men rape you!" Sergio threatened. "Until you open your fucking mouth! Is that what you want?"

Alex was silent. She closed her eyes; she didn't fight back when they loosened the tape around her ankles and the first man attacked her—a fat, slimy guy who stank like sweat and garlic. The edge of the metal table rammed painfully into her back with every thrust. Without a word, Alex endured the pain and humiliation. She stopped counting after the third man. She just heard Sergio's angry voice from a far distance. Nothing mattered anymore. She was just a numb shell. The minutes stretched into hours, and Alex felt like she was looking at herself from above. She saw her injured body, her face swollen and disfigured by the beating. Her thoughts wandered to Nick. Not even this brutality could defile her memory of the most beautiful night of her life.

"And?" Alex heard Sergio's mocking voice. "Do you like it? Or do you finally want to talk to me?"

If it would have helped her at all, she would have told Sergio everything. Yes, she would have begged him, beseeched him, done everything just to live. But he would kill her anyway. She needed to remain strong. She knew her pride would drive him crazy.

Speechless with anger at her persistent silence, Sergio watched as one man after the other lustfully pounced on Alex. The sight of these men panting like animals, taking possession of the body of this woman he'd once truly loved, filled him with disgust. There were even worse methods for forcing a person to talk, but something deep inside made it impossible for Sergio to have them sever Alex's limbs or mutilate her.

"She stopped breathing," one of the men said. He leaned over Alex and felt for her carotid artery. Sergio jumped up from his chair. He stared at Alex's lifeless body. The humiliation he'd suffered in front of his men drilled into him like a barbed hook. Nevertheless, he felt respect for this woman who dared to defy him. She wasn't afraid of him. He ran both hands through his short hair. Alex had been right. Nelson had given him bad advice. What a great companion she would have been to him! She would have remained loyal if he had only allowed her to stand by his side.

Sergio's anger suddenly subsided and made way for a leaden fatigue. Beautiful, passionate, brave Alex! He would never meet a woman like her again. She dealt him a major defeat with her death. But above all, his feeling of invincibility had died with her. Alex had beaten him. In every sense.

"What should we do with her?" Luca asked. Sergio winced. Impatiently, he chased away these sentimental feelings. This little whore deserved to die. She had lied to him, betrayed him, stolen from him. *Basta.* Life goes on. He needed to clear his head.

"Throw her in the river," he said coldly. Then he turned on his heel and walked out.

Nick didn't get a wink of sleep all night. Shortly before one thirty in the morning, he had left the US Attorney's Office and walked the two blocks to city hall as it began to snow. He could no longer stand to just sit there and wait. And he could hardly bear how Jenkins and Engels talked about Alex. She was nothing more than just a witness to them. They didn't care that she was a human being. They were completely indifferent to whether she was innocent or guilty. They'd certainly solve the corruption case without Alex. Nick had a feeling that Vitali would manage once again to squirm free. His high-powered lawyers would squash every allegation, and he'd probably intimidate anyone who considered revealing anything to use against him. But Nick didn't really care about Vitali. His thoughts revolved around Alex. Where was she? What had they done to her? Was she still alive?

Nick knew that he wouldn't be able to cope if something happened to her. His intense feelings were completely different than the love he had felt for Mary. He couldn't quite explain it to himself either. But his attraction toward Alex was far more than the desire of a man over fifty trying to regain his youth.

He entered city hall through the back door and walked to his office. The security guards greeted him respectfully. No one asked him what he was doing here at this time. He strode into his office and switched on the small lamp that drew a warm yellow circle of light on his desk. Nick sat down in his wet coat. His gaze wandered over the spacious office and landed on the framed portraits of his predecessors. This office was the place he had wanted to be ever since he was a little boy. It was his dream, and he had achieved it. He had spent so many nights working, neglecting his family. Nick was used to fighting, but now he was tired. There was a different life out there, one without politics, outside the public eye. He intensely longed for this life more than ever before. He sighed despondently. He had achieved so much, but he'd lost even more. He hadn't watched his son grow up because he had no time. He knew the New York TV stations better than his own home, and some reporters were more familiar to him than his own son. His days were ordered by his schedule, from early morning until late at night.

And then Alex appeared in his life, and she succeeded in doing what Mary had tried in vain for so many years: Nick started to take a hard look at himself. Suddenly, he no longer understood the driving force behind his crazy ambition—what his enemies had labeled his "obsession." Why had he been so unwilling to compromise? It was Alex who had made him take a critical look at himself. And when he did this, he realized that, during all those years of fighting, he had completely forgotten to live.

No, Alex couldn't be dead! It simply couldn't happen. Nick wrapped his arms around his chest, doubling up.

"Dear Lord," he whispered in desperation. "Please, don't let her die…"

Travis Stewart cursed. On the short path from the car to the docks, the wet snow had soaked through his jacket and the wind was icy cold. To make matters worse, he had overslept. Dawn would break in about a half hour, and cops would be teeming everywhere. He needed to hurry. He cursed as he climbed down the quay wall's rusty ladder and jumped into the small motorboat. He pulled out a metal briefcase from beneath the oiled tarpaulin, and he was about to climb up the ladder again when he heard engine noise above him.

"Shit," he whispered. If that was the cops and they caught him with a briefcase filled with drugs, then he'd go back to the slammer. Travis stuffed the briefcase under the tarp and cowered in the boat. Car doors slammed, and he heard male voices. Suddenly, silhouettes appeared farther down the quay wall. Travis saw them razor-sharp against the brightening night sky. They carried a heavy bundle that they dragged to the edge of the old pier. People often threw garbage in the river here because the current was strong. But that wasn't garbage! For a split second, Travis could see a person's body being dumped into the water. He ducked down automatically. If those guys saw him, they wouldn't hesitate to kill him as well.

But they didn't see him. They disappeared immediately. Travis stared at the dark-gray water and saw wildly flailing arms in the current. There was no doubt that this was not a dead body drifting in the ice-cold water, but a living human being! He really shouldn't care. Helping people only caused trouble. He strained to stare into the water. A head suddenly emerged just six feet from his boat's bow. Travis threw himself forward with such force that the boat nearly capsized. Now he was completely soaked, but his fingers closed around a handful of wet hair. Then a hand grabbed for his. A woman's face appeared. She coughed and spat water. Her eyes were wide open. The woman was more dead than alive, and she lost consciousness as Travis pulled her into the boat—but she was alive! He stared at her in surprise. She was completely naked. He took off his army jacket and placed it over the woman's shivering body, which was covered with cuts and bruises.

It wasn't easy to climb up the slippery rungs of the rusty ladder with her weight on his back. The snow was falling heavier around him as he stumbled to his car, which was parked a few hundred yards away at an abandoned storage shed. Then he opened the door and placed the lifeless woman on the passenger seat. He grabbed an old wool blanket from the trunk and wrapped it around her. The last thing that he needed now was for her to kick the bucket in his car. He put the car in reverse, turning it around.

"Nick?"

Nick jerked up, dazed and confused. He needed a moment to realize where he was. He remembered that he had gone to his office last night, and apparently he'd fallen asleep at his desk. Then he remembered Alex.

"Hello, Frank," he said. "What time is it?"

"Almost six." Frank stood in front of the desk.

Nick sat up straight.

"Do you know if they found Alex?"

"I don't think so." Frank shook his head. "I heard an announcement on the radio that she was missing just before I got here."

He noticed his boss's reddened eyes, his tormented face, and wondered why this woman affected Nick so deeply.

"I need to call Connors," Nick mumbled.

"You should get some sleep," Frank said. "You look terrible. Have you been sitting at your desk all night?"

"I came here at one thirty. I was with Connors until then."

"Do you think Sontheim is still alive?" Frank asked.

"I don't know," Nick whispered.

"That would be bad. Without her testimony—"

"Damn it!" Nick cut him off harshly. "I don't give a shit whether or not she testifies! I just pray to God that she's still alive!"

Frank stared at his boss in concern. He slowly began to understand that this was no longer about Vitali or uncovering this whole scandal. At this point, Nick only cared about this woman's life.

Nick's face looked desperate. He turned away from the lamplight and stroked his forehead.

"Frank…I…" His voice was hardly more than a whisper. His dark eyes were black with despair. "I…I fell in love with her, when she came to me at the cemetery and listened to me. She…she was understanding and compassionate, and suddenly I could bear everything that had happened to me. She gave me the courage to keep living; she even saved my life."

He took a sobbing breath, and Frank understood at once that Nick wasn't just feeling wretched about Alex's disappearance; he was also tormented by feelings of guilt about Mary. He watched a tear flow down Nick's cheek.

"I couldn't bear to lose Alex now as well."

Frank had never seen Nick Kostidis cry before, and to see this man whom he admired and truly liked in such pain hurt him to the depths of his soul.

Sergio sat in his office at the VITAL Building and watched a photo of Alex flash on the news. They could keep frantically searching for her all they wanted, because they'd never find her. The telephone rang. Sergio looked up. It was his private, tap-proof line that he used only for special calls.

"It's me," a male voice said on the other end of the line. "What about the woman?"

"She won't talk again," Sergio replied.

"Good. I have my hands full putting the brakes on the deputy US attorney and the mayor. It's inevitable that some people will have to be sacrificed."

"It's all right," Sergio replied calmly. "De Lancie wasn't that valuable anyway, and Whitewater was about to retire."

"Connors arrested Harding. I couldn't do anything about it."

"Harding was arrested?" Sergio froze.

"Yes, but that won't be a problem either. He won't utter a word—he's too smart for that."

"And too greedy." Sergio relaxed a bit.

"Maybe," the man laughed.

"The important thing is that you keep me out of this mess."

"Don't worry. I'll take care of it. Once enough heads have rolled, the president and the public will be satisfied. There will be heated discussions, some people will pack their bags, and then everything will be business as usual again."

"What about Kostidis?" Sergio asked.

"What about him?"

"Don't underestimate him."

"Kostidis isn't involved in the investigation, and the deputy US attorney does as I say."

Sergio nodded. "What should I do?"

"Just act normal. If the woman doesn't reappear, then the US Attorney's Office has nothing concrete but the statements. And as long as no one spills the beans, there's no trail leading to you."

"How sure can I be about that?" Sergio furrowed his brow. "They'll pressure people."

"No, I'll make sure that it doesn't happen," the man said with a quiet laugh. "We've fixed bigger things than this before. Just think of the Iran-Contra affair, or Kennedy, or Watergate."

Sergio laughed too.

"All right," he said, "everything else should be as we discussed. Once this unpleasantness is water under the bridge, then we'll take on Ortega and you'll be a hero."

"Very nice. I'll call you when I hear something new."

"Thanks," Sergio said, "I'll see you soon."

He hung up, grinning in satisfaction. That pathetic idiot from the US Attorney's Office and this bastard of a mayor should just try to keep on him! Neither of them would even get close.

Tate Jenkins entered Connors's office with a cup of coffee in his hand. The deputy US attorney sat at the conference table with a bleary-eyed expression in front of a stack of files.

"How far are your people with the indictments, Connors?" Jenkins inquired, sitting down.

"They're working on it," Lloyd Connors replied and leaned back. "But without Alex Sontheim's testimony, we have nothing but speculation."

"That woman doesn't matter anymore," Jenkins said. "The material we have is enough to remove half of the city's political elite. We already have a dozen confessions. What else do you want?"

Connors looked at the deputy director of the FBI, astonished. "I want the people who pull the strings," he said. "I want the mastermind behind this, not just the small fries."

"I don't know whether you can call the police commissioner of New York or the US attorney for the Southern District 'small fries.'" Jenkins raised his eyebrows. "Get your people moving, Connors. I don't feel like waiting until Christmas. I want the indictments on my desk by tomorrow."

"But I can't possibly go public with this whole thing tomorrow!"

"Why not?" Jenkins took a sip of coffee from his plastic cup. "We have bulletproof evidence; we should pounce before anyone disappears or blows their brains out."

"I want the mastermind," Connors persisted, "and in my opinion, that's Vitali. If it says in the newspaper tomorrow that his bribery scheme was busted, then he'll cover his tracks. We need Sontheim as a key witness against him."

"And what if she took off and doesn't surface again?" Jenkins asked. "How much longer do you want to wait, Connors? Until the whole case goes up in smoke?"

There was an awkward silence before Connors responded.

"But I—"

"Let me tell you something," Jenkins interrupted him. "Let's wait another twenty-four hours. We'll go public if she doesn't show up by then. I'm getting pressure from above. The president expects something to happen, you understand?"

"Yes, of course," the deputy US attorney said with a helpless shrug, "but if we don't get to the root of this, after a brief interruption things will just be the same again."

"You've got twenty-four hours to find the woman," Jenkins cut him off. "One full day, and not a minute more. Then we'll step in front of the press."

Jenkins finished his coffee. Connors turned to his files again. He was dead tired, and not particularly optimistic about the case. If Alex didn't show up soon, then Vitali would get away again unscathed. Connors thought about Nick, and he slowly understood his frustration. Vitali was slippery as a fish.

Alex scanned the small room. It was daylight behind the dirty curtains. She moved carefully, and sharp pain flashed through her body. She looked at her wrists and saw the blood-encrusted wounds where the restraints had cut deeply into her flesh. And suddenly the memory was there again, and the horror returned in a vicious wave, bitter as bile. She remembered all of the gruesome things that had happened to her. A tear ran down her disfigured face. She had experienced the worst things imaginable to any human being, and during those horrifying hours—where she thought she'd go crazy out of fear—something had irrevocably broken inside of her. To be at someone's mercy, the futility of being unable to defend herself, had been worse than the pain, even worse than realizing that they were trying to kill her. The wounds and bruises would heal, but what about the trauma? Just a few days ago, she was one of the highest-paid investment bankers on Wall Street, juggling billions of dollars. She knew the most important people in the city, in the entire country. Until recently, she had a bright future ahead of her. Now she had nothing left but her bare bones, and even that wouldn't be worth much if Sergio found out that she was still alive. He'd do anything to finally finish her off.

Alex curled up beneath her blanket and sobbed. Her life would never be the same again. The spirits that she had called upon herself would haunt her for her whole life. She saw no future; there was no one she could trust. Alex suddenly paused. Yes! There was someone who cared for her, someone who could possibly help her. She lay motionless in her sagging bed, the thin mattress's springs cutting into her back, and she stared at the dirty ceiling that had turned yellow from the nicotine of thousands of cigarettes. She needed to call Nick. Right now.

"Nick, I can't wait any longer," Lloyd Connors said in an emphatic voice. "I know what it means if we make this affair public today, but what the hell am I supposed to do?"

The deputy US attorney was a shadow of his usual self.

"Jenkins gave me an ultimatum, damn it! Time's running out!" He ran his hand across his exhausted face. He had come to see Nick at city hall to escape the tension in his own office for a while.

"Vitali will slip through our hands again," Nick muttered in a dull voice, "just as he has so often before. I knew it."

Connors sighed. In the past hours, he had thought about nothing else except how they could prove Vitali's involvement in the bribery scandal. But it was almost impossible without Alex Sontheim. Even van Mieren's video testimony was unlikely to be allowed as evidence in court if there weren't any other witnesses confirming his statements. And Jenkins forbade him to look for exactly that. "Focus on solving the corruption case," he had said.

Connors knew that Vitali's clever lawyers would tear him apart if he charged him without ironclad evidence. This would probably mean the premature end of his career; the other side would bombard him with actions for libel and other damages until he gave up. If Alex remained missing, then Vitali had managed to save his neck once again.

"I've got only one chance to bring him before a court," Connors said tiredly. "There's the murder case from 1963, with that Stefano Barelli who van Mieren claims Vitali shot dead. There's no statute of limitations for murder, and maybe we can find that witness van Mieren mentioned."

Nick made a resigned gesture.

"I've only got eight hours left, Nick," Connors said, leaning forward. "I'm supposed to step in front of the press and make everything public tomorrow morning."

The mayor nodded. "I understand."

"If we at least had a trace of Alex," Connors said, slamming his fist on the table, "at least a tiny clue, but we've got nothing. She simply vanished from the face of the earth."

Nick remained silent. It had been three days since Vitali got hold of her. He'd certainly killed her, because he knew how important she was to the US Attorney's Office. She was a threat and had to be eliminated as such.

"We made a big mistake involving the Feds," Connors said gloomily. "They have no interest in uncovering the whole thing."

"Of course not," Nick replied bitterly. "It's all about cover-up. Damage control. It's always been like that. No one had any interest in uncovering this bribery scandal. Everyone was afraid to be sucked into the maelstrom. Especially now that the president has major foreign policy issues, he can't afford these domestic problems. If it got out that the corruption reached as far as federal departments and the Senate, the public response would be explosive."

"But we can't just pretend that nothing happened!" Connors was appalled.

"Yes," Nick said, nodding wearily, "we can. And you will. How many times do you think I felt like I was tilting at windmills? It's not easy to do unpopular things, and there's hardly anything less popular than a bribery scandal. I've fished in troubled waters many times, and time and again I had to realize that what felt honest and seemed like the right thing to do was never appreciated by the big bosses. Politics is dirty business. Everyone gives and takes. That's how politicians and their old-boy networks survive."

"I refuse to accept that!" the deputy US attorney protested.

"I used to be as idealistic as you are, Lloyd," Nick said, shrugging his shoulders, "but if you want to have a career, then you have to learn to act against your convictions."

"Of all people, I can't believe that you would say something like that!"

"Why not? For years, I've fought for what I felt was right, and I've made many enemies. It was lucky that I was often fighting things that also bothered politicians in Washington and Albany: organized crime, insider-trading scandals on Wall Street, common criminals in New York City—all of these issues were things that had the government's support. I was fighting the small guys without a big lobby: Mafia bosses, criminal stock brokers and bankers, murderers, rapists, drug dealers. But this time we're stepping on the toes of respected politicians." Nick sighed. "One crow doesn't peck another crow's eyes. It's always been like this."

Outside the window, snowflakes fluttered from the slate-gray December sky. Nick used to love the weeks before Christmas: the festively decorated city, the shop windows, the snow in Central Park, the eagerly expectant children's eyes at the huge Christmas parade, and the ice-skaters at Rockefeller Center and at Wollman Rink. Around Christmas, the hectic pace of the city seemed to slacken for a few days every year, and the people seemed a little friendlier than usual. But Nick didn't notice any of this today. There was no Christmas tree at home, and instead of Mary, members of his staff took care of writing the Christmas cards this year. For the first time in twenty-five years, Nick wouldn't spend Christmas with Mary's family in Montauk.

Nick's direct line buzzed on his desk. He picked up.

"Mr. Kostidis?" Nick didn't recognize the female voice on the other end.

"Yes, speaking."

"Is it really you?"

"Yes, of course. Who am I speaking to?"

"One moment," the woman said, "stay on the line. There's someone who wants to talk to you."

Connors watched Nick's changing expression. His hopelessness and exhaustion vanished instantly; the mayor immediately sat up.

"Nick?" He heard her voice and he almost died of relief. It was her!

"Alex!" he exclaimed. Connors jerked upright. "Where are you? How are you doing?"

"Nick," Alex said in a thin voice, "can you come get me?"

"Yes, of course!" Nick exclaimed. "Where are you? Tell me! I'm coming right away!"

"I'm in Brooklyn," Alex replied, slurring heavily. "It's a bar called Blue Bayou at the docks near the Brooklyn-Queens Expressway."

"I'll find it. I'm leaving right away." Nick's whole body trembled.

Alex whispered, "Please hurry."

Nick jumped out of his chair. He was dizzy with relief and happiness. She wasn't dead!

"We need to drive to Brooklyn immediately!" The deputy US attorney looked at him with hope, but also suspicion.

"It sounds like a fucking trap to me," he said. "You won't go there alone. I'm calling Spooner. I want him to go with you."

Nick stared at him. In his relief, he didn't even think about the possibility that someone could have forced Alex to call and lure him into an ambush. If that was the case, then Alex's life was still in danger.

"Nick, please!" Connors already had the telephone receiver in his hand.

"Let's bring him then," Nick agreed reluctantly.

The Blue Bayou turned out to be a sleazy dive bar at the docks. The colorfully lit letters of its neon sign somewhat disguised the seediness of the joint, but it was definitely the place that Alex had told them about.

"She's supposed to be here?" Spooner raised his eyebrows.

"Is there another bar with this name near here?" Nick snarled at the officer impatiently.

"We'll check the establishment," Spooner said. "Stay in the car."

"No," Nick said as he opened the door and got out. "You stay here, Spooner."

"We have strict orders to protect you, Mr. Kostidis," Spooner's colleague Khazaeli interjected. "If this is a trap—"

"Then I have shitty luck!"

Nick slammed the car door shut. Didn't Alex risk her life for him once? He owed it to her to come to her without the two US marshals at his side. But Deputy Spooner stepped in his path.

"Mayor or not," he said, "I have my orders, and I don't feel like being suspended because of your stubbornness."

"I don't give a damn," Nick replied. "Let me through!"

He pushed the US marshal aside and walked around the building until he found the kitchen door. Under no circumstances did he want to be seen by a dozen people at this bar.

Nick knocked on the door, and Spooner and Khazaeli stood behind him.

"At least keep your weapons out of sight," Nick asked them.

"So that these guys can gun us down?" Spooner cocked his Glock. "I don't think so!"

The door opened a crack, and an unshaven, pockmarked man peeked out suspiciously.

"Are you…?"

"Yes," Nick replied impatiently. "I'm Nick Kostidis."

"And those guys?"

"US marshals," Spooner said. "Open the door, pal!"

Nick rolled his eyes. Deputy Spooner was as diplomatic as a steam-roller.

"Come in," the man said, opening the door, and Nick entered the incredibly dirty kitchen. The place made a mockery of New York's health regulations.

"Hi, Mayor Kostidis." A fat woman with a cigarette hanging out of the corner of her mouth appeared in the doorway. "I can't believe it! We all voted for you—me and my regulars."

Nick forced a smile. "I want to see Ms. Sontheim."

"Unbelievable. Ain't it, Travis?" The corpulent woman rammed her elbow into the pockmarked man's side. "The mayor himself in my place."

Nick shook with impatience.

"Travis here pulled the girl out of the river," the fat woman said, patting the man's back. "She was butt naked and half dead—the poor thing."

Nick turned pale. Had Vitali really tried to get rid of Alex in the river in classic Mafia style?

"Come with me, Mr. Kostidis." The fat woman waved to him. She planted herself in front of the two US marshals.

"You stay down here, boys," she said with an authority that tolerated no dissent. "The babe's in pretty bad shape, as you can imagine. And I'm sure that she doesn't want to see any cops."

"But—" Spooner was about to protest.

"Nope. You stay here." She heaved herself up the narrow staircase, and Nick followed her along a dimly lit hallway to a door.

"You better be nice to her," the fat woman said in a quiet voice. "She got roughed up pretty good, the poor thing. Lost her memory and had a high fever. But she's doin' better since midday today. She remembers what happened now."

Nick nodded. His heart was racing, and he would have loved to charge past the big woman.

"Hey, sweetie," she said in a surprisingly gentle way, "you got a visitor."

She stepped aside, and Nick entered the room. He didn't notice the greasy wallpaper, the worn-out carpet, the nicotine-yellow curtains, the decrepit furniture, or the red lamp that made this room what it was in the evenings: a pay-by-the-hour motel. Nick only had eyes for the slender figure that sat at the head of the bed with her arms wrapped around her knees.

"Alex! Oh my God, Alex."

Her face had been mangled terribly, looking like one big bruise. Blood had dried on her cheeks, chin, nose, and busted lips. Burst blood vessels surrounded her eyes.

"Nick," she whispered. Her eyes were filled with fear and looked nearly dead. Only a picture of misery remained of this beautiful young woman. He knelt down in front of the bed and looked at the wounds on Alex's wrists. She was wearing a jogging suit that was much too large.

Nick had a feeling that more had been destroyed than just her beautiful face. A broken human being crouched before him.

"He came to the hotel," Alex whispered. "I thought that you had come back, that's why I opened the door."

Nick frowned as he tried to hold back the tears. This was all so simply horrifying. Tears of anger rose in him and a lump caught in his throat. What unfeeling animals could do such a thing to a woman?

"I didn't tell him anything. Not a single word," Alex continued.

She was speaking mechanically; her expression was empty, trance-like.

"They beat and raped me. He said that he would kill me. I couldn't defend myself. He sat on a chair and watched, and then he…*laughed*…"

Her voice failed her. She swayed back and forth while the tears ran down her face. Nick felt a wild, powerless anger. Sergio Vitali—this brutal, merciless monster without regard for human life—had destroyed Alex. And then Nick's heart tensed when he remembered her expression of happiness back on the beach in Montauk. That seemed like light-years ago.

"Come with me, Alex." Nick extended his hand.

"If he finds out that I'm still alive," she said, her gaze wandering around the room aimlessly, "then he'll try to kill me again."

"I'll look after you, I promise you." Nick's voice sounded brave. He extended his hand patiently to her, until Alex finally let go of her knees and grabbed it.

"Oh, Nick," she suddenly sobbed. "Why did all of this have to happen? Why?"

She threw her arms around his neck, pulled her sobbing body toward him, and buried her face in his chest.

"I'll take care of you, Alex." Nick pressed his face into her hair. "I promise you, my love. I'll protect you."

He held her tight, cradling her in his arms like a baby, letting her cry. Once she calmed down a bit, he picked her up and carried her out to the hallway, where the fat woman was still on guard. Nick's eyes met with hers.

"Thanks," he said. "Thank you for your help."

"It's okay," the woman replied and stroked Alex's stringy hair. "Take good care of her."

He carried Alex down the stairs, past the marshals to the car. In the car, Alex cuddled in his arms. Her whole body shivered even though the car was warm and she was wrapped in a wool blanket. Nick murmured senseless, calming words that one might say to a child; his sympathy for her was so deep.

"Where are we going?" Deputy Spooner asked curtly.

“Goldwater Memorial on Roosevelt Island,” Nick replied, “and keep a low profile, please.”

“Of course, sir.”

As the car drove off, Nick stroked Alex’s beaten face and held her tightly in his arms. He searched for consoling words, but there was no solace. Nick remembered his own emotions all too well. In the days following Mary’s and Christopher’s deaths, he couldn’t bear to be spoken to. The lights of the Brooklyn Bridge illuminated the injuries to Alex’s face. Nick wished that he could spare her everything that was waiting for her. She would have to endure endless questioning by the US Attorney’s Office, the SEC’s investigation unit, the NYPD, the doctors, and especially the FBI. Time and again, they would force her to remember what she probably wanted to forget. Often enough during his tenure as a US attorney, Nick had had to ask such questions. He had never realized how painful they could actually be.

The news that Alex had surfaced again put Lloyd Connors into a state of sheer euphoria. His exhaustion was forgotten. With fiery zeal, he and his staff worked overnight on the indictment against Sergio Vitali. However, Alex’s murder charge had to be redacted for her to be a credible witness of the prosecution. But Oliver Skerritt’s testimony would prove Vitali’s guilt, along with St. John’s documents, and—last but not least—Nelson van Mieren’s confession that now had unexpected weight because Alex was alive. Alex had witnessed a hired assassin reporting the killing of David Zuckerman to Vitali. Vitali could not possibly wrench himself free from this accusation. It was six forty-five when Tate Jenkins stepped into Connors’s office accompanied by two men.

“Your time is almost up now, Connors,” the deputy director of the FBI said with a patronizing smile. “How far along are your people with the indictments?”

"Done," the deputy US attorney replied. "We're ready to go whenever you give the signal."

Jenkins nodded in satisfaction.

"What does your plan look like?"

"We have signed confessions from fifty-three bribed individuals," Connors explained. "There are eleven more people on the list we haven't spoken to; Whitewater is dead, and Harding still refuses to cooperate. I plan on doing nothing."

The smile vanished from Jenkins's face.

"What do you mean?"

"After talking to Mr. Engels, I've decided to investigate this without going public," Connors countered in a calm voice. "The Department of Justice shares my opinion that it's better if we don't raise too much dust. We're going to offer a plea bargain to those willing to cooperate. They'll avoid tax-evasion charges by paying the back taxes that they owe. We will refrain from prosecuting on criminal corruption charges as long as these men voluntarily resign from office and never run in the future."

"But—" Jenkins's jaw dropped in astonishment; he was struggling for words.

"Engels has spoken to the president's advisor Jordy Rosenbaum," the deputy US attorney continued, "and the president prefers this quiet solution to avoid an emotional public discussion."

Jenkins was silent for a moment. Relief was clearly etched into his face. At that moment, Connors knew for sure that his instincts hadn't failed him, and that Nick was right again. It was unbelievable. Jenkins was in league with Vitali.

"What about Vitali?" Jenkins actually asked.

"Nothing," Connors said, shrugging his shoulders. "What can we do? Given the current evidence, we can't prove anything. Until this woman reappears, I won't even think about preparing indictments that would just be thrown out due to a lack of evidence."

It was silent in the large office.

"Oh well." Jenkins cleared his throat and then smiled. "It appears I'm no longer needed in New York. However, I want you to update me regularly about the progress in this case."

"Of course." Connors nodded. "I'll keep you posted."

Nick Kostidis stood at the frosted door of the private internal medicine ward on Goldwater Memorial Hospital's third floor. He stared out the window. Ever since he'd found Alex in that sleazy dive, something had changed inside of him. The sight of her battered face, the fear and horror in her eyes, made him forget his own sorrow. Now, he felt a hot, raging fury, a wild thirst for revenge. His time of paralyzing numbness was over, and Nick knew with certainty that he wouldn't allow Vitali to get away unscathed this time.

The sun pushed through the thick cloud cover and shone on the skyscrapers behind the United Nations. Somewhere over there, Vitali was sleeping calmly, thinking that Alex was dead. Just as dead as Mary and Christopher, Britney Edwards, David Zuckerman, Clarence Whitewater, and Zachary St. John. But he was mistaken. Alex was alive and would soon overcome her shock. And he—Nick Kostidis—would do everything in his power to support her in her testimony.

Nick's eyes burned from exhaustion, but there was no time to sleep. Lloyd Connors and Gordon Engels had come to the hospital the very same night. They agreed to keep Alex's reappearance hidden for the time being. Nick and Connors managed to convince Gordon Engels that Jenkins was no longer on their team, and Engels had called the president's chief of staff and the attorney general—both of whom gave a green light to a strategy excluding the FBI from the investigation.

A few days earlier, Connors had hired a private detective to find the eyewitness to the murder Vitali had committed in 1963—at least according to van Mieren's testimony.

"I don't just want to throw Vitali into prison," Connors had said. "I want him in the electric chair." He was deeply shocked to see how brutally Vitali had treated Alex.

The frosted glass door opened, and Dr. Virginia Summer, senior physician of the internal medicine ward, stepped out. She balanced two paper cups of hot coffee. Nick had known Ginnie Summer for a long time. She'd been a friend of Mary's, and her husband was a senior partner at a much-respected law firm. Nick had studied with him back in the day at NYU. "Hello, Ginnie," Nick said. "How's Alex?"

"As good as can be expected under the circumstances," Dr. Summer said as she handed him one of the coffees. "She has broken ribs and severe contusions, but fortunately no life-threatening internal injuries. With a few days of rest and good medical attention, she'll be over the physical part of this very soon."

The doctor gave him a scrutinizing glance.

"And you?" she asked. "How are you?"

Nick looked at her; he shrugged his shoulders and stared out the window. The city that he had always loved, that he'd always fought and lived for, felt hostile all of a sudden. A sip of the hot, strong liquid revived his spirits.

"I'm doing pretty well," he replied. "I'm slowly getting used to Mary not being there when I come home."

He swallowed hard. Was it unfair to Mary that he had fallen in love with Alex? Would it have happened if she hadn't lost her life?

"You look very tired," Ginnie determined. "Go home and get some sleep. Ms. Sontheim is in good hands with us."

"I know." Nick smiled tiredly. "That's why I brought her here."

The doctor nodded.

"You seem to truly care for her," she said. "Is it true what they say about her on TV?"

"No," Nick said, shaking his head, "none of that is true."

He sat down awkwardly on an orange plastic chair, and the doctor sat next to him.

"I've never before seen you so worried," Ginnie said, "and so compassionate."

Nick turned his head and looked at her in astonishment.

"You've changed," the doctor said.

"Have I?"

"Yes," she said. "Since I've known you—almost thirty-five years now—you've always been self-involved. Many ambitious men are selfish, but it was more than that in your case. I never envied Mary being married to you."

Nick sighed.

"I admired you, regardless," Ginnie continued. "You had a vision that you fought for with all your might. You always succeeded in inspiring people with your ideas. But sometimes you were downright self-righteous and inconsiderate."

"I've realized that," Nick admitted. "I was too uncompromising and made many mistakes."

He turned the coffee cup in his hands.

"And now? Has something changed?" the doctor asked.

"Oh yes," he said. "I've been punished severely for my arrogance, and I'll have to live the rest of my life with the guilt of knowing that Mary and Chris died because of me."

He was silent for a moment.

"Alex came to me at a time when I was seriously contemplating suicide. She came and listened to me like no one else did. She wasn't afraid to talk to me. All I heard from our friends were empty phrases. All of a sudden, everyone seemed afraid of me. Only this woman, whom I hardly knew, came to me and she helped me to survive. I'm deeply indebted to Alex. She saved my life in two ways."

"I get it," the doctor said quietly.

"Do you?" Nick looked up, and Dr. Summer saw the agony in his eyes. She grabbed his hand. This revelation that he had true emotions, was capable of acting without expediency, suddenly made him likable in the doctor's eyes.

"Mary was a friend of mine," she said quietly. "I liked her so much. But she's dead, and you must live on. No one expects you to mourn forever and be lonely."

Nick stared at her. Then he frowned, as if he were about to burst into tears. He watched Ginny Summer leave behind the frosted glass door, and then he turned toward the window and leaned his forehead against the cold glass. *Self-righteous and inconsiderate. An egoist.* Yes, that's what he was. Filled with conviction about the righteousness of his actions, he'd never even considered the feelings of all the people he indicted and prosecuted. He'd been too enamored by his own success and reputation to even evaluate himself. Now, he'd received a painful lesson in humility. Fate had punished him severely for his mistakes, but it had also given him a second chance.

The posh St. Regis Hotel had become a major construction site ten days before Christmas. An army of interior decorators and craftspeople worked at full speed to transform the foyer, the ballroom, and the adjoining conference rooms into a magical winter wonderland. Truckloads of fir trees, fake snow, and countless lights hinted at how the finished space would look on Saturday evening.

The chief designer—a young interior architect with a serious face, who chain-smoked and wore her dark hair in a ponytail—walked around the hotel with a clipboard under her arm. She had the chaos totally under control, directing the electricians, the painters, the carpenters, and the decorators.

Sergio smiled happily as he saw what a work of art was being created solely for his charity ball. “Hello, Sharon. You’re doing wonders.”

“Oh, Mr. Vitali,” Sharon Capriati replied with a mixture of impatience and awe. “Do you like it so far? Just wait until everything’s finished.”

Sergio gave her a look that, in his experience, no woman could resist. The young woman threw him a cutting look and then laughed. Her austere face was pretty. Sergio wondered what she was like in bed. He examined her firm, small breasts beneath her gray T-shirt and her well-shaped behind in her skintight jeans.

“Stop!” Sharon Capriati suddenly turned around and waved at two men transporting large wall pieces on a lifting cart. “The pavilion goes over there! Next to the fir forest!”

She turned toward Sergio again, smiled apologetically, and made a note on her clipboard.

“Maybe you should have invited your guests to the Caribbean,” she said. “This is going to be quite an expensive affair.”

“That doesn’t matter,” Sergio said, shrugging his shoulders. “I want everyone to still be talking about this next year. I booked the best bands, and the food will leave everyone speechless. What about the champagne fountain?”

“It’s going to be right at the center of the ballroom,” she answered, absentmindedly sticking a pencil behind her ear. Sergio examined her closely.

“You’re doing a great job,” he remarked. “Would you like to join me for lunch today?”

“That’s very nice of you.” Sharon Capriati smiled the same impersonal smile that Alex had mastered so perfectly. “But I’m very busy. After all, you want to have a party here in twenty-four hours.”

"Maybe another time?"

Sergio felt a prickling feeling of excitement rise inside of him. This woman was a completely different type, but somehow she reminded him of Alex, with her pronounced self-confidence and professionalism. Unexpectedly, the idea occurred to him to take her to the ball as his date. He stepped closer toward her.

"I'm terribly busy before Christmas," she said, not even looking up from her clipboard and shrugging her shoulders, which annoyed him. What, was she a lesbian?

"Why don't you accompany me tomorrow evening at the party?" he said.

But instead of excitement, he received polite testiness.

"Listen, Mr. Vitali." Sharon Capriati sounded like a kindergarten teacher talking to a slow-witted child. "You hired me because I'm the city's best interior architect. I'm doing my job. That's what you pay me for. Let's leave it at that."

This clear-cut rejection left Sergio speechless.

He nodded and raised his eyebrows. "Whatever you say. I won't bother you any longer."

"Okay then." She smiled briefly, but she had already turned away and walked over to a group of electricians installing spotlights for the stage.

"Dumb bitch," Sergio muttered, offended. He walked up the stairs leading from the foyer to the ballroom and turned around on the last step. The view was just as grand as his first impression. Sergio could already tell that his party would be a success. It was the pinnacle of the holiday season in New York, and nearly a thousand guests would be arriving from all over the United States and even Europe. New York VIPs, politicians from Washington, Hollywood movie stars, famous athletes, and corporate bosses from all over were expected. But Sergio would be attending by himself, with no woman on his arm this year. Constanzia had vanished, and Alex—who had accompanied him last year—was dead. Sergio's face darkened thinking about her, and he turned around so abruptly that he almost collided with Luca.

"What's the matter?" Sergio asked him, still rankled by the interior designer's rejection. He looked Luca up and down. The otherwise calm and cold-blooded man seemed agitated.

"I just got a phone call from Sandro Girardelli," Luca said quietly. "He works in the administration of Goldwater Memorial."

"And?" Sergio suddenly had a queasy feeling in his stomach; he was overcome by a sense of foreboding.

"A woman was admitted during the night three days ago," Luca continued. "She was immediately brought to the private ward of a Dr. Virginia Summer, and the hospital administration doesn't know who she is or why she was admitted. No one from the hospital's staff is permitted to enter the room. It seems as if no one is supposed to know she's even there."

"Continue," Sergio prompted him, looking suddenly petrified.

"Two US marshals guard the room around the clock," Luca said, "but the woman has a visitor every night. It's none other than Mayor Kostidis."

"You told me that you dumped her in the river!"

Sergio struggled to keep his voice down. Alex was supposed to be dead! He'd seen with his own eyes that she had stopped breathing. There was no way she could still be alive.

"My men dumped her into the East River—at the Brooklyn docks where the current is the strongest," Luca reaffirmed. "I swear to you that she was dead."

"If this woman at Goldwater Memorial is Alex," Sergio replied grimly, "then she certainly wasn't."

Sergio's thoughts somersaulted in his head.

"I have to call Jenkins," he said, biting his lower lip. He walked quickly through the foyer of the St. Regis. Then he stopped and turned around to Luca.

"A hospital is a wonderful place to make someone disappear," he said. "You do it, Luca. You and Silvio. I don't want this to go wrong again. Go over there and blow her away. And this time, I don't want to hear any bad news, *capito*?"

Harvey Brandon Forrester was used to tracking down people who had disappeared. He had founded a private investigation practice twenty years ago, and he specialized in lost causes. His four partners preferred to limit themselves to easier cases, like following unfaithful spouses or finding defaulted debtors, but Forrester liked the more complicated cases. Strictly speaking, he was more of a bounty hunter than a private detective. Because of his excellent connections with the US Attorney's Office and many renowned law firms in New York, he couldn't complain about a lack of work. His search for the eyewitness in the 1963 murder of the gangster Stefano Barelli turned out to be more difficult than expected. Difficult because Forrester could hardly investigate in Little Italy. His client wanted to avoid anything becoming public about this investigation. Forrester had spent two long days searching the police files they'd provided him. He read the interrogation records and indictments, looked at pictures, reconstructed the sequence of events, and finally reached the conclusion that there had to be not just one eyewitness but at least six or seven. But the US Attorney's Office was looking for one man in particular: the son-in-law of the owner of the small trattoria where Barelli was shot. His name was Vincente Molto, and he'd been missing since that day.

Forrester combed through documents and electronic records to find more information about the eyewitness. Vincente Molto was born on July 24, 1940. He married Lucretia Amato in May of 1962 and left New York with his wife on May 28, 1963, for an unknown destination. So the man had to be sixty years old. Forrester browsed the police computer and got lucky. Vincente Molto had been convicted of a crime in 1961—aggravated assault. There was a picture, fingerprints. And a note in the file stating that he was suspected to be a member of the Genovese family.

Harvey Forrester spent three sleepless nights; he tapped all available sources, spoke to reliable informants, and finally traveled to Florida where he actually made a find. In Tarpon Springs, a small town outside of Tampa, he found Valentine Mills living in a small house with a view of the Gulf. Forrester watched the man for a full day before was he sure that he'd found the right person. Although Vincente Molto had gained a hundred pounds since his mug shot had been taken, the unusually bushy eyebrows and the receding chin were the same. Forrester called Lloyd Connors on the phone.

"I found your man, boss," he said. "He's living under a false name in Florida, near Tampa."

"Are you one hundred percent sure?" The deputy US attorney's voice sounded tense.

"One thousand percent," Forrester replied. "I'm never mistaken."

"Okay," Connors said, "I'll send two US marshals. Don't do anything that could give him advance warning."

Lloyd Connors could hardly believe his luck. He hadn't had particularly high hopes that Forrester would find the man that Nelson van Mieren had mentioned in his testimony. If this Molto—now Mills—was also willing to testify against Vitali, then everything would be clear-cut. The deputy US attorney smiled grimly. Maybe he could charge Vitali with the murder of Stefano Barelli. This murder, committed on March 17, 1963, was definitely a case for the electric chair. Van Mieren claimed that Barelli had tried to push Vitali out of the business. So Vitali killed him with a shot to his neck. The murder charge would be the icing on the cake when seeking a warrant for Vitali's arrest. Connors picked up the telephone and called Nick Kostidis, but his secretary said he was out of the office taking care of private business. The deputy US attorney dialed Nick's cell phone number.

"I'm on my way to the hospital right now," Nick said after he heard about Forrester's find. "I think we should move Alex to a different location."

"Is she capable of answering some questions tomorrow? I want to arrest Vitali tomorrow evening at his grand ball, and I urgently need her testimony for that," Connors replied.

"I think she's ready," Nick said.

"Good," the deputy US attorney said as he leaned back, "she's my best trump card against Vitali. Take good care of her."

Two paramedics in scrubs entered Dr. Virginia Summer's private ward at Goldwater Memorial Hospital. One of them pushed a stretcher, while the other held a clipboard under his arm.

A young doctor came out of the nurses' station.

"Hello, can I help you?" he asked.

One of the paramedics, a stocky man in his midforties, smiled in a friendly way and looked down at his clipboard.

"We're supposed to transfer one of the patients in your ward to another hospital," he said. "Ms. Alexandra Sontheim."

The doctor gave him a suspicious look.

"We don't have a patient with that name. Can I see your papers?"

The paramedic standing behind the doctor reached into his jacket pocket and pulled out a revolver with a silencer. While the doctor stared at the papers, he raised his weapon and pulled the trigger. The stocky man caught the young doctor and placed him on the stretcher, while the other entered the empty nurses' station to check out the ward's patient listings.

"Room 16 is the only one that's allegedly empty," he said.

Both men walked along the hallway until they reached room 16. They didn't waste time knocking, but entered immediately.

"Best regards from Sergio," Luca said. From a distance of about six feet, he aimed at a patient lying beneath white hospital bed linens and fired four times.

"That's it," he said, putting the weapon in his jacket pocket. Both men left the ward unseen and took the elevator to the ground floor.

Nick Kostidis and Frank Cohen entered the foyer of Goldwater Memorial Hospital accompanied by the US marshals Spooner and Khazaeli.

"Fucking idiot!" Deputy Spooner grumbled. "That guy almost hit my brand-new Dodge."

Khazaeli tried to calm his colleague down. A dark Lincoln had suddenly pulled out of a parking spot and almost hit Spooner's car in the hospital parking lot. The driver—a fat paramedic—didn't apologize and simply drove away.

"He's still an idiot!" Spooner shook his head. At that moment, the beeper on his belt went off.

"It's the head office," he announced after a quick glance at the device. "Shit. My cell phone doesn't work in the hospital."

He turned away and walked to the desk to make a phone call. Nick, Frank, and Khazaeli waited in the hall until he was done. When he saw Spooner's face, Nick was overcome by a strange feeling—a kind of dark premonition. He felt like someone had punched him in the stomach.

"What's the matter?" he asked the US marshal, struggling to control his voice.

"Something's wrong," Spooner responded with a grim face. "Boyd and Roscoe are unreachable. They're not at their post."

"Who are they?" Nick asked impatiently. Spooner didn't answer, but he disengaged his Glock's safety catch and rushed to the staircase.

"The marshals guarding Sontheim," Deputy Khazaeli said. He also pulled out his gun and pressed the elevator call button. Nick turned ice cold. All the color vanished from his face.

"What's that supposed to mean?" Frank asked as they got into the elevator with two nurses, who were staring aghast at Khazaeli's pistol.

"I don't know," the US marshal replied. "Both of you wait in the elevator until we figure this out."

Nick's whole body began to shake. The elevator stopped on the third floor with a quiet ring.

"Stay here!" Khazaeli repeated, but Nick shook his head.

"I certainly won't," he replied.

"Damn it!" Tension was etched into the US marshal's face. "I don't want to argue with you! Do what you want!"

Frank objected, but Nick wasn't listening. "Nick, maybe we really should—"

Nick's dark eyes were black with fear. He felt like charging past the officers. At that moment, the private ward's glass door was flung open, and a young nurse came out screaming.

"Dr. Walters!" she screamed. "Dr. Walters is dead!"

Spooner and Khazaeli ran past her, with Nick and Frank following. In front of the nurses' station a collapsible stretcher held a man whose eyes were wide open. Blood dripped from his half-closed mouth onto the light-gray linoleum floor. Terrified doctors and nurses were shouting hysterically and some were crying. Frank, who couldn't stand the sight of blood, fought his nausea and turned away.

"Which room is Sontheim in?" Deputy Spooner yelled at Nick.

"Sixteen," Nick whispered. His heart was racing: his mind refused to accept what seemed obvious after seeing the murdered doctor. Vitali had heard that Alex was still alive and didn't hesitate. His killers had already finished their bloody job. Ginnie Summer was suddenly standing in front of him. Her usually friendly face looked shocked, terrified.

“Nick!” she shouted in a shrill voice, grabbing his arm. “What’s going on here?” Who did this?”

“I…I don’t know.” His watched as the two marshals as they ran down the hallway, then returned his gaze to the dead doctor. He didn’t want to know what had just happened in room 16. He didn’t want to see Alex’s body riddled with bullets. He had failed once again. Hadn’t he promised that he would protect her?

“Nick…” Frank touched his arm, and the mayor flinched.

“Mr. Kostidis!” Deputy Spooner shouted at the same moment and waved to him.

“No,” Nick whispered, “please, please don’t…”

The few steps to the door of Alex’s room felt like miles to Nick. But he registered that Spooner looked relieved; soon he was staring uncomprehendingly at a bed riddled with bullets.

“Someone stuffed blankets and pillows beneath the bedding,” Deputy Khazaeli explained. “The killers probably thought it was a human body and blazed away at it.”

“But where is she?” Nick whispered.

“Here,” Spooner said, “she seems to be okay.”

Alex cowered on the floor of the adjoining small bathroom, her arms wrapped around her knees, staring at him with wide, frightened eyes. When she realized it was Nick, she silently extended her arms, and he fell on his knees in front of her. His relief was overwhelming as Alex flung her arms around his neck and pressed her face against his chest.

“I’m so sorry,” Nick whispered in a tearful voice. “I’m so sorry. I promised that you would be safe here.”

“Please get me out of here.”

“I will,” Nick said as he stroked her hair. “Don’t cry—everything will be all right.”

Gordon Engels accompanied them out to the hallway with five US marshals.

"Is she all right?" he inquired.

"Yes," Nick replied, "but what about your people who were supposed to guard her?"

"They're both dead," Engels said, his expression frozen. "I don't know yet how it happened, but they were both shot in the neck just like the doctor. We found their bodies in the laundry room."

Nick felt Alex shudder in his arms.

"I know who shot them," she whispered. "I was just about to leave the room. I don't know why, but I had a really strange feeling. Then I saw the doctor standing in the hallway with two paramedics. One of them suddenly pulled out a gun, and from behind, he shot the doctor in the head. I knew they were here for me because I recognized them."

She started sobbing.

"Who were they?" Nick asked in soft voice.

"Sergio's closest men. Luca di Varese. Silvio Bacchiocchi."

The bloody murders at Goldwater Memorial Hospital dominated news broadcasts that day. Camera teams from all over the country besieged the hospital building. Gordon Engels decided to disseminate false information in order to protect Alex. He announced to the waiting television reporters and journalists that unidentified perpetrators who fled the scene had shot two police officers, a doctor, and a hospital patient for no apparent reason. Engels assumed that both perpetrators wouldn't go into hiding because they believed they were unidentified; he knew they'd be arrested the following evening. Nick took Alex to the St. Ignatius monastery. She'd be safe behind the Jesuit monastery's fortresslike walls.

Alex wore a gray hooded sweatshirt and jeans. Her hair was tied in a simple ponytail. Traces of terrible abuse were still clearly visible on her face. For the questioning by the US attorneys, the Jesuit fathers provided a large room, empty save for a table and chairs. Punctually at seven in the morning, Lloyd Connors and Royce Shepard from the US Attorney's Office arrived at the monastery accompanied by Gordon Engels and Truman McDeere. Nick and Frank Cohen were there of course, and Nick felt a sting in his heart as Alex entered the room accompanied by Oliver Skerritt. He had his arm protectively around her shoulders and only reluctantly let go of her when the questioning commenced. The deputy US attorney introduced himself and his colleagues and then asked Alex if she had any objections to them recording the conversation on tape.

"Ms. Sontheim," Lloyd Connors began, "because of the urgency of this situation, we've decided to postpone the questioning by the SEC. Mr. Kostidis told me that you waive your right to legal representation. Is that correct?"

"Yes." Alex's voice sounded firm. She sat upright, her hands placed on the table in front of her, looking at the deputy US attorney attentively.

Connors cleared his throat. "The sole purpose of today's questioning is to compile evidence of Mr. Sergio Vitali's involvement in this bribery affair. You could potentially serve as the prosecution's key witness should there be a court trial. At this point, you may be the only person testifying. Please tell us briefly about your job at LMI."

Alex nodded and gave them the information they needed. She recounted Levy's propositions. She recalled all of the deals she had closed for LMI, and identified those from which Levy and Vitali illegally profited, with the help of St. John. She told them about the first time that she suspected someone was conducting secret deals with her information behind her back, and she described the trap that she'd set for St. John with Syncrotron. She made no secret of her relationship with Vitali. Then she told them about the birthday party at his house in Mount Kisco, where she accidentally overheard the conversation between Sergio and the man with the yellow eyes. Truman McDeere frowned, but he remained silent. Alex spoke in an emotionless voice, never averting her eyes from Connors.

"What can you tell us about the night Mr. Vitali was shot?"

"Everything," she said. "I was there."

Alex told them how Nick had warned her that afternoon about Sergio's conflict with the Colombian drug cartel. She gave a detailed description of the assassination attempt and described the warehouse in Brooklyn where she'd been taken. Gordon Engels had been silent until then, but he asked a few questions.

Finally, Connors asked her to tell them how she became aware of the corruption conspiracy. Alex drank a sip of water and then recounted her inquiries and how they all led to dubious stock purchases through an investment firm called MPM. She told them about her trip to MIT, where she learned about the secret accounts on Grand Cayman and Vitali's involvement in MPM. The deputy US attorney appeared to be satisfied with her statement.

"Let's go back to the events of the night that Mr. St. John was shot dead," Connors said. "What really happened?"

Alex related all the significant details.

"Why didn't you inform the police?" Royce Shepard asked.

"I knew that Vitali had paid off the police commissioner and also the US attorney. I was afraid of him."

"Where did the money go?"

"I changed the transactions to my name," Alex said. "I knew who the money belonged to, and I thought that it might come in handy as protection. It was clear to me as I read the e-mails on his computer that St. John didn't commit suicide. Vitali had him killed because he feared that he'd blow everything up. He planned to disguise his death as a suicide, but then he had a better idea. He could kill two birds with one stone by pinning the murder on me. St. John was dead, and I'd be discredited as a witness."

"Where's the money now?"

"I placed it in foreign accounts."

"Why did you leave the country even though St. John's statements proved you were innocent?" Engels asked.

"Who could I have proved it to?" Alex frowned, shrugging her shoulders. "No one would have believed me because Vitali had the right men on his side. I would have been arrested, and Vitali's people would probably have killed me while I was in custody. Think about what he did to his own son."

"What happened the day you disappeared from the Portland Square Hotel?" Connors inquired, and Alex lowered her gaze. Nick felt horrible. In the past, when he'd asked questions like this, he had no idea how painful they were. Each answer forced the person to relive the dread and horror.

"Mr. Vitali barged into my room with four of his men." She spoke in an expressionless voice. "He beat me and had them tie me up. He left no doubt that he would kill me as soon as he heard everything that he wanted to know."

All of the men in the room were silent.

"Vitali tried to force me to tell him everything that I'm telling you now. Then he beat me again and had his men beat and rape me. When he thought I was dead, they dumped me in the East River."

Nick couldn't take it anymore. For the first time since Alex had entered the room, she looked at him and saw that he seemed almost as tormented as she did.

"It's okay, Nick," she said quietly. "I want this guy prosecuted."

"I'm sorry we couldn't spare you this, Ms. Sontheim." Connors's voice sounded apologetic. "But with your testimony, we'll be able to charge Mr. Vitali with multiple crimes. I don't want to risk letting him slip through our fingers again."

Alex nodded.

"Are you willing to testify against him in court?"

Alex nodded again.

There was complete silence in the large room.

"Are you aware how dangerous such a testimony could be for you?"

"Yes," Alex replied calmly, "I am. But I'm not afraid anymore. I won't hide, and I don't want a new identity. He will find me wherever I go. I'll testify against him."

The interrogation ended at twelve thirty. Nick and Frank drove to city hall, and the US attorneys started to prepare the arrest warrants. Alex not only identified David Zuckerman's killer in photographs, but also the men who had raped her. She also identified Luca di Varese and Silvio Bacchiocchi as the murderers of the US marshals and the doctor at Goldwater Memorial. After that, twenty-three attorneys worked nonstop on the indictments and the arrest warrants until evening. They would drop the bomb in a few hours. Vitali had no clue that many of his "friends" had come to the St. Regis that evening because the US Attorney's Office had forced them to. Very soon, the handcuffs would click around his wrists. Connors was determined to make sure that Sergio Vitali would never ever get out of prison.

Nick left his office at city hall in the late afternoon accompanied by two bodyguards. Connors asked Nick to come with him to the St. Regis to witness Vitali's arrest, but Nick declined. He was tired, burned out. It suddenly seemed that he'd been robbed of all perspective, and he lost his ability to make even the simplest decisions. The past weeks and days had drained him, and now—with the goal that he'd doggedly pursued for so many years finally within his grasp—he realized that it no longer mattered to him. The price he had paid was too high. There was no one left with whom he could share the triumph of Vitali's arrest.

And then there was Alex. Nick had a feeling that she would leave the city when this nightmare was over; he could understand why she wouldn't want to live in this place anymore. She was still young and could start a new life somewhere else, allowing these ghastly events to become a dark shadow of the past. Maybe she had a chance with Oliver Skerritt, who apparently loved her and wasn't leaving her side.

As his limousine crawled across the Brooklyn Bridge, Nick contemplated his own future. He still had one more year ahead of him as the mayor of this city that he both loved and hated. He would get through this year, because he owed it to the people who had elected him. Then he would be fifty-five years old. He could join a law firm, or even turn his back on New York and start a new life somewhere else.

His thoughts involuntarily drifted back to Alex. How strange life is! He ultimately had Vitali to thank, of all people, for having met her. Dusk was falling as the limousine passed through the entrance gate of the St. Ignatius monastery. Before Nick went to Father Kevin, he turned into the cloistered courtyard to visit the cemetery. There was no one left for him to talk to, but he felt that Mary listened to him when he visited her grave.

As the door to the cloister opened, he caught sight of Alex and Oliver Skerritt sitting on a bench beneath the bare branches of a mighty chestnut tree. The courtyard they sat in was illuminated by the last rays of the setting December sun. He felt a painful sting in his heart when he saw Oliver putting his arm around Alex's shoulders. He stared at them for a moment; then he closed the door silently and took a different path to the cemetery.

On that bench in the courtyard, Oliver silently held Alex's hand. Too many horrible things had happened, and the memories were too fresh to talk about.

"Why didn't I listen to you?" Alex said in a quiet voice. "All of the things that happened to you were my fault. Mark and Justin might not even be alive."

Oliver turned his head and looked at her. Everything that had happened between them seemed like a different life.

"Mark knew what he was getting himself into," he replied. "Justin did too, and so did I. You never left any doubt that things could get dangerous."

She didn't react to his words; it was almost as if she hadn't heard them. There was a lost expression on her pale face. Oliver put his arm around her shoulders again. She leaned slightly against him and closed her eyes.

"What will you do once all of this is over?" he asked.

"I don't know," Alex replied tiredly. "I don't know anything anymore. How about you?"

"I'm finished with New York," Oliver said. "I'll sell my loft and go back home to my parents. My dad's getting old, so maybe I'll take over his fishing fleet. And write a book. I definitely have enough material now."

Alex smiled softly and opened her eyes again.

"Come with me to Maine," Oliver suggested, "at least for a while."

"To Maine," Alex said and sighed. "That sounds far away enough from all of this."

They were silent for a while. The pale December sun vanished behind the monastery's church tower. It grew cold.

"I know that this probably isn't the right moment," Oliver whispered, "but I want you to know how much I care for you."

Alex bit her lip and swallowed. Then she looked at him.

"I really like you, Oliver. But..." She fell silent searching for the right words.

"Alex, I don't mean to put you under pressure in any way. You don't owe me anything, but you should know that you're the most wonderful woman I've ever met. I could live with it if you told me you didn't love me, but I wouldn't forgive myself if I didn't try."

He smiled sadly, and she turned and looked at him.

"You love Kostidis, right?" he asked quietly. He found no answer in Alex's green eyes, but then she slowly nodded.

"I think so," she replied.

"He loves you. I probably don't have a chance against him."

Suddenly, Alex wrapped her arms around his neck.

"I wish that we'd met under different circumstances. I wish that I'd stayed away from Vitali. I wish that I never heard of LMI, SeaStar-Friends, and all these things. Sometimes I wish that I had never come here from Germany."

Oliver took her in his arms and held her tight.

"Who knows what good any of this did." He gently lifted her face and looked at her for a long time.

"Do you promise that we'll remain friends?"

"Yes." Alex nodded seriously. "I promise you that. We will stay good friends. Forever."

He smiled and carefully kissed her cheek.

The church bells started chiming.

"We should go inside," Oliver said. "Otherwise, we'll catch cold."

They stood up, and Alex put her hands into her jacket pockets.

"I'm going for a little walk," she said. "I need to be alone for a few minutes."

Oliver looked after her as she crossed the courtyard, disappearing in the cloister's darkness. It hurt him to see her so broken, so tormented, but he had long since realized that he wasn't the one who could give her the comfort that she needed.

On the way to his family's gravesite, Nick Kostidis didn't encounter a single soul. The noise of the city was muffled by the thick walls. A few mockingbirds argued loudly in the tall yew trees, and two gray squirrels chased each other in the tops of the old oaks. The sun had melted the snow and left just a few remnants beneath the trees and in the shadow of the wall. It would snow again that evening. The clear, cold air smelled like it. Nick sat on the bench and stared at the gravestones, etched with the names of his entire family: his father, mother, two brothers, and now also Mary and Christopher. The pain of their loss overcame him so unexpectedly and violently that tears sprang to his eyes. He bent his head back and stared up at the sky. It was almost dark in the east. The first stars sparkled coldly and inaccessibly from afar, and the pale crescent moon announced the coming night. This was the night that would bring Sergio Vitali's demise. An airplane passed silently, high above in the sky. The setting sun illuminated it and made its metallic body sparkle. How wonderfully quiet it was here! The cemetery was an oasis of peace and tranquility. Nick wasn't frightened by the thought of sitting among all these dead people. The prospect of one day overcoming all doubt and sorrow calmed him.

"They'll arrest him tonight, Mary," he said quietly. "Today is the day that I've dreamed of for so long. Maybe I should rejoice, but I can't. This was supposed to be my victory, but the victory is bittersweet."

Nick shivered in the cutting cold of the December evening.

"Oh, Mary," he exclaimed, "why didn't I take more time for all of you? I keep thinking that I didn't give you a good life. Why did I work so much and leave you alone? In all those years, you never complained."

A tear rolled down his cheek.

"I always thought that we had so much time left, but suddenly… suddenly we ran out of time. Can you forgive me, Mary? I know these are just empty words, but if I had a chance to do things differently, I would."

He felt so completely alone; he covered his face with his hands and sobbed. His guilty feelings were worse than the loss, even worse than his own terrible regrets. He was forced to suffer for everything that he'd missed out on with Mary. And still, Nick couldn't help it that his grief for his family was mixed with a longing for Alex. It seemed inappropriate to him, almost like a betrayal, to be thinking about another woman at his wife's grave.

He suddenly noticed a movement in the distance and raised his head. His heart started pounding when he saw Alex, strolling along the path, her head lowered and her hands dug deep in the pockets of her jacket. When she noticed his gaze, she walked over to him.

"I didn't even know you were here," she said quietly. "I thought you'd be there for the arrest."

"No," Nick said, shaking his head and quickly wiping away his tears with the back of his hand. "That's none of my business anymore."

Alex looked at him for a long time.

"Sit down," he invited her. She hesitated.

"I don't want to bother you."

"You're not bothering me." He reached out his hand for her, and she sat next to him on the edge of the bench. In the fading daylight, her face looked almost as beautiful as before. They sat there in silence for a while.

"You should be there tonight," Alex finally said. "You fought for this for so many years."

"Did I really fight for this?" Nick shrugged his shoulders. "If I did, then I was wrong. It cost me everything I had."

Alex turned toward him, and their eyes locked.

"Nick," she said, almost shyly taking his hand, "I want to thank you—for everything that you've done for me."

The sad, depressed expression in her eyes seemed to mirror the state of his own soul. Here they were now—two human beings treated unpleasantly by fate. After just barely escaping death, both of them would never view life the same way again. Both were devastated—marked forever by their experience, now condemned to be outsiders. For Nick, everything that was essential to him before now seemed unimportant: his reputation, other people's opinions, absolute justice. Nothing was perfect or absolute in this world. Nick could live with this. He had no other choice. He'd lived the majority of his life, had celebrated great successes and triumphs over the course of a distinguished career. He was thankful for everything. He had more modest plans for his future, but what about Alex? She was still so young! Could she keep living with what she had experienced? Was she strong enough to forget what had happened?

"Why didn't I listen to you before?" Alex broke the silence.

"You mean when we met at the Plaza?"

"Yes. You warned me about him, but I didn't want to listen."

Nick shrugged his shoulders.

"We have to have painful experiences on our own. Well-meant advice doesn't replace life experience."

"I did everything wrong," Alex said and sighed. "I was arrogant and vain and enamored with success."

"Don't blame yourself. Vitali and Levy are criminals, and they'll get their just punishment. St. John also knew what he was getting himself into—trust me. Sooner or later, Vitali's entire empire would have collapsed anyway. Not only because of you, but thanks to Nelson van Mieren's testimony."

"I'm still so discouraged. I can't stand the guilt."

"I also keep blaming myself," Nick said. "I wonder why my family had to die and I'm allowed to live. There's no answer."

Alex gave him a steadfast look.

"On the evening when you returned to the city," Nick said quietly, "I was so happy. I was so relieved that nothing had happened to you. I was totally overwhelmed by my feelings. But then I felt guilty, because Mary is dead and will never feel happiness again."

Alex sighed. Her breath drifted like a white cloud in the ice-cold air.

"Do you think that they will convict Sergio?"

"There is no way out for him this time," Nick said with conviction. "I'm sorry that you have to go through all of this. The trial, the media hype, the slander of the defense trying to discredit you in every possible way."

"I don't care." Alex let go of his hand. "It will give me satisfaction to see him tried. He hurt and humiliated me so deeply that every part of me is screaming for revenge. Something inside of me is broken forever. How could things get any worse?"

She shuddered.

"You're cold," Nick observed. "Let's go inside."

They stood up and walked slowly back to the monastery buildings. When they reached the church's side entrance, Alex stopped. It was almost dark now.

"Will I see you again?" she asked. Alex's eyes seemed unnaturally large in her pale, thin face. Nick thought about Oliver Skerritt. How he sat on the bench earlier today with his arm around her shoulders.

"I don't know if that's a good idea," he replied.

"But I want to see you again," she whispered.

After hesitating briefly, Nick nodded. "I need to go to Father Kevin, but it'll only be for an hour."

They entered the church. A slight smell of incense and fir boughs was in the air, reminding them that Christmas was just around the corner. The old Jesuit priest's steps on the church's polished marble floor echoed. Behind the high altar, they turned into the church's side aisle. They entered the cloister through a small gateway connecting the church with the other monastery buildings, and went their separate ways.

Walking to her room in the monastery, Alex thought about Sergio. Today was his big day. She had accompanied him to the ball last year, and she remembered the magnificent party vividly. How arrogant and confident she had been back then! And Sergio…she felt a chill as she thought about him. At this moment, he was probably about to leave for the St. Regis looking handsome, meticulously dressed, and in the best of moods—with no clue what awaited him tonight. Or did he have a premonition? Had something leaked through somewhere? Maybe he had been warned and was on his way to South America or Europe. Alex felt a chill at the thought that he might escape. As long as he was free man, she wouldn't be safe anywhere. Not even here behind the thick walls of this monastery.

Sergio Vitali stood in the gallery of the grand ballroom, looking around in satisfaction. The big charity ball had been organized by his VitalAid Foundation on behalf of disabled children. It was in its fifteenth year and was already a complete success. Every year was more magnificent than the last and its invitations more coveted. Sergio smiled. Even though Sharon Capriati had turned out to be a bitch, she was a true master of her trade. She had created the perfect scenery in just forty-eight hours: snow-covered pavilions and small forests, ice sculptures, and millions of Christmas lights and candles had transformed the bland ballroom, foyer, and adjoining rooms into a winter wonderland. The buffet table was loaded with the most exquisite delicacies prepared by the chefs of the hotel's own posh Lespinasse restaurant, and the most expensive French champagne bubbled from the fountain.

Sergio Vitali couldn't care less that Vincent Levy didn't attend the ball this year. Clarence Whitewater was also missing and—unfortunately—also Nelson van Mieren. But that's the way things were. Some people left, others joined. Sergio understood perfectly well how to select new people he could use. Even if some ambitious, young US attorney tried to shake his throne, it didn't bother him much. Nick Kostidis had tried to take a crack at him in the past; now it was someone else. But none of them stood a chance. He had the better connections, and this ball was the ultimate proof of his unshakable power. Storms came and went. Some people were sucked up by them and swept away. But he—Sergio Vitali—withstood them all. He was untouchable.

Four men sat in an inconspicuous dark Chevy across from the St. Regis and observed the guests' arrival. They didn't talk much, and their faces were tense. Shortly after ten, the message the men were waiting for was transmitted over the radio.

"All units are at their posts," the voice squawked from Deputy Spooner's radio. "The entire building is sealed off."

"What about Vitali's people?" the US marshal asked in return.

"They won't notice. They're busy with the events at the hotel."

US Attorney Lloyd Connors exchanged a glance with Gordon Engels.

"Okay. We're going in," he said curtly, grabbing a briefcase that was sitting by his feet. His heart was beating in his throat, and he noticed his palms were clammy from the excitement. The time had come. Nothing should go wrong. Deputy Spooner pressed the button on his walkie-talkie.

"To all units," he said. "We're coming in through the main entrance. Team C and D will follow, and secure the entrance, the elevators, and the foyer. Keep it low-key, understood?"

He waited for acknowledgment from his men, and then he nodded. The four men got out and crossed Fifth Avenue at Fifty-Fifth Street. Then they entered the Beaux-Arts-style hotel. Another group of four men got out of a vehicle parked further up the street. As was typical of a big society event held in New York, onlookers and press people were gathered behind barriers. Vitali's security personnel denied access to any unauthorized person, but Spooner had prepared for that in his minutely detailed operation plan. Each of his men knew the stakes. They were intercepted at the magnificently decorated foyer's entrance by these men, who'd exchanged their regular suits for tuxedos on this festive occasion.

"Can I see your invitations, please?" one of the bodyguards asked.

"US Marshals Service." Engels pulled out his badge.

"I can't let you in if you don't have an invitation." The blond, broad-shouldered man shrugged apologetically.

"Step aside," Lloyd Connors said, "I'm the US attorney for the Southern District of New York. I'm here on official business."

"Sorry, but I have orders—"

"What's going on here?" A brawny, grim-faced man with a walrus moustache appeared behind the blond giant, reinforced by an army of bodyguards.

"Who are you, and what do want here without an invitation?"

"We're here to see Mr. Vitali," Lloyd Connors countered.

"Mr. Vitali is busy at the moment," snarled the fat guy—who wasn't the least bit intimidated by the appearance of multiple US attorneys and US marshals. "Come to his office on Monday."

"Fine, if you want trouble." Connors smiled thinly. "Deputy, arrest these men for obstruction of justice."

He pushed his way through the group of bodyguards, who watched with dropped jaws as handcuffs clicked around their boss's wrists.

"Wow." Deputy Spooner whistled through his teeth as he stepped into the ballroom. "So this is what a party for the upper crust looks like! Holy smokes!"

With fully loaded trays, liveried waiters made their way from one magnificently decorated table to another as ladies in the finest designer gowns and gentlemen in tuxedos with tails enjoyed lobster bisque, salmon mousse, filet mignon, and truffles.

"I prefer a comfortable barbecue," Lloyd Connors answered dryly, looking around the gigantic ballroom.

A full orchestra played onstage, and the guests sitting at tables on various levels of the ballroom were in a splendid mood.

"I'd like to know how many insurance companies are sweating blood tonight that all this stuff gets returned safely," Deputy Spooner observed with his usual sarcasm.

"Keep your eyes peeled for Vitali," Connors said. "I don't want anyone to warn him before we find him."

The US attorney was trembling with excitement. If something went wrong and Vitali escaped, every effort of the recent weeks would be in vain—not to mention the fact that he might be forced to resign tomorrow.

"Over there!" Royce Shepard whispered. "The table at the very top of the gallery. That's him."

"I see him." Connors nodded with grim determination. "Come on, let's get him!"

They shoved their way through guests, who responded with indignant remarks and looks.

"The complete corrupt gang in one pile," Deputy Spooner said with a grin. "A thousand years of prison time sitting here. It's too bad that we can't take all of them with us at once."

The monastery's guest room was slightly larger than the simple cells in which the Jesuit priests lived. It had its own shower and toilet, which was an unheard-of luxury for the priests. That morning, Frank Cohen had brought Alex the suitcase she had left behind at the Portland Square Hotel. Alex stepped under the hot water of the shower. She still thought she smelled the sharp stench of men's sweat on her skin. Just as she was drying herself off, someone knocked on the door. She wrapped the towel around her body and opened the door just a crack. Her heart jumped when she saw Nick in the dim of the hallway.

"Wait a second," she said.

After she got dressed, he came inside.

Alex realized that she wasn't the only one who had gone through hell in the past days. She could see the exhaustion in Nick's face, his tired eyes and the dark circles beneath them.

"You look very tired," Alex said quietly.

"I am," Nick admitted. "I'm very tired. I'm longing for the days when I can get some sleep again."

He sighed.

"Come and sit down for a moment," Alex offered. Nick sat down on the edge of the bed. There was no other place to sit in the small room.

"I can handle it pretty well during the day because I'm distracted, but the loneliness sets in at night, and the nightmares full of explosions come with it."

There was no bitterness in his voice, just resignation. Alex nodded slowly. She knew all too well what Nick was talking about because she felt the same way. The demons were faint during the day, but they came to life in the darkness and silence of the night. Then she heard the laughter of the men and their voices and saw their cruel, indifferent eyes.

"You're freezing," Nick sensed. It was cold in the small room because the heater gave off very little warmth. "I…I should leave now."

"No," Alex said and pleadingly put her hand on his arm, "please don't. Stay awhile."

Nick thought about Oliver Skerritt. It wasn't right for him to be here.

"Alex," he said, "I don't want to—"

"Just wait a moment," she interrupted him. "Please. I'll be right back."

"Okay." Nick still hesitated, but then he nodded. Alex disappeared into the tiny bathroom and dried her wet hair. When she returned after a few minutes of primping, Nick was stretched out on the bed, sound asleep. Alex felt a deep tenderness for him. Should she wake him? No. He was so tired, so exhausted. She carefully took off his shoes, loosened his tie, and covered him with a blanket.

Then she sat on the floor, leaned against the wall, and wrapped her arms around her knees. So this is where they'd ended up. Nick Kostidis, one of the city's most powerful and famous men, and Alex Sontheim, clever and intelligent Wall Street star. Like Icarus, they'd aimed too high and crashed. What was left of their former glory? Alex could hardly comprehend what had driven her to work those hundred-hour weeks. There wasn't much left of the enticing feeling of success besides a bad aftertaste. Fueled by her ambition, she had refused to look beyond the shiny facades of material success. She had ignored every warning. Alex thought about Mark, Justin, and Oliver—who had confessed his love to her…Should she go to Maine with him?

Nick shifted a little. Asleep, he looked more relaxed and peaceful than she'd ever seen him before. He was no longer a stranger to her, but this had nothing to do with their night of passion. Their friendship had just gotten deeper that night. Alex felt safe and comfortable in Nick's presence. She trusted him like she'd never trusted anyone before. She didn't have to pretend around Nick; with him, she could be who she really was. And although Alex knew that she loved him, she was aware of the wide chasm that divided them. All of New York City stood between her and Nick Kostidis. She needed to turn her back on this city if she wanted to have a future, and that's exactly what Nick couldn't do. New York was his life, and Alex had accepted that long ago.

It was almost midnight, and Alex was so tired that she could barely keep her eyes open. She switched off the light, and the bright moonlight cast a dim glow over the room. Alex lay on the bed next to Nick. She felt his body's comforting warmth, and as he moved in his sleep, she wrapped an arm around him. She was determined to stay awake to enjoy these precious hours, but after a few minutes she fell asleep.

Sergio Vitali sat between a princess from Monaco and Cassandra Goldstein, billionaire Simon Goldstein's widow. He was in a splendid mood. His table guests included New York construction tycoon Charlie Rosenbaum, the oil billionaire James Earl Freyberg III, Secretary of State Oliver Kravitz, Senators Ted Willings and Fred Hoffman, Governor Rhodes, *Time* magazine publisher Carey Newberg, and Hollywood diva Liza Gaynor.

Lloyd Connors wasn't particularly surprised to see Tate Jenkins also sitting there. The deputy director of the FBI certainly was astonished to see the US attorney coming up the small stairs leading to the gallery. Jenkins turned pale. Connors stepped toward the table, and the orchestra stopped playing abruptly, as though it had been given a signal.

"Mr. Vitali?" Connors cleared his throat. He noticed that his nervousness had disappeared. He had imagined this scenario hundreds of times. He felt like an actor playing a well-rehearsed role at the premiere, but the play had become reality. Sergio Vitali looked up indignantly.

"Lloyd Connors from the US Attorney's Office in Manhattan."

"I know who you are," Vitali replied, his smile failing to reach his cold eyes. "I don't remember seeing your name on the guest list."

"That's right," Lloyd Connors said, "I'm here on official business. I'd like to talk to you for a moment."

From the corner of his eye, he saw the awkward faces of Governor Rhodes and Senator Hoffman—both of whom would have loved to crawl into a hole in the wall. Vitali didn't seem to be particularly disturbed by the US attorney's appearance. No one could have ratted him out.

"Can't you see that I have guests?" he said condescendingly. "I'm busy now. But help yourself to the buffet. It would probably be a welcome change from the cafeteria at the US Attorney's Office."

Only Charlie Rosenbaum and James Earl Freyberg III laughed.

"I must insist that you—"

"Listen, Connors." The mask of friendliness fell off of Vitali's face. "I don't have time right now."

His eyes narrowed as he saw Gordon Engels coming up the stairs in the company of Spooner and Khazaeli. His gaze drifted to Tate Jenkins, but the man was staring down at the table looking petrified. All conversation around the table fell silent.

The US attorney shrugged his shoulders. "Fine, if you prefer it this way. Mr. Vitali, I have a warrant for your arrest."

"Excuse me?" Sergio Vitali froze, his face flushed. "You're joking, pal! Leave with your people before I have you thrown out!"

Unmoved, Connors unfolded the paper.

"Mr. Vitali," he said in a businesslike voice, "you're under arrest for the murder of Stefano Barelli."

It was dead silent around the table.

"What the hell?" Vitali's face turned a darker red.

His guests avoided looking directly at their host. Spooner and Khazaeli walked around the table and stood behind him.

"US Marshals Service." Spooner held his badge under Vitali's nose. "Would you stand up please?"

Vitali gesticulated as if chasing away an insect, but he stood up.

"How dare you?" he exclaimed. "This is absolutely ridiculous!"

His face alternated between red and pale, and fine beads of sweat appeared on his forehead.

"Come with me, Mr. Vitali." Connors said coldly. "You're under arrest."

Sergio Vitali turned toward his guests.

"This is a regrettable misunderstanding that will be cleared up very quickly."

Spooner took advantage of the opportunity and clicked the handcuffs around Vitali's wrists, causing him to turn around angrily.

"Come on, mister," he said, "let's go."

"You have the right to remain silent..." Deputy Khazaeli started with the usual admonition, but Vitali interrupted him angrily.

"Save your breath," he snapped. "I want to speak to my lawyer immediately!"

In the meantime, the news had gone around that something unusual was happening at the host's table. A pin drop could have been heard in the gigantic ballroom.

"This will have consequences for you!" Sergio Vitali hissed as Spooner led him past Connors. The US attorney simply shrugged his shoulders. He was about to turn away, when Gordon Engels held him back.

"Wait a moment," Engels said. "I need to take care of something else."

Connors looked at Engels in astonishment as he headed toward Tate Jenkins.

"Mr. Jenkins," Gordon Engels said, "you are also under arrest. You're charged as an accessory to the murder of David Zuckerman and with aiding and abetting organized crime."

The deputy director of the FBI stood up without saying a word. His expressionless face showed that he understood. They had his number. Connors stared at Gordon Engels open-mouthed.

"Deputy Khazaeli," the US attorney general said to his officer, "arrest this man and read him his rights."

"Gordon," Connors murmured, "I don't quite understand."

"We have suspected Jenkins for quite a while," Engels replied quietly. "Two nights ago, we tapped a phone conversation between Jenkins and Vitali. That was the final proof we needed. Jenkins has been Vitali's man for years."

"I can't believe it." Connors shook his head in disbelief. "Nick's really been right all along."

"Yes," Engels replied, "Kostidis had been right all these years. But his hard luck was that he lacked hard evidence."

The guests of the VitalAid Foundation's charity ball watched in shock as their host and his guest were led though the large hall in handcuffs. No one moved from their seat, and the room remained dead silent until the men walked out to the foyer. Only then did people awake from their shock, and all hell broke loose.

Connors could hardly suppress a smile. His triumph was complete. Of course, he could have made his arrest more discreetly, but he had very deliberately created this humiliating scene for Vitali. The US attorney only regretted that Nick couldn't witness Sergio Vitali's arrest in the public eye.

Massimo Vitali suddenly appeared in the foyer. "What's going on here?" he exclaimed when he saw his father and Jenkins in handcuffs.

"Who are you?" Lloyd Connors asked.

"I'm Massimo Vitali."

"We arrested your father," the US attorney said. "You should get him a lawyer as soon as possible."

Vitali's eyes flashed angrily at Connors; he was furious to be in this very unflattering situation. Deputy Spooner pushed him along.

"Papa!" Massimo exclaimed in agitation. "What should I do?"

"Call Bruyner!" his father shouted. "And…"

And? Nelson wasn't there anymore, and Judge Whitewater was also gone. Tate Jenkins, his valuable connection at the FBI, walked handcuffed behind him, and even John de Lancie didn't seem to be in his post anymore. The seriousness of his situation slowly dawned upon Sergio. He had a feeling that he wouldn't get away so easily this time.

"Papa!" Massimo's voice sounded desperate.

"Come on," Deputy Spooner urged, "go, go!"

Massimo stared after them helplessly. Sergio's security personnel and the hotel staff were also paralyzed, and the crowd of guests curiously gathering around the ballroom's doors whispered in excitement.

"Is that really necessary?" Sergio Vitali protested as Spooner directed him toward the main entrance. "Can't we at least exit through the back?"

"Oh no, sir. You'll get the full program." Spooner grinned with satisfaction. "Like a man of your status deserves."

Vitali put on a grim smile and straightened his shoulders. He kept a stony face in the flurry of flashes, showing his contempt for the reporters, the TV cameras, and the gawking crowd. Royce Shepard opened the back door of the limousine, and Spooner pushed Vitali into the backseat.

"Don't touch me!" Vitali snapped. "I'll make sure that you're writing parking tickets in the future!"

"I'm looking forward to that," Spooner replied calmly. He joined Vitali in the backseat, while Connors gave a brief statement to the agitated reporters. Sergio Vitali's face was frozen solid. As the reporters knocked against the window to get a good shot of him, he didn't turn his gaze once. Lloyd Connors sat in the front seat as the car drove off with a flashing red light and wailing siren. Gordon Engels and Tate Jenkins followed in a second car, and there was a full convoy behind them.

Connors exhaled a deep sigh of relief. He'd done it! He had doubted the success of this operation until the very last second, but he'd finally accomplished what Nick Kostidis had tried for so many years: he had arrested Sergio Vitali—the secret godfather of New York City. The evidence was overwhelming, and the prosecution's key witness was alive. The message that di Varese and Bacchiocchi had also been arrested came over the radio. Vitali didn't react at all.

"You're getting a big kick out of this, aren't you?" he said after a while in a disdainful tone. "That pathetic bastard will piss his pants in joy once he hears about it."

"Who are you talking about?" Connors asked coolly.

"That damned son of a bitch Kostidis." There was a glow of murderous rage in Vitali's eyes. "I likely owe this entire spectacle to him!"

"You've been arrested," Lloyd Connors said as he turned around, "because you killed *at least* one person and brutally abused Ms. Alex Sontheim."

"That's bullshit," Vitali said, shaking his head. "Where are you taking me? I have a thousand guests, and you've got nothing better to do than to arrest me because of a little whore who stole from me and lied to me! I'll complain to the attorney general himself about this!"

"Complain to whomever you want." The smile vanished from Connors's face. He thought about Alex's disfigured face. He thought about Mary and Christopher Kostidis, who had to die because Nick stood in Sergio Vitali's way. He thought about David Zuckerman and Zachary St. John, both sacrificed by Vitali after they'd outlived their usefulness and possibly posed a threat to him. He thought about the lawyer in Los Angeles who had been murdered in such a brutal way, and the many other people who'd died because this man had ordered it.

"We're going to take some fingerprints now, and a few pictures," Connors said, "and then you can spend a night on the taxpayer's dime. It certainly won't be as comfortable as you're used to, but maybe you'll learn to like what's waiting for you for the next hundred years."

"I won't stay in jail for more than twenty-four hours!" Vitali hissed, but his arrogance was gone and his anger had given way to a helpless embitterment.

"The judge will decide that tomorrow morning," Lloyd Connors replied in a calm voice. "Not you and not me."

Nick Kostidis was startled out of his sleep in the middle of the night. It took him a few seconds to comprehend where he was and he realized in surprise that he wasn't alone. Alex lay next to him sound asleep. Then he remembered that he had visited her. He'd simply fallen asleep in sheer exhaustion, and Alex had taken off his shoes and put a blanket over him. Nick smiled. The dial of his wristwatch indicated it was two thirty in the morning. He thought about Lloyd Connors. Had the US attorney managed to arrest Vitali? Nick got up carefully in order not to wake Alex and tiptoed over to the small bathroom. He closed the door and switched on the light. Stepping in front of the mirror, he stared at his face. He had spent the past six months in a world of nightmares, but now he had awakened from them and knew that he wanted to live again. And he owed it to Alex. The strong feelings he had for her seemed like a tender glowing light at the end of a long night, a thin, bright beam of hope that could lead him away from his vale of tears. In the face of these incomprehensible and irrevocable experiences, he had submitted himself to senseless self-pity for much too long. Now it was time to make a decision about the future. He wouldn't go the US Attorney's Office tonight as he had initially promised Connors. He didn't want to see Vitali, and he didn't care to know what had happened. It was strange, but he was really completely indifferent. He would hear about it all tomorrow morning.

Nick switched off the light and quietly went back to the bed. In the dim light coming in through the small window, he saw that Alex had woken up.

"Nick?" she whispered sleepily.

"Yes," Nick said as he sat down at the edge of the bed and looked at her.

"I let you sleep," she said quietly. "You were so exhausted."

"Thank you," he replied. Alex smiled. She really was enchanting.

"What time is it?" she asked.

"Quarter to three."

"In that case, we can sleep a few more hours." She lifted the blanket, and Nick slipped beneath it.

"Do you think they arrested him?" she whispered.

"I don't know," Nick answered. "Probably."

The church bell chimed the quarter hour.

"Nick?"

"Yes?"

"I'm glad you're here."

He pulled her close. Thanks to this woman, his heart, which had turned into an icy block, had melted again. "I'm happy too," he whispered, and carefully stroked her battered face.

"Will we ever be able to lead a normal life again?"

"I hope so," he replied quietly. "I really hope so."

Her eyes were close to his, and they looked at each other for a while, not saying a word.

"What are you going to do now?" Nick finally asked, though he feared her answer.

"I think I need to leave the city," Alex responded. He nodded slowly.

"I understand that," he said, his voice husky. "Where will you go?"

"I'll probably go home for a while to my parents in Germany. I need some time to think," she said. "And Oliver invited me to go to Maine with him."

"And? What will you do?" Nick didn't feel pain or disappointment. He knew she would leave. She needed time to heal her wounds.

"Maybe I'll go. Oliver is a really good friend," Alex replied. "What will you do?"

"I'm still the mayor for another year," Nick said. "Someday, all this will be water under the bridge. Life goes on, and I'll keep doing my job."

"You'll never leave New York, will you?" Alex asked quietly.

"I've thought about it," Nick admitted. "I've never wanted to live anywhere else, but after everything that's happened, I sometimes think that it would be better to move away from here."

"The city would lose the best mayor it ever had." Alex reached out her hand and tenderly touched his cheek, "and you wouldn't be able to cope for very long without the hustle and bustle, the noise, the skyscrapers, and all that."

Nick laughed quietly. "You think so?"

"Yes," Alex said and smiled. "This city is like a disease. Once you're infected by it, you can't get rid of it."

"And what about you?" he asked. "Do you have the disease?"

Alex turned her face so that she could better look at him. Her smile had vanished.

"I think I have a different disease. It has a lot to do with this city."

Nick felt his heart start pounding. "Aha. And what disease is that?"

Alex rested her face on her hand.

"I'll tell you," she said quietly, "if you don't tell anyone."

"I won't breathe a word. What is it?"

"I fell in love with the mayor of New York City," Alex whispered.

"Really?"

Alex nodded silently.

"Imagine," Nick said, his voice hoarse, "and he fell in love with you."

An enchanting smile brightened her face, and he was suddenly filled with such a rush of happiness that it almost hurt. He leaned over and kissed her gently.

"Could you imagine returning to New York one day?" he asked. Her smile widened, and her eyes looked deeply into his.

"If I can't have you without this city," she replied, "I may have to accept it for better or worse."

On hearing these words, a wave of delight overcame Nick, and his heart jumped so wildly and happily that he thought it would burst. He put his arms around her and pulled her closer to him. Alex loved him the same way that he loved her. Even if she left tomorrow, he knew that it wasn't the end, but a new beginning.

EPILOGUE

Alex and Oliver sat in the monastery's lounge and watched the morning news. There was an extensive report on the shocking nighttime arrest of Sergio Vitali. Footage showed him leaving the St. Regis, handcuffed and escorted by authorities to a waiting car. Alex saw his expression, his murderous rage. She shuddered because she knew this look all too well. She felt no triumph or joy, but just a deep sense of relief. It was over. US Attorney Connors had Vitali arrested in front of all his guests at his big charity ball, and the reporter recounted all of the criminal charges. He mentioned Alex and even showed a small picture of her. The murder charges and all of the other allegations against her had been cleared for good.

The next report showed Sergio on his way from the arraignment to jail. He wasn't wearing a tailor-made tuxedo, and he didn't look furious anymore, just grim. He had to know that his bribery scheme had been busted. Maybe he even knew about van Mieren's confession and the arrest of his henchmen di Varese and Bacchiocchi. Fourteen of his men plus Vincent Levy—who had attempted to escape to Europe—had been arrested last night.

But the best news was that Mark and Justin were alive. The police had found them exhausted, but unharmed, in Vitali's warehouse in Brooklyn. Nick Kostidis, the mayor of New York, appeared on the screen standing on the steps of city hall. Alex smiled when she saw the face of this man whose arms she had woken up in that morning. He looked almost the same as he had in earlier days. His eyes shone, he was full of energy and vigor, and he was confident and strong.

"Alex?"

Alex flinched and looked at Oliver.

"I think this nightmare is finally over." He smiled and reached out his hand toward her. She returned his smile and grabbed it.

"Have you thought about coming to Maine with me?"

Alex's smile widened.

"First I'm flying home to my parents."

"And then?"

"Then I'll have time to catch lobster with you."

"There's more to Maine than just lobster," Oliver said with a grin. "I'd like to show you everything."

"I'd like that, too." Alex smiled, and then her gaze fell on the television. Nick was still on the screen. Someday the shadows would disappear and this nightmare would be just a distant memory.

"Maybe I'll come back to New York one day," she said.

She stood up and switched off the television.

ABOUT THE AUTHOR

Photograph © Felix Krumbholz

Nele Neuhaus, a longtime resident of the Taunus Mountains, is one of Germany's most widely read crime authors, thanks to her thrillers featuring the investigative duo of Oliver von Bodenstein and Pia Kirschoff, which were recently launched in English with *Snow White Must Die*. Her novels have been translated into twelve languages. To learn more about her, visit www.neleneuhaus.de.

Made in the USA
Charleston, SC
25 January 2014